Private Lives

www.penguin.co.uk

Also by Emily Edwards

The Herd

Private Lives

EMILY EDWARDS

bantam

TRANSWORLD PUBLISHERS

UK | USA | Canada | Ireland | Australia
India | New Zealand | South Africa

Transworld is part of the Penguin Random House group of companies
whose addresses can be found at global.penguinrandomhouse.com.

Penguin Random House UK, One Embassy Gardens, 8 Viaduct Gardens, London SW11 7BW

penguin.co.uk

Penguin
Random House
UK

First published in Great Britain in 2025 by Bantam
an imprint of Transworld Publishers

001

Copyright © Emily Edwards 2025

The moral right of the author has been asserted

Typeset in 13.5/16 pt Garamond MT by Falcon Oast Graphic Art Ltd.
Printed and bound in Great Britain by Clays Ltd, Elcograf S.p.A.

The authorized representative in the EEA is Penguin Random House
Ireland, Morrison Chambers, 32 Nassau Street, Dublin D02 YH68

A CIP catalogue record for this book is available from the British Library

ISBNs
9781787636958 (cased)
9781787636965 (tpb)

To my sisters

The dogs of Waverly are the first to sense something is wrong.

Then a group of people, confused by what they heard, congregate in the dark roads, wrapped in dressing gowns, feet shoved into gardening clogs.

'Retribution.' A man nods, knowingly, his phone in his hand like a prayer book. 'Makes sense, doesn't it?'

The others stare at him and then nod at each other, their faces glowing and uncertain beneath the street lamps, sirens already screaming close by.

Someone's taken this too far. Much too far.

'You see it on the news all the time, don't you?'

Some think it was shots they heard, a gunman rampaging through cobbled streets, some loner in military gear, ammunition looped like beads around his neck. A few weeks ago they might have guessed it could be that guy who works at the newsagent's but never talks, maybe. Or what about the drunk who is often weeping, always alone in the park? But now, of course, they know exactly what this is about.

'But *Waverly*?' they ask each other. 'I never would have thought anything like this could happen in Waverly!'

What they really want to ask is: does this mean their luck's run out? Has the good fortune that led them all to this historic town, snuggled away from the chaotic world, safe and warm as a pocket in a cashmere cardigan, finally soured?

Others briskly close their curtains, shake their heads at the noise and say, 'It's a trick, that's all. Just a stupid trick.'

But the air is grey with flotsam, full of loss.

'We mustn't feel guilty!' a woman says, putting her arm around her neighbour, who shakes then nods her head, unsure in her confusion how to agree.

Some silently reach for the hands of loved ones, while others stand alone.

'I mean, the stuff they've been saying online – it was really only a matter of time . . .'

And they all do their best to ignore their quietest voice, the one that whispers from deep within them that they might not have been the ones who lit the match – but that doesn't mean they didn't all have a hand in burning that family to the ground.

Chapter 1

Seb and Rosie walk in silence, side by side, to Eddy's party.

Eddy adores his birthday, but it has been the same every year for the last decade. In the weeks leading up to it, Eddy will shake his curls and say he doesn't want to celebrate, but then a few days before he'll tug his beard and change his mind. And on cue, every year, his wife, Anna, will pull together a last-minute dinner party.

Now, outside their friends' Victorian terraced house, almost identical to their own, Rosie turns to Seb and offers him the tennis racquet she wrapped with their four-year-old daughter that afternoon. 'Here, you give it to him – it was your idea.'

The wrapping paper gapes and bags around the thin frame like ill-fitting clothes. Their fingers briefly touch as he takes it, and Seb catches a flash of panic in her eyes, as if she's worried, worried he's going to bring up everything from last night. She just shakes her head and turns towards the gate. This is their dynamic now. Their relationship more like that of passive-aggressive colleagues than the happy couple they lead everyone to believe they are. It's normal, Seb silently reminds himself. They are just relearning how to be together without their three kids – Sylvie, eleven; Heath, nine; and

Greer, four – dangling off them, screaming and needing them. That's all. So normal.

As he follows behind her, stepping over a compressed mash of autumnal leaves, he runs through his options to lift the mood. In the final moment before they reach the front door, he opts for a classic.

'Hey, Ro,' Seb says, suddenly a bit shy as she turns back to him. 'You look beautiful.'

Rosie looks down at herself. Perhaps a little surprised and a little disappointed to see herself still there, dressed in her favourite black jeans and blue silk shirt. 'My body feels like a bag of spanners,' she says glumly.

Seb laughs. Relieved she's making a joke. 'Well, I adore every single one of the spanners in your lovely bag.'

Rosie smiles, grateful, and Seb reaches for her hand, the one not holding a wine bottle, and squeezes quickly. He feels another wash of relief, because looking into her dark eyes in that moment they silently agree to let last night go.

The door opens with a big whoosh and Seb and Rosie lift their arms to the sky, calling in sing-song voices, 'Happy birthday!'

'Friends!' Eddy's laughing, folding them both into his big arms, pulling them close, smacking his lips to their foreheads like they're his grown children who have at last come home. 'Thank God you're here.'

Eddy keeps his hand on the back of Seb's neck as Anna hurries pink-faced towards them from the kitchen, lifting an apron over her blonde head. Her feet are bare and her arms – just like Eddy's – are open wide to Rosie.

'Hi, loves!' she squeals like she hadn't seen them both only yesterday at the school gates.

Rosie bends down towards Anna but as they hug, one of Anna's dangly gold earrings catches in Rosie's hair. 'Ow!'

They release each other quickly, Rosie touching the top of her head.

'Oh God, sorry! Bloody things!' Anna says, pulling a few strands of dark hair from the complicated hoops.

Rosie shakes her apology away, keen to move on from the awkwardness, and reaches for Anna's hand. 'That dress looks fab on you.'

Seb looks at his wife, his gorgeous, kind wife. She is next to Anna who is now on tiptoes, twisting her curvy hips from side to side, showing off her fitted black dress, delighted, and Seb marvels at Rosie's apparent ease in giving others what they need.

'Thanks. Spanx are the best,' Anna says, snapping the elastic under her dress, before turning to Seb, opening her arms again.

'Sebbo!' She pulls him down firmly towards her. She smells warm, of spices simmering in a stew. Eddy and Anna have been together for twenty years, and Seb's known her for longer than he's known Rosie. Although he feels brotherly towards her, he will always find a reason to pop out into the garden when Anna gets too much. Eddy can be similar. Seb often finds himself missing easy shots on the tennis court because he's zoned out of Eddy's constant chatter. Releasing him from her grip, Anna starts telling Seb about their cat leaving a bird's decapitated head on the kitchen table. Meanwhile Eddy takes Rosie's coat with a twinkle in his eye, a telltale sign that he is already at least two drinks down, and ushers her into the sitting room.

'Oh wow!' Rosie starts laughing as soon as she enters

the room. It's a blurt of a laugh, uncontrolled, one of Seb's favourites.

Seb follows a couple of paces behind and starts laughing with Rosie. The room is plastered with photos of Eddy. The same extreme close-up of Eddy's grinning, bearded face has been stuck up on the walls, over the fireplace and is even dangling from the lampshade over the large, carefully set dining table.

'Welcome to heaven,' Eddy says, raising his hands, grinning widely as Anna starts passing around champagne flutes.

'Jesus. I had a nightmare like this once,' Seb says, turning around the room slowly.

'Ha!' Eddy laughs, his palm reaching to stroke Anna's bottom as she passes.

'It was my idea,' Anna says to Rosie, whose favour, even after all these years, she still seeks out. 'He's always prattling on about not getting enough attention, so . . .' Anna gestures at the room as though this should be enough to satisfy any attention deficit.

Seb glances at Rosie. 'See?' he wants to say. 'See? It's not just us!'

Rosie's holding out her glass to Eddy, who is pouring sparkling wine too fast, the bubbles foaming up and over, wetting her hand. She licks the rim of her glass to stop it spilling to the floor. Seb watches her tongue flick and where he would once have felt a snap of desire, he now just feels a dull thud. But Eddy's turned, proffering the bottle towards Seb, so he keeps smiling as he offers up his own glass. When all their glasses are full, they lift them in a high salute as Seb says, 'To Eddy!'

They turn to each other, carefully making eye contact with

each member of their group, clinking glasses and chorusing, 'To Eddy!'

When the other couples arrive soon after, there's more kissing, more whoops of surprise, more drinks handed around. Seb doesn't like the start of these things – the high-pitched greetings, the charge of nervous anticipation as everyone attempts to adapt to each other again.

He falls into conversation with Patrick, a friendly, enthusiastic man with a daughter at Seb's school, married to the officious and slightly intimidating Vita. They talk about the local tennis club and the plans for resurfacing the older courts. Changing the subject, Patrick asks, 'So, how does it feel being at the helm?'

Seb became headmaster at Waverly Community Secondary School three weeks ago, at the beginning of the autumn term. It's what he's wanted since he was a kid. Back then, Eddy laughed at him and told him to keep it quiet, because what kind of geek wanted to be a head teacher at twelve? Far better, Eddy said, to want to be an astronaut.

Now, whenever anyone asks about his job, Seb feels a lightness in his chest, a sense of pride.

'Yeah, it's good. I'm enjoying it. I mean, it's obviously a big shift from teaching to doing a load more managerial stuff . . .'

'That's great, really great,' Patrick says, his gaze sliding over to the women. 'Essie loves school, you know. Adores it.'

Seb decides to give Patrick the gift he knows all parents crave, especially from a head teacher. 'Well, Essie's great. Such a kind girl and so hard-working.'

Patrick looks back at Seb, his eyes full of wonder and gratitude, because Seb's seen what Patrick's known all along – there's some special kind of magic in his Essie.

'She is, isn't she?' Patrick says, his voice a little watery with feeling.

Seb gets it. All three of his kids are at the Old School House, the primary feeder school across the road from Waverly Community. Greer, their youngest, is only three weeks into Reception and he can't stop himself from seeking a smile, a nod, a secret transmission from her exhausted teacher that he is right. Greer is unusually bright for a four-year-old.

Seb half listens as Patrick begins to rattle away about Essie's GCSE choices and his son's rugby obsession before they're interrupted by Anna, her voice high, loud, demanding attention as she shrieks, 'A bird's head!'

'And that is exactly why we're never getting a pet,' says Vita, before making a vomiting gesture.

Eddy puts his arm around Vita's thin shoulders, agreeing. 'I'm with you. Worst decision of my life, getting that cat.'

'Yesterday, you said having Albie was the worst decision of your life,' Anna shrieks in faux-outrage, whacking Eddy on his round stomach.

'OK, the cat was the second-worst decision, and don't hit the birthday boy.'

From the kitchen, an alarm starts to ring.

'Oh, that'll be the dauphinoise!' Anna says, putting her glass down on the table. 'Everyone, find your seats. Ro, will you give me a hand?'

Rosie is sitting on the arm of the sofa, her phone in her hand, typing. Smiling the far-away smile of someone enjoying a private joke. She doesn't hear Anna.

'Rosie Kent, are you messaging your new girl crush?'

Again, Rosie doesn't hear, so instead Anna turns back to Seb and says, 'Unbelievable! Is she like this at home, Sebbo?'

Seb doesn't want to be publicly disloyal, but Rosie is of course being rude, so he shrugs, nods and shakes his head. Abi is new in town and Rosie has taken it upon herself to show her the ropes. Rosie has lots of friends and acquaintances in Waverly but none of them make her smile like this or pull her phone out to message when she really shouldn't. It's like watching the first rumblings of love, and it makes Seb feel swampy with jealousy.

Seb still hasn't met Abi even though her eldest daughter is at his school. Abi had cancelled a meeting they'd arranged last-minute, and it occurs to him now that he should make an effort to rearrange. That meeting with Abi might bring him a little closer to unlocking whatever is going on with Rosie.

From the sofa, Rosie looks up. 'Sorry, I just had to reply to something . . .'

'So it *is* Abi you're texting?' Anna asks, eyes still wide with disbelief to hide any genuine hurt she might be feeling.

'Sorry,' Rosie repeats, dropping her phone back in her bag. She glances briefly to Seb for backup; he smiles at her but she immediately looks away, back towards Anna, as she says, 'Sorry, Abi was just asking about after-school clubs for Margot . . .'

'Oh, well then.' Anna crosses her arms under her large chest. 'You should have said it was something so incredibly urgent. I honestly don't get what all the fuss is about. I mean, Abi seems nice but . . .'

Rosie pouts out her bottom lip, gets up from the sofa and puts her arm around her friend. 'Oh, Anna, don't be jealous – you're still my number one,' she says in a soppy voice, too theatrical to be true. The truth, which Seb knows, is that Rosie enjoys Anna, loves her in her way, but probably wouldn't have chosen to be friends with her were it not for Seb and Eddy's long-standing friendship.

'Hmm,' Anna replies, like she understands she will never see all of Rosie, but that's OK because right now Rosie's arm is round her. Seb watches Anna's shoulders drop with relief.

Anna and Eddy are the same in that respect, needing constant reassurance. Their huge personalities, like fur coats, belying the sensitive, brittle little creatures inside.

Then Patrick turns to them, nose twitching, and asks, 'Is that burning I can smell?'

'Shit! The dauphinoise!' Anna says, grabbing Rosie and pulling her towards the kitchen.

The rest of them shuffle around the table looking for their handwritten place cards. Seb is sitting next to Lotte, another parent from the school.

Lotte and her husband, Richard, are opening a new restaurant in town called PLATE (the capitals were Lotte's idea) and Seb finds that Lotte is – as usual – in a chatty mood. She grasps Richard's hand, which is balled in a tight fist on top of the table, as she tells Seb how Richard poached an excellent London chef – 'Diego someone, have you heard of him?' Richard smiles reflexively but pulls his hand away from his wife and turns his attention back to Eddy, who is asking him something about the wine. Seb makes sure he keeps nodding as Lotte chatters about tile options for the restaurant toilets, and he feels the rush as a great wave of loneliness rises up within him. Rosie appears holding a platter of steaming pulled pork, she must feel him looking – she smiles briefly, like he's an acquaintance she's just spotted in the street.

'Hope everyone's hungry!' Rosie says, leaning over the table to put the meat in front of Anna's place at the head, next to a bowl of bean stew for vegetarians Patrick and Vita.

Lotte picks up a serving spoon to dish out the potatoes that Anna places in front of her as she asks Seb, 'Has Rosie told you that we're employing – on Diego's insistence, actually – her new friend, Abi? She's going to be our restaurant manager.'

'Oh?' Seb says, accepting a spoonful of sloppy, creamy and only slightly blackened potatoes. Rosie hadn't told him – but that's hardly remarkable, a bitter little voice reminds him inside.

'Yeah,' Lotte replies. 'I wasn't sure about her at first, I thought she had a bit of a too-cool-for-school vibe, but I think that was just because she's from Hackney, you know? Tattoos, cropped hair, you know the type. Now, of course, I love her. She's super cool.'

'Give it a year or two in Waverly and that'll change,' Vita says across the table, holding up her plate to Lotte before turning, like a hunter spotting a deer in the woods, towards her husband. 'Patrick, is that meat on your plate?'

Patrick pinks but doesn't look up before sliding the small piece of meat on to Rosie's plate next to his, muttering, 'Sorry, sorry, V.'

Vita shakes her head at the table, as if she blames all the other carnivores for Patrick's momentary lapse of judgement. Poor Patrick.

Anna whoops again. 'Shit! The gravy!'

This time Seb stands quickly; he's closest to the kitchen and needs a break. 'I'll get it.'

Anna blows him a kiss. 'Love you, Sebbo.'

*

The kitchen is chaos. It looks like Anna's used every utensil, every pan. Seb spots the gravy bubbling on the hob, picks up a cleanish spoon, tastes, before adding more salt. He goes to the cupboard for the cow-shaped gravy boat he remembers from Sunday dinners made by Eddy's mum long before her dementia set in. Just as Seb's about to pour the gravy into the boat, the back door opens, and Blake appears. At fifteen, his godson's got the same body Eddy had as a teenager, before beer and a desk job filled him out. Blake's tall and solid; he seems to take up half the kitchen.

'Hey, Blake,' Seb says, meaty steam from the gravy billowing around him.

'Hey, Mr . . . I mean, Uncle Seb.' Blake kicks off his trainers without undoing the laces, leaving them and his sports bag by the back door. 'Mum always forgets the gravy. Need a hand?'

Without waiting for an answer, Blake, sweet boy, holds the ceramic cow steady while Seb slowly pours from the pan.

'Thanks, mate,' Seb says when they're finished. 'How was football?'

'Yeah, all right, one all. Greenwood did some dodgy sliding tackles, though.'

'God, they're still doing that? They were like that when your dad and I used to play them thirty years ago.'

Blake smiles and shakes his head, amazed by the vast swathe of time. 'I thought football wasn't around back then.'

'Oh yeah, it was right after the ball had been invented, although of course all we had to kick were pig's bladders, so . . .'

'With your bare Neanderthal feet.'

'That's right.' Seb laughs now, thinking how he'd stay here in the kitchen talking with Blake all night if he could.

From the sitting room Anna calls, 'Seb! Gravy!'

Seb widens his eyes at Blake and Blake laughs again. With a flick of his head, Seb asks, 'You coming in to say hello?'

'You think I'll ever hear the end of it if I don't?'

'Nope,' Seb says, smiling.

Blake breathes out.

'Come on, then,' Seb says, picking up the gravy boat.

As Seb follows Blake back into the dinner party, Eddy looks up at them, his eyes glazed and shiny with wine. 'What secrets has the spy been sharing with you, Blakey?'

'Spy?' Patrick asks, taking a bite of his bean stew as Seb places the gravy boat on the table and decides to say nothing. Lotte and Rosie turn to Blake, asking about his football practice. But Richard is one of those people who always dawdles a beat behind everyone else.

'Why's Seb a spy?'

Eddy stands, picking up the bottle, and starts refilling everyone's glasses before he comes up behind Seb, squishing his cheeks together with one hand, and says, 'Because no man can be so good and so bloody pretty, that's why. It has to be an act.'

Seb pushes his hand away, saying, 'Didn't you used to think Anna's dad was a spy, too?'

'No, Grandad Mike always wanted everyone to think he was MI5 but actually he was just the local busybody . . .'

'Eddy!' Anna interrupts; she has always been defensive of her beloved dad. 'He had good reason to be protective. You don't know what it was like growing up in Ruston!'

Eddy wipes away an invisible tear and Anna rolls her eyes before turning to Vita, telling her the story of how she was raised just a few miles down the road in Ruston. Once a lovely local fishing village, it was slowly destroyed by poor planning, a corrupt council and all the usual cruel accoutrements of poverty. Her dad fought hard to protect the town he had been raised in, costing him his physical and mental health, before finally accepting defeat and moving to a tiny cottage in rural Hampshire.

Eddy ignores Anna and instead calls out to interrupt his son. 'Blakey. Hey, Blake. Tell everyone, why is Uncle Seb a spy?'

Blake glances at Seb apologetically. 'Oh, Dad and I just came by his office one day and he slammed his laptop closed as soon as he saw us. It was pretty sus.'

Seb's throat tightens, he feels his smile shake, and he keeps his eyes on his plate of food in front of him.

'No, you're not telling it right, Blake,' Eddy says as he puts the wine back on the table and sits down. 'It was funny because Mrs Greene appeared and suddenly it all made sense to me. Mrs Greene isn't who she says she is, she's not a secretary but the boss, like . . . what's her name? N? The one from Bond? Anyway, she appeared in a puff of—'

'Oh, I remember what I wanted to say!' Anna interrupts, making everyone turn to her. 'Did everyone see the news today? The story about the poor TV presenter – Max Harting? I mean, what a fall! He was basically a national treasure.'

Eddy throws up his hands in exasperation at being talked over. 'Fine. Everyone ignore the birthday boy.'

So they do.

'It's his wife I feel sorry for. I always said he was gay . . .' Lotte adds.

'Oh, live and let live, I say,' Anna returns. 'He hasn't done

14

anything illegal. I mean, I bet the boy's parents are pissed off, but they should just sort that out between themselves . . .'

'I'm going to go up,' Blake says.

The women blow him kisses and everyone calls out good-night as Anna checks Blake found his plate of food in the kitchen, and Eddy gets up again to bear-hug his son.

Later, after they've eaten and watched Eddy open his gifts – 'It's not . . . it can't be . . . it is! The fucking Slazenger! Thank you, you beautiful people' – and everyone is sloppy with wine, Anna squeezes Rosie's hand and says to her and Seb, 'I was doing that thing of hating my kids all day, then scrolling through baby pictures of them all night, and look what I found . . .'

Anna holds up the screen for them to see a photo of two naked, creamy babies with arms like fat, buttery croissants, sitting opposite each other in the bath. Baby Albie – Eddy and Anna's younger son – and baby Heath – Seb and Rosie's middle child.

'I mean, just look at them! Such little puddings.'

A warm longing floods Seb because there he is, their baby son. He glances at Rosie, too; she's smiling but it's a sad smile, like she wishes she could reach into that photo and hold her beautiful baby one last time.

'Flick to the next one,' Anna says. It's a photo of Rosie holding a naked baby on a towel on each leg, having just lifted them out of the bath. Rosie frowns at the screen, like she can't quite place herself from eight years ago. Anna's turned away from them now, laughing at something Vita and Eddy are arguing about, so Seb and Rosie look at the photo together.

'Look at you, so beautiful,' Seb says, resting his hand on her lower back. Close, but hopefully not too close.

'You reckon?' Rosie says, doubtful, cocking her head to look at the photo from a different angle. 'I was thinking how knackered I looked, and I think that's breast milk leaking through my T-shirt.'

'Still totally gorgeous,' Seb says, before adding, 'That photo must have been taken before we moved down here.' He remembers back then; they were still living in London. He'd just started teaching while studying at the same time, Sylvie a boisterous toddler and Heath crying with reflux all night. They'd spend most weekends trekking down to stay with his mum, Eva, and he longed to move, craved the simpler, safer life Waverly offered his young family. Now, living in Waverly, just a ten-minute walk away from his mum and with so much to be grateful for, Seb still feels hungry. It seems he is always yearning for something.

Next to him, Rosie sighs, her eyes fixed on herself in the photo, the woman she hardly recognizes. The wine is making her maudlin. For a mad moment he thinks about picking her up and carrying her home. He wants to lie skin to skin, wants to feel the mysterious electric pulse of her, the pulse that will remind him of his own precious aliveness. Rosie glances at her phone and he knows she doesn't want that. She never wants that any more. As she reads a message, he looks at her and tries to imagine how it used to be, Rosie naked and lovely on top of him, her head thrown back, immersed in pleasure. For a long time, that image had been almost painfully erotic but now, mostly, it makes him sad. He'd tried everything he could think of. He'd tried talking, not talking, he'd back off and then he'd come on strong – buying Rosie an expensive silk nightie he thought she'd love but which she said made her feel like mutton – and so he'd retreated into despair. He was usually so good at being who people wanted him to be, expert at denying himself to make others happy, but this – this sex thing – and Rosie's complete detachment – no, her complete rejection of him – gnawed at him until he felt he was disappearing inside his wanting.

In the first few months they hadn't had sex, she said she was 'touched out' – the kids still grabbing, so demanding of physical touch. Now they are all at school, she has more time without them, but nothing has changed. She still flinches every time he even touches her hand. It's the confusion that is slowly dissolving him. The feeling that she is wilfully keeping him from understanding. She says it isn't that she doesn't desire him, it's that she has to relearn what she wants, what will turn her on. She needs time to figure that out. That's as far as they've got and nothing – as far as Seb knows – has changed in months. What has become clear – crushingly, devastatingly clear for Seb – is that sex, and specifically their sex life, is, for Rosie at least, simply not that important.

Vita and Patrick shift furniture around to make a tiny dance floor and Eddy puts a Prince record on. He's trying to pull Anna up to dance with him, but she's squirming away, saying, 'No, Eddy! I don't want to, stop!'

Eddy gives up on his wife and instead grabs Rosie's hand. Rosie drops her phone back into her bag again and because it's Prince and because it's Eddy's birthday, she lets herself be led to the makeshift dance floor in front of the sofa. Rosie loves to dance. Her body flows like liquid, natural and free as she lets the music pour through her. Seb looks at Rosie – she's laughing and for the first time tonight she seems at ease, like she's shrugged something heavy off her shoulders – and, as he looks at her, he feels for an insane moment like he might cry, because all he can think, when he sees his wife's happiness, is:

How could you, Sebastian?

How fucking could you?

Chapter 2

'Taadaa!' Rosie says, turning her palm skywards, revealing Waverly to Abi like a flamboyant waiter. It's hot, one of those syrupy summer days of autumn, and they're puffed and sticky from walking up the steep footpath to the best viewing spot in town. Abi makes her way to a bench, reading the little inscription, says, 'Thanks, Barry,' before she sits down.

'It's gorgeous.' Abi extends her legs, crossing them at the ankles. She lifts her arms to get the breeze in the hollow of her unshaved armpits, dropping her denim jacket on to Barry's bench. She's wearing Birkenstock sandals, her feet tattooed in a beautiful lattice-like design, her skin still tanned, carrying the memory of summer. The letters 'L' and 'M' are tattooed on her inner arm. There's something wonderfully unstudied about Abi that makes Rosie want to stare. She has a tousled look to her but whenever Rosie looks into Abi's eyes she knows the other woman is as solid as a rock.

Rosie sits next to her feeling pimply and pale but glad to be here, away from the kids, away from work, away from Seb. Just here with her new intriguing friend.

They met a few weeks ago – as so many parents do – through their kids. Margot and Greer are in Reception together and have become firm friends. Rosie noticed the way Abi shrank back at the school gates from the noisier, shrill women Rosie calls 'friends'. The ones who talk in high-pitched whispers about other people's kids and marriages. It was a quiet thrill for Rosie to leave those women and stand with Abi instead; she hasn't made a new friend, independently of Seb, for so long. Rosie offered Abi help in navigating the town, recommending the best kids' swimming lessons, after-school clubs and the places to avoid. They had a couple of play dates in the park and while the girls dangled from monkey bars Rosie found herself telling Abi things she hasn't even told Anna. How disconnected she feels sometimes from her own life, how her days feel like an endless 'to-do' list. Abi sates a part of Rosie she hadn't even known was starving. Some little forgotten wisp of her that had been banging a tiny internal cymbal, a lone protestor demanding attention. Rosie hasn't talked to anyone like this for so long. Abi must have been an amazing therapist, her job for years in London before moving to Waverly.

Today, for the first time, Abi and her kids are coming back to Rosie's after school. Seb is picking up a takeaway from the local Thai on his way home as a treat for the three adults.

'Everything looks so simple from up here, doesn't it?' Rosie says, noticing the perfect neatness of the doll's house town, a place where nothing bad could ever happen. She automatically places the Old School House, where all three of her kids will be, and, just across the road, Waverly Secondary, where Seb is at work. Strange to think of everyone she loves muddling their way through another day down there. Abi doesn't reply because she's rummaging around in her rucksack for something, before offering Rosie a bright-pink mini macaroon out of a small Tupperware.

'I was going to save these for pudding when we're back at yours, but sod it. Fancy one?'

'Ha!' Rosie laughs. 'Wow! Hell yes, I do!'

She bites into the fluorescent sugary flakiness before the sting of the bright raspberry cream fills her mouth. 'Jesus – they're insanely good.' She immediately wants another.

'Well, they were my first attempt – I don't know. I think maybe next time I—'

'Wait. Are you telling me you actually *made* them?'

Abi shrugs. 'Food's my thing. I love making new stuff.'

'Yes, but come on – you're a single parent with two kids, you've just moved town, changed career and you're making *home-made bloody macaroons*? Honestly, you're showing the rest of us up.'

'Well,' Abi says, inspecting a macaroon before popping it into her mouth, 'at least it explains why I don't have time for dating.'

Rosie takes another macaroon. 'Ever thought about going pro? Being a chef?'

Abi's face twists as she tongues her back teeth, freeing them of stuck sugar before she says, 'Oh, when I was, like, twelve, I thought about nothing else.'

'Twelve!'

Abi laughs before she pops another macaroon into her mouth, chewing slowly, considering how much to tell Rosie. She swallows, runs her fingers through her cropped fair hair and says, 'We were living on an estate in Hackney and a fancy chef set up a pop-up restaurant in an old service station – remember disused spaces were all the rage in the noughties? Anyway, I was twelve and they paid me a fiver an hour to wash up – totally illegal, of course, but I loved it. Some of the chefs would sneak me this insane food – beef cheeks cooked for twenty-four hours and baked oysters, stuff I never knew existed. The place became my way of escaping. I guess for some kids it's books or video games. For me it was always food.'

'What were you trying to escape?' Rosie asks, emboldened by Abi's honesty. Rosie has shared much more in this new friendship so far.

'Oh, I don't want to go all *Angela's Ashes* on you,' Abi laughs, 'but we didn't have much. My mum drank, my dad left. Same old, same old.'

'Do you still see them?' Rosie asks, quietly, like she doesn't want to talk loudly and disturb these precious things Abi is sharing with her.

'My dad not at all. Couldn't even tell you where he lives. My mum – well, it's complicated. We haven't spoken in a long time.'

Rosie wants to ask more about her parents, but Abi looks back at the view before closing her eyes, feeling the sun on her face. Rosie won't push it so instead she asks, 'How did you go from being a kid washing pans to a therapist?'

Abi opens her eyes, looks briefly to the sky, turns back to Rosie and, smiling, says, 'I went through a few wild years. Got really into boys – too into boys, my mum would say – partying, all that stuff, and then when I was eighteen found out I was five months pregnant. So, yeah, Lily was the wake-up call.'

Rosie can't help it. She wants to know. 'Did your parents help?'

Rosie notices for the first time the strain behind Abi's equanimity.

'God, no. Mum was often drunk and, like I said, things

are complicated between us and Dad wasn't around, so . . . no. No, they didn't. I mean, there was this charity that helped quite a bit so, yeah, I had that . . .'

Abi's silver bangles chime as she brushes bright-pink crumbs off her T-shirt, waves her arm in front of them and says, 'And now, incredibly, we live here in this beautiful place.'

They both look again at the view. Talking about Abi's difficult childhood in Hackney, Waverly seems claustrophobic and almost offensively twee, crammed as it is between the vast expanse of hills and sky. Rosie knew early into their relationship that if she was going to love Seb, she was going to have to love this ancient, eccentric little town with its narrow streets and malty air from the brewery. Seb was a bit like one of those people who marry the Eiffel Tower or the Statue of Liberty – but his lifelong love was a whole town. And Rosie had come to love it too, in her own way. 'How did you become a therapist?'

Abi smiles again, but the corner of her mouth shakes and she keeps staring at the view. 'Oh, I did the training online, like a night-school thing. Turns out I had a kind of natural ability for it so, yeah, I set up my own practice, working when Lily was sleeping or in nursery, and it just grew and grew. Covid was obviously a boom for therapists.'

'I bet you were brilliant. You must have helped so many people.'

Abi smiles in acceptance of the compliment before she asks, 'How about you? How's architecture?'

Rosie groans. 'It's not architecture. It's a glorified admin role. I went back part-time when Greer was two and my salary covers the mortgage so it's worth it financially, but the job is definitely not the reason I spent seven years training to be an architect.'

The only good thing about Rosie's job is its flexibility: she can always be available for sick days and dentist's appointments. Rosie is constantly on call. Her nervous system braced like a vigilant guard, always ready for the next minor family emergency. The job itself is just the bullshit no one else wants to do.

'What would you be doing if you could do anything?' Abi asks, and Rosie's mind snaps straight to the Instagram message she received this morning from Maggie. She tells Abi how she and Maggie studied architecture together in London and while Rosie got married, had kids and moved to Waverly, Maggie emigrated to Sydney and set up her own architecture practice. She tells her about the photo Maggie sent her this morning of a huge partly demolished warehouse next to a sparkling slip of coastline – the plot her company is developing into a new eco art gallery and hotel. And as she talks, she knows she's smiling, feels her heart flood with possibility. She looks back at Waverly, back to the school playground where her healthy, happy children play, and feels her shoulders drop, her heart wither again. Jesus, she's selfish, dreaming of a different life when she has so much. Is envied by so many. What is wrong with her?

Abi, her arm still tucked over the back of the bench, looks right at Rosie but doesn't say anything. Rosie can feel Abi listening and she feels exposed, flashing the most secret parts of herself.

'Sorry, I'm really going off on one. Of course it makes sense, the focus being on Seb's career, you know, while the kids are small. I think something had to give, right?'

'Hmm,' Abi says, neither agreeing nor disagreeing.

They sit in silence, and for a moment Rosie feels the eternal pacing inside herself rest. But it doesn't last long, the disquiet from the night before Eddy's birthday seeping into Rosie's stillness.

They'd been on the sofa. Seb was finishing off some work admin before putting his glasses and his school laptop – the one he uses for everything – on to the floor and opening his arms to Rosie. She leant into him, putting her head on his chest so she could feel, hear and see his heart beating, steady and true.

He started stroking her hair, the way he knew she liked. She wished more than anything that that could be enough, but it never was for Seb. Sure enough, his hand moved, quickly slipping under her shirt and into her bra, searching for her. And as his body grew, she felt her own shrinking, curling away, searching for somewhere to hide.

'Seb.' Her voice was a warning. 'Seb, I think Sylvie's still awake.'

'Well, let's go up to bed, then,' he said, his mouth in her hair.

She sat up suddenly, clumsily pulling herself away from him.

'No, I – I should just go up and check on her.'

Seb's head drooped. 'Ro, we need to talk about this . . .' But Rosie was already at the door as he tried again. 'Rosie, it's been a year.'

'What?'

'It's a year, sweetheart, since we last . . . made love.'

Rosie's always disliked the phrase 'making love' – it sounds weedy to her, the sex equivalent of a limp handshake. She'd rather 'have sex' or even 'fuck'.

'No, it isn't,' she replied, unsure, trying to remember. They'd argued about their sex life so much recently. She couldn't bear to go over it again, what Seb wanted versus what she felt she could give. She'd told him so many times to watch porn, to satisfy himself however he wanted, just not to put any pressure on her.

Gently, he started, 'It was just before Eddy's birthday last year; the kids were staying at Mum's.' She remembered the night. Greer had only recently – at long, long last – started sleeping through the night. Rosie's body felt like it was finally coming back to her after so many years of the kids needing it. For years, she'd been an incubator, a feeding machine, a comfort blanket, a punch bag and a carrier. Her body jangled with their fears, their joys, their anxieties along with her own and now, at last, she'd thought that night, she could return to herself. She wanted to get reacquainted with her body when she was ready, privately, on her own. But Seb had stroked her, just like he'd stroked her the other night and as he'd become more alive in his body she'd felt a deadening, a closing down. She'd been wrong. Her body was not her own. It never would be.

A year ago, she couldn't face letting him know that she didn't want sex. She couldn't deal with his disappointment, didn't want to have to reassure him again and again that it wasn't him, that it really was her. She couldn't face how sweet she knew he'd be about it. So instead, she'd let him have sex with her. She'd ignored the deadening feeling and forced herself to put on a show for him, sighing like she couldn't hold her pleasure in, rubbing her weary breasts, telling him she was about to orgasm when really she felt hollow. She told herself it was just a little white lie, a necessary one, because that was what they both wanted, wasn't it? He'd had his orgasm believing she'd had hers, and they'd cuddled and then her body was her own again. At least for a few hours until the kids woke up.

26

The next time, a couple of weeks later, when Seb had started stroking her again, something had happened. The deadening feeling wouldn't be buried. Her body refused. Her body felt like a great iron door, locks fully engaged. She simply could not comply any more. She could not satisfy Seb's needs to the detriment of her own, no matter how much she loved him. She tried, she really did, to lie there, but it felt like she was abusing herself. There was no way. She leapt away from Seb's touch. He'd known that something wasn't right.

'It's OK,' he said after listening to her, 'let's just hold each other.'

They did just that, the first and second time, and then what could she do? She started lying. She'd heard Greer call out, she'd tell him, she had her period, a headache, the prolapse from the three births had returned, she simply didn't want to. That's when the rowing started. Quiet, bitter words, knifing each other from both sides of the bed. Continuing until one would leave to curl up on the spare mattress in Sylvie's room. The next morning Rosie would always regret the things she'd said, but at the time there was a kind of heady joy, a release, in telling Seb he was a self-centred narcissist, a pathetic, fucking typical man. It almost felt good to hear Seb shout back that she was messed up and needed help. It made them more real somehow. Seb would always apologize first thing the next morning with a coffee, a quick kiss, and they'd promise to talk about it properly, to get help, counselling if necessary. But sex never felt so important in the daylight hours and Rosie never liked the look of the counsellors Seb contacted, so the issue slipped again and again.

It wasn't, Rosie told herself, such a big deal, was it? Lots of couples were the same, weren't they? She couldn't imagine buttoned-up Vita and Patrick having sex. Anna had made Rosie think she and Eddy were always doing it but maybe that was just what Anna wanted people to think.

And besides, didn't Rosie show Seb intimacy in other ways? She liked a cuddle on the sofa, enjoyed feeling his feet curl against hers under the duvet, but the problem was that the cuddle would always lead to his hand down her top, his foot would start stroking her leg. What she offered, what she felt she could give physically was never enough. She'd never been abused or suffered any childhood trauma but felt like her whole life her body had existed for other people, never for herself. She'd begged Seb for the time to figure out her new relationship with her body. She'd told him she was in some kind of transition that she herself didn't fully understand yet. It was true, but it was also true that Rosie had no energy or time to try to figure out what kind of metamorphosis her body was going through and what to do about it. And all the while there was Seb pushing and whining.

Last week Seb had said, 'I don't want to be in a sexless marriage, Ro.'

She looked at him then, imagined his disappointed dick creeping back into itself, and she had an overwhelming urge to kick him hard between the legs because after everything her body had done for him, for their family, how fucking dare he keep whining for more?

So, she said the thing she knew would upset him more than any kick, the thing she'd said to him many times already.

'Do what you like, Seb. I really don't care.'

Rosie has never said anything about the problems between her and Seb to anyone. Even thinking all this next to Abi, sitting on Barry's bench, feels like a betrayal. Abi's eyes are closed and Rosie wonders where she's gone. Whether Abi, like Rosie, tries to swim away from the dark water within herself. Feeling Rosie looking, Abi opens her eyes, smiles sleepily before she glances at her watch and says with a groan, 'Urgh. It's quarter to three. We should get going.'

It's slow progress walking home with all the kids. Anna and Albie join them for a short while, Anna telling Abi about all the other restaurants in Waverly before PLATE and why, in Anna's opinion, they failed. Heath and Sylvie bicker and Greer cries for an ice cream, Abi placating them all with a macaroon as Rosie trudges behind, a donkey beneath the kids' coats and bags, any lightness from her walk with Abi already evaporated. Things settle as soon as they're home. The kids all thump up the stairs as Abi follows Rosie into the kitchen extension.

The extension had been completed before they bought the house five years ago. It wasn't done well, in Rosie's professional opinion – the kitchen is now divided in half by two supporting pillars which the previous owners presumably hadn't been able to afford to replace with steels. The extension has a sofa and armchair at one end and the big oven at the other, with French doors leading to the garden in the middle. The older half houses the large family table, sink, fridge and the rest of the kitchen units. It creates a feeling of two distinct spaces, the pillars obstructing the view of the rest of the kitchen from the sofa and vice versa. When they bought the place, Rosie had started saving to remove the pillars and to put a skylight in the extension roof, but the increase in the cost of living and Greer's nursery fees have emptied the pot.

Upstairs, the girls are clattering about; Abi glances up,

smiles at the sound of them laughing. Heath's up there too, playing with his Lego, while Sylvie can be heard occasionally bossing the younger girls about.

Abi looks around at the framed baby photos of the kids, the drawings and calendars on the fridge. 'Anna seems interesting. Her energy's . . . lively.'

Rosie is opposite Abi, standing by the oven, pouring pasta into a pan of boiling water. 'Yeah. I mean, I love her, but she can be exhausting . . .'

'Hmmm,' Abi says, like she wants to say more but chooses not to. Rosie glances round as Abi picks up a framed photo from the bookshelf behind her. It's from Seb and Rosie's wedding day almost twelve years ago. It's a close-up of Rosie in flattering black and white, Seb out of focus, slightly behind her. Seb likes the photo because you can't see the silver scar that runs from his nostril to his upper lip. He was born with a cleft palate and had corrective surgery as a baby. In the photo Rosie looks like she's about to explode with laughter, but she can no longer remember what was so funny; maybe the photographer had asked her to laugh.

'What a gorgeous pic,' Abi says, peering closer. 'You look so happy.'

'Yeah,' Rosie says, turning back to the pan, 'it was a long time ago.' She shakes her head. 'That came out wrong' – thinking she should explain – 'we've just been together for a long time.'

It's over fifteen years since they met at a friend's party in London. They didn't have the ripping-clothes-off, breathless, can't-live-without-you kind of falling in love that Anna describes having when she met Eddy, but rather a slow, gentle tumble. A dignified dawning that they wanted complementary lives; a strong, dedicated relationship, children, security. Seb, who had grown up with all those things, wanted to replicate what he'd had. Coddled in the rolling hills of Waverly with strong, dynamic Eva at the helm and his kind, steady older dad, Benjamin, as second mate. Rosie, in contrast, had grown up in Stoke Newington with her two present but distant academic parents and older brother, Jim, who moved to Hong Kong ten years ago and whom they still haven't visited.

There's an explosion of giggles as the girls burst into the room in a puff of taffeta, calling out, 'Get ready for the fairy show!'

They watch three chaotic shows, all of which involve at least one of the girls pouring 'fairy flying dust' over their heads and leaping from chairs, arms flapping to show off their flying. Abi opens wine while the girls swap fairy costumes and Rosie dishes up the spaghetti bolognese and calls for Heath. She notices how she barely needs to bend down to kiss his head any more – he's growing so fast.

Lily arrives after walking herself back from school where she stayed late. Sylvie pats the bench next to her and says shyly, 'You can sit here, Lily,' and Lily, kind girl, does.

'How was your life drawing class, Lily?' Rosie asks, delivering water to the table.

'Great, thanks. We had a new model, she was lovely.'

Sylvie giggles into her hand and assuming his sister is laughing at him, Heath remarks, 'What?'

Sylvie looks to Lily, checking in with the older girl that her stupid little brother can handle the truth. Lily just smiles at her, shrugs, and Sylvie turns back to Heath and says with authority, 'Life drawing means drawing *naked* people.'

'What?' Heath repeats, spaghetti falling from his mouth. 'You're lying.'

Sylvie widens her eyes and nods her head, replying with worldly authority, 'They draw *everything*.'

'No, they don't,' Heath insists.

'Sylv . . .' Rosie interjects, but Abi approaches the table and she's nodding at Heath.

'It's true,' Abi says. 'Penises, bottoms, vulvas and breasts.' Rosie's kids shriek, cover their eyes and mouths and dissolve with horror and delight. Abi laughs along. 'Yeah, it's pretty funny,' she says before adding, 'but those bits aren't the hard bits, it's the proportions that's tricky with the body – isn't that right, Lily?'

'The position they're sitting or lying in totally changes the shape of their body and, like, the shadows and everything . . .' Lily says, but Heath interrupts her, his face wrinkled with distaste as he says, 'Not the balls, though. You don't do balls, do you?'

After the kids have eaten, Heath, Lily and Sylvie go up to draw and Rosie puts *Frozen* on for the little ones.

Abi's telling Rosie about Diego's current boyfriend – an adorable-sounding man called Stephen who likes to dress like it's the 1950s and keeps a house rabbit – when the front door opens and Seb calls out his usual self-deprecating announcement, 'Only me!'

'Hi, love,' Rosie calls back, adding, pointlessly, because she's always in the kitchen, 'we're in the kitchen!'

She hears Greer calling, 'Daddy! Daddy!' and Rosie listens to the creak of the floorboards as he moves towards the kitchen, Rosie and Abi sitting up a little on the sofa, and she can tell Seb's in a great mood.

'Hi, guys!' he calls to them. 'They had to double-bag the takeaway, so I hope you're both feeling hungry!'

She hears the rustle of paper bags as he puts the takeaway on the kitchen table before he turns into the extension, and Rosie sees him in the way she thinks Abi will see him. His tall, solid Danish frame made stronger by hours of tennis, his smile still warm even after a long day. But there's a scream followed by a great thud from upstairs and both Heath and Sylvie start shouting. Shit. Bad timing. Rosie looks to Seb; usually he'd be halfway up the stairs by now to sort out the latest drama but he's just standing in the extension. He looks confused, panicked, like he's forgotten Abi's name, so Rosie decides to help him out. 'Seb, this is Abi. Abi, this is Seb.'

Heath shouts something indistinguishable and Rosie rolls her eyes at Seb before turning to smile apologetically at Abi who doesn't notice, because she's frowning, staring at Seb.

Sylvie howls, 'MUM!'

'Coming!' She rushes past Seb towards the stairs, calling behind her, 'Sorry, guys, back in a minute.'

The problem is that Sylvie had taken Heath's special sketching paper, which he got for his birthday last year, without asking, so Heath had jumped from the bed, tearing up Sylvie's drawing. Lily steps in to save the day, ripping out some pages from her own sketchpad, giving them each a few sheets and challenging them to draw their feet. Rosie thanks Lily and leaves the three of them miraculously quiet and sketching side by side again after just a couple of minutes.

Downstairs, Seb is still standing in the extension, but he's turned to the side, his hands on his hips, and Abi is in front of him, her hands raised, fingers flexed, whispering urgently. Seb hears Rosie first and he turns quickly towards her, takes a step back, away from Abi. His face is pale, his eyes wide, like she, Rosie, frightens him. Rosie would usually laugh at him, but she doesn't because Abi immediately turns to Rosie. She looks strange, too. Her eyes are bright, her face flushed, but she doesn't seem frightened like Seb. No, she looks fucking furious.

As she glances from her new friend to her husband and back again, Rosie makes herself smile. 'You guys OK?'

Seb spins around towards the table and immediately starts pulling chopsticks and small cardboard boxes out of the take-away bags behind him, saying too brightly, 'Yeah, good!'

Abi and Rosie are left blinking at each other before Abi says, 'Ro, I'm so sorry. I was just telling Seb I got a message from Lotte – there's an urgent issue, at the restaurant; I'm going to have to go.'

And before Rosie can say anything, Abi turns away, gathering her denim jacket and rucksack, passing Rosie and squeezing her arm briefly as she walks past. 'I'll message you, yeah?'

Everything is changing too quickly for Rosie. She feels like she's just woken up on stage in the middle of a play and has no clue what all the other actors are talking about, how she should join in, if she should join in or if she should just watch. She follows Abi dumbly to the bottom of the stairs as Abi calls up for Lily. Abi hardly seems to hear Rosie as she tells her the girls can stay here until she's finished whatever she needs to do at the restaurant, that they can heat up the take-away, save it for later, maybe?

But Abi keeps moving, gathering coats and school bags and telling a grumbly Margot to please hurry up before ushering the girls outside and turning to Rosie on the doorstep. 'Thanks, but I don't know how long this thing at the restaurant will take to sort out, so better if the girls are home.' Rosie hears Seb walk down the corridor behind her, feels him stop close, too close; she can feel the breath of him in and out even through their layers of clothes. She feels herself suspended, sandwiched between the two of them, like an intruder. Abi's eyes are hard as fists as she looks at Rosie's husband, and whatever has just happened, the mammalian part of Rosie's brain recognizes it as no good, so she doesn't say another word as Abi looks back to Rosie and says, 'Bye, Rosie.' Then Abi and her children disappear into the inky twilight.

As soon as she closes the door behind them, Rosie turns around to face Seb. 'I thought you guys hadn't met before?'

Seb blinks but keeps his eyes fixed on her. 'No! No.' He shakes his head, a little too firmly. 'I told you: she cancelled a meeting a couple of weeks ago, but we have been exchanging emails. Stupidly, I hadn't realized Ms Matthews – the woman I've been emailing – was your new friend. It's a . . . it's a school thing, an issue with her daughter. She expressly asked to keep it confidential, so . . .'

Seb shrugs his shoulders, tries to smile at Rosie, an unconvincing flicker of a thing, before he says, 'We should eat before it gets cold.'

Rosie is still confused. 'Why didn't she mention that to me?'

Seb turns around to walk back to the kitchen and either he doesn't hear her or he pretends not to, as Rosie's words fall into the empty space between them.

Standing there, Abi walking away from her outside, Seb walking away from her inside, Rosie is left with the creeping, shuddery feeling that something significant has just happened but that both Abi and Seb want to keep her far away from it.

Chapter 3

Abi blamed herself. If she'd met him, as originally planned, at the new-parent meeting, things would have been different. She'd have known how to handle herself. But having Lily and Margot in the same house, so close to the truth, had been horrifying. Abi was in too much shock to talk after they left Rosie's, but listening to Margot and Lily chatting about *Frozen* kept her feet on the ground, kept them shuffling towards home. Without knowing they were doing it, her girls saved her. They always saved her. Margot took Abi's and Lily's hands so they could swing her along the pavement, Margot kicking her little feet into the air and calling, 'Higher, higher!' The weight of her, feeling Lily on the other side, knowing they needed her to be strong, to keep going with her plan, kept Abi from falling to her knees.

What the hell was she doing?

It wasn't until the girls were in bed that she paced, swore and tried to work through all the different scenarios of what could be going on. None of them were good for Abi or the girls.

She woke early, still furious and still afraid. But really, what was new?

Margot had crept into her bed at some point during the night, bringing her little body close. Her presence helped Abi ignore the question that had been circling in her mind all night: *What will he tell Rosie?* She had no idea. So she did what she had done for years. She pushed her rage away and, weak with fear and exhaustion, she did what she had to do to feed her children.

She knew he'd come; she just didn't know when.

She'd held Margot close, kissed her cheek. Smiled and waved to Lily at the school gates. She hid her fear behind her smile, because pretending was Abi's thing. She kept her face impassive as she walked away from school, imagining what he could have told the other parents, told Rosie.

The thought of Rosie made Abi wilt. She was surprised by how much she wanted to be friends with Rosie. She hadn't made a new friend in so long, but Rosie intrigued Abi; she'd never actually known anyone like her. Someone who seemed to be gliding along on an escalator through life while the rest of them trudged up mucky steps that smelt like piss. Rosie had the kids, the husband, the sighing complaints about the kitchen extension. To Abi, Rosie's life seemed so calm, so exotic in its ordinariness. But Abi knew now there was sadness too, a weariness that wore at the edges of Rosie's dreamy set-up and made her face fall into worry when she thought no one was looking.

Abi arrives early at the restaurant. There are hundreds of forks, knives and spoons that need unpacking, washing, drying, polishing and putting away. This is the kind of monotonous work she can handle today. While Richard and Lotte sweep around the restaurant arguing about where to hang an oil painting, screaming at each other over a wine order, Abi keeps to the kitchen, hunched, working her fingers raw.

She wishes Diego were here, but he isn't arriving for another few days and, besides, she probably shouldn't tell him. He is moving for a new start both professionally with PLATE and with his partner. It'd disturb him, the past stalking them like this.

Abi stays in the kitchen, working and listening to Richard and Lotte's latest row about the reservation system when suddenly the swing doors sigh open and Lotte stalks stormily into the room. She kicks herself up on to the stainless-steel countertop and holds her head in her hands, groans dramatically, 'Urgh. Men!'

Abi stops drying a platter.

'I honestly think doing this on my own would be easier than doing it with him. It was such a stupid idea, thinking we could cope working together.' She turns to look at Abi. 'I mean, look at you, a working single parent. You're better off without a man, aren't you?'

Abi breathes out, fiddles with the bangles round her wrist, wrestling with the urge to tell her boss to fuck off, but reminds herself this is what women like Lotte do: they chat.

A few months ago, when she first arrived in Waverly for her interview, she noticed how Lotte's smile had faltered. The way Lotte's mouth crumpled as she took in her tattoos, her freshly cropped hair.

But Richard and Lotte had spent months wooing Diego to leave London and head up PLATE, and Diego had been unwavering: he'd only accept the offer at PLATE if Abi had a role too. She's promised Diego she'll do her best to fit in.

Abi forces a smile. 'Well, it hasn't always been easy.'

'No, of course it hasn't,' Lotte states, before curiosity gets the better of her and she asks, 'Does their dad help?'

Of course. This is what Lotte wants. A slice of Abi's history.

'Well, they don't have the same dad.'

'Oh,' Lotte says. 'They're half-sisters.'

'They're just sisters.'

Lotte nods like Abi's confirming what she already knew. 'Of course.'

Lotte's eyes still on her, Abi gives in to the pressure to offer her half of the story.

'I got pregnant with Lily when I was eighteen – it was just a casual thing. He's been all right, really – paid maintenance, did the bare minimum – but he's never really been Lily's dad.' Abi looks steadily at Lotte, hoping to pre-emptively neutralize any pity. 'He lives in Scotland now; he's got other kids, his own family, which is fine.'

Lotte nods, like this is all as she anticipated but she's impatient to hear the rest of the story. 'And Margot?'

Abi picks up a few spoons, starts drying them, unsure how this is going to go. 'I knew I wanted another child, so I used a sperm donor.'

Lotte's jaw actually drops. 'I was not expecting you to say that,' she says, her eyes blinking with surprise.

'No one ever does.' Abi shrugs and picks up some more spoons to keep her hands busy. Although it was never a motivation, she has to admit there is some satisfaction in challenging the bleak single-parent narrative. People always think Margot must have been 'another mistake' but the truth is the opposite. Abi loved being a mum and she was bloody good at it. She wanted another baby and Lily wanted a sibling. She'd waited until Lily was old enough to understand, until she had savings and could take a few months off work, could support the three of them, and then she'd tracked her ovulation and bought some sperm. The whole thing was straightforward, and Margot made her presence known as a little blue line after only two months of trying.

'Wow,' Lotte says, sitting up straighter on the counter and shaking her head. 'I have so many questions, I literally don't know where to start.' Abi realizes that her honesty has made Lotte relax, and she smiles as she feels Lotte arrive fully in the room.

'What about you guys?' Abi asks.

'Oh, we just did it the boring old sex way.' Lotte laughs and then quickly settles herself. 'You mean, why didn't we have another kid?'

She says it in a way that suggests she assumes this is what people want to know about her but most dare not ask. It makes Abi want to howl and laugh at the same time because women's lives are never immune to scrutiny – even the choices of married, straight, solvent mothers like Lotte.

The bell from the front of the restaurant sounds, Lotte rolls her eyes and Abi freezes.

'Bet he's forgotten his bloody keys.' Lotte jumps down from the countertop, padding out of the kitchen.

Abi silently prays that Lotte is right, that it is Richard or another delivery person, but her veins shrink as she hears Lotte squeal, 'Sebbo!'

She's not ready, not at all, so she closes her eyes, listens in darkness as Lotte and Seb talk, their voices indecipherable

40

murmurs. His voice, the brutal unfairness of the whole thing, makes her grab the side of the sink and kick, hard, against one of the new units. She hasn't, she tells herself, strictly done anything wrong, *she* hasn't hurt or betrayed anyone, and yet, and yet . . .

Their voices are getting louder now, they're coming for her, and she remembers her golden rule. Don't let him see that you're scared.

The swing doors to the kitchen open and Lotte's soprano sing-songs, 'Abi! Sebbo needs to have a word about school.'

She is ready.

Abi walks, wiping her hands on her apron, into the main restaurant. It's bright compared to the cool, dark cave of the kitchen. Lotte is talking, something about being sent burgundy aprons instead of the magenta she ordered, but Abi hardly notices because there, fragile as a reed, is the man who with just a word could destroy her new life in Waverly. Their eyes meet and she settles a little because she knows he doesn't have the strength to break her – not today, anyway.

'Hello, Seb.' Her voice is clear.

He twitches at the sound of his name on her lips. 'Hi, Abi, sorry to disturb you at work, but I thought it best to discuss the matter I mentioned without the children around.' He's practised his lines and looks nauseous now that showtime has arrived.

Something through the window catches Lotte's attention. 'Oh shit, is that a traffic warden?' She's spotted a man in high vis, standing perilously close to her car. 'Shit!' she screams again before flying out of the door towards the warden.

The sound of the door banging closed seems to wake Seb

up. When he meets Abi's stare, his eyes have changed; now they're full of anger. *Welcome*, Abi thinks, *to my world.*

'What the fuck were you doing, *Abi*?' He moves closer to her, saying her name like she repulses him. 'In my fucking house? What is this? Some fucked-up bunny-boiler stunt?'

She hates him, then – hates him from the very root of her being.

'Trust me, *Mr Kent*, this is just as uncomfortable for me as it is for you.'

He shakes his head, looks like he wants to rip hers from her shoulders, but his voice quakes. 'I doubt that. I doubt that very much.'

Abi is careful to keep looking straight at him as she says, 'Look, I had no idea you lived in Waverly, no idea you were Rosie's husband.'

'Bullshit.'

Rage takes her then, shakes her body and pushes her in the last direction her fear wants to move: even closer to him. 'You piece of shit. I have just as much right to be here as you.'

'Why the hell are you here?' he demands, tiny flecks of spit exploding from his mouth.

'Because this insanely privileged fucking bubble of a town is my chance to change my life. Waverly happens to be the best opportunity for my kids to live somewhere beautiful. Where people bitch about slugs in their allotments and their biggest issues are dog shit and potholes. OK?'

He looks startled, appalled perhaps that she is a person with a life, responsibilities, desires. He starts breathing quicker then, hyperventilating, heaving around his words. 'I have children, too. A wife. God. I could lose everything.'

Abi stands back as he bends forward, hands on his knees,

his breath coming in painful-sounding gasps. She watches him fight to control his breathing. When he looks up, there's sweat on his brow, spittle at the corners of his mouth; his face has turned an unnatural red, just a shade lighter than the scar on his upper lip, the scar that had given him away in Rosie and Seb's warm kitchen. Abi is worried he'll need an ambulance if he doesn't calm down. She pulls out the nearest dining chair.

'Sit,' she says, 'for God's sake.'

He does as he's told, elbows on knees, starts sobbing into his hands, making a quiet choking sound. Abi glances out of the window to where Lotte is now shrieking at the poor traffic warden. They still have a couple of minutes. Abi turns back to Seb coming undone in front of her, wishes she could simply leave him here, walk away. But the rubble of his life is now mixed up with the rubble of hers. She has to stay.

'Listen, Seb,' she says as clearly as she can, 'I haven't come to Waverly because you're here. I have no interest in hurting you. I'm not going to blackmail you or cause any trouble for you or your family. What happened between us was . . . well, it's in the past.'

He looks up at her, his eyes swollen and raw. 'What do you want, then?'

'Like I said, I just want the same as everyone else. The opportunity to change my life. To be someone else.'

Listening to herself, she realizes how badly she wants to be here, to be part of something. It is only now, living in Waverly, that she appreciates how painful life was in London, always on the periphery.

'I tried your phone – your old number,' Seb says weakly.

'I don't use that number any more.'

'So, you've totally changed?'

43

She wants to scream at him. But she knows she can't. Not here, not in the fresh Waverly air, not with him in the clothes where he probably has a snack for his kids in the coat pocket, or when he can still feel the press of Rosie's mouth on his cheek.

Abi knows better than to say 'never', so instead she shrugs and asks, 'You?'

Seb stares at her, grinds his jaw. He swallows and says, like it absolves him of everything, 'I love my wife.'

Abi doesn't point out that that wasn't what she asked.

He looks at her, brow furrowed, disgust twisting his mouth. It's a look Abi knows well. Revulsion. Still, she'll just about take it over pity. 'Don't you dare look at me like that.'

Seb hangs his head again and says, 'Look, I'm sorry. I'm sorry. All I want is to understand why you're here. What it means. Obviously, no one knows.' He glances again at her, hoping she'll let him off, but she won't. She's been letting men off for years. She stares at him to make him keep talking and he does, but so quietly she can barely hear.

'No one knows about us.'

'Same here.'

He looks at her, startled. 'What about your friends, your family?'

She could tell him the truth: that her only friends are her kids and an unpredictable Mexican chef who is also now her boss, and that her mum, still living on the estate where Abi grew up, hasn't spoken to her for years. But she won't tell him any of it because there's already sorrow rippling across his brow and the truth would probably tip him over the edge. Just because she can cope with her story doesn't mean other people can.

She just shakes her head.

44

'Why are you here – in Waverly, I mean?' he asks again.

She motions to the restaurant. 'Like I said, for the opportunity. For my girls. For all of us. It was just time for me to move on. Just like you.'

He nods slowly, taking it in, taking the time to process the startling fact that she is just, well, ordinary.

'What did you tell Rosie?'

He breathes out quickly and for a moment Abi thinks he's going to start hyperventilating again, but he manages to keep himself steady. 'I told her I had a migraine, that I had to lie down.'

'She believed you?' Abi knows the answer; Rosie isn't stupid. Seb shakes his head.

'After you left, she knew something was off. She asked if I knew you. I told her there was an issue with your daughter at school – a confidential thing – that you'd had a disagreement with one of the teachers and, well, that we'd had an awkward email exchange.'

'Oh God.'

'What was I supposed to do?'

'Don't bring my children into it!'

'I'm sorry. I was in shock; I wasn't thinking straight.'

'She won't believe it. I would have mentioned something like that to her before meeting you.'

It is clear then that Seb might be many things, but he isn't good at lying.

'Rosie messaged me this morning,' she continues.

Seb looks up. 'What did she say?'

'She invited me and the girls over on the weekend and, no, I haven't replied yet.'

'What are you going to say?'

'I'm not sure yet.'

45

'Don't – please don't be flippant. This is my life, our lives we're talking about.'

Abi's about to ask whether he's referring to him and her or to him and Rosie, but her eyes catch movement outside the window. The traffic warden is walking away from Lotte now, shaking his head, Lotte waving her arms, still ranting behind him.

They don't have long.

Abi closes her eyes briefly. The veil between her old and new worlds is, in this moment, gossamer thin. She needs this to stop.

'Look,' she says softly but clearly, 'we've got the same problem. It would be better – much better – for us both if no one finds out what happened.'

Seb nods. 'I agree. I completely agree.'

Cool relief washes through Abi's body.

'I need you to distance yourself from my wife.' Seb adds, 'Please. No more messages, no more walks and no more invites to dinner.'

Anger ripples through her. She hates him, hates any man, especially this kind of man, dictating what she can and can't do, but she concedes with a bow of her head. Friendship with Rosie – real, true friendship – is no longer possible anyway. How could it be when she'd previously washed her husband's semen from between her legs? Another wasted relationship to add to the pile. But Rosie isn't Abi's focus now.

'What about Lily, school?'

Seb puffs out his cheeks, glances briefly at the ceiling. 'I'll be professional.' He looks Abi in the eye as he says, 'I promise I won't treat Lily any differently because of all this. She's a good kid, talented; she's got nothing to do with any of this.'

Abi looks back at him and for the first time she thinks she might cry; kindness has always moved her more than cruelty. But she reminds herself now, looking at Seb, that kindness can be just another act.

'Don't ever tangle my girls up in another lie.'

He nods. 'I'm sorry I did that. I won't do it again.'

Then he lifts his hand to his face, and he starts to sob again, little whimpering sounds.

The whimpering turns into a kind of growl before he does something unexpected: he moves closer, towards Abi.

'I'm sorry. I'm so sorry.'

She's confused. What's he apologizing for? For the unfair distribution of luck? Or is he apologizing for something more mundane, more familiar to Abi; is he apologizing for the ugly thoughts he has about her? Or for wishing she didn't exist, because the very fact of her reminds him of what he's capable of, his duplicitous nature, the part of himself he has to work so hard to smother in all his fucking goodness?

She doesn't know and, really, it doesn't matter. Let his thoughts be his own. She wants nothing more to do with him. They both turn to see Lotte walking back towards the restaurant, her face gripped in anger, a yellow parking ticket twisting in her hand.

Abi takes a step back, away from Seb. 'OK.'

She wants him to leave now but he asks again, needing more reassurance, 'You won't say anything?'

She looks at him one last time, directly into his pitiful, scared eyes. 'No, Seb, I won't. Just know that I'm protecting my children in this – not you. Is that clear?'

He nods and she's glad he can't say anything else even if he wanted to because Lotte's back, a ball of spitting outrage as it turns out the laws of the land also apply to her and her Land Rover.

Neither Seb nor Lotte notices as Abi walks away from them both, back into the cool darkness of the kitchen.

Chapter 4

Rosie knows as she walks down the stairs – even without seeing her or hearing her – that Eva has arrived. The air feels calmer, and the kids have stopped bickering; they talk rather than whine and have become the kind of children Rosie imagined having before she actually had any. Today, Eva's arrived with a jigsaw puzzle she kept from Seb's childhood, and the four of them are already gathered round the table sorting out the pieces. The kids kneeling on the chairs, bums in the air, hovering over the table.

'*Min skat*,' Eva says when she sees Rosie, reserving her Danish words of endearment for those she loves best. Rosie bends to kiss her mother-in-law's soft cheek. It's as soft as the kids' skin but no longer springy, more like something worn and loved for a long time. She smells of fresh air and shortbread.

'Thanks so much for this, Eva.'

Rosie is digging through a pile of dirty washing, left in a heap outside the machine, to see if her swimsuit is hiding in there.

'I can't think of anywhere I'd rather be,' Eva says, acknowledging Greer with a nod as she passes her a corner piece of the puzzle. After more than five decades in the UK, Eva still sounds Danish, her accent warm like hot chocolate poured over words. They all adore her. Even though she's faced a few hard things in life – fertility issues, grief and living away from her beloved Denmark – she is still determined to experience joy whenever it comes her way. She'd met Seb's dad, Benjamin, when she'd sat down in one of his economics lectures at UCL, having got lost on the way to her English lecture. He'd drawn her a little map of where to go so she wouldn't make the same mistake the following week and, in a moment of uncharacteristic bravado, he'd written his number at the bottom. Seb had the map framed after Benjamin died, peacefully at home, from cancer. He'd never seen Eva sob the way she sobbed when she unwrapped the frame. Now it hangs in her bedroom, above the side of the bed where Benjamin slept next to her for so many years.

Rosie discovers her swimsuit at the bottom of the washing, curled and limp like discarded skin, and decides it's best not to smell it before putting it in her tote bag along with her towel. 'I'll only be a couple of hours.'

'Take your time, *elskede*. Don't rush for us.'

Rosie puts her hand on Eva's shoulder and Eva squeezes Rosie's arm. Now Eva is here, the need to leave suddenly seems less urgent. Having Eva in her life is like having a second chance at being a daughter. But Anna will be waiting, so Rosie kisses all four of them again before she leaves, her heart aching with love as they call out their goodbyes.

At Anna's gym, Anna strips her clothes off in the communal area while Rosie dips into one of the cubicles.

'Ro, there's no one here!' Anna laughs, muttering, 'Prude,'

as she undoes her bra, her breasts pouring into her hands. Rosie peers at her friend like she's snooping on a bathing nymph. Anna's naked body spills and sways and sinks as she rummages in her bag for her swimsuit, but the main difference between them is that Anna wears herself proudly, luxuriously, while Rosie beetles around, eyes swivelling in the shadows. Rosie bets Anna masturbates regularly. Anna would probably tell her if she asked, not that she ever would. Rosie is sure friendship is easier, clearer when some things, intimate things, remain private.

Rosie comes out of her changing room while Anna's bent over. She's stepping into her costume, pulling it up, groaning 'Bloody thing,' at the twisted straps, the complicated design.

Rosie moves forward to help and they're both soon shaking with laughter as Anna puts her head through the wrong hole so when she pulls the costume up, her enormous breasts are forced out either side of the fabric. They're hanging like water balloons, almost under her armpits, and Anna slides her goggles on and while Rosie doubles over, stamping her foot and shaking with laughter, Anna says, 'Perfect! Let's swim!'

And Anna starts to walk, duck-like, tits swinging free, towards the pool.

'God, I honestly can't remember the last time I laughed like that,' Rosie says after their swim as she lies back on the bottom shelf of the wood-panelled sauna while Anna, breasts now safely contained, lies on the top. Anna doesn't say anything, but Rosie knows she's smiling, glad. She loves to make people laugh. Rosie bubbles up with giggles again before they both settle into a delicious, endorphin-charged quiet.

After a couple of minutes, her face just a few inches from the ceiling, Anna says, 'You said you had something you wanted to talk about?'

For a moment, Rosie can't remember what it was she'd wanted to discuss with Anna, but then the weird disquieted feeling blooms up in her again. 'How often do you and Eddy have sex, Anna?'

Above her, Anna laughs.

'Quite an opener,' she says, but Anna doesn't squirm like Rosie when sex is mentioned. 'Umm. Once a week, every Sunday. He reads the papers, I read the supplements and then we have sex.'

Once a week?

'How about you guys?' Anna asks back.

'We're going through a bit of a dry spell, actually. I'm just kind of trying to get back into it, I guess.'

'Oh, babe.' Anna twists around, peering down at Rosie between the slats. 'That's so normal, especially with young kids. I wouldn't worry about that. How often do you have sex?'

Rosie feels her veins leap before rushing with shame. She's never talked with anyone about the drought, only argued with Seb about it. She can't go straight in with the truth. She needs to ease in gently. 'Umm, maybe it's been three months?'

Anna's eyes widen. 'I prescribe a maintenance shag. It's worked for us before. Even if you don't feel like it, gets you back on the horse as it were,' she says with a snort of laughter.

'Yeah,' Rosie says, irritation nibbling at her now because all the sex she's ever had has felt like a maintenance shag. She'd been trying to uphold and maintain some false version of herself – Rosie the sexual, generous, intimate lover – when really she had no idea who she was sexually. No idea what turned her on or even how she liked to be touched any more.

Above her Anna is quiet, so she adds, 'Yeah, that's probably a good idea. Thanks, Anna.'

Rosie wants to ask, but could never without confessing how long it has been: is a year really *just* a dry spell? Sure, after each baby they didn't have sex for a few months. A couple of months after Sylvie, around three after Heath and even a bit longer after Greer. And perhaps this longer drought is simply an expression of their lives becoming fuller, busier.

Seb acts like sex is as urgent and necessary as breathing, something that keeps him alive. Rosie is sure she used to like sex, but she's never felt like that about it. Never felt like she'd fade away without it.

'I remember you saying that as soon as you saw Eddy after Singapore you knew something had happened.'

Anna peers down at Rosie again, wondering why Rosie's asking this now. This time, Rosie avoids her eye completely.

'Yeah. I did. He stepped through the front door and I knew something had happened before he even took his coat off. He had nervous energy; he'd spent the whole flight home trying to figure out what to say, eaten up with guilt.'

'As he should!' Rosie adds.

'Yeah,' Anna agrees, wiping sweat from her brow. 'Women's intuition, I guess. I knew something had changed.'

'He told you right away?'

'Yes, right there in the kitchen, and then I threw a plate at him.'

A drop of sweat falls off Anna's chin as she shakes her head and half smiles at the memory.

It had been on one of Eddy's flashy business trips two years ago.

Eddy runs a company specializing in car tech design and is frequently put up in five-star hotels, encouraged to order whatever he likes at the bar. This trip had been to Singapore and the woman perched on the hotel bar stool next to Eddy laughed at everything he said. Eddy told Seb that the woman was the opposite of Anna – dark, thin, spiky. He knew she was bad for him in the way he knew smoking or having another whisky would make him feel awful the next day. But Eddy was a glutton. He couldn't – and he didn't – resist. The flight home was the worst day of Eddy's life. It never crossed his mind to lie. Eddy was many things – selfish, an impossible flirt, arrogant – but he was not a liar. He could never lie to someone he loved.

Forgiveness took time. Anna and Eddy had counselling and Eddy – for a few months at least – gave up drinking and cut back on the business trips. Both Rosie and Seb knew but never said aloud that Anna wouldn't end their marriage. For all his flaws, his maddeningly selfish behaviour, Anna loved the idiot.

An unexpected outcome of Eddy's infidelity had been that for a time, at least, Rosie and Seb had been closer. Rosie remembers feeling like a bit of a traitor, Anna going through the worst time of her marriage while Seb and Rosie were briefly golden. For a few nights, after the kids were asleep, they'd sit in the bath together and talk. Then they'd wash each other, shining and buffing the untarnished commitment between them. They'd been beautiful, those baths and, yes, a couple of times Rosie thinks the slow washing had led to them having sex. She remembers how connected they felt then, how easy it had been to fall asleep wrapped up in each other. Why couldn't they go back there now?

'Why is this coming up now, babe?' Anna asks gently.

Rosie tells Anna about how she convinced Abi to stay for dinner, how Seb came back with straining takeaway bags, how when she came back down after the kids' row upstairs, the atmosphere was weird, and how Abi immediately said she had to go. Seb told her later that there'd been a minor disagreement with Abi, some school issue about Lily, that he hadn't realized the parent – Ms Matthews – he'd been exchanging terse emails with was also Abi, Rosie's new friend.

'OK, what's the problem?' Anna asks.

Rosie lifts her hand to her sweat-slick brow, feels the flesh on her legs swing as she bends her knees.

'It's a bit weird, isn't it, that Abi didn't mention this thing with Lily? I mean, I'm not saying I expected her to tell me everything, you know, if it was confidential, but Abi could have just flagged it, don't you think?'

Rosie doesn't tell her that Abi has suddenly gone cold on messages. Saying she's too busy to come for dinner but will be in touch. She's told herself Abi probably wants to wait to hang out again until this school issue with Seb is resolved.

Anna adjusts her position again, leaning back on her arms.

'It's a bit odd,' she agrees. 'Yes, I know you like Abi, but, to be honest, I've been getting some strange vibes from her. I told you I asked her if she could mind Albie after school for me and have him just for an hour on Thursday? Well, I suggested I bring a bottle of wine over, so we can have a glass when I collect him – you know, get to know each other a bit – and honestly, she looked like I'd just slapped her. Just grabbed her kid and disappeared.'

Anna is prone to hyperbole but still Rosie can picture the scene, Anna widening her eyes at Abi's retreating back, turning to the parent next to her, mouthing, 'Rude!'

Rosie wants to step in, defend her new friend. Anna has done this before, asking for help with childcare from women she just wants an excuse to interrogate. She can be too quick to form an opinion and despite whatever happened the other day, Rosie still feels drawn to Abi.

'Maybe she's just getting used to how it is down here. You've got to admit, it's pretty different and she's Hackney through and through, right?'

'Hmm,' Anna says, unconvinced, before adding, 'she just seems a bit aloof. I can't help but feel like she's patronizing us, treating us like sweet little provincial wives. You know, the other day she asked me if I work? I was like, "Hell yes, I work!"'

Anna works in communications for a hedge fund. Three mornings a week she gets the 6.30 a.m. train to London and can often be found on the 7 p.m. back to Waverly, still tapping away at her spreadsheets.

'Oh, Anna,' Rosie scolds, 'the woman has just upended her whole life, changing town, jobs, and doing it all on her own with two kids. I mean, imagine! Maybe don't write her off just yet.'

Anna lies back down; Rosie watches the flesh on her back fill the spaces between the wooden slats like rising dough.

'Saved by the bell!' Anna says, relieved, lifting herself immediately up again, sweaty face glistening, illuminated by a call coming through the screen of her smart watch.

Rosie shuffles over so Anna can clamber down, Anna's bum and legs branded with red welts from where she's been pressed against the wooden slats.

'I'll be out in a mo!' Rosie calls after her but Anna doesn't acknowledge her. As the sauna door slowly closes, Rosie can see her friend already searching the pocket of her dressing gown for her phone. She watches Anna for a moment through the square sauna window, pacing by the showers, her eyes swivelling around the echoey swimming pool.

Rosie, her head back against the wooden slats, feels her sweat run down her body, and she wonders at Anna's fragility. Her friend is loud and bright, but easy to bruise and quick to judge. Abi, with her different approach to life, would trouble Anna. How delicate it could be, sharing lives so closely but resisting the urge to collapse into each other's prejudices. Rosie feels in her root that she is more aligned with Abi, but time and conditioning have made her twist and grow alongside Anna. She'll text Abi later, see if she's up for going for a drink soon.

Rosie sits up, her body feeling like a long-burnt candle collapsing in on itself, and she stumbles out of the sauna into the coolness of the pool. She's surprised to see that Anna's standing across from her, call finished but holding her phone over her heart like a nun with a Bible, her head tipped to one side like she's trying to solve a problem she can't quite see, staring directly at Rosie before she blinks and points towards the showers.

Once they're dressed again, they sit side by side in front of a large mirror, Rosie towelling her hair while Anna massages cream on to her face.

'Bloody hell, I look like a boiled ham.' Anna laughs, before adding, 'That was Lotte calling while we were in the sauna.'

'Oh yeah?' Rosie replies. 'Is she OK?'

'She's feeling stressed about the restaurant. Apparently, her and Richard have been rowing loads, which is kind of predictable.'

'Yeah,' Rosie agrees. Lotte is always moaning about Richard.

'She was asking if we could get there for seven thirty p.m. sharp next Saturday. The opening-night nerves have definitely set in, she's already having nightmares about no one turning up.'

'OK, I'll ask Eva if she can come earlier and do bedtime.'

They're both quiet. Anna applies her trademark red lipstick while Rosie tips her head to one side and runs her fingers through her damp hair, strands catching in the webbing of her hands like weeds. Next to her, Anna's reflection stills in the mirror; she smiles with freshly painted lips but her eyes are weighted, sad. Rosie stops towelling her hair and asks, 'You all right?'

Anna shakes her head softly. 'Yeah, sorry, it's just a work email. It's put me in a funny mood – my fault for reading it now.'

'You've got to stop doing that,' Rosie agrees. 'Boundaries,' she reminds her friend.

'Boundaries.' Anna nods, gathering her make-up before she stands and moves behind Rosie, her hand on Rosie's shoulder. They stare at each other in the mirror; they look like a staged photo from a hundred years ago – Anna fair and flowing, her full arm reaching up for her dark-haired friend. They've shared so much. Thanks to Eddy and Seb, they'd had no choice, really; they had to be friends. They've babysat each other's kids; Rosie knows their alarm code and the trick to opening the sticky back-door lock. Anna knows the names of Greer's favourite cuddly toys and that Rosie is allergic to penicillin. They are more than neighbours and more than friends. Bound together, living life side by side.

'You know I love you, don't you, Ro?' Anna says, her eyes shining in the mirror.

'Course I do,' Rosie says, patting her friend's arm. 'What's brought this on?'

'I just want you to know that I'm always here for you.'

'OK!' Rosie says, smiling and turning to face her friend. 'And I'm always here for you. Come here.' She opens her arms and, as they hug, Rosie feels how tightly her dear, bold, emotionally brittle friend clings on to her.

None of her kids move their eyes from the TV as Rosie kisses them hello, offering only monosyllabic answers to her questions about their afternoon. She picks up a discarded mug, a few plates scattered with crumbs, and puts Heath's abandoned school rucksack on a peg in the hall before she walks into the kitchen. Seb is wearing the 'Kiss the cook!' apron Eva bought him for Christmas a few years ago. He's bent over the kitchen sink, frowning and scrubbing something hard. He turns towards her, holding his hands in Marigolds in the air, like a surgeon pre-op.

'Hi, love,' he says. 'You OK?'

'Yeah, fine,' she replies before she leans forward and gives him a bouncy kiss on the lips. She notices his eyelid twitch as he turns back to the sink.

'Think I found some bacon from 2006 on this pan.'

'Still tasty?' she asks and he laughs.

'Delicious.'

'How were the fajitas?'

'Well, Heathy and I loved them, the girls not so much. We

set the smoke alarm off again, though, and it's a bit mangled, I'm afraid.' He looks over to the table where the alarm sits, an alien mess of cables.

'Jesus, did you just yank it out of the ceiling?'

'Ro, it was uncontrollable – it was only charred chicken. Greer was screaming and the big kids started beating each other up in the garden – what was I supposed to do?'

She stares at the broken alarm. 'Um, press the "stop" button, remove the batteries . . . basically do anything else than pull our house apart.'

His eyelid twitches again, his jaw pulses. He sounds like it's very much a big deal even as he says, 'Look, it's not a big deal. It's been glitching for ages; we had to do something about it eventually, didn't we? I've already called someone; they're coming over tomorrow to replace it.'

There is a brief pause, then over his scrubbing Seb asks, 'How was it? Anna OK?'

Rosie laughs into the glass cupboard at the memory of Anna's breasts bursting out either side of her costume. 'Yeah,' she says, 'Anna's great.'

Seb turns and smiles at her; he once told her he loves watching her laugh.

As he looks back down at his pan, Rosie keeps her eyes on him, noticing how quickly his smile drops. It's as if he is suddenly lit differently, new, unfamiliar shadows darkening his features.

She moves towards him, puts her hand on his scrubbing arm, feels his tendons leap against her touch as he stops abruptly and she asks, 'You OK?'

He turns, just slightly towards her. Their eyes don't meet but his voice is unusually sharp as he says, 'Yes, of course. Why wouldn't I be?'

She pulls her hand away. 'You just seem a bit . . . I don't know, a bit tense.'

'Do I?' He lifts the pan out of the sink, suds running, his eyelid pulsing. 'Well, yeah, sorry. The smoke alarm thing put me on edge, to be honest, and, you know, Sylvie and Heath arguing the whole time.' He stares at the still-blackened pan in his hand and says, doleful, 'I think we're going to have to throw this away, sadly. What a bloody waste.'

He carries it across the kitchen, splattering water on the floor as he opens the back door. Rosie watches as he props it up in the pile of stuff they've been saying they'll take to the tip for months, silvered now by hungry autumn snails.

Heath slides sloppily into the kitchen, caressing a rugby ball between his hands. Rosie kisses the perfect freckles on his perfect nose and Heath nudges Seb with the ball, code for them to go outside. Seb musses his son's hair before kissing Rosie's cheek.

'Glad you had a good time, love.' He follows their son, who is now chattering away about rugby, out into the garden. Rosie turns on the outside light for them, smiles at their retreating backs and thinks, yes, she's right not to worry. Everything is fine. Everything is absolutely fine, isn't it?

Chapter 5

Seb perches on the edge of his desk and looks at the cocky young man staring at him from under a curtain of dark hair. Seb starts to fold his arms together but stops himself, places his palms flat on the desk behind him instead. Ethan stares at him, his expression strangely knowing, and panic suddenly licks inside Seb's stomach. He drops his eyes as Ethan says, 'I know what you're going to say, Mr Kent.'

'Oh yeah?' Seb addresses the floor in front of Ethan because he's slime, and this kid is amazing.

Ethan keeps staring at Seb as he says, 'Yeah. You're going to say that I'm letting myself down getting rubbish marks, that I'm going to mess up my GCSEs if I don't sort it out.'

At the end of last term, Ethan was top of every subject and now he's right at the bottom. Today he hasn't handed in his GCSE coursework, without offering an explanation. Seb has talked to his mum, asked if there's anything going on at home, but she said everything is steady on that front. No changes.

Seb lifts his eyes up to Ethan as he says, 'I just wanted to ask how you're doing.'

It's Ethan who looks away this time, towards the door, then back to Seb. Seb gets it. He wants to run away, too.

In front of him, Ethan shrugs. 'I'm just not as clever as I let on, I suppose.'

'That wasn't what I asked.' Seb's voice is gentle, but he has to force himself to keep looking at the teen. 'How are you doing, Ethan?' Seb asks again.

'Fine.' Ethan lifts his chin to Seb, warning him to back off. 'How are you doing, *sir*?'

Seb glances out of the window at the football pitches, thrumming with players. For a second, he wonders what would happen to Ethan's young face if he told him the truth. Would it lift with shock, cresting into laughter, or would his expression twist, sour with disgust as his brain processed the truth?

Of course, Seb won't tell the whole truth. He seldom does these days. 'I'm finding life quite intense at the moment, actually.'

Ethan raises his eyebrows.

'Don't tell anyone, but I'm worrying a lot. Worrying I'm not doing a good enough job as head teacher. It's a big responsibility, this job. I worry sometimes that I'll let you guys down.'

Ethan stares at Seb and, as he talks, Seb notices something waking up in Ethan. He's listening, not just staring dully, but really listening. It's like Seb can feel his words trickling into Ethan's ears.

'I'm trying my hardest, but I worry it's not enough.'

Ethan nods slowly, thoughtfully, and Seb wants to grab him by his shoulders, shake him and tell him to wake up! He needs to learn when he's being lied to! He just keeps talking, like he always does, like he's thinking aloud, like he's forgotten Ethan's right there, in front of him.

'I'm seeing my mate after school today, actually; he went to school here with me and now we play tennis together. I've been thinking about talking to him . . .'

Ethan keeps his eyes on Seb. 'That sounds like a good idea,' he says.

Seb nods his agreement slowly, thoughtfully.

'I know what you're trying to do, by the way.' Ethan narrows his eyes at Seb, cynicism back in place.

He wants to laugh, thinks, *Glad someone does, because I have no fucking idea!* He stops himself, keeps Ethan away from the truth and instead lies again.

'I'm honestly not trying to do anything, Ethan. Trust me, I know how hard it can be to talk about feelings. Just know, I'm not going anywhere. I'm here if anything changes and you want to talk.'

Ethan nods, shoving his rucksack back on his shoulders. 'So, I can go now?'

Seb nods. Wishes he could swap places with this kid who can just walk so easily away from his troubles.

'That's it?'

'That's it.'

Ethan dips his head towards Seb, but before he opens the door, he stops. 'I'll bring my coursework in the day after tomorrow.'

'That'd be good.'

He nods again and before he leaves Seb asks, 'Ethan, don't tell anyone what I said, will you?'

Ethan turns to look back directly at Seb, his eyes surprised, but there's a small smile on his lips as he replies quietly, 'Course I won't.'

*

The court floodlights switch on as Seb sits on the bench outside Court Five and waits for Eddy. They try to play at least twice a week – always on Wednesday and Friday – more when their schedules allow. They've been playing tennis together since they were twelve and they think of Court Five at Waverly Tennis Club as 'their court'. Eddy always says when he writes his memoir he'll call it *Court Five*, and Seb always assumes – hopes – he's joking. But you never really know with Eddy.

This seventy-eight-by-twenty-seven-foot tarmac rectangle has been a silent, constant witness to their friendship. It was on Court Five that Seb finally broke down after his dad died. It was on Court Five that they asked each other to be godfather to brand-new Blake and then, a few years later, to Sylvie. And it was on Court Five, a couple of years ago, that Eddy told Seb that he'd cheated on Anna. Of all the memories, Seb thinks about that one the most.

Eddy's game was off that day. He'd got two double faults in a row, which was unlike him. During a break Seb put his hand on the back of his friend's neck and asked, 'Ed, you OK?'

Seb couldn't have known, but the combination of that touch, those words in that exact moment made Eddy crumple. They hadn't played a second set; instead, Seb held Eddy, tried to make his arms strong, capable, like those of the fathers they both missed. Underneath the humour, the piss-taking and bravado, Eddy was as soft as a peach.

From the bench, Seb watches Eddy arrive in his black gear, socks pulled up his calves, waving to a couple of other players they know, rolling his shoulders, swinging his new racquet, already warming up. What, Seb wonders, would happen if

Eddy put his hand on the back of Seb's neck – just like Seb did a couple of years ago – and asked him if he was OK?

Would he collapse into the truth, just like Eddy did that day, or grit his teeth and cling on to his lie that everything was fine?

Just fine.

No. He won't say anything. Eddy is the talker – not Seb. In the fifteen years they've been together, he's never had a reason to talk about his relationship with Rosie in any detail with anyone. What would he even say? That his body feels as if he is slowly starving to death from lack of touch? That he's terrified Rosie will never desire him again? That on some subtle, mystical level she's discovered the truth? That Seb is disgusting, unlovable, that he's tricked the whole world into believing he is something else, something good? Even if he did share any of this, then how could he possibly ever come back? Eddy would know too much for everything to stay the same. As a kid, Seb never excelled at any one thing, so he made his goodness his superpower. He'd always offer him-self up to be in goal when no one else wanted to be or he would accept the smallest ice cream. He'd smooth arguments between friends and as a teen clear up the bathroom after Eddy had puked stolen spirits everywhere.

'The Slazenger's maiden battle,' Eddy says by way of greet-ing, kissing his new racquet before jabbing it gently into Seb's ribs. 'Ready for a battering, Sebbo?'

Eddy doesn't notice Seb's unsmiling eyes, the panic flut-tering up his spine, down his limbs, so what can Seb do? He stretches out his quads briefly before putting a couple of balls in his pocket, ignoring the wild hammering in his chest as he jogs on to the court.

After they've warmed up, they break for some water and Eddy looks closer at his friend.

'Jesus, mate, you're a sight for sore eyes,' he says, adding, 'I never really understood that saying. Does it mean I've got sore eyes and you're making them hurt more because you look like shit?'

Seb stares at his friend, supposedly his best friend, and wonders how the hell Eddy can't see that he's slowly dying.

Eddy bounces a box-fresh, bright-yellow ball, testing its springiness, before putting it in his pocket. 'Whatever it means, I suppose what I'm getting at is – I hope you play as badly as you look. C'mon, let's do it!'

Seb loses the first three games with Eddy breaking his serve easily, something he hasn't been able to do for months. Seb feels like an out-of-control marionette doll, strings loose, clattering unsuccessfully after every ball. From the other side of the court, Eddy becomes quieter; he stops bouncing on his heels and after he wins the third game without breaking a sweat, he calls out to Seb, 'Right, that's it.' Eddy waves his new racquet. 'Break.'

Seb gladly obliges, walks slowly back towards the bench and takes a swig of water.

'Shit, mate. I'm sorry I forgot; Anna said you had a migraine this week. That explains your rubbish play . . .' Seb looks at Eddy, his face full of worry suddenly, and he starts laughing quietly because it's just so absurd that Eddy thinks Seb's falling apart because he had a headache. It hurts his throat, his chest, his heart to laugh but he does it anyway; he wraps his arms around himself and convulses with joyless laughter. Eddy stands opposite, frowning, a little scared. And then Eddy does the only thing Seb needs of him right now: he steps closer, so their chests beat side by side, and he opens his arms, pulling Seb towards him.

Held at last, Seb's shaking doesn't stop; in just a few short breaths it turns into sobs. He hasn't ever cried like this before, rattling with shame from an unknown place within him, a place where previously he thought he was just bone, tissue and blood. He couldn't hold back even if he tried and Eddy takes it all. Even when Seb stills a little, Eddy keeps his body strong, braced for another wave which comes again and again until at last he's empty and a new stillness, heavy and sad, fills his chest. He keeps his eyes half closed as he pulls away, sinking to the tarmac. Eddy steadies Seb first and then comes to sit next to him as he slowly opens his eyes fully, wincing against the court floodlights, Eddy's unusually calm face coming into gradual focus.

They sit in silence, breathing together, until Seb takes a longer, deeper breath on his own and says the words Eddy's said to him many times before: 'I've really fucked up.'

Seb rolls his lips together, between his teeth, unsure of the words but unable to stop them.

'I cheated. On Rosie.'

Eddy's eyes are soft, his gaze gentle. He knows this territory. 'You had sex with someone else?'

Seb nods, feels the tears start to roll again. 'We hadn't – Rosie and I – we hadn't had sex in so long. We kept arguing about it, I tried to make things better but no matter what I . . .' Seb shakes his head, swats the tears from his eyes. 'It's been a year now, but even back then I was . . .'

'A year!'

Seb feels a shift in Eddy, like Eddy is coming back from wherever they just journeyed together.

Now he's started, Seb can't stop; he has to get the words out of his body. His voice is quiet but calm as he says, 'Eddy, I . . .'

'Tell me, mate.' Eddy's eyes are wide, ready.

'I found her online.'

Eddy stumbles and asks, 'Were you drunk?'

'No, I . . . We met in the day.'

'You *planned* it?'

Something in Eddy's tone pulls Seb back.

'How many times did you do it?' Eddy is needy, wanting the facts fast before Seb changes his mind and clams up.

'Twice, only twice, a few months ago.'

'Ah. OK.'

Seb watches as Eddy battles to keep his expression neutral.

'Are you going to tell Rosie?'

'No. No, definitely not.'

Eddy's forehead lifts in surprise.

'Why are you looking at me like that?'

'Mate, I'm not looking at you like . . .' Eddy starts defensively, but then changes course, saying more gently, 'It's just a lot to take in, that's all. So this happened a little while ago?'

Seb glances at the sky. He's come this far and, besides, this whole thing has only become a big issue since he came home and found her in his fucking house.

'She, um, the woman, she turned up . . .'

But Seb's talking too slowly for Eddy, who asks loudly, 'Turned up where, mate?'

Seb looks at Eddy, his face frozen, greedy for whatever bombshell is next. Seb realizes that Eddy is only impatient for the explosion; he doesn't care what damage it may cause. Seb had thought, with Eddy's arms around him, when their breath felt like the same breath, that he'd tell Eddy everything. That he'd chosen her from hundreds of profiles, that she'd moved to Waverly, that he'd come back with a takeaway to find her drinking wine with his wife. But now he knows it's not safe. It's not safe to tell Eddy any more, so when Seb rolls on to his knee to stand, dusting grit from his legs, Eddy follows his lead and says, 'What were you going to say, Seb – where did she turn up?'

'It was just a message, that was all, a text she sent. I've blocked her number. I won't ever see her again, I can promise you that.'

Eddy looks numbly at Seb, disappointed, like he knows he's being lied to.

'Look, mate, I'm sorry to lay all this on you. I've been stressed, with the new job, tensions at home. I suppose it just got too much.'

Eddy nods. 'Are you going to find someone else?'

'No!' Seb shakes his head, appalled. 'No. I don't want anyone else; I've only ever wanted Rosie. I want to fix my marriage.'

He should never have told Eddy; it was a mistake, a huge mistake. He'd thought he'd feel better for sharing, that his brotherly camaraderie with Eddy would relieve some guilt, but Eddy's clumsiness has only made him feel grubbier than ever. Thank God he didn't tell him everything.

Eddy looks like he's about to ask another question but thinks better of it and shuts his mouth.

Seb looks towards the tennis club building. They usually play until they're kicked off by the next booking, but even though no one's walking towards them, swinging racquets, he says, 'We're probably running out of time.'

Eddy nods; he wants this to be over, too.

'Eddy, I can trust you, can't I? With what I've just shared.'

'Of course you can, mate, of course.' But Eddy can't quite meet Seb's eye as he says, 'Listen, Seb, trust me on this one. You've got to tell Rosie.'

Now Seb's shaking his head; he needs Eddy to shut up. Eddy doesn't understand, doesn't know the real reason why he can never tell Rosie, but Eddy keeps talking, ignoring Seb. 'The only thing that convinced Anna to give me another chance was the fact that I came clean, that I told her as soon as I walked through the front door. I told her. Really. It's a way of showing respect, proving you want to work on your marriage.'

You fucking hero, Eddy, Seb thinks cruelly, but he keeps his voice gentle as he says out loud, 'Good advice, mate, thank you.'

Eddy cups his palm around Seb's shoulder. 'You're my best friend, Seb, always have been. I only want to help. You know you can trust me, don't you?'

Seb nods without saying anything and Eddy pats him on the back. Seb has to resist the urge to shrug his warm palm off him.

'You'll tell her, right?' Eddy asks and Seb still doesn't need to say anything, just nods before he starts to pack their balls and racquets away in silence and they walk side by side back towards the pavilion. Usually, at the end of a game, Eddy opens his arms to commiserate or to congratulate Seb, but tonight he looks unsure. Instead, he holds Seb's upper arm. 'Well done for telling me, mate, and good luck with Rosie. Call me anytime, yeah?'

Seb slings his tennis bag over his shoulder and starts walking home, the night closing in around him. He has the urge to keep walking, to never stop, to walk until his body – his stupid, needy, traitorous body – dissolves into the human sludge it really is. A car passes him, the driver waving, and even though he doesn't know who it is, he automatically waves back, because it'll be a parent or one of his mum's friends, someone he's known for years. As he walks, he feels like he's carrying all the people he loves on his shoulders. They're all stacked in a precarious pyramid with Seb wobbling and straining at the bottom, trying to keep them all up. But tonight, by telling Eddy, he's started to tremble under the weight, and Seb knows he's not strong enough to keep them all from falling.

Chapter 6

Eddy can't wait to get home from tennis; he wants to feel Anna, his soft, warm, loving Anna, in his arms. Blake's staying at a friend's tonight and Albie will be upstairs in bed already. Anna's sat at the kitchen table, a bottle of wine open before her, and the radio's on so she doesn't hear him come in straight away. After his party, she'd stuck a few of the printed photos of his stupid, grinning face in different places around the kitchen: one on the fridge, another one on the corkboard with the takeaway menus and old appointment reminders. It's disconcerting, accidentally making eye contact with himself constantly. When Anna does turn to him, her eyes are swollen, bloodshot. What is it with tonight?

'Anna, love, why are you crying?'

He hates it when she cries. It makes him feel so useless.

'You're home early,' she says, and she gestures to the chair opposite for him to sit. Eddy pauses. Maybe he should hug her? No, no, he should let her talk while she's in the mood. He sits and tries to make his face open, neutral, like the expression their marriage counsellor always wore during a session. But stillness for Eddy is exhausting; his facial muscles were made for movement. He gives up, takes a gulp of her wine and says, 'Anna, I've had a hell of an evening already. Please, just tell me why you're sad.'

Anna runs her palm over her face and breathes out. 'Rosie told me that something weird happened with Seb and Rosie's new mate, Abi? Anyway, it made me start thinking about everything' – she gestures to Eddy and back to herself, a tissue scrunched in her hand – 'that happened between us and, well, I started thinking through some things and I noticed . . .' She makes an exasperated groan, glancing at the ceiling as the tears come again. 'I noticed some condoms were missing from your bathroom drawer.'

Eddy wants to laugh but forces himself not to. His darling Anna. He's pretty sure her hyper-vigilance, her anxiety, is a kind of love.

'Missing?'

'Four of them,' Anna croaks before starting to cry in earnest again.

Eddy stands and moves to kneel before her, like he's about to propose. He looks up at her, not breaking eye contact, and feels himself swell with something unfamiliar – innocence, perhaps – as he says, 'I promise you, Anna, I promise on our sons that I know nothing about those missing condoms.'

Anna looks down at him. 'Really?' She sniffs. 'You mean it?'

He holds his arms out again, trying to show her he has nothing to hide. 'I mean it, sweetheart. I really do.'

Then he does what he's been yearning to do all evening. He puts his head in her lap, closes his eyes, and she strokes his face with her warm, soft hands as her tears fall on to him.

'Oh, Ed, I'm so relieved. It's just that Rosie was telling me weird stuff in the sauna yesterday about Seb and then Lotte called, to confirm the reservation, and she said something strange too . . .'

Eddy's eyes open. 'What stuff with Rosie and Seb?'

Anna doesn't answer right away. Eddy lifts his head to look at her and he realizes with clashing certainty that Anna knows something.

'Eddy, don't, don't do that, please. I'm not supposed to say anything . . .'

'What, even to me?'

'Well, yeah, I think so, I mean . . .'

'Anna, I'm Seb's best mate. Don't you think I'd know if something was going on?'

Anna looks at him steadily then and Eddy realizes his stupid face is going to give him away. He drops his brow, erases his smug smile, but it's too late. Anna's on to him.

'What? What did he tell you?' Anna's stopped crying, quickly tipping into anger.

Eddy freezes, stares up at his wife, feeling like a chastened dog on the floor.

'And don't say "nothing", Eddy. I swear I'll fucking scream if you say "nothing".'

He looks away, feels his heart thumping, like it too is taunting him. What are you going to do, Eddy? What. Are. You. Going. To. Do?

'Look. Look, all I know is that Seb intimated there might be problems.'

'Go on . . .'

'That's it.'

'Did he mention Abi?'

'That new woman you said Rosie was really into?'

Anna nods.

Eddy lets the genuine surprise show on his face. 'No. No, he didn't. Why would he mention her?'

Now it's Anna's turn to decide what's more important – loyalty to her friend or interest in the truth. She doesn't weigh it up for long.

'Rosie told me that Seb came home when Abi was at their place. She said it was weird. Rosie had to go upstairs to stop the kids arguing and when she got back they were whispering to each other. She said Abi became awkward, made some transparent excuse and couldn't leave quick enough, that she's been off with her ever since.'

Eddy's face puckers in surprise. 'That's unlike Seb.'

'Yeah.' Anna agrees, enjoying herself a bit now. 'It gets weirder. Lotte called me when we were in the sauna to confirm our reservation for opening night next week. We were chatting and she said that Seb turned up at the restaurant, totally out of the blue, to talk to Abi. She said she watched them a bit, said it looked like it was getting really heated, that afterwards he was completely flustered and left in a real hurry. Which, again, isn't at all like Seb, is it? I decided not to say anything about Lotte's call to Rosie, didn't want to add to her paranoia.'

What was it Seb said on the court? He said this woman had 'turned up' and then he tried to backtrack, lied and pretended she'd only messaged, because he didn't trust Eddy with the truth. The truth, Eddy realizes now, is that Abi is the woman he met online, the woman he had sex with.

He stands up because this is beginning to feel a bit much.

Anna stands with him, her eyes never leaving his face because she knows everything he's feeling will be written there.

'Eddy, what is it?' she's saying again and again, and all Eddy can mumble is, 'Bastard.'

Eddy's stomach squirms, not for Abi or Seb but for himself, because Eddy's always found his role in any situation the most interesting. Why didn't Seb trust him with the full story? Eddy has trusted Seb with everything, always, but Seb has been duplicitous, keeping his secrets to himself. He hadn't said anything about the problems with Rosie – that they haven't had sex for a year – and how many games of tennis had they played in that time? Besides – and here Eddy really starts to feel like he's falling – who even is Sebastian Kent if he's the kind of man to find a woman online for sex? Twice! Sober! And still, he hasn't confessed to Rosie? He's most definitely not the person Eddy thought he was. The perfect person he'd made them all believe he was. Why should he, Eddy, have to lie to his wife simply because Seb doesn't have the balls to come clean?

Slowly he turns to Anna, blinking, and only still half believing it himself he says, 'I think Abi and Seb had an affair.'

Anna laughs, loud and involuntary, but then one look at Eddy and her face falls.

'Oh God,' Anna groans, lifting her hand to her mouth. 'You're serious.'

He tells her everything Seb told him on Court Five, starting with Seb's uncontrollable sobbing and then his half-confession. How it felt to Eddy that there was more to the story, more that Seb wouldn't share.

'I mean, why, after months of keeping this all to himself, does he choose right now to tell me? The timing's too convenient, and now all this strangeness with Abi . . .'

Anna's eyes are round with wonder; she reminds Eddy of eight-year-old Albie last year when he discovered the truth about Santa. 'Sebbo wouldn't, I mean, he couldn't . . .' she's mumbling, pouring herself more wine, sloshing some on the table but not bothering to wipe it up.

'Anna, he literally just told me tonight. They haven't had sex for a year. He said he got desperate; he met her online.' Since his own indiscretion, Eddy usually cowers away from any conversation about infidelity, especially if Anna's within earshot, but he can tell from Anna's rapt expression that for once she's not thinking about what he did.

She shakes her head and stares at Eddy as she says, 'Online? He planned it?'

Eddy nods his head. 'And he was sober.'

'Is he going to tell Rosie?'

Eddy looks away from Anna, catches his own eye in the photo Anna had slung over the hook where they hang aprons. 'He said he wasn't going to.'

'What?'

'I know. I know,' Eddy agrees, looking back at her shocked face, and, while it doesn't feel entirely unpleasant for his perfect, handsome best friend to fall a few thousand feet in his wife's estimation, Eddy can't completely eviscerate him, so he shifts the perspective. 'It makes you think about what the hell is Abi playing at? Turning up in Waverly – is she blackmailing him or something? That's what I keep thinking.'

Anna shakes her head and says, 'She could be a psychopath.' The force of her words takes Eddy by surprise and then suddenly, out of nowhere, Anna starts crying again, and again Eddy feels useless.

He takes her in his arms, his muscles remembering Seb's weight as he clung on to him. Anna's voice is soggy as she says, 'Oh, Rosie. Poor, poor Rosie.'

Eddy steers them through to the sitting room. Anna sits on

78

the sofa first and by the time he's brought her wine and the vape she keeps hidden at the top of the dresser 'for parties', she's calmer. Her eyes are glinting and alive as Eddy sits next to her, and he knows she already has a plan.

'What are we going to do, then?' she asks.

'What do you mean, sweetheart?'

'Well, I have to tell Ro. Obviously.'

'Really?' Eddy sits up; he needs to see Anna's face.

'Eddy. There's no way I'm keeping this from her. I mean, we really don't know what Abi's up to. You've seen *Fatal Attraction*. We have no idea what she's planning. It's not safe.'

Shit. This is getting out of control.

'My God, he could have been talking to her that time you and Blake went into his office and slammed his laptop closed, remember? You know, when you first called him a spy?'

'Wait. Anna, slow down. Look, the first thing I need to do is talk to Seb, see if our suspicions are correct. Then . . .'

'Then we have to tell Rosie . . .'

'Let's give Seb the chance to tell her himself first? I'm sure he'll tell her when he finds the right time. We owe him that much, at least.'

'He's had months, Ed! How much time does he need?' Her pitch has crept higher and higher. She can't maintain it; she pauses, resets herself and comes back steadier, lower as she says, 'When all that shit happened in Singapore, one of the only things that made it easier was knowing you'd told me straight away, that it only happened once and that it was you being drunk and out of control. Seb *knows* that. I remember telling him that.'

Eddy almost reminds Anna of the Seb he's known for more than half his life. Seb, the boy who swapped his brand-new bike for Eddy's old one when they were thirteen because Eddy was trying to impress the first girl he fancied, Seb who literally dragged Eddy across the finish line at the London Marathon, Seb who occasionally leaves them home-made loaves on their doorstep, Seb who writes Blake, his godson, beautiful letters every year for his birthday. But somehow, Eddy knows reminding Anna of that Seb now will only make him fall from her grace harder.

Instead, on the sofa, Eddy keeps his arm around his wife and they talk through their shock, each asking questions they know the other won't be able to answer. They stay like this until they've finished the wine and then they lie back, their bodies pressed against one another, stretched along the full length of the sofa.

Eddy feels weary in both heart and body, but still, sex is probably a good idea. It'd reassure Anna, remind her that they're OK, that they're solid. He pulls her hair to one side, starts kissing her neck until she makes those little sighing noises he loves, and she reaches for him. When they're finished, they lie back again on the sofa and Eddy strokes her hair and she massages his hand as she says, 'I think it was Blake, by the way.'

'Blake?'

'Who took those condoms.'

'Ahh, of course!' And Eddy adds, because he knows Anna will like it, 'I'll chat to him.' Even though he probably won't.

Against his chest, he feels her smile. He's glad they've shared their secrets with each other tonight, and their unscheduled sex reconnected them. The dynamic between Eddy and Seb has changed, in a way he could never have anticipated, but

Eddy's never been able to function on his own – now he'll need Anna more than ever.

He kisses the top of her head and says, 'Love you, A,' and he feels her smile again so he closes his eyes, content and safe, knowing he is loved.

Just after midnight they go to bed and Eddy wakes in the morning with his arms still around Anna. She's the only woman he's ever been able to cuddle while he sleeps, one of the things that made him realize she must be 'the one'. He's working from home today, so he's in no rush to get out of bed. Eddy pretends still to be asleep as Anna gets up and pads downstairs. He listens to her unloading the dishwasher, boiling the kettle, and then hears her chatting to Simon, the postman.

'Morning, Si. Heard about your back, you poor thing.'

A couple of minutes later she walks back upstairs, putting a cup of tea on Eddy's bedside table. He's about to talk to her, but she's on the phone already. She likes to call her sister, Sami, who lives in the Lake District, first thing in the morning. His eyes only open a sliver, he can see she's still in her dressing gown, staring out of the window, as he listens to her leaving a voicemail.

'V, it's me, Anna. Listen, I need to ask you a favour – would you be able to collect Albie after school and have him at yours for about an hour today? I know it's last minute, but I can explain everything when I see you, and Albie would love to show Luca his new Lego car. Sorry to ask, but I have a meeting and predictably all the after-school clubs are booked . . .'

Eddy's eyes fly open. What the hell is she doing? Albie is supposed to be going over to Abi's, isn't he? She turns around as he sits up in bed and mouths, 'What the fuck?' which makes her stumble and rush her sign-off: 'Message me to let me know this is all fine.'

Before Eddy can open his mouth, Anna beats him to it. 'It's not safe, Eddy. I can't risk Albie getting into a precarious situation.'

'What are you talking about, "precarious situation"?'

Anna tilts her chin up; she really gets the hump if she feels like she's being patronized. 'Abi, obviously.' She glances at the door. It's open a little, so she goes over to close it, which is unnecessary as Albie's downstairs listening to a football match, quietly munching through the seven Weetabix he eats every morning. 'I can't trust her with Albie.'

'You can't trust her with Albie?'

'He's a child, Eddy, my little boy – I won't let a possibly unhinged bunny-boiler we barely know look after him. And besides, what will Rosie think when she finds out that I let Seb's mistress look after Albie!'

'Anna, you're overreacting.' He thinks about adding 'as usual' but knows that would totally derail the conversation.

'I'm not, Eddy. Think about it. She's obviously turned up here to blackmail Seb – she might be some kind of scammer or catfish; she might have done this many times before.'

'Anna, we hardly know the woman! And besides, you can't warn the whole town off her. This is irrational—'

Anna waves her hands, talks over him. 'You're right, Eddy, completely right! We hardly know the woman and that's exactly why she shouldn't be looking after our son. It's my fault and I won't ask people we don't know well for help with childcare again, OK?'

She's wired and Eddy knows she'll have spent the early

hours going over and over her arguments. He feels weak and unprepared, so he nods to show he accepts everything she's said. Anna kisses him and says, bouncy again, 'I'm going to get in the shower.'

Eddy leans over for his tea and, as he sips, acknowledges that he's not feeling good. Not feeling good at all.

In their en suite, he hears Anna turn the shower on. He shared too much last night and now he's hungover from too much honesty; his thoughts feel like scuttling mice in his head. Did he really have to tell Anna everything? He loves her – of course he does – but she isn't known for her discretion and, besides, her loyalty lies more with Rosie than with Seb. But shouldn't Eddy's loyalty also be with Rosie? After all, Seb has acted and is acting like an absolute idiot. Last night, he felt so connected to Anna, good about himself, but now, in the cool, blue morning light, the revelations feel too real, too grubby, the consequences too big to comprehend. Next to him, on the duvet, Anna's phone starts to ring. Eddy looks at the screen, the letter 'V' illuminated, covered in hearts. With a groan, he pulls the duvet over his head and waits for the noise to end.

Chapter 7

It's raining again, so everyone's hurrying, not wanting to stop and chat, when Abi goes to pick up Margot from school. It's sad – the community she once yearned for while living in London is now something she's actively hiding from.

After the incident at Rosie's house, and Anna's stiff voice-note telling her that she no longer needs Abi to take Albie home after school, she wonders if she's someone who could ever feel like they belong in a community like Waverly. Anna who had only the other day been overly matey and keen to be friends, now sounded like she was firing a nanny. Abi replied simply with a thumbs-up.

Why should she care about Anna's opinion of her, anyway? It was odd, Anna asking for help when their kids aren't even in the same year. It felt more like a ploy to get inside Abi's house, a chance to get the scoop on the newcomer. She finds Anna uneasy, nosy in a way that feels untrustworthy.

But still, Abi spent the whole of yesterday afternoon cleaning the maisonette ahead of the visit, scrubbing the mouldy grout around the kitchen units with an old toothbrush. She even hammered a few framed prints on to the walls, including her favourite, a poster advertising a Picasso exhibition from the 1960s. While the flat will never be beautiful, it is at least clean and warm. It's as good as she can manage. Better, she reminds herself, than anything she ever had growing up.

Margot takes the news about Albie with surprising stoicism, when Abi tells her by the school gates. She'd been so excited about having someone over, something she'd never been able to do when they lived in London. But Margot simply thinks for a few seconds, before shrugging her little shoulders and asking practically, 'Can you do my shop with me, then?'

At home, she peels off her raincoat and school shoes in the tiny hall and thunders up the thin stairs to the cardboard shopfront she painted this morning, while Abi makes a start on the fish pie she's planned for dinner. 'Shop's open, Mum!'

Abi spends the next hour carefully being instructed on exactly what to say when buying imaginary vegetables and being told off by Margot when she gets it wrong. When Abi was younger, being 'nice' was the most important thing and it meant being quiet and doing whatever someone else wanted. Abi learnt to play on her own, so she could make her own rules. She didn't know then, of course, that these were skills she'd depend on as an adult.

It is this kind of moment, rain beating against the window, laughing with her kid while the delicious smells of dinner fill the flat, that Abi had dreamt about ever since Lily was born. Abi would take Lily out in the pram, given to her by a new mothers' charity, and would ride the number 19 bus for hours. It was cheap and the rhythmic motion soothed Lily, allowing nineteen-year-old Abi to sit and flick through food magazines she'd shoplifted from Smith's. She loved the shining photos of Christmas roasts and delicate canapés, art she could taste through the page. When she didn't have a magazine, she'd stare out of the window, her gaze always finding the other mums who seemed like a different species, their designer prams laden with Waitrose bags, feeding their kids in expensive cafes and not caring if their toddler's £10 macaroni cheese ended up on the floor. Those mums in their space-themed yoga leggings, sipping their green juices, made Abi hold Lily to her chest and whisper apologies into her tiny, curled ear. Because, somehow, this perfect child had been made by Abi. Abi who slept on a mattress on the floor in their bedsit, Abi whose own mum cuddled bottles of cheap Polish vodka and didn't notice if Abi went to school or not. Abi who had tried to hide her pregnancy from the restaurant where she washed the huge greasy pans until she'd practically given birth on the floor. She apologized to her daughter for all those nights out when she hadn't known she was pregnant, apologized to Lily for all that she was and all that she wasn't, and then she'd stare at those other mums and her apologies would morph into promises. Promises about decorated Christmas trees, bouncy castles on her birthday and delicious, hot food made by Abi, in a real oven not a microwave. Abi promised Lily all these things, as despite her own lonely childhood she was still a dreamer and had started to feel the tug of possibility, the whisper of a better future for herself. She just needed to figure out how they were going to go from riding the number 19 for an entire day to taking a table in one of those expensive cafes.

While Margot is happily serving imaginary customers, the front door flies open.

'Hi, Mum,' Lily calls, the door clicking shut behind her.

Abi stops stirring the white sauce and watches her beautiful

Lily, a flash of long red hair and silver jewellery. She waits until Lily's ready before she opens her arms and holds her. She smells earthy and a little chemical from the art studio and Abi whispers in her ear the words that she never heard as a teenager, 'Sweetheart, I'm so happy you're home.'

Lily sits on the cheap plastic countertop, kicking her legs against the cupboards, and begins telling her mum about the other kids in art club, while Abi finishes up the fish pie.

'You know that boy, Sam, I was telling you about?'

'The quiet kid?'

'Yeah, that one. Well, it turns out he's the one who does those incredible architectural drawings.'

'Nice!' Abi says, passing Lily a pot of hummus.

'And that football guy came by the art room today,' Lily says, a little quieter, her eyes fixed on the hummus, smiling.

'Oh yeah?'

Lily has mentioned him a couple of times already, said that the popular footballer had noticed her artwork up around the school, asked if she'd show him more.

'What's he like?' Abi knows to keep grating cheese, to not look up; it's such a fine line, showing interest but not making Lily feel pressured.

Lily pauses, thinks before she replies, 'He's sweet. I think lots of people think he's just a football cliché, but, I dunno, I think Blake's actually really cool, sensitive, you know?'

Oh fuck. Abi balks as she realizes who Lily's first crush really is – Blake. Blake, Anna and Eddy's son. Not only that, but Seb's godson.

'Ow!' Abi shouts as heat slices through her thumb, the length of it white and clean where skin should be. Lily leans over, stares too as the blood starts to seep.

'Owww,' Abi wails as Lily jumps to the floor, turning the kitchen tap on and ushering her over. Abi grimaces as the cold water rushes over the cut.

'Owwwww,' she wails again and Lily fusses around, finding the wound spray and plasters. When Abi's pulsing thumb is wrapped, Lily makes her a cup of tea before scattering the cheese over the top of the pie and sticking it in the pre-warmed oven.

An hour later the three of them are eating around the tiny Formica table that came with the flat. They're taking it in turns to answer 'Would you rather . . .?' They are deep in a discussion about Margot's question, 'Would you rather have a tail like a monkey or kangaroo legs?' when, on the side, Abi's phone lights up with a call from Diego.

'Hey, Diego,' Abi says into her phone as the girls chorus behind her, 'Hi, Uncle D!'

'Hello, beautiful girls!' His rich Mexican accent booms through the receiver. Abi tells the girls that she'll just be a moment and moves to take the call in their boxy sitting room.

'Have you arrived?'

'Got to the restaurant about twenty minutes ago.' Typical Diego, going straight to work on the day he's moving. 'Listen, sweetie, are you busy?'

'You want me to come in, don't you?'

There's a pause before Diego says, 'Nooooo,' in a way that they both know means, 'Yessss.'

'All right. Let me finish up here, sort the girls out and I'll be over in an hour.'

'You're the best.'

'You're the worst.'

'Tell the girls I love them and that their Uncle D will be over soon, OK?'

'There you are,' Diego says, shoving a pencil behind his thick black hair before kissing Abi efficiently on both cheeks, looking her over like one of his beautifully made plates before service. He's in work mode, not friend mode now.

'You're tired.' He's not asking, he's telling her.

'Hi, *abuela*.' Abi hangs up her coat. It feels good already: having him here, calling him 'granny', the nickname they use for each other now their partying days are behind them and they both like to be in bed by ten p.m. on a day off. 'How was the drive?' But Diego isn't listening; he's walking to the kitchen and Abi knows he wants her to follow.

The issue is the flow of the kitchen, he explains. The largest pots and frying pans are stored too far away and the kitchen appliances aren't organized properly. Removing his pencil from behind his ear, he leads her back into the dining area as he talks through the new plan he's already sketched out. His way would mean having to bring the carpenter back in to make some cupboards larger and others smaller, but Diego just shrugs when she tells him this – so be it. Abi is going to have to get used to playing middlewoman between Diego and Lotte and Richard.

'So that's it,' Diego says when he's finished. 'Can you let Madam know?' Diego loves giving people nicknames; not even his employers are immune.

He pauses, distracted by a huge abstract oil painting that Richard insisted on hanging on the largest wall next to the toilets. 'Apart from this absolute monstrosity.'

'Don't!' She laughs. 'They almost came to blows over it.

At least it's better than the photograph of a load of men in tuxedos surrounding a naked woman that was his first choice. That one was unbearably creepy.'

'Jesus.' Diego shakes his head, still staring at the weird bull.

'We're really doing this, aren't we?' he says, putting his arm around her shoulders, and Abi breathes out in a great sigh. She closes her eyes briefly and when she opens them, Diego is staring at her, his lovely brown eyes soft, thick dark eyebrows knotted.

'We really are,' she replies, giving his warm hand a squeeze as they both look around the empty, perfect restaurant. Their shared vision finally coming to life after so many years of planning, saving and sacrifice. Lotte and Richard had never been part of the dream, but when they approached Diego, and the negotiations began, Diego had been clear there was no way he was accepting without Abi.

They stand in the restaurant's soft light in silence for a little longer, taking it all in, before Diego squeezes Abi's hand and announces, 'This is the right moment.' He disappears briefly before returning, already opening the bottle of Moët he's carrying. 'It's from Stephen,' he says.

'Oh, you should save it, really, have it with him later . . .' Abi starts but it's too late. The bottle opens with a loud *pop*.

They sit up on the bar top, their feet dangling like kids', turned towards the restaurant as she pours the champagne into tumblers. Proper flutes are one of the things Abi has on her list to chase tomorrow.

They raise their glasses to each other and Diego says, 'To dreams coming true.'

They talk shop for a while – discuss Diego's concerns about the butcher Richard's insisting on using and the need for another hire – before Diego turns to Abi. 'How are you settling into this peculiar little town?'

Diego's switched to friend mode and Abi takes too long figuring out how to answer. 'Yeah. Fine.'

Diego raises his perfectly groomed big eyebrows. 'Don't lie to me, Abigail.'

'It's fine. I'm here for this,' she says, gesturing to the restaurant, 'and for the girls.'

'Missing London?'

'Missing being invisible, yeah.'

Diego winces. 'Urgh. Are all the people here as boring as I said they'd be?'

Abi laughs, widens her eyes in a way that shows Diego he's got it exactly right, and he groans. 'Well, it doesn't matter,' he says, putting a reassuring arm around her. 'We've got each other. We're not here to make friends.'

For a moment, she thinks about telling him the truth about Rosie, about Seb, and how this whole new life suddenly feels vulnerable.

But even though it could be her only chance, and even though she's suddenly desperate to ask him what the fuck she should do, she knows Diego hates messes he can't easily wipe away. Besides, the more she dwells on the whole thing, the bigger an issue it will become. She'll stick to her plan: she'll focus on work and the girls and stay out of Seb and Rosie's way. In time, all this will be so buried it'll feel as though none of it ever happened at all. The woman she used to be will fade and maybe one day Abi will struggle to remember what she was like, what her name even was. She kicks her legs, sips her champagne, forces herself to forget yesterday, and does what she's always done best: she dreams about tomorrow.

Chapter 8

Seb catches himself whistling down the corridor, notebook and pen in hand, making his way through the science block that hasn't changed in decades. He's meeting with some of the Year 11 parents to discuss how best to prepare and support their children through their GCSE year. It's one of the changes he promised during his interview and a proposal that Harriet – the chair of governors – especially welcomed. As head teacher, Seb wants to have more direct communication with the parents, especially during important exam years. Yes. Seb is back on track – all that bullshit last week was scary and no doubt it will continue to be awkward when he sees Abi at the school gates, but they've promised to stay out of each other's way and, most importantly, Rosie seems to believe his lie about Lily and a situation at school. Eddy is his best mate. He'll keep his secret and there's no need for Rosie to ever know the duplicitous man she married. He's going to let all his grubby secrets go. From now on, this new, reborn Seb is going to appreciate the extraordinarily good fortune of his life. He's going to love Rosie better, actually book that romantic weekend away instead of just planning it in his head. From now on he'll be more patient with the kids – perhaps they could introduce a day when all five of them play board games all day and paint pictures of each other. Maybe that last bit is optimistic. Maybe it should be just half a day but, whatever, Seb is feeling good and believes for the first time that he is going to survive everything that's happened. Better than survive, in fact – the whole experience is going to make him change his ways.

Even though it's a school rule that no teachers use their phones outside of the staff room, he can't resist texting Rosie a quick, *LOVE YOU*. The capitals are accidental, but he decides not to change them. From now on he is going to love her loudly.

He reaches classroom 6D where Harriet is standing in front of a few rows of parents. Harriet – a retired teacher herself – likes to be involved.

Harriet turns and says, 'Afternoon, Mr Kent. Good to see you.'

Seb walks confidently into the classroom, smiles at the whole room and says to Harriet, 'Please call me Seb.' He addresses the seated rows of parents, all of whom he recognizes. 'Afternoon, everyone.'

Eddy and Anna are both working so can't come along. But that's OK; they are reassured Seb will be looking out for his godson.

'We were just running through the agenda.' Harriet beams at him and raises a hand towards the empty chair positioned next to her own at the front of the classroom. Seb nod-walks to his seat as Harriet turns back to her notes.

He sees her as soon as he sits. She's in the third row, close to the window, a denim jacket slung over her lap, her ringed hands loosely clasping each other, her head tilted to one side, and that mouth – oh God, that mouth that made him do unspeakable things – is smiling at him.

She must be mad.

Seb stares at Abi; it's like she's got her hand around his windpipe and is squeezing.

What does she want from him?

He remembers her voice. The faint rasp of it.

Hey, try and relax . . .

Seb leans forward, over his knees, coughs into his hand. Harriet starts fussing about fetching him a glass of water but he waves his hand at her, feels his eyes bulging in their sockets, his neck straining against his collar, looks up at the gently concerned faces before him and says, 'Excuse me, sorry everyone.'

When she's reassured that he has recovered, Harriet says, 'Well, maybe that's my cue to hand over to you, Seb, and ask you to address our first item: exam anxiety; how to spot it and support your child through it.'

Standing, Seb plugs his laptop into the classroom's interactive whiteboard and immediately launches into his slideshow, never once looking back at Abi.

The meeting rumbles along, the parents take notes and ask questions, then finally they get to 'AOB'. Harriet turns to him, smiling so widely Seb can see the silver fillings at the back of her mouth before she says, 'I just wanted to feed back some of the responses we've been getting from parents about your first few weeks in the post and they are, of course, unanimously glowing. We know you're still finding your feet in your new role but your commitment and enthusiasm for the school and, most importantly, the students is palpable and, really, that is all the parents' – Harriet points to the room before indicating herself – 'and us governors can ask.'

The parents look to one another, unsure whether they should clap, so Seb saves them all by saying, 'Thanks for making me blush, Harriet! No, that's good to hear, and thank you, everyone, for coming along,' before starting to pack up his laptop. Seb makes sure his smile doesn't slip once as everyone files out of the room. He asks Abi if she has a moment to chat privately, his face aching.

He ensures the door is closed behind Harriet, the last to leave. He's stronger than when they spoke at the restaurant; she's clearly fucking with him, and he needs to be absolutely crystal clear with her this time. He stands solid and firm. 'What are you doing?'

Abi runs her fingers through her short hair, standing opposite him. 'I was invited. That's why I'm here. I have the same rights as everyone else, even if it makes you uncomfortable.'

He forces himself to sound calm. 'We said we'd stay out of each other's way, Abi.'

Abi's forehead wrinkles; she shakes her head. 'We agreed we'd stay out of each other's private lives.'

Seb lifts his face to the ceiling, shakes his head and whispers, 'Fuck's sake.' He opens his arms, indicating the classroom, the entire school. 'This is my life. This is my work. Don't ambush me at work.'

She stares at him, and he has to resist the urge to look away. She's everything he despises about himself.

'Then why are you and your wife and friends coming to the opening night of the restaurant? If you're allowed to show up at my work, then why can't I show up at yours? Unlike you, I've done nothing wrong. I haven't betrayed anyone.'

His stomach twists with revulsion for her, for himself, as the meanest, cruellest part of him snaps, 'Tell your kids that.'

95

She comes so close he can feel the heat off her. 'Don't think for a moment I don't know what I'm doing, Seb. I've known men like you my whole life. And you should know, I've got my own tussle going on' – she knocks her knuckles gently against her chest – 'because let me tell you, there's a part of me that would love to tear your privileged bullshit life apart. Would love to tell the world what a fucked-up little liar you really are. You're the one who came looking for me. Remember that.'

She gathers up her bag and jacket, ignoring Seb's hurried, quiet apologies as she walks quickly away.

Later that evening, steam billows from the oven as he opens the door and pulls out the celebratory moussaka he made earlier for Eva's birthday. Seb always makes moussaka when there is something to celebrate. The tradition started when Rosie went into labour with Sylvie; Rosie had gone to sleep but he needed something to do. Twenty-four hours later, in bed, they'd eaten it, with Sylvie sleeping in the crook of Rosie's arm. He makes it for special occasions and the kids, incredibly, have yet to tire of it.

The kids are upstairs playing while Seb and Rosie are getting things ready for Eva. Rosie's hanging their trusty silver 'Happy Birthday' banner over the table while Seb makes a salad dressing. Once he's done, he glances at his phone; there's another message from Eddy waiting, unread. Seb puts it back on the table, screen down. Eddy will just be whining about Seb missing their game again. Eddy, for once, can wait.

Seb loosens his jaw; he needs to talk to Rosie now. This could be his only chance.

'Hey, Ro,' he says, turning towards her as she sticks candles into the shop-bought cake he picked up on his way back from school. 'I've been thinking about tomorrow night.'

She tilts her head to show she's listening but keeps counting candles. 'Do you think she'll mind having thirty-seven candles? Half of her real age?'

'No, she won't mind at all.'

'I mean, I could chop them all in half, I suppose – we never use the whole candle anyway – might look a bit odd . . .'

'Ro, please, it doesn't matter about the candles,' he retorts sharply, taking her hand. She turns in surprise, taken aback by his tone.

'Sorry. It's just, I want to talk about tomorrow night before Mum gets here.'

'OK,' Rosie says, still frowning at him. 'What's up?'

'Well, it's . . . I'm . . . I just don't think we should go.'

'Why not? It's been in the diary for ages! Eva's coming over to do bedtime, Lotte and Richard are expecting us and so are Eddy and Anna. They'd all be pissed off if we cancelled so last-minute!'

Seb looks away, worried about what Rosie will read on his face: his fear etched in the crease of his brow, the sadness in his eyes, the betrayal stiff around his mouth. 'I know. It's just that this thing with Abi and her daughter still isn't resolved, so . . .'

She takes a sharp little breath, her face strangely expressionless, her voice low, as if she's speaking from a dark place within herself. 'What is this really about, Seb? Ever since you met Abi in our kitchen, I feel like you haven't been honest with me.'

Seb recoils, a part of him shocked because they come easily, these lies.

'Ro, I told you! It's just this ongoing thing . . .'

'You promise me there's nothing else I need to know?'

She looks desperate suddenly, a little teary. He's making her feel mad but what choice does he have? He's not lying to protect himself; he's lying to protect her and their whole family.

'Ro, please. Come on. You know I'm crap at lying.'

He tries to take her arms, tries to hold her, but she resists. 'Fine. If you don't want to go, I'll just go on my own.'

Panic glistens through him. This hasn't gone well. The only thing worse than going to the restaurant would be Rosie going without him, especially now that Eddy knows what happened. Well, a version of what happened. If he has any hope of containing this thing, stopping them from figuring out the whole truth, he must be there tomorrow.

The doorbell shrieks through the house and the kids start shouting, 'Granny!' They race to the front door and Rosie starts singing 'Happy Birthday' as she follows behind them. Seb watches this bundle of people in the hall, his heart a ball of pain in his chest, and marvels at how even as everything is dismantling itself all around him, nothing, absolutely nothing, has changed.

Dinner is the usual mix of cajoling food into Greer's mouth, trying to ignore Heath as he dissects his plate to ensure he won't accidentally eat anything green, and listening to Sylvie's long and detailed description of the book she's been reading. Eva looks happy, smiling as the kids moan, her love for them all so uncomplicated, so easy. No one seems to notice the force field of tension Seb can feel crackling around him.

The kids whoop when it's time for cake and ice cream and

argue over whose turn it is to light the candles, while Eva gamely pretends she has no idea what's going on.

Sylvie wins the candle row while Greer cries on Seb's lap and Heath chips a spoon like a pickaxe into some frozen vanilla ice cream. Rosie goes to the loo and when she comes back to the kitchen announces, 'Guess who I found skulking outside the front door?'

'Uncle Eddy!' Greer exclaims, like he's a present she's just unwrapped. Seb's stomach plummets as Eddy shuffles forward in his tennis gear, holding a box of chocolates and offering the room a little wave. 'Hi, everyone.'

Seb stares at Eddy, watching as he wraps his arms around Eva. 'I had to come and give the birthday girl a kiss!' Eddy hands Eva the chocolates.

'Edward!' Her palm against his face, just like she does to Seb. 'You look tired!'

'I always look tired, Mrs K. I think I was just born this way,' he replies, which makes Eva pat his cheek, laugh and tut all at the same time. Eddy briefly hugs each of the kids before he slaps Seb on the back, and Seb feels the eyes of his children, his mother, his wife on him and so he pats Eddy's back in return.

'You want some food, Edward?' Eva asks, already half standing, holding the edge of the table for support, to make him a plate.

Eddy stops her and shakes his head while next to him Heath says, 'No, Granny, he just wants cake and ice cream. Don't you, Uncle Eddy?'

Heath always treats Eddy like he's one of the kids. But Eddy's still shaking his head, running his hand over his beard, keeping his eyes on Seb as he says, 'Actually, guys, my own dinner is waiting for me at home, so I just came by really quickly to say happy birthday but also to ask your dad something.'

'Is it because he's head teacher?' Greer asks Eddy, her expression serious.

Eddy smiles at her and lies, so easily, 'Yes. Yes, it is.'

Greer nods, satisfied, before looking down at her bowl and crying out in outrage, 'Heath! You gave me a tiny bit!'

The inevitable battle over ice-cream portions ensues and Eddy beckons Seb, who mouths, 'Sorry,' to his mum as they back into the hall, Eddy waving them all a quick goodbye.

Eddy opens the front door, steps outside, and Seb has an urge to slam the door behind him, to leave Eddy in the chilled air, alone. But he resists and stands opposite Eddy, who nods, breathes out. 'Look, mate, I've been feeling pretty weird since our chat last week.'

Everyone Seb loves is just a wall away and stupid Eddy is too entranced by his own feelings; he hasn't even considered how precarious this is for Seb. Eddy knows too much, he must be placated, so Seb closes the door behind them and gestures for Eddy to move down the path a few paces away from the house.

They stand and face each other just outside Seb and Rosie's front gate, where Seb asks, 'What's going on, Eddy?'

Eddy swallows, glances over Seb's shoulder back at the house and says, 'You have to tell Rosie before tomorrow night.'

'What?' Seb feels his face twist.

'I know it won't be easy but it's not right, Seb, Rosie not knowing. You must see that.'

'Eddy, you don't get to come and tell me what to do in my marriage.'

'Anything else, anything else I'd agree with you, but she's my friend too . . .'

'I trusted you.' Seb hears his own voice, too loud, too dangerous, too close to everything he loves. He forces himself to quieten, moves closer to Eddy as he says, 'I trusted you with my biggest secret. I'm not proud of what I did, you know I'm not, but it's up to me to figure out what to do, what's best for my family. Not you.'

'It's Abi isn't it? Abigail Matthews.'

Everything around Seb – the whistling birch trees, Eddy, the cool autumn air – seems to slow and blur. The shock of her name makes Seb forget what his face is doing and as Eddy slowly comes back into focus opposite him, he knows he's given himself away, knows there's no denying what Eddy now knows to be true. Eddy shakes his head. 'Shit, Seb. What a bloody mess you've made.'

'How did you . . .?'

Now Eddy can't meet Seb's eye and Seb knows, of course, knows immediately that it was Anna who figured it out, and for some reason this makes Seb laugh, hard and joyless.

'Anna,' Seb says, her name like a claw in his throat. 'You told Anna. How fucking dare you, Eddy . . .'

Eddy freezes; there's heat rising in his cheeks, too.

'You betrayed me. Betrayed my trust. All these years of promising me that I could tell you anything . . .'

'Listen to yourself, Seb.' Eddy's shaking his head, eyes wide, appalled by the stranger in front of him. 'That's not the betrayal here, the betrayal is that you cheated on your wife – our friend, Anna's best friend – and you're not coming clean.

Frankly, I don't give a shit what you think about me; it's Rosie I'm thinking about. She's the reason I'm here. We won't let you humiliate her . . .'

'Your hypocrisy is unbelievable.'

'Seb, what I did was a momentary lapse of judgement. I was so drunk I could hardly stand, it was . . .'

'So that makes it OK, does it?'

'No. Of course not, but at least I didn't shop around online, at least I didn't plan it, and at least I had the balls to tell Anna as soon as I could—'

'Yeah, Eddy, you're a real saint . . .' Seb interrupts but Eddy ignores him, ploughing on to his headline point.

'. . . Which is why I'm here to ask you to please tell Rosie before tomorrow, because if you don't then Anna will and, trust me, it'll be . . .'

'Fine. Fine. Yes. I'll tell her. OK? I'll tell her . . .'

'What are you two plotting?' Seb spins around; Rosie is standing in the doorway. She's staring directly at Seb, her head to one side, her voice light, but she's frowning. She's too far away; she can't have heard anything.

'Tennis,' Eddy says, unconvincingly. 'We're talking about our last tennis match.'

Rosie moves forward, towards them, her hands resting on the gate between them. 'Was one of you cheating again?'

Seb stares at his beautiful, smiling wife and he feels the first wash of tears as Eddy says, 'Something like that, but it's all sorted now.'

'Oh, good. You two are both such bad losers.' Then she turns to Eddy and asks, 'Ed, can you please convince him to stop being an arse about tomorrow night? He keeps saying he won't come and . . .'

102

'Ro, please stop. I'll be there.'

She raises her eyebrows before immediately wrinkling her forehead. 'Good.'

They say goodbye quickly and Seb keeps his hand on Rosie's back as he guides her gently inside.

That night, Seb lies sleepless in bed next to Rosie. He wants to stay there, next to her, as close as she'll allow, but she must feel his buzzing mind because one of her eyes cranks half open and her voice is heavy with sleep as she slurs, 'Get up if you can't sleep.'

He does as he's told. Pulls on tracksuit bottoms and a T-shirt and pads barefoot through the kitchen into the garden.

He lifts his face to the clear sky, to the stars and the moon; the air smells rich, of distant bonfires. He used to do this, stand in the garden alone at night, when he was just a kid. It started when his dad got his cancer diagnosis, and they'd had no idea how long he'd survive. His dad had asked him to be good, to help Eva, not to cause any problems. And that's what he'd done. He'd tried so hard for so long to keep himself neat, to do the right thing, and now all that effort is dissolving, revealing Seb for who he really is, a mess of wants and desires.

His mind keeps playing forward to tomorrow, to the opening of the restaurant. He can't go, but he also can't risk Rosie going without him. Eddy will be there, licking his lips, ready to tell Rosie he cheated. But he only knows half the story – what if Abi reveals the other more shameful half tomorrow night? At least if Seb is there, he can try to protect Rosie from Eddy and Anna. And what about Anna and Eddy knowing it was Abi? She'll assume it was Seb who broke their agreement, Seb who told them. She'll have no reason to protect him and, more importantly, no reason to protect Rosie. She won't go quietly; she promised him that.

There is, of course, the other way. A cleaner way. He could tell Rosie tonight, as he promised Eddy he would. He could tell her. He could open himself up, tell her everything, pluck out his deceitful, broken heart and let her do what she will with it. He can do no more. He's done.

The house is quiet. He takes the stairs three at a time; he needs to move quickly, outpace his fear, his doubt. It'll be over soon.

In their bedroom, Rosie is fast asleep, but while Seb's been gone, Greer's taken his space. They're like two apostrophes in the bed facing each other, their arms entwined, beautiful. He tries to move Greer away, but she moans and clings tighter to her mum. He can't wake either of them without waking the other. He can't ruin Rosie's life without also destroying his daughter's.

He leaves them to sleep as he collapses on the floor, next to the bed, and he holds his disgusting head in his hands as he feels himself break.

Chapter 9

Rosie tries on a few different outfits, eventually settling on a fitted knee-length crêpe dress she remembers her own mum wearing in the nineties. Greer is sitting on the bed, attempting to untangle a large clump of beaded necklaces.

Rosie looks at herself in the mirror and she can admit, in the right light and from the right angle, she looks good.

She picks up her phone to see if Seb's been in touch, opens Instagram and is immediately distracted by the computer-generated photos Maggie has posted, plans for the new gallery.

She shakes herself to bring her back from Sydney to Waverly again. 'Where's your dad?' Seb went for a run over an hour ago and they're due to leave for the restaurant in fifteen minutes. The phone rings, but instead of Seb, it's Anna. Again. She's tried to call twice already; clearly whatever she wants isn't going away. Rosie squeezes her phone between her shoulder and ear.

'Ro, hi, babe.' Anna's tense, her voice strained. 'You OK . . .?'

Usually, she doesn't wait for a response, but tonight she does.

'I'm fine, thanks, Anna. Why?'

'Just checking that you're OK coming tonight . . .'

'Why wouldn't I be?' Rosie frowns as she opens an old shoebox; it's a pair of ancient leather brogues, not the silver boots she was hoping for.

'I just have something I want to talk to you about – maybe we could walk to the restaurant together?'

'Fine. I can ditch Seb, but I will have Sylvie with me. I'm dropping her at a sleepover on the way.'

'Oh.' Whatever it is Anna wants to talk about, she clearly doesn't want Sylvie within earshot.

'What is it, Anna?' Rosie's body tightens as Seb, sweaty and breathing hard, walks into the bedroom, already peeling off his damp running top.

'Daddy!' Greer squeals, jumping to stand on the bed. 'Daddy's home!' On the other end of the line, Rosie knows Anna is listening.

Rosie moves past Seb and Greer, out into the hall.

Once she has more privacy, she whispers into the phone, 'Anna, what's this about? Has something happened?'

When Anna speaks again, she sounds small, far away. 'Oh, no, no, nothing. I just wanted to talk to you about this silly falling out I've had.'

'Well, you can tell me tonight, can't you?' Rosie suggests as Anna says at the same time, 'I should finish getting ready, see you there.'

And suddenly, Anna's gone.

Seb carries Sylvie's rucksack and is silent on the short walk to her sleepover. Just as Sylvie disappears into her friend's house, Seb pulls his eldest daughter in for a hug, whispering something in her ear, Sylvie replying, 'Me too, Dad.'

As the lights from the restaurant come into view, Rosie knows Seb is miles away; she's walking next to an empty body. It's frightening. She doesn't think as she reaches out for his hand. Her touch brings him back and he looks sad, incredibly sad. She's about to ask him what's wrong when he says, 'I love you, Rosie.'

His intensity makes her laugh a little.

'You do know that, don't you?'

'Yes, I know, Seb. I do.'

He nods, lets their hands drop, and whatever it is that's going on with him, Rosie has a feeling that she's about to find out.

'Hi, Rosie. Hi, Seb.' Abi's gorgeous in minimal eye make-up and bright-red lips. Rosie had fantasized about her and Abi being close friends, but Abi has essentially ghosted her. Tonight, an iPad tucked under her arm, Abi hardly looks at Seb. Instead, she fixes her eyes on Rosie as she asks, 'How've you been?' She's professional, exuding a quiet confidence.

'Fine, thanks, fine.' Rosie feels like she's tripping up inside herself. Had she done something without realizing it, to make Abi act so cold suddenly? Or is Abi like this with other people, too?

But Abi's all smiles as she says, 'Here, let me take your coats.'

Once they've gone through the clumsy coat-removing motions, Abi says, 'Eddy and Anna are already here, so just follow me.'

Lotte's given them a prominent table in the middle of the small restaurant. As she follows Abi, Rosie immediately notices that their table is strangely silent. Their friends turn to look at them as they approach. Eddy and Anna, usually the first to speak, look away, grimacing at the sight of them. Eddy drinks his wine and Anna looks at her hands folded on her lap.

'Hi, guys,' Rosie says, frowning, and they both look up, nodding and mumbling polite hellos as Rosie and Seb take their seats. Once seated, they turn towards Abi standing under a soft spotlight, the only one seemingly at ease.

'So delighted you're all here,' she says, looking them all in the eye. 'Your menus are on the table.' And while Abi tells them about the specials and the free opening-night cocktail, Rosie looks around the group.

Anna is scowling, like she's trying to stop herself from spitting in Abi's calm face. Eddy is scratching at something invisible on the tablecloth in front of him. And Seb, opposite her, looks like he's about to puke.

No one is behaving normally and it's in that moment that Rosie knows she is alone. Alone in her confusion, alone in her ignorance. She looks to Seb and he's staring directly at her, directly *into her*, and he smiles but it doesn't make her feel any better.

'I hope you all have a wonderful evening!' Abi concludes before walking away, shoulders back, head high, towards a newly arrived couple at the door.

Left alone, the friends size each other up as if they were strangers.

'Isn't it amazing what they've done to this place?' Rosie says, looking at Anna who still has thunder in her eyes.

'Yeah, it looks great,' Anna replies flatly, glancing around briefly. No one is talking as their waiter arrives with their free cocktails. Eddy finishes his wine, immediately picking up the martini glass that's placed in front of him.

'What shop was it before? I can't remember,' Rosie asks out of desperation, before Anna picks up her hint and the two of them quietly start rowing about whether the unit used to be a craft shop or a newsagent's. Seb looks around, almost as though he's checking how and where to make an emergency exit.

Suddenly, Richard and Lotte appear by their table in a great puff of ego and cologne. Richard puts his hand on Rosie's upper back; his palm burns through the fabric of her dress. They're grinning from ear to ear and Rosie wonders if they've taken something as Richard exclaims, 'Wonderful to see you lovely people here!'

Lotte makes a great show of going around the table, kissing each of them, chattering the whole time, not pausing for breath, until she gets to Seb and, making sure the whole table can hear, she says, 'Mr Kent, headmaster, absolute legend!'

Then Richard slaps his forehead and says, 'Mate! I'm so sorry, I've been meaning to message and say I'm so glad the sports pavilion is finally being sorted out. All my not-so-subtle hinting finally worked, I guess. I want to give you something to say thank you. Let's have a bottle of champagne, shall we?' He nods at Abi and says, 'Champagne, please, Abi – a bottle and six glasses.'

Seb mumbles something about it not having much to do with him, that the staff and students were the ones who . . . but Lotte waves his modesty away with a manicured hand – 'Oh, pfff' – and Richard starts telling Seb how next he hopes he'll get rid of grumpy old Mrs Greene. 'Early retirement, maybe?'

They don't notice as Eddy stands, a little unsteady, and starts to walk towards the toilets. Rosie watches as Anna leaps up after him and, just before he goes into the men's, pulls his arm. They're in the middle of an argument, that's clear, but whether it's about how pissed Eddy already is or something else, Rosie can't tell.

Then Abi appears back at the table, obscuring Rosie's view, condensation dripping from the bottle of champagne she's holding. She opens it in one smooth motion.

'So cool,' Lotte says, like she's flirting. 'Wish I could open champagne like that! You'll have to teach me one day, Abs.'

Abi smiles, a little taut, replies with a wink, 'Lots of practice.'

She's about to place the bottle on the table next to the champagne flutes but Lotte says, 'Pour it out, would you, Abs?'

Rosie wants to tell Lotte to be more respectful because now, being back in the same room as Abi, Rosie is still drawn to her. She watches her pour, froth billowing up the glasses, and Rosie feels again with certainty that tonight, something's going to change.

The evening inches along. Eddy, Anna and Seb stare at each other blankly, like they're engaged in some intense poker game. The food arrives, and it is – as promised – magnificent, which is a relief as it gives them something to talk about. Towards the end of the meal, Rosie decides she's had just the right amount of wine, she's feeling bold enough to go and talk to Abi. Either she'll clear the air and find out she was being paranoid all along or Abi can tell her to her face why she's suddenly stopped messaging her, why she didn't say anything about the emails she'd exchanged with Seb.

'Just going to the loo,' she tells the table as she stands, already looking around for Abi, but she can't see her. Suddenly, there's a hand pulling her arm and Rosie turns, hoping it's Abi but finding Anna.

Anna's flushed face is staring up at Rosie. 'Ro, babe,' she says, her eyes filling with tears, 'we have to talk.'

Rosie backs away from her, shaking her head because Anna's unsmiling, so serious, and whatever it is, Rosie doesn't want it. She feels her heart pulse in her temples as she walks quickly back to the table. Anna is still at her side and Seb's also staring at her, his face full of sorrow. She realizes it then: whatever it is, this thing, Seb knows it too.

'You guys ready to order pudding?' Eddy's voice is thick with wine, but everyone ignores him. Seb gently pulls Rosie away from Anna, towards the door, grabbing their coats from their hooks. Everything and everyone passes Rosie by in a blur on their way out.

Then they're outside and it's just the two of them and Seb is trying to pull her away, further away from the restaurant, but this isn't what Rosie wants. She doesn't want to be dragged or pulled any more. She twists her arm, yanking it away from Seb. 'What the hell is going on, Seb? Why is everyone so strange tonight?'

'I'm going to tell you, Rosie. I want to tell you everything,' he says, glancing back to the restaurant like he's worried they're about to be set upon by their friends, 'but not here. Please, we have to go home.'

'No, Seb. Whatever it is, judging by tonight, it seems Eddy and Anna already know.'

Seb looks to the sky and then to the ground, as though asking the great mystery above and below for answers. He swallows, looks at Rosie. 'That night, when Abi was at ours . . .'

Rosie doesn't say anything, she just stares at him, watches him collapse a little more with every word.

'We'd met before. Abi and I.'

'At school?' Rosie hears herself, a little desperate now.

'No. We met a few months ago. Twice. In London.'

He can't look at her and she can feel his shame and suddenly Rosie sees it. She sees it all.

'You had sex with her,' she states, her mouth dry and hard.

Seb nods his head, his eyes fixed on the ground.

'You love her,' she says, a statement, because she's done with questions, done with others having control.

At last, he meets her eye. 'No, Rosie. I promise you. It wasn't an affair.'

'I don't believe you.'

'It wasn't an affair, Rosie. Because . . .' He whispers, 'I paid her.'

Rosie feels the earth beneath her tilt at a new angle and everything goes quiet. For a moment it's a wonderful relief but then she stumbles, and Seb leans forward to steady her as Rosie hears herself scream, 'You paid her? You fucking *paid* her?'

Somehow Eddy and Anna are there already, disgust twisting their mouths and Anna asking again and again, 'What? What did you say, Ro? Ro! What did you just say?!'

Seb's reaching for her now and she pulls her arm away hard, shouting, 'Don't you touch me! Don't you fucking touch me,' and Anna's by her side again and she's crying and screaming at Seb to get the fuck off Rosie and Seb's saying, 'Calm down, Anna, you need to calm down.'

Which makes Eddy lurch forward and, pointing a sloppy finger at his friend, say, 'Back off, Seb. Anna's just being a good friend.'

And suddenly Richard is standing at the top of the steps,

outside the restaurant, and calling, 'Oi, what's going on? What about the bill?'

Everyone is shouting and no one notices as Rosie turns and starts to run.

She runs without knowing where she's running to. Pedestrians step into the road to let her pass, shaking their heads at the unpleasantness, the shock of a middle-aged woman who has clearly lost control, a woman who should know better. Rosie doesn't care. She runs until her heart screams and her body shakes. She realizes she's close to the train station. She envisions herself getting on a train, escaping, leaving Waverly and everyone in it behind. It is the only thing she can think about, this need to leave.

It starts to rain, and she starts running again. The first ticket machine is broken. She kicks it and moves on to the next. Without looking at the time she buys a ticket to London and runs down the ramp to the platform. It's only then that she notices that the platform and the one opposite are empty, that the whole station is deserted. The only movement is the text from the service announcements, scrolling along the station screens. She glances down at her ticket, realizes she's just missed the last train.

She bows her head, the rain like tiny, cold kisses on her scalp, and she feels something break within her. She turns her face to the chilly night sky and makes a strange, high-pitched groan. Her rage is ancient and brand new, it's hers alone and belongs to every woman who has ever lived, it is in every fibre of her being and it's in every breath of air she breathes. It burns out of her in great fiery clouds, and she lets it, at last, at long last, rip through her. Her shouts and screams change shape, soften a little, and suddenly she's crying, silent racking sobs that feel like they could crack the fragile basket of her ribs in two. She stumbles to a bench; it's soaking, but she doesn't care. She lies down, her cheek pressed against the sodden wooden slats, and she lets the rain and her tears fall together.

'Excuse me, sorry, are you OK?'

From where she's lying on the bench, she sees his sensible-looking black boots first and then his high-vis jacket. The security guard is young, still spotty, using a gloved hand to shield his face from the rain.

Rosie doesn't want to scare him, so she sits up, her wet hair sticking to the side of her face. He bends down a little so he can see her. 'Sorry, but you're not allowed to sleep here,' he says, loud and slow, like he assumes she can't understand him.

'I wasn't sleeping,' Rosie says, 'I was crying.'

'Oh.' He takes a step back, rummaging in his pocket until he finds what he's looking for. 'Here,' he says, thrusting a card towards her. It's rain-splattered but Rosie can read the words, 'Desperate? Suicidal? Alone? Whatever you're going through, we'll listen.'

'The number is on the card,' he says, still enunciating every word, 'but you can't cry here.'

It's only when she's standing outside the train station again that she realizes she's soaking and numb with cold. The streets are empty now and for the second time that night she starts moving without knowing where she's going. It's a new lone-liness, not knowing where to go so her heart can break.

She's only been stumbling for a few minutes when a woman shouts from the other side of the road, 'Rosie? Rosie, is that you?'

Anna discards her umbrella as she runs across the road towards her, Eddy a few paces behind.

Rosie's too numb to push her away so she lets Anna hug her.

'Shit, you're freezing. Ed, take your jacket off. Quickly!'

Rosie can't do anything as her own unbuttoned, wet coat is pulled from her shoulders and Anna wraps her in Eddy's body-warm wool coat.

Anna's hand rubs circles on her back; it's supposed to be comforting but it just stirs up Rosie's rage.

'God, we've been so worried,' Anna says. 'Where've you been?'

Rosie shakes her head: it doesn't matter.

'Come on, I'm taking you back to ours.'

And with Anna hugging her arm on one side and Eddy on the other, Rosie lets herself be led like a fugitive with two arresting officers. Anna, with strange joviality, chatters away, telling her the places they've been looking for her, that they were close to calling the police, while Eddy, with his arm around Rosie for warmth, makes a phone call. 'Seb, hi, we've got her. Yep, wet and cold but think she's OK. We're taking her back to ours. Yup, OK, I'll be in touch later, then.'

As Rosie listens, she realizes that this is what's been happening for who knows how long. Have her friends been talking about her, privately laughing – 'Poor Rosie!' – while she blindly blundered on?

She stops walking. 'You knew. You both knew what he'd done.'

For the first time, she looks at them, notices the panic crackle between them.

'Let's get you warm and dry first and then, if you want,

we can talk, OK?' They try to pull her along, but Rosie can't move; she won't be their prize.

'No. I want to talk now.' She looks directly at Anna, make-up melting down her face. 'You knew, you both knew?'

Anna glances, briefly desperate, at Eddy, who gets the hint and says, 'We didn't know she was a prostitute, Ro.'

'But you knew he'd had sex with her, and you didn't tell me?' Rosie would shake them if she wasn't so cold, wasn't shaking so much herself.

'When we were in the sauna, Lotte called. She mentioned that Seb went to the restaurant to talk with Abi. She said it felt like a row. That's when we figured it out but, Ro, I promise, I tried to tell you earlier tonight – when I called? But Greer was there and . . . Eddy wouldn't let me tell you any sooner. He wanted to give Seb the chance to come clean first.'

Eddy, sober now, looks sharply at Anna. Rosie turns to him. 'Was it you, Eddy? Did you tell him to pay for the shag he couldn't get from his frigid wife?'

'Ro, no, please don't—'

'Tell me!'

'I had no idea, Rosie. I think what he's done is disgusting, I do. There's no excuse. I'm ashamed of him.'

Rosie looks at him, sees the way he squirms away from meeting her eye, the way Anna is frowning at Eddy, and she realizes there's no love here, not between any of them. There can't be with all this anger and mistrust.

'What kind of friends are you?' She pulls her arm from Anna's, moving away from them both.

'Rosie, we need to keep going, please, you're freezing . . .'

'I'm not going with you.'

'What?' Eddy glances nervously at Anna.

'I don't want to be near you. Either of you.'

'Rosie, come on, that's a bit dramatic . . .'

'Don't you fucking dare call me dramatic!' Rosie's voice is a shriek. 'You came into my house, Eddy, you were with my kids, and all the while you knew what he'd done and you said *nothing*?'

Eddy looks at the ground.

'Anna, you could have told me on my own. You could at least have let me have that.'

Anna starts crying, which makes Rosie want to scream in her face, but instead she says, 'Tell Seb I'll get a room at the Travelodge. Tell him I don't want to see him. That I'll come home tomorrow. When I'm ready.' She takes out her phone and searches for the number for the hotel.

'Rosie, it's late, you don't have any stuff . . . There might not be a room . . .'

But someone, thank God, answers and her voice only shakes a little as she asks, 'Oh, hi there, please can you let me know if you have a room available for tonight?'

She lets Anna and Eddy walk her the short distance to the hotel, but she won't talk, won't answer any of their questions. Eddy reluctantly takes his coat back as Rosie goes to get her key. The receptionist smirks at her wild hair, her running make-up, and Rosie smirks back, emboldened by the drama of it all. As the door clicks shut behind her in her small, blank room Rosie's heart fills with pain and suddenly she realizes it was always there. This feeling, the subtle vibration that she was being lied to, that she'd tried to ignore for so long. But now there's no hiding because there's no one she can call, no one who can help. She's alone with it now and all she can do is climb into the tightly made bed, curl up into a ball and let herself go.

Her phone wakes her, rattling on the table next to her head. Seeing it's Anna, she doesn't answer, but then a few seconds later the phone in her room starts ringing. Her children flash into her heart and with a heavy arm she lifts the receiver.

'Good morning, it's reception.'

It's immediately clear from the receptionist's chirpy tone that none of her children are in hospital or in danger.

'Hi.' Rosie's voice is gruff from her night of crying.

'Just to let you know that your friend is here and she's . . . oh, hold on . . .'

On the other end, Rosie can hear Anna saying, 'Tell her I don't need to come up, tell her I'm only here to drop off a bag of stuff for her . . .'

'She says she has a—'

Rosie cuts her off. 'Can you leave the bag outside my room, please?'

And then she hangs up.

She thinks of her children. Panics that they'll be worrying and feels herself harden against her own sorrow. She looks for her phone on the bedside table, but as soon as she picks it up, the battery goes dead.

She urgently wants to know the time so she can place her children in their Sunday morning, know whether Greer has had a good breakfast and if Heath will be out playing football already; will Sylvie be back, exhausted from her sleepover? Or will they be collapsed, sobbing, trying to understand what's going on, why Rosie isn't home? She opens her room door and there is Anna's favourite overnight bag. She pulls it inside and rifles through it, ignoring a handwritten note, clothes and toiletries until she finds a phone charger.

As soon as her phone is plugged in, it lights up with a call. Seb. She pauses but the pull towards her children is even greater than her rage. She answers, 'Seb,' just as her son in his high voice says, 'Mummy?'

Rosie's heart somersaults and before she's even said anything, he starts crying. As he sobs, she can't help but lie to him: 'It's OK, my love, it's all going to be OK.'

When he calms a little, he asks, 'What's happening, Mum, where are you?' But Heath's never been good at waiting for anything, so before she can answer he says, 'Dad was standing in the garden this morning – I watched him. He'd been crying, Mum. He couldn't stop. He said you'd had a row, that you would be back soon.' Now Heath's started talking, his words avalanche. 'He keeps crying, Mum, I don't know why. He's let us watch TV for ages, which never, ever happens. He said he'd talk to us later, when you're home and things are a bit clearer, so can you come back? Please. We just need to know what's going on.'

She pictures him, standing in the corner of the kitchen, the phone pressed close to his mouth, his beautiful brown eyes full of too much worry for someone so young, and she aches to be with him. She swallows hard so she doesn't cry and says, 'OK, darling, I'm coming home, I'm coming home now.'

She showers quickly and dresses in Anna's softest clothes, tucking her crumpled dress into the bottom of the bag and ignoring the receptionist as she rushes out into the grey, expressionless morning.

*

Heath is waiting for her at the front door when she arrives, and they hurry to hold each other. His body is tense, full of shock, and she tries to soften her own to calm him. Heath has always feared anything he can't control. Across the road, their neighbour Martin, his youngest daughter hanging off his arm, calls her name. She waves, briefly, and says to Heath, 'Come on, let's go in.'

Heath holds on to her, like he's worried she'll make a run for it if he doesn't cling on. The house feels empty even though it's not. Greer has fallen into a slack-faced, wide-eyed trance in front of the TV. Rosie kisses her and now it's Greer's turn to cling to her. Upstairs, Rosie can hear Sylvie singing to herself. They're all here. They're all fine.

'Dad's probably still in the kitchen,' Heath says, still holding her hand.

Rosie kisses Greer's forehead again and gently pulls her hand away from Heath. 'Give us a couple of minutes to talk, OK, sweethearts?' Heath looks worried, thinking they'll argue, that Rosie will run again, so she explains. 'We need to talk so we can figure out if we're ready to say sorry,' she says and he nods in agreement before he slumps down on the sofa next to his little sister.

Seb is still in his pyjamas, sitting on the sofa in the extension, his legs wide and his elbows balanced on his knees, his fingers in his hair. He looks up at the sound of her footsteps and in his weary face Rosie sees her own fear and confusion reflected back. He stands up. 'You're here.'

'Heath called.'

Seb pats his pockets, realizes he doesn't have his phone. 'I'm sorry, I didn't know . . .'

'Doesn't matter.' Rosie shakes her head; she doesn't want to be distracted when they only have a few minutes to figure out how they're going to break their children's hearts. 'They know something's happened. We need to work out what to say.'

Seb nods. 'I'll go along with whatever you want to tell them.'

'I want to tell the older two the truth,' she says with a snap.

Rosie closes her eyes and hates Seb and what he's done anew for putting her in this position. Because what, really, would her children do with the truth? She doesn't even know if Heath knows what sex is yet. But they know what a liar is – how would it break them if they knew their daddy was one of the worst?

'Wait,' Rosie says, holding up her hand; she's too angry to make such huge decisions. 'I need more time.'

Seb nods.

They stand in silence before she asks, 'What do you think would be best for them?'

Seb glances around the kitchen as though the answer might be hiding under the table or on top of the dresser. 'I think we should buy time so you can figure out what you need.'

She wants to kick him, but instead her body sobs, 'How?'

'We confirm what they already know. That we've had an argument, but we're trying to work it out.'

'If we tell them that, they'll panic, think we're splitting up.'

Seb doesn't say anything, and Rosie can't bear to look at him, so she closes her eyes again as she says, 'We're going to do what we've always done.'

Seb widens his eyes, needs her to explain.

'Pretend,' she says, coldly.

Seb grimaces.

'Don't act like you don't know how, Seb.' He looks to his

feet as she keeps instructing him. 'We'll pretend we've made up, that everything is normal, and we'll put on a united front until we figure out how to tell them.'

'How to tell them . . .'

'That you've betrayed us all, that you've destroyed our marriage in the seediest way possible.' She's surprised the words come so easily. But isn't this always the way? That the truest things are often astonishingly simple.

Seb lifts his hands to his temples to squeeze either side of his head. 'It's the worst feeling, knowing how much I've hurt all of you . . .'

'Save it!' she says, holding up her hand again. His mouth makes her feel physically sick. 'You found her online, presumably?'

Seb looks at her, alarmed by this sudden change of topic. 'Um, no, it was at that awards thing, with Eddy.'

Albie had been unwell, and Anna needed to stay with him so Seb had hired a tux and gone as Eddy's plus-one.

'One of Eddy's bosses showed me her website,' he mumbles, like this was all against his will, and Rosie wants to punch him right in his disgusting, lying, sucking mouth, imagines the crunch as his teeth loosen against her knuckles.

They both look up as Greer cries, 'Mummmmmyyy,' from the living room, already making her way down the hall towards the kitchen. 'Heath just pinched me!'

'I didn't! She's lying!' He's coming after his sister, because that's what big brothers do, but also because he needs Rosie to deliver on her promise, to prove that everything is OK. They only have this moment, she knows, to convince them, so Rosie does the opposite of what she wants: she moves towards Seb and whispers quickly, before the kids arrive, 'Stay at your mum's. I don't want you here.'

She keeps her hand on his back so when their children burst into the room, the first thing they see is their parents holding each other but they don't hear as she whispers to him, 'I'll never forgive you for this.'

Greer claps her hands, delightedly shouts, 'You're friends again!' She presses her little body against Rosie's back to join in the hug and Heath does the same, and Rosie didn't hear Sylvie come down the stairs but she's there too, staring at them, unsure, before breaking into a grin and piling on. The kids start laughing and Rosie knows then that they believe everything is healed, and the five of them stay like that, clinging on to each other in the kitchen, until at last Heath, his voice muffled, asks, 'What's for lunch?'

Chapter 10

Seb had been close to tears when he got back home from the restaurant, dripping wet, waking Eva who was asleep in the living room. 'Have you seen Rosie, Mum? Is she here?'

That night he'd got away with telling Eva he and Rosie had just had a row, that everything would be fine. Eva didn't believe him, of course, but it was late. When Eddy rang to say that Rosie was safe, Eva knew without asking that Seb needed to be alone.

'Try to sleep,' she said before she left.

Tonight, when he lets himself into her house, she's sitting next to the flickering wood burner, a handmade quilt over her knees, almost as if she had been expecting him. As she slowly closes the book on her lap, clocks the overnight bag slung over his shoulder and turns her strong blue eyes on her only child, he knows that he's going to have to tell her everything.

He sits down opposite his mum, pressing the heels of his hands into his eye sockets so he doesn't have to look at her, and tells her a version of the truth. He tells her that they hadn't had sex in so long, that Rosie seemed simply disinterested in their marriage, in him. He hears the pathetic whine in his voice as he says those words. He tells her what he told

Rosie, that Abi's website had fallen into his lap. He tells her how sorry he is, how much he regrets it.

He doesn't tell her there were so many times he nearly turned back. How he was close to not calling Emma – Abi's work name – from outside the cafe as she'd instructed him to do. Almost didn't press the buzzer to the flat and almost didn't walk up the flights of stairs to the tiny central London studio. But his body kept pushing him forward like it had already disassociated entirely from his brain. He'd noticed his wedding ring just before he knocked on her door. What a fucking cliché. He slipped it into his coat pocket and managed to smile back at the blonde woman who answered the door in a silk kimono. Her feet were bare, tattooed in complicated patterns. So different to Rosie's; he couldn't stop looking at them.

'It's your first time?' she asked, still smiling, once they were both inside.

Seb tried to talk but just kind of spluttered and nodded, which made her smile more. He fumbled with the money which she took from him with ease, tucking it into her pocket.

'It's OK to be nervous,' she said. 'Would you like some fizzy water?'

He was glad to bookend the appointment with a shower, washing both the before and after Seb away so when he left the apartment he wasn't sure who he was any more. He was just a man who in ninety minutes had replaced his desperate craving with something new, a dull ache he couldn't name. As he waited for a train back to Waverly, the thought occurred to him that perhaps what he had just done wasn't so bad after all. Emma was bright, kind and, yes, very attractive, but the whole thing was transactional. She was entirely attentive, but he knew that she didn't have any more feeling for him than the basic affection she'd maybe feel for a cafe barista. Perhaps he could think of sex with Emma as a kind of physical therapy – relief for body and spirit. Something Rosie might not need but he did, like visiting an osteopath or getting some acupuncture. All the fierce moralizing about it was a waste of time, a cultural obsession that had surely caused a lot of harm and done little good. As an affair was a relationship – that meant being attentive to the subtleties of someone else, their smell, their sense of humour, their values, and sharing those same intimacies with that person – it would engage brain and heart. That was the difference, he told himself. That reasoning was what made him visit a second time.

But now, lying in the gloom of Eva's spare room, he realizes it doesn't matter what he thought about it. For Rosie, it wasn't about Seb and his body, it was about her and it was about him, and now it's about her friend. There is no justification or explanation that will change that. From her point of view, he has betrayed her in the most degrading way possible.

Seb wakes at four a.m., pulls on tracksuit bottoms and a faded T-shirt, lets himself out and walks home. The air is chill, and Seb starts to panic as he walks, picking up the pace, imagining getting home and finding empty beds, missing passports. As soon as he's through the front door he takes the stairs three at a time, but there, of course, they are. Rosie and Greer fast asleep, Rosie clinging on to their daughter like she's charging her own gravitational force, the one that will keep her from drifting away from them all entirely. He strokes Greer's hair, and she stirs slightly before he goes to check on her brother and big sister.

He goes downstairs without turning on any lights, sits on the kitchen sofa and looks up how to delete the search history on his phone. He waits for his phone to finish deleting everything, all those women lurking in its synthetic memory, and where he used to feel a spike of excitement, he now just feels hollow.

Electronically cleansed, he waits for the first glimmer of sunrise before getting up to unload the dishwasher, put the kids' porridge on, fold the washing, just about outpacing his despair with order and movement. He hears Greer laughing first, and then Heath grumpily shouting at her to be quiet. They'll all be awake now. His hand shakes as he carries a mug of tea upstairs to Rosie.

Greer is sitting up in bed, her hair a tangled halo, a schoolbook in her lap. Rosie is lying on her back, listening.

He's a shit.

'Daddy!'

'Morning, my loves.' Seb watches Rosie turn to look at him, her hand shielding her eyes, weak protection against the morning light. Her face is creased with sleep. She looks exhausted, confused. 'Let's let Mummy sleep a bit more – why don't you read to me downstairs?'

'This book is boring.' She throws it on the floor as she starts to shuffle off the bed. 'Can we play witches' school instead?'

'We can play whatever you want.'

While Greer is cutting out a green frog for her cauldron and Heath is flicking through a magazine at the table, Rosie comes into the kitchen. She's showered, perfumed, dressed for work and is moving quickly. The Monday morning panic snapping at her heels, she's already fighting the brand-new week.

'Where's Sylv?' she asks Seb, her voice crackling with tension.

'She's not down yet.'

Rosie tuts and turns to the bottom of the stairs. 'Sylv, you up?'

Sylvie shouts something indecipherable back, which makes Rosie tut again. Seb moves to the kitchen door. He asks quietly, 'I thought maybe we could not go to work today?'

She looks at him, but he can tell she can't see him; she's blind with anger. 'Why?'

'I was thinking we could talk . . .'

She looks like she wants to spit in his face. 'I don't want to talk.' She pushes past him, reminding Heath, 'Sweetheart, it's Monday, you're supposed to be in your football kit, remember?'

Sylvie finishes her geography homework at the kitchen table while Seb changes into work trousers and a shirt. The thought of staying here, his betrayal everywhere, fills him with more dread than going out into the world. He'll go to work. He loads the dishwasher while Sylvie looks up facts about volcanoes on his phone. 'Oh, you got a new message, Dad. Auntie Anna says, "Seb, we need to talk . . ."' she reads before he clumsily snatches the phone, knocking her hand too hard.

'Ow, Daddy!' She flinches dramatically, rubbing her arm, his phone clattering to the tiled floor. He picks it up but doesn't read the message from Anna, lets it rest on top of the other unread messages and calls from Eddy.

'Sorry, Sylv.' His hand is shaking as he comes towards her, reaching to touch her, but she pushes him away before leaving to walk to school.

When Seb opens the front door, their neighbour Martin is shepherding his daughters along the bumpy pavement on their pink bikes.

'Morning, Seb!' Martin says, smiling from his crouched position next to his youngest, who is balanced on stabilizers at a precarious angle. 'Good weekend?'

Seb manages to nod and say, 'Fine, thanks, Martin. You?'

Martin grimaces and says something about his in-laws before he stands up straight and shouts at his elder daughter, 'Jessie, I asked you to wait!'

Seb gratefully turns left, away from Martin, taking the longer route to school.

He isn't walking alone for long before Vita calls his name. 'Sebbo!' She crosses the road towards him, her son, Luca, silently following.

Seb looks at the squirming kid first. 'Morning, Luca,' he says while Vita arranges herself on Seb's arm.

'So, how was it?'

Seb, blank, replies, 'How was what?'

'PLATE!' Vita squeals while simultaneously rolling her eyes. 'I'm so jealous you got that reservation, but Anna's always so on it, isn't she . . .' And while Vita witters away, they greet other parents. Seb scans their faces, and he is relieved to notice that nothing's changed. Some, like Vita, perform friendship; others are slightly formal. The world is turning, just as it should, but no one else apart from Seb seems to notice the strange new tilt.

Mrs Greene is already at her desk and, like every morning, she stands to slide open her little glass doors fully as soon as she sees Seb. 'Morning, Mr Kent,' she says, smiling. She's not once called him Seb.

She takes her glasses off her face, like she wants Seb to see her eyes, to better see the faith she has in him pouring out of her. She sometimes reminds him of Eva and at the thought of his mum, how she'll be waking this morning, trying to digest everything he told her last night, Seb thinks his knees are about to give way. He holds on to the reception counter and hears himself croak, 'Morning, Mrs Greene. How are you?'

Mrs Greene waves his question away as the school phone starts ringing; she doesn't have long. None of them do first thing in the morning. 'I just wanted to remind you to mention the work starting on the sports pavilion.'

Blankness again, and Mrs Greene's smile widens because she knows how busy he is – it's only natural he'll forget the odd thing occasionally.

'In assembly?' she offers and Seb's organs drop.

It was his own stupid initiative. Once a month the whole school congregates in the hall. First a different year group performs something – music, maybe a poem – and then the kids can ask Seb questions about the school or raise any concerns they might have. It's part of his plan to make sure the kids feel ownership over the school, like they have some agency in how it is run.

'Just be ready for some questions about the sports pavilion from the students, mostly around what's going to be in the vending machines.' Mrs Greene wrinkles her nose and puts her hand on the still-ringing phone.

'Thanks for the heads-up, Mrs Greene.'

She glows a little brighter at him before putting her glasses back on and answering the phone. 'Waverly Community Secondary, good morning.'

Usually, he goes to the staff room first, makes tea for anyone who wants one and chats to his colleagues, but this morning he goes straight to his office. As he fumbles with his keys, he feels the air shift as someone stands right behind him.

He turns, and staring at him with a look of pure revulsion is Anna.

'We need to talk,' she says, keeping her arms folded.

He nods, turns back to the lock and says, 'OK. Come back at lunch . . .'

'No, now.'

'Anna, it's assembly in ten minutes . . .'

He pushes his office door open, and Anna ignores him, follows him straight into the stuffy, boxy room. She turns towards him, proud and livid, a righteous representative for every woman who has ever been hurt by a man. He closes the door slowly before coming to sit on the edge of his desk, keeping his eyes low as he says, 'I can see you're upset, Anna.'

Anna laughs joylessly.

'You should know that I'm doing everything I can to make things right.'

Which must be the wrong thing to say because Anna's shaking her head. 'Not even you can make this right, Seb.' Her voice is practised, calm, but she's still shaking her head at him. 'What you've done is unforgivable.'

'I'm sorry you feel that way, Anna.'

'No, no, Seb. It's not that I feel that way, it's the truth.' She's actually shaking now, vibrating with indignation, with rage. 'You think there's any way we can be friends again when you pretend to be this holier-than-thou person, but all along you treat women like things that can be bought and sold – just *things* to fulfil your pathetic needs?'

'Anna, that's not fair, you know I don't . . .'

'No, Seb. The person I thought I knew could never, *ever*

demean women like that. But you did. You made an *appointment* to abuse a woman – not once, but twice. Honestly, it sickens me. You – the real you – sicken me.'

That isn't him. Seb is slowly finding out that he is many inglorious, ugly things, but Anna is wrong. He isn't an abuser. But Anna's got too much to say; there's no room for Seb to defend himself.

'You know I grew up watching women sell themselves at the end of our road? I'd be drawing my bedroom curtains and see them get into strangers' cars. They were all addicts, Seb, all of them painful to look at, and I'd hate those men then just as much as I hate them now, because even back then I couldn't understand how they could ignore the sadness in those girls' eyes, ignore the fact they were hurting them even more than the needles they stuck into their arms . . .'

'Look, Anna. I know you're angry, I know you're hurt, and perhaps you have a right to be, but it wasn't like that. I didn't abuse anyone. She was doing that work legally and of her own volition . . .'

'That's what you have to tell yourself, isn't it? That she actually enjoyed it? That she chose to have dick after disgusting dick inside her?' Anna moves closer to Seb. 'I don't think you're that stupid or that naive. I think you know she hated every second of it, that she was doing it for drugs or because she was abused as a child, probably both. But still you went along with it, you still paid her so you could rape her, and that makes you a monster.'

Seb's never heard his darkest fears spoken out loud before, even by himself, let alone someone else. These screaming accusations should turn him to ash, but they don't because Seb is certain that the person Anna's describing is not him.

What she's describing is not what happened in that tiny, soul-less W1 studio. He knows it, and he also knows that there's no way he can prove it.

Instead, he does the only thing he can.

'That's enough.' He moves to open the door for her to leave, but she grabs him by the arm, her sharp nails digging painfully into his skin.

'No, you fucking don't. I'm not finished yet.'

Seb pulls his arm away from her. 'Anna. Stop. I know you're upset, but that's enough. I have done something wrong, you're right. I betrayed my wife, broke promises we made to each other – I get that. I regret it bitterly but I'm not going to stand here and let you call me a monster. What happened was legal and it was between two consenting adults.' He pauses for a bit, thinks, *Fuck it*, before adding, 'In a way, there's no difference between what Eddy did in Singapore and what I did.'

Anna's face turns a strange puce colour; she looks like she's about to vomit. 'Eddy didn't pay, he didn't abuse anyone.'

'No, he didn't pay, but he did flirt, laugh and, let's be honest, he definitely didn't mention your name.'

A sob rises in Anna's throat then, winding her and making her fall forward. She shakes her head at him, like she can shake his words out of her ears. 'Eddy's different now.'

'OK, Anna.'

She starts crying – big, angry, rasping sobs – but Seb holds himself steady, stops himself from comforting her.

She holds up her hand, making a small space between her thumb and forefinger. 'I'm that close, I swear to God, I'm that close to telling everyone what a shit you really are.'

Seb stares at her and tries to feel if this threat is genuine or not. He forces calm into his voice and says, 'I have a right to a private life, Anna.'

'And I have a right to ensure my kids are guided by some-one who isn't a liar and who doesn't abuse women. And now, knowing what I know about you, I have a duty to all the other parents who have a right to know who you really are, the real man making huge decisions about their kids' futures.'

'Anna . . .'

'The only reason I haven't so far is because of Rosie and the kids, of course.'

Seb's heart sinks. His poor children.

'I think you know, deep down, that you're not fit to lead this school, Seb.'

'Anna, what I did has no bearing at all on my position here. That hasn't changed. I'm still just as capable, I'm still the same person . . .'

'Not to me you're not. And if you stay in your position, you'll leave me with no choice.'

'You're threatening me?'

'If that's what you call it. I don't care. I'm just looking out for the children. All our children.'

'What do you want, then, Anna? Seriously, what do you want from me?'

She doesn't pause; it's like the words are right there, waiting for her. 'I want you to know that we've had enough. Men like you pretending you're safe, feigning friendship, when you're the worst abusers of all. Men like you – entitled, educated, privileged men – can't keep treating women like we're dolls to be played with when you feel like it. I want you to feel what it's like to be publicly shamed and then I want you to disappear.'

The bell rings for the school to gather for assembly but

Anna doesn't take her eyes off Seb. 'You should come clean, Seb. Tell the whole school that you can't continue as head teacher. It's your one chance to do something that is truly right, and if you don't, then I will.'

She turns and, with one last disgusted glance at him, opens the door and walks away.

Seb stays perched on his desk, holding his head in his hands, adrenaline flooding his body, his thoughts like fire ants. Anna hadn't shut the door behind her and suddenly Mr Clegg, the geography teacher and deputy head, pokes his bald head into Seb's office and asks, 'You all right?'

Seb looks up at him and, standing, says, 'Yeah, just a bit of a headache, that's all. I'll take some paracetamol.'

Mr Clegg nods, backing out into the hall.

Seb nudges his office door shut. He is right, isn't he? Everyone's entitled to a private life. Even teachers, even head teachers. What if Mr Clegg secretly loves dressing up in leather and being spanked with a paddle? That's none of anyone else's business. Would that make him unsafe to do his job? No, no, of course it wouldn't. Anna is wrong. He can be both: a reliable professional and a fallible man who messed up big-time. Anna is always so ready to explode, so full of rage. Eddy will help calm her down, just like Seb calmed her down when she found out about Eddy's affair. All Seb has to do is call Eddy and ask. He just needs to get through the next few days. Just needs to help Rosie understand that he did what he did because he felt so stuck, so scared, so lonely. If he can find the softness in himself to share all that with her then maybe, just maybe, they can heal together.

He picks up his notepad and a pen, and takes a sip of water from the glass that has sat stale on his desk all weekend.

When he enters the hall, he feels every one of the six hundred pairs of eyes on him.

He lets his gaze blur as he turns towards them. *Just get through this.*

'Morning, everyone,' Seb says, his mouth twitching. 'I hope you all had a good weekend . . .'

He swallows, the saliva bitter in his throat.

'We're starting today with an assembly from the Year Nines with a "celebration of autumn", which sounds wonderful. So, over to you, Year Nine.'

Before he leaves the stage, he looks up briefly at the blur of young people in front of him, and one face lifts into focus. Lily. She's sitting next to Blake, at the back, looking at him like everyone else, but she's serene, composed, smiling faintly, and Seb knows he not only holds his own fragile family's future in his shaking hands, but also that of this talented young woman. His body fills like a sack of wet cement; he can't sit where he's supposed to but rushes out of the side door, the sniggers and whispers from the students like falling arrows at his back.

Chapter 11

Abi spent the whole of Sunday at home with her girls. They are good at spending a day together, just the three of them, with no need for anyone or anything else. They built a den, watched a movie, did a bit of yoga, cooked. It was slow and it was simple, the perfect antidote to the intensity of the restaurant opening. Every now and then Abi could feel herself drifting back to the previous night, remembering what one of the teenage waitresses had told her, about the middle-aged couples who left abruptly, their dessert menus abandoned on the table, who went outside to scream at each other while Abi was in the wine cellar searching for a bottle. Abi had smiled even as she felt cold stones drop into the well of her stomach; they could have been arguing about anything, she told herself strictly, but she didn't believe it. Then Margot would stick her head up in the den to complain, 'Mum! You're not listening!' And she'd be brought back to the present. Saved by her girls again.

On Monday morning she keeps herself busy and heads into the restaurant. It was, Richard gloats, rocking in his leather boat shoes, a resoundingly successful evening but there is so much, of course, to improve.

Lotte pops into the restaurant briefly to refresh the flowers, fussing with the display on the reception table while Abi is on hold with an IT team.

'You heard, did you, Abs, about the row outside?' Lotte's eyes gleam. Abi hates being called 'Abs'; it makes her feel like a member of a nineties boy band.

With the phone to her ear, Abi nods. 'Any idea what it was about?'

Lotte scrunches up her face. 'Nope. You?'

Abi shakes her head and Lotte turns, a little disappointed, back to her flowers, plucks a couple of wilting roses from the vase before adding, 'I'm guessing it'll be something about Eddy – it usually is. He had an affair a couple of years ago that ricocheted around the town. So much more embarrassing with it being so public.' Lotte shudders, then keeps talking. 'I bet he's been up to no good again and that's why Anna's not returning my calls. I never understood why she forgave him in the first place, to be honest. But anyway, I'll keep trying and, trust me, the truth will come out. It always does. Especially in Waverly.'

Abi walks to pick up Margot from school. It's a beautiful afternoon, gold pouring from the sky, the air fresh, the earth partying with a few more bursts of light before the long rest. A few parents glance at Abi, smiling easily when she makes eye contact, which is a good sign. There's no problem here, she chants to herself, the row wasn't about her. There's no problem here.

She's outside the school a bit early, so she thinks about going to the park opposite to sit in the sun and crunch through some of the pistachios she bought for Margot's snack. She notices a Volvo estate indicating to turn into the car park, waiting for Abi to cross. Suddenly the driver leans forward, nose practically touching the windscreen, staring at her. It's Rosie. Abi can tell from the way Rosie is staring at her that she knows. Rosie knows, because she's staring at Abi like she's the most dangerous and the most fascinating thing she's ever seen.

Abi moves first, lifts her hand to Rosie, breaking the silent, clear channel of understanding between them. They'll mess it all up with words now. Rosie leans over to the passenger side and opening the door says, 'Would you get in, Abi?'

She doesn't want to, she wants to run as fast and as far away as she can, but there's something in Rosie's voice, like she used her last ounce of strength to say those words. Rosie desperately needs this and so Abi reluctantly gets in.

Rosie turns the car around quickly and they drive in silence to a quiet cul-de-sac just a few yards away. It's double yellow, but Rosie pulls in anyway. She yanks the hand brake, cuts the engine and turns to face Abi. Her skin is white, her eyes wide. She looks like she can't believe what she's doing.

'I was coming early to have a quick chat with . . . Doesn't matter. I didn't think I'd see you.'

Rosie's hair glows in the afternoon light; her eyes are darting, her mouth pinched, knitted with tension. She's nervous. But that's OK. Abi's nervous, too.

'Rosie, I . . .'

'You were never a therapist, were you?'

Abi looks at Rosie before she looks out of the car. So, there it is. How simply, how easily her new life could be destroyed.

'No, no, I wasn't.'

Abi can't look directly at Rosie but out of the corner of her eye she can see she's biting her bottom lip, the surface crisp, flaky. She senses Rosie needs to keep leading, so she lets her.

'My husband paid you to have sex with him.' Rosie's voice is calm, her words simple, but she's breathing heavily.

'Yes,' Abi replies carefully.

Rosie lifts her hand to her sore-looking mouth and sobs briefly, into her palm, before swallowing, turning to look at Abi fully. 'You fucked men for money.'

It's a strange relief to have another woman say the truth out loud so plainly. Abi nods. 'Yes.'

'Why?'

'Because I needed the money, Rosie. Because I couldn't exist on handouts, and I couldn't raise my kids the way I wanted if I was working all hours for minimum wage.'

Could she tell her that scrubbing other people's shit off toilets for ten hours a day was, for her, worse than taking men like Rosie's husband in her arms? Would she understand? Would she try?

'The truth is I sold sex because it was a better option, for me, than any other at the time. I know I was one of the lucky ones. It was a choice. I sold sex because I got to choose when I worked, how much I was paid, and because I got to choose my hours and, in all honesty, I was good at it. Did I love it? No, not really. Did I sometimes hate it? Of course I did. But you know what? Most of the time it was just like a lot of other jobs. It was fine. It paid the bills. It served a purpose.'

She was one of the more vigilant workers. She had to be. She'd heard the horror stories of kids being taken into care. She could never risk being arrested or spending time in a hospital because who would look after her girls? She made sure she worked legally, which eventually meant working alone, which, ironically, was more dangerous. She devised a raft of safety checks before she'd accept a new client, installing a camera outside the studio flat she rented for work, putting in an alarm button that looked like it was connected to a security company but was actually just a dummy, hiding a can of pepper spray under the mattress.

But now she realizes she has no checks or alarms against the good people of Waverly. It is another irony that she feels more afraid of women like Lotte and Anna, stuffed full of centuries-old prejudice, fascination and derision, than the men who used to knock on her door to forget their loneliness for a little while.

'He paid you,' Rosie repeats, carefully. 'You had sex and now you're here, in our lives – why? What do you want?'

Rosie narrows her eyes at Abi, who shakes her head.

'Nothing. I don't want anything from you. I'm here because I needed a change, just like everyone else. That's all. I wanted this job, and I wanted my girls to have a better education, more choices. It's that simple.'

Rosie forces a laugh, hard and disbelieving. 'You expect me to believe that?'

Abi keeps her mouth shut, worried she'll shout if she doesn't. Why is it so hard for Rosie to believe that Abi could want the same things as most other people? That she too wants the chance to make changes in her life? Why is it so hard to believe that she is just fairly ordinary?

'If you don't want to blackmail us and you don't want to be with Seb, this is all just really fucking unlucky?'

Abi nods, breathes out through her mouth. She notices how Rosie is watching her now, seems to be studying her mouth, her hands. Imagining all those things her mouth and hands have done, all the licking and sucking and stroking.

'Did you never think about us? The families, the marriages you'd be wrecking?'

Abi looks at Rosie and suspects that deep down Rosie knows the answer.

'Rosie, I was never a threat to your marriage—'

But Rosie shouts, interrupting Abi, 'My husband paid you for sex – of course you were a threat to my marriage!'

Abi mustn't say any more. She needs this to end. 'What do you want, Rosie?'

Abi thinks Rosie isn't going to answer, so she's surprised when Rosie, her voice taut but clear, says, 'I want to know what he wanted. I want to know what you did with him.'

'Oh, Rosie,' Abi says, her heart aching for them both, 'please don't . . .'

'Tell me!' Rosie says, angry suddenly.

Abi tells her the truth. 'I don't remember much.'

Rosie's face lifts with shock before her eyes narrow, disbelieving, repulsed. 'You don't remember?'

'I saw hundreds of men, Rosie. Hundreds. All kinds of men with all kinds of issues. I'm sorry to say your husband, with whatever marital stuff he had or has going on in his privileged life, didn't make a huge impression.'

Careful, Abi, she sounds too prickly. Rosie's jaw hangs and Abi tries to backtrack. 'But the fact I don't remember means it wasn't remarkable – it was probably vanilla, over quickly.'

Abi worries she's overdone it, but she's started telling the truth now and doesn't want to stop, not yet. She glances at Rosie who is frozen, appalled but gripped, so Abi keeps talking. 'The reason I remembered him that night at yours was because of his scar.' Abi points towards her lip. 'My grandad was born with a cleft palate, so . . .' She shrugs again.

'Get out,' Rosie says quietly. 'I need you to get out now.'

Abi understands. Rosie doesn't want Abi to see her scream or cry or do whatever she needs to do.

Abi reaches for the door handle and is about to do as she's told but stops, because she needs something from Rosie too, and Rosie hasn't asked, hasn't bothered to think about Abi's needs in all this. 'Rosie, there's something I have to ask of you.'

They look at each other and, embarrassingly, Abi feels her own eyes burn. They always do when she thinks about her girls, the years of lying.

'If you're going to tell everyone about Seb and about what I used to do, then please' – she forces the words out – 'please give me the chance to tell my girls before the whole town knows. Please.'

Abi hoped that saying goodbye to Emma, her old persona, meant she'd never have to tell the girls. That with Waverly, their new schools and friends, her girls would lose any interest in their old lives in London. The past wouldn't exist any more, even to Abi, and they could all live like young children, focused only on the day in front of them.

But it isn't up to Abi any more. It's up to Rosie and her friends. Rosie looks away as tears rise in her eyes and Abi knows she can't talk, all she can do is nod, which will have to be enough for now.

'Thank you. Thank you, Rosie.' And as Abi steps out of the car into the syrupy light she hears Rosie cry out, angry, right before the car door closes with a thud, sealing Rosie and her misery away so her sorrow won't muck up the clean Waverly air.

*

Abi makes roast chicken in milk with lots of bay and nutmeg, but Diego is, as always, late and the girls are hungry, so the three of them eat without him. Half the chicken is gone, and the girls are already talking about what flavour ice cream they're going to have with their fruit salad when Diego enters the tiny kitchen, arms outstretched, holding a bottle of what Abi immediately recognizes as an excellent Sancerre.

The girls talk over each other, Margot trying to tell Diego about her new friend Luca while Lily asks him if he'd like to see her life drawing sketches and Abi tries to shoo them away, so Diego can at least take off his jacket.

He's here, like a human blanket; Abi wants to wrap herself in him, safe from the world. She hadn't realized until now how much she needs her friend, how different it is when they're at work. In a restaurant kitchen Diego is focused, concise, unsmiling – a typical chef. But outside of work he laughs loudly and easily; everyone wants to be close to him.

Diego and Abi had met in a members' bar in central London over ten years ago. The much older men they were both with – a client of Abi's and one of Diego's boyfriends – knew each other from working together in a bank years ago. While the old men reminisced, Abi and Diego found themselves next to each other on a sofa and spent the evening slagging off the bar menu, drinking outrageously priced cocktails and trying to impress each other with their knowledge of food. That first night they argued about where to get the best oysters in London, told each other what their Death Row meal would be (mole poblano 'with a twist' for Diego, and a seafood lasagne from Milan for Abi), and the evening ended with Diego begging to cook for Abi. A week later, Diego arrived in Abi's Zone 5 flat and, over his osso buco with fried polenta cake, they'd started planning their restaurant.

He knew about her work, of course, but gay men, Abi found, understood the nuances of sex and the complex power plays. Apart from occasionally checking she was safe, Diego didn't ask too many questions.

Now, Diego glances around the little kitchen, nods and smiles approvingly at the Picasso poster he bought for Abi's thirtieth a couple of years ago. Margot pulls him into a chair so she can clamber on to his lap and give him one of the mermaid tattoos he sent for her when they moved.

'Do you like yellow or brown hair best, Uncle D?' she asks seriously, turning his forearm over in her lap.

'On men or mermaids?' Diego twinkles in reply, his accent making his words rise and fall like music.

He tickles Margot, who squeals, 'Mermaids, silly!'

'Oh, yellow. Definitely yellow.'

'They seem well.' Diego is smiling as he walks back into the kitchen in his slow, sloping, graceful way, helping himself to more wine. He's been upstairs reading Margot's bedtime stories and then with Lily looking at her new sketches while Abi, trying to be patient, tidied the kitchen. Diego picks at the chicken carcass Abi left on the side, which she knew he'd go looking for. 'Lil mentioned a boy – Blake someone?'

Abi nods but she doesn't smile and her voice is strained as she says, 'It's her first proper crush.'

'Uh-oh.' Diego can tell she's not happy about it. He wiggles his dark eyebrows at her. 'Is he an asshole?'

Sometimes Diego sounds just like the kid he used to be, the kid who taught himself English from watching American films in the eighties in Mexico City.

Abi shakes her head because she doesn't want to talk about

Blake or even the girls. She steps towards Diego who drops a wing on the counter and opens his arms before wrapping her up, tightly. She lets her head rest on his chest, feels her body exhale, relieved not to be responsible for holding herself up. Diego kisses the top of her head, then rests his chin in the spot he just kissed and asks, 'What's wrong?'

And for the first time in years, Abi cries. Her fat tears soak Diego's shirt, and he holds her and rocks her and keeps kissing her cheek, keeps muttering, 'Baby, poor baby,' until her tears transform into big, billowy breaths. He pours her a glass of water and helps her to the table.

'I'm sorry,' she mutters, wiping under her eyes. 'I know we're supposed to talk about work.'

Diego ignores her and keeping his fudge-brown eyes on her says, 'Tell me everything.'

She tells him about meeting an ex-client in her new friend's kitchen, the shock of realizing he was not only Rosie's husband but also Lily's head teacher. She tells him about the agreement she had with Seb and then about the row outside PLATE. She tells him about her strained conversation with Rosie.

Diego sighs, winces and says, '*Dios mío.*' Then he asks quietly, 'You spoken to him since?'

She shakes her head. 'Haven't had the chance and, besides, I don't really know what I can say, other than beg him to keep me out of it again, which isn't just down to him any more. What if everyone finds out, D?'

Diego looks steadily at Abi. 'You do what you've always done. You tell everyone to fuck off and live your life.'

Abi smiles briefly because suddenly Diego sounds decisive and clear, like he's at work in a kitchen.

'Yes, but it's not London down here, D, it's different. I tell someone to mind their own business and then I've got to see them twice a day at school for the next however many years. I don't want my life, my kids' lives to be painful and lonely just so everyone else can learn something about tolerance.'

'Hmmm,' Diego agrees before adding, 'And they'd probably be bullied.'

Diego, a gay boy growing up poor in machismo culture, knows about bullying.

Abi clasps her forehead and groaning says, 'I think I have to go back to London, D. I don't think I can do this . . .'

'Hey, hey.' Diego shakes his head and puts his hands on her shoulders. 'Come on, now. I've never heard you talk like this – you've never been ashamed of who you are.'

'Not until now. Not until moving here.'

Abi thinks about Lotte, how delighted and appalled she looked when she told her that Margot was a donor child. She'd likely combust if she found out about Abi's past.

'No, Abi.' Diego holds up his hand in refusal. 'You've worked too hard, too long to give up so easily. This is your time, your chance; you deserve your chance. You can't let other people's small-mindedness, their prejudices, stop you from doing what you have wanted for so long. It might be hard, sure, but you've done much, much harder things in your life.' He pauses before he adds with a little smile, 'Good speech, hey?'

She nods, wishes she shared his conviction.

'But I do think if anyone else finds out then maybe tell Lily.'

Adrenaline shoots through her as she imagines the conversation. Lily pulling her hands away from Abi with a look of confusion, revulsion. What if Lily looks at her the way Rosie looked at her today? The way her own mum looked at her. That would kill her.

'What about the restaurant?'

'What *about* the restaurant?'

'Well, if people find out about me, they might, I don't know . . .'

'Want to book a table because not only is the food magnificent but the people working there are also interesting, real people?'

Abi tries to smile at her friend's efforts, but Diego has only just arrived in Waverly. He doesn't understand. Abi is pretty sure Anna, Lotte and the rest would rather see her lynched for her past than help her succeed in her new life. Women, especially mothers, are never let off the hook easily.

'Come here,' Diego says, and they stand to hug again. He kisses the side of her head and his deep voice tickles around her ear as he says, 'I mean it, though. You can't give up so easily. Besides, think of all those dicks you've had to suck to get here.'

She whacks him in the side then and he starts picking at the chicken again while she goes upstairs to kiss Lily goodnight.

Chapter 12

It's Tuesday morning and Anna's still asleep as Eddy flicks the kettle on. Yawning, he starts up her laptop on the kitchen table. She'd spent most of the night down here, tapping away while he pretended to sleep upstairs. Since Singapore he's often caught her reading messages on his phone, emails on his laptop. Of course he doesn't like it, but he lets it go. Their therapist had said that rebuilding trust required effort on both sides. His effort is practising patience and if that means letting Anna snoop from time to time, then so be it. He's never felt the need to spy on her in return, but since she came back from talking to Seb she's been muttering about 'doing something' and Eddy is pretty sure whatever it is she's planning is laid out on her laptop.

Albie sloshes milk all over his Weetabix and flicks through an old Lego magazine while Eddy taps 'Smithson' – Anna's maiden name – into her computer and the screen lights up with a Word document.

He rubs the coarse hair of his beard, the words blurry without his glasses; he can only make out a few: 'unethical behaviour', 'unsafe' and 'immediate removal'.

'What the fuck,' he mutters, and Albie looks up at him

sharply. 'Sorry, Albs,' Eddy says to his littlest one as the kettle comes to an angry boil. 'I'm just going to take Mum a cup of tea, I'll be back in a minute.'

Albie doesn't lift his eyes from his magazine; he just nods as Eddy tucks the laptop under his arm and carries two cups of tea upstairs. Blake's door is still closed – he'll still be fast asleep – but Eddy doesn't have long before Albie will need him again, he doesn't have long to find out whatever it is Anna's planning.

Anna's sitting up in bed, blinking against the brightness of the day. She eyes the mug in Eddy's hand. 'Thanks, sweetie.'

He reaches to his side table for his glasses and sits on the edge of the bed. She smiles when she sees the laptop; she seems glad, flattered even, that he's been poking around.

'You read it?' she asks.

'Not yet.' He puts on his glasses and starts reading. '"Petition to remove Sebastian Kent as head teacher from Waverly Community Secondary School." Anna,' he says, the vowels long and full of warning, 'you want to get Seb *fired*?'

'I was hoping he'd resign before it came to that,' Anna says defensively.

For as long as Eddy can remember, Seb had always wanted to be head teacher. Eddy never understood it, even tried to turn Seb's head by showing off his own larger paycheques, the company car, the flashy business trips. Seb had been appropriately impressed but had stuck to his course. When he'd told Eddy he'd got the head teacher job just a few months ago, they'd held on to each other's arms and jumped about Eddy's kitchen, whooping, until Blake came in and told them, smiling, that they were both acting like kids.

Now, Eddy is reading a document his wife has written to

bring all that to an ignoble end. The petition reads like a fever dream; she hasn't bothered with punctuation.

It's a relief she doesn't mention exactly what it is that Seb's done, but still, it's written to incriminate him, written to show him in the worst possible light.

'Anna, you can't really think he's not safe to do his job . . .'

'If he worked in a factory or was an IT guy, then sure, whatever. I wouldn't care. But he doesn't, does he? He's a teacher, our son's head teacher. He should be a role model, lead by example. He has a responsibility to our children, to our whole community, to act with integrity with . . .'

Eddy holds up his hand and interrupts, 'Yes, fine. I agree, I do, but when he's not at work then surely he can do what he likes as long as it's legal. Think about that presenter guy who was caught messaging younger men at work, Max . . .'

'Max Harting.'

'That's it. Didn't you say that you didn't like what he was doing, didn't agree with it, but that it wasn't illegal so never mind?'

He sounds desperate, but it isn't fair, he wasn't prepared, and Anna has been up thinking about this all night. She enunciates her words carefully as she says, 'What if Seb was a far-right lunatic in his spare time, had a swastika tattoo and posted awful stuff online – would you want to know about that?'

Eddy pulls a face. 'Of course I would,' he says gruffly.

'Yeah, but all that's legal, so . . .' Anna makes her eyes wide, shrugs, like, 'what's the problem?' She's made her point. 'Well, I'd want to know if he slept with prostitutes, and I think other women would agree with me.'

Eddy stares dumbly at the laptop screen, silent for a

moment. He doesn't want to get into an argument about gender. About why this prostitute thing is worse, more offensive – or so Anna seems to be suggesting – to women. He'll certainly lose.

Eddy knew some of his colleagues, on work trips to faraway places, would sometimes pay. But Eddy had never considered it; the best part had always been the chase, the 'will we, won't we?' Paying for it – he imagined – took all the magic, all the sexiness away. But he won't mention any of this to Anna. He needs to keep his own name as far away from all this as possible.

'What does this mean, then, for our family, for Blake?'

'Well, I think if we can't get rid of Seb then we're going to have to find somewhere else for Blake, even if it's further away. Brighton has some good places . . .'

'Brighton's half an hour away!'

'We'll make it work.'

'Anna, all his friends are here, he's happy at Waverly, we can't just . . .'

'Then for once in your life, Eddy, support me! The petition will get rid of him, everyone will sign it – trust me. We'll get a new head and then we won't have to move Blake.'

'But Seb's his godfather . . .' Eddy replies meekly and Anna reaches for his hand, squeezes, like she's full of regret about that choice they made fifteen years ago, too. He can't say out loud what he's really thinking, the feeling that crowds out almost everything else. The panic that he'll lose Seb. His best friend and perhaps, he realizes now, the truth sinking within him, his only real friend. Anna will tell him he's being selfish, thinking only about himself again, like always. So instead, Eddy asks, 'And what about Abi and her girls, the repercussions for Rosie? It's not just Seb who'll be impacted by this.'

Anna just nods, sadly. 'I know. I'm going to try and talk to Rosie today, let her know that we'll be there for her . . .'

'She can't possibly think this is a good idea.'

Anna breathes out gently, tries to keep herself calm, reminding Eddy that she's an expert in this particular kind of heartbreak. 'Look, Ed, Rosie's in the denial stage now. I remember it myself. She can't think straight about anything, but when she's processed some of her own feelings, I think she'll understand where I'm coming from with the petition.'

'And Abi? What about Abi?' Eddy asks, clutching for the thing that will make Anna stop or at least pause, but he hasn't found it yet because Anna replies, 'I don't name her; I don't even mention exactly what he did.'

Eddy tries to ignore the strange slippery feeling in his stomach. He noticed the way Blake blushed and looked away when he mentioned Lily's name the other day. Blake has a crush on Lily, which Anna doesn't know about and which only serves to complicate everything even more.

'Yes, but it will come out, won't it? She'll be implicated . . .'

'Well,' Anna sniffs, 'excuse the pun, but she made her bed, didn't she? I'm afraid I can't protect everyone.'

He can't help it. He has to say something about the cost to his own life.

'And what about my thirty-year friendship?'

Anna breathes out; Eddy's exasperating her now. 'I don't know, Ed. That'll be up to you guys to figure out.'

Eddy's head feels like an untethered balloon, bobbing around; he knows he should say something, but he can't find any thoughts, just air where thoughts should be, so he pleads, 'Can you just let me talk to him first, please, before posting this?'

Anna props herself up on her elbows a little, considering, and says, 'I tried that already, didn't I, Eddy?' Her eyebrows slant together which means she's about to say something difficult. 'Look, Ed, I didn't want to tell you this, but when I spoke to Seb he compared what he's done with what you did, in Singapore. He said it was the same thing.'

Eddy wilts. 'What?'

Anna nods. 'I'm sorry. I know it's not, of course. You didn't plan to be unfaithful, you didn't pay a poor, desperate woman for sex and you came home and told me straight away about what you'd done, so . . .'

Eddy can feel her eyes on him, anxious for his reaction. Anna's quiet for a moment, staring at him, before she glances at the laptop balanced on his knees and her face lifts with excitement. 'Oh my God, Ed!'

'What?' Eddy says, nervous again.

'You remember when you and Blake saw Seb at school and he slammed his laptop shut and you started that whole stupid "Seb's a spy" gag – can you remember whether it was his school computer?'

Where feelings should be, Eddy's mind is completely blank. He looks at his wife, mystified, shakes his head, blows out to show that he has no idea, absolutely none.

'It probably was? He uses it for everything, I'm pretty sure. What difference does it make?'

'What difference? Ed, if he was looking for sex workers, literally shopping for women to abuse and using school property to do it, then he really is a danger to kids . . .'

'What? How?'

Anna rolls her eyes at his slowness. 'Imagine if a child came into his office, if they'd seen those images . . .'

'Anna, come on, that's pretty unlikely . . .'

But Anna doesn't care what Eddy thinks because she keeps talking, 'He's being paid by the taxpayer, literally funded by us, the hard-working public, and he's using that time on school property to look up women to abuse.'

Anna's talking herself into a rage and Eddy knows that the thrill of it is too alluring for her, he won't be able to reason with her now, so it's a relief when a small voice from down-stairs calls up, 'Dad . . . Daddy?'

He clears his throat and calls back, 'Coming.'

'You OK, Eddy?' Anna asks, clasping his hand briefly, as he stands up, readjusts the tie on his dressing gown to go to their son, while Anna stares at him, her eyebrows lifted in concern.

Eddy nods to show that yes, of course he's fine, when they both know he's not. He's really not fine at all.

Eddy has a lunch meeting with a client in London and while he's standing in front of the open wardrobe trying to choose a shirt for the day, Anna comes in and immediately hands him the light-blue shirt he'd been looking for. 'I'll drive you to the station.'

Eddy frowns; the station is just a short walk away.

'I've got something I want to show you on the way. Come on.'

'But my train isn't for an hour, and I've got a couple of . . .'

'You can send emails while I drive. Please, Eddy. It's important.'

Ruston is only five miles south of Waverly, but as Anna's parents moved almost twenty years ago to a more salubrious village in Hampshire, they have no reason to visit. Eddy has

155

come once or twice to buy paint in one of the big industrial estates that seem to be engulfing the small town, but other than that he hardly thinks about the place and Anna almost never mentions it.

Anna is quiet on the drive. Eddy focuses on his phone and does his best to ignore the anxiety nibbling away in his stomach.

Even with the sun shining and autumnal leaves falling soft as snowflakes, Ruston is still an armpit. The centre of town is strangled by a one-way system and many of the shops are boarded up. The only places open are betting shops, take-aways and tired-looking budget supermarkets selling more booze than food. Kids bunking off school and drunks con-gregate outside, like these grubby places are their church and they're seeking redemption in a bottle of cheap whisky or energy drink.

A skinny mum pushes a bored-looking toddler and a wall-eyed baby in a pram. She moves like she's angry, ready for a fight, stopping next to another woman with greasy hair and a pushchair, smoking at a bus stop. It's jarring thinking about their lives in Waverly occurring at the same time, just five miles down the road.

'Why are we here?' Eddy asks nervously.

'Wait a moment,' Anna says, keeping her eyes on the road. Eddy notices how tightly she grips the wheel. This is hard for her. She wants to be here even less than Eddy but she's pushing through her discomfort because whatever this is, it's important.

They stop outside a row of red-brick houses that doesn't look so different to their own terrace in Waverly. But these houses have broken kids' toys in tiny overgrown front gar-dens, weeds sprouting out of the roof tiles, and one of the windows has been barred up with a metal grate. Anna points to a house in the middle. It has grey net curtains hanging in the window that look like they were once white.

'That was ours. Number sixteen. And that' – she points to the scrubby patch of grass opposite the row of houses – 'is where I used to watch them. They used to call out to my dad asking if he wanted a blowjob for breakfast, laughing at him as he walked me and my sister to school. Dad used to get so angry. When it first started getting bad back in the late nineties, Dad would come out here with a litter picker and a bin bag every weekend to pick up the used condoms, but he stopped after a while.'

'Why?' Eddy asks weakly. Horrified for his upright, dignified father-in-law and appalled for little Anna.

Anna shrugs and just stares blankly, like she doesn't want to see the place in focus even from a car window. 'I think he just gave up. It almost destroyed him, you know, watching this fishing village he grew up in become one of the most deprived towns in the country.' Anna folds her lips against her teeth. 'It got worse. Once, Sami opened the door to a pimp looking for one of his girls. Sami and I weren't allowed out on our own after that, even though we were teenagers. We were bullied at school for being stuck up, for having this overprotective dad. Then one day I recognized one of the girls; she was only two years above me at school and she was standing out there in just her bra and short white skirt. She went missing a couple of weeks later. I remember her mum asking if we could put a "Find Charlotte" poster in our front room. We did, of course, but then a few days later I heard my mum crying in the kitchen; the poster had been taken down. No one said why and we moved soon after.'

Eddy doesn't know what to say but knows he should say something. 'God, Anna, I'm so sorry.'

Anna turns in the driver's seat to look directly at him. 'This is what I'm afraid of, Eddy. Of this same thing happening to Waverly.'

The thought that Waverly with its tourists, art galleries and lazy brunch cafes could ever fall like Ruston is almost laughable, but Anna's face is so serious and she seems to read Eddy's thoughts as she says, 'I mean it, Ed. Ask my dad. He always says that if this could happen to Ruston, it could happen anywhere.'

Eddy thinks about pointing out that her father had told him the reason Ruston fell so hard was because the community was dependent on the fishing industry and when their small boats were overtaken by the huge trawlers, they didn't stand a chance. Overnight, it seemed, everyone was unemployed, which of course led to poverty, which in turn led to all the other problems. But one look at Anna and he can see that she won't want to hear it. Her reasons are emotional; she is motivated by trying to protect her sons from some of the things he now knows she experienced in her own childhood. Her fears might not be grounded in reality, but that doesn't make them any less important.

He takes her hand where it rests on the gear stick between them. He feels a wonderful tenderness. He can respect, even love her fire about this whole Seb mess now he knows where it comes from. 'Why didn't you ever tell me any of this, Anna?'

She shakes her head, sadly. 'I don't know; they're not the best memories. I try not to think about it.'

He nods. He knows those reasons all too well.

She turns to him, curious to see if he understands her

better now, and he smiles at her and nods to show that he does.

'I just want to protect my community and our kids' childhoods for as long as I can. And if she hasn't been forced into it, then she is simply a woman who makes bad choices. Most women' – Anna says the words carefully, implying that what she means is 'most *good* women' – 'most women would do anything other than sell their bodies. I'd stack shelves, clean toilets, whatever, if I had to. You know I would,' she says, warming to her own righteousness. 'But Abi didn't. She chose to open her legs for whoever paid her, putting herself and her own children in danger. If she's capable of doing that, then she could be involved in anything – organized crime, drugs – and God knows what she's like when it comes to parenting. Thank God I cancelled Albie going over to their place when I did. It would break me if the same thing happened . . .' She glances towards the door that used to be her front door but there's a crack in her voice, she can't keep talking, so he leans towards her, takes her in his arms, clumsy over the gear stick, and he kisses the side of her face and doesn't make her finish, but instead he says, 'Come on, I can't miss that train.' And Eddy keeps his eyes on the road and neither of them talks as they drive back to the safety of their lovely little town.

Eddy waits on the platform for his train and after checking there's no one around who might overhear him, he calls Seb. Just when he thinks Seb's answerphone is going to click on, like it has every other time Eddy's called since Saturday night, Seb picks up. 'Hi, Ed.' His voice is flat, his tone grey, exhausted.

'Seb. Mate, good to hear you,' Eddy says and out of habit adds, 'You OK?'

'Um, not really, no, not really. Look, Ed, I really want to talk, I've got something to ask you, something you can do to help this whole horrible thing, but I'm about to meet with a parent so only have a couple of minutes . . .'

'That's fine. That's fine.' Eddy knows he should start by telling him how sorry he is that all this is happening, gently ask what Seb's plans are, perhaps suggest that he take some time away from work to focus on his family, prepare the ground for Eddy to imply that he should resign. Or perhaps he could tell Seb that he's just been to Ruston, the things Anna told him, the things that helped her reaction make more sense to Eddy. But those words are jostled and pushed to one side, making way for other, more boisterous ones that leave Eddy in an undignified whine, 'Listen, Seb, I . . . Anna told me that you think what happened in Singapore was the same thing as . . . you know, this thing that you've done.'

There's a brief pause on the other end of the line, Seb doing that thing where he quietly considers what's just been said.

'Ed, you know I'm going through a horrific time, I don't really have the energy for your relationship prob—'

'You meant it?' Eddy can't help it; he cuts Seb off.

But Eddy stops talking because to his dismay and irritation, on the other end of the line, Seb starts laughing.

'What? What's so funny, Seb?' Eddy squeaks, sounding like the twelve-year-old he was when they first met at the bike park.

But Seb can't answer because he's laughing too much, a little manic.

He takes a couple of deep breaths to calm himself before he says, 'That is literally the most selfish thing I've ever heard. My life is falling apart and you want to talk about *yourself*?'

Now it's Eddy turn to pause.

He's selfish? Seb's calling *him* selfish when Seb's the one who has lied again and again, Seb's the one who rented a damaged woman, like that girl, Charlotte, Anna told him about, and Seb's the one who gambled his children's well-being for a quick shag? For most of Eddy's life, Seb has been the golden boy – athletic, clever and kind – while Eddy felt like a grasping, hunched, lowly sidekick whose only attribute was to do the stupid stuff others were too frightened to do and to say the stupid gags to make people laugh – and, even then, only sometimes. But now, with these revelations, Seb has fallen from his cloud with the other rare angels, face first into the mud where Eddy has always stood.

'My life, everything I love is hanging by a thread and you, my best mate, are worried about something your insane wife said about you?'

That word, 'insane', kicks Eddy in the guts. Seb doesn't know Anna, not really; he doesn't know that she knows more about the dark side of prostitution than any of them. What it can do to people, to a place. He thinks again of Charlotte.

'That's not fair,' Eddy says, his jaw tense.

'No, Ed, I'll tell you what's not fair. Being hounded by your wife at work when I need friendship, support more than ever. What's not fair is my best mate thinking only of himself . . .'

Eddy hangs up.

He thinks about his arthritic, white-haired father-in-law slowly clearing away used condoms in the jacket and tie he always wears. Of Anna's young face watching girls being driven away by strangers, that poor, poor girl Charlotte, and then he thinks about Seb. The circumstances might have been a bit different but he still knowingly got involved in an industry that treats women like commodities, like some kind of human spittoon. Anna is right: he isn't so different to any of the men driving those desperate young girls away somewhere quiet and lonely where no one would hear them.

His phone buzzes with a message from Anna: *I'm going to publish the petition, OK?*

Eddy types out, *Fine*, but then he deletes it because Seb has been his best mate for longer than he's known Anna. He types out, *No, Anna. Please don't*, but just as he's about to press send he changes his mind, deletes that message too, because how long had Seb been lying to them all? And besides, doesn't Anna need his support now? He throws his phone back into his bag and gets on his train and decides to do absolutely nothing – which is, he decides, a decision in itself.

Chapter 13

Seb works from home on a Tuesday; with his new open-door policy at school, it made sense having one clear morning to tackle budget admin and staffing issues, and make confidential phone calls somewhere he wouldn't be disturbed. When Rosie gets back from drop-off, she finds him hunched over his laptop, long legs splayed at the kitchen table, his head snapping up from the screen as she enters.

'Ro, sorry, I thought you'd be at work.'

Rosie flicks the kettle on and looks at Seb. God, his earnest expression is so transparent; nervously touching the scar on his lip.

'I've taken the rest of the week off work,' she says, her tone bland, emotionless. 'Good old Norovirus.'

'You didn't tell me,' Seb says, a whine in his voice, eyes blinking from behind his glasses.

Rosie snorts a fake laugh and Seb at least has the decency to look away, abashed. That was an idiotic thing to say.

His work phone starts ringing; he looks down. 'Sorry, it's Harriet, I'm going to have to take this.'

Rosie shrugs and turns her back to him to get a mug and teabag as Seb stands and walks out of the kitchen to take the call upstairs, saying, 'Morning, Harriet,' to the chair of governors as he leaves.

Once he's gone, Rosie turns back round to face the kitchen table, ignoring the kettle as it spits and bubbles behind her. As she hears Seb move around safely away upstairs, she stares at one thing. His school laptop. Seb thinks she doesn't know his password, but she's watched him open it enough times that she knows it's their kids' initials followed by the year. He is vigilant about protecting his students' and teachers' confidential information, but not vigilant enough. Fucking Seb. Fucking upright, law-abiding Seb. She moves across the kitchen, sits down on the still-warm chair. Seb. So good when it came to everyone else and such a traitorous slimy shit when it came to her – his wife. Rosie taps in his password, and the screen comes alive.

Above her, the floorboards groan. He's pacing around. She feels her hands moisten, nervous suddenly at what she's going to ask them to do; they've never done this, never snooped before. But she didn't listen to her instinct before, when she suspected something more had gone on between Seb and Abi, and look where it has left her. Betrayed in the most degrading way. She remembers Blake and Eddy's story – how Seb had slammed his computer shut when they'd disturbed him at school. She won't ignore her instinct again. She clicks through to the computer's history easily, and the screen fills with an incredibly young-looking Asian girl, peering over her shoulder, looking back at Rosie, around her pert, naked bottom the words 'GeeGee is ready to play!' Rosie whimpers and clicks on the next page. This time it's a white woman with long brown hair in a squat over a chair, bronzed, doughy breasts pushed up, masturbating, her eyes closed, her lip slightly curled, furiously focused on her own pleasure. 'Discounted rates! Only £130 for the first hour!!!!!'

Rosie clicks on more and more pages. Where was she, she wonders, when Seb was staring at them? Was she putting their kids to bed? Cleaning the bathroom? Folding fucking laundry?

Rosie sits back and lifts her face to the ceiling, feeling herself drop fully into what she suspected to be true. Seb is a liar, a perpetual liar. He'd been shopping online for people just like how she'd buy toilet roll and tomatoes. He hadn't just stumbled on Abi's website like he said. He'd hunted for her, hunted specifically for Abi with her brown eyes, toned legs and perky breasts.

Upstairs, on the phone, Seb laughs, and Rosie feels like she's suddenly no longer made of bone and muscle. No. Now she's all rage.

She stands, knocking the chair over but not caring; she can't sit with him smiling and laughing, thinking he's got away with this sick *browsing*. She leans over the laptop, palm pressed against the table, hunched as she keeps clicking. He'd considered hundreds, not caring how cheap or young or desperate their eyes looked in the photos. He couldn't have called them all, but can she, Rosie, ever be sure he didn't? How can she ever know for certain that he didn't go and visit the thin Black girl with fake breasts, stilettos and huge, sad eyes? Her hand reaches for her shoulder, her forearm slung across her own slack breasts like she's protecting them from the perfect twenty-year-old breasts on the screen. She feels her own vagina pressing chubbily, falling out of itself against her old cotton pants, the creeping hair, a different species to the impossibly neat slit of these women. She bets they all smell lovely, those tidy, hairless vaginas, like perfect, silken closed mouths despite the grind of their endless, tiring work.

'Rosie?'

Rosie's head snaps up from the screen as she slams the laptop closed. Eva is standing in the back doorway, holding something wrapped in a tea towel and looking quietly at her daughter-in-law.

'You scared me!'

'Sorry,' Eva says, addressing the toppled chair on the floor before looking back up to Rosie. 'I did knock but you were miles away.'

Eva's eyes move from Rosie's face to her hand, her finger-tips resting on Seb's laptop, the Waverly Community Secondary School label stuck on top.

'Yes, I was just . . . Seb's upstairs on a call. I'm actually about to go out. I want to go for a swim and then I promised I'd see Anna.' Rosie had, in a weak moment, finally given in to Anna's incessant requests to meet and talk.

'That sounds like a good idea.' Eva nods approvingly and Rosie knows she's referring to the swim rather than to Anna, whom Eva has never really connected with. Eva is one of those people who believes cold water cures everything from dry skin to a broken heart. 'I just wanted to see if you needed anything – a chat, maybe, or food or help with the children . . .'

'No, I'm fine. Thanks, Eva.'

Still on edge from almost being caught out, Rosie can't return Eva's smile as she passes Rosie the warm bundle she's been holding.

'Here – I baked it this morning. It's the one with cheese and chives.'

Heath's favourite.

Eva glances again at the laptop on the table, like she's think-ing about saying something. It makes Rosie bristle.

'I'm so sorry this has happened,' she says, quiet but steady.

Rosie doesn't want Eva's calm now, not when all those websites are spinning so wildly in her brain. She puts the bread on to the work surface and grabs a tote bag from the hook by the back door before shoving in a still-damp towel from the drying rack.

Eva says nothing, knows Rosie well enough to know when to back off.

'Seb probably won't be long,' Rosie says, bending down to pick up the fallen chair.

'No, I won't wait for him. It was you I wanted to check in on.'

Rosie doesn't know what to say so she just nods furiously and says, 'Yes, well, I'm fine. Fine!'

She heads out of the back door, leaving Eva to deal with the human maggot she raised whom she can still hear, laughing, above their heads.

Rosie walks quickly into the water and the cold screams through her as she wades up to her hips. A huge wave, made up of a million angry foaming mouths, rises to bite, but she dives underneath it. The freeze makes her retract into herself so she can hardly move at all. Then a great pull drags her up and out and she surfaces, screaming, swearing, and she's so fucking small but she'll keep fighting because there's nothing else. Another enormous wave roars towards her, a great salty mouth howling for her. This time, she lets it take her, pulling her into its mess, its rage, and while it plays with her, rolling her around with its watery tongue, there's a moment of immense silence, of such elemental gentleness that Rosie doesn't feel scared, she doesn't feel anything and, for a second, she disappears. Then, without warning, the sea starts chewing her again, her lungs panic, heave, and suddenly the sea is done with her. It spits her out, a diner spitting a bone out of a stew. She's left in the shallows, spluttering and breathing hard. The water has worked smooth Rosie's jagged edges like sea glass. She isn't thinking about Abi and all those other plastic women online and for a moment she's left with just the clean, simple realization: Seb was never good. He'd been yearning and suppressing and hiding himself all along. He'd had secrets. And she loves him, and she hates him and she loves him and she hates him, and she has no idea how they're going to survive.

She doesn't dry herself well so she's shaking with cold by the time she gets back to the car, but this is the best bit, her skin tasting of salt, the sparkle and fizz of blood in her veins. Her phone buzzes with more missed calls from Seb and one from Eddy and then a text comes through from Anna.

Just got to the cafe, babe. Will order us some tea. Love you. X

Anna has been ending every message to Rosie with 'love you' since Saturday, which to Rosie feels more indicative of Anna's guilt, for not telling Rosie that Abi and Seb had had sex, than genuine love for her. Rosie wishes for the millionth time that, apart from Maggie, her architect friend in Sydney, she hadn't let her old friendships from school and university fade over time. She'd known it was happening, especially after they moved to Waverly, but her children were so young, her life already overly stuffed with people. She couldn't handle any more, so letting those relationships splutter and die had felt more like a relief than a loss. Until now. Now she just has Anna and a handful of other Waverly women whom she calls

168

friends, who no longer feel safe. Especially not now when she really needs help.

Rosie dresses, for once not caring that her dimply bottom and sagging breasts are on display. She slowly makes her way along the beach to the cafe; it's windy so she clamps her arms around herself in a hug to try to keep warm. Her hair is cold and wet, like seaweed dangling around her face. She's shivering by the time she arrives at the almost empty cafe and sees Anna sitting at a table for two in the far corner by the window, a pot of tea and two mugs in front of her. Anna stands and opens her arms as soon as Rosie walks through the door. The young girl behind the counter glances up from her phone to look at Rosie, but the screen drags her eyes back immediately.

It's good to feel Anna's soft, warm body against her own. Anna kisses the side of her face and Rosie shakes her head so Anna knows it's not her fault as she whispers, 'I'm so sorry, I'm sorry about all this, Ro.'

When Rosie at last pulls away, Anna rubs Rosie's upper arms and says, 'You've been swimming!'

Rosie nods. 'I had to clear my head.'

Anna's doing her best to hide it, but Rosie can still feel her excitement, the anticipation just behind her gentleness. It's in the way she smiles, the spark in her eye. Anna's always loved drama.

They sit and Anna pours tea, adding two spoonfuls of sugar to Rosie's mug without asking before handing it to her.

The hot mug in Rosie's hands feels wonderful. Anna settles back in her seat, spine straight, braced and waiting, which Rosie knows is challenging for her. They don't mention how upset Rosie had been that Anna hadn't told her earlier about Seb; Anna has already explained her reasoning in texts and, besides, there are more important things to talk about now. When Anna can't take the silence any more, she leans in and says, 'I want you to know, anything you tell me won't go any further. I won't tell anyone. I promise.' Adding as an after-thought, 'Not even Eddy.'

Anna says it like she's bestowing a great gift on Rosie rather than offering her the simple dignity of confidentiality. Still, Rosie remembers how hard it was talking to Anna after Eddy's affair, the pressure she felt to find the right words, so she nods and mutters, 'Thanks,' before adding with a sigh, 'I talked to Abi the other day, just before pick-up.'

'Fuck.'

'Yup.'

Anna's eyes pinball around Rosie's face, trying to keep her talking, but she doesn't, so Anna says, 'Well, I hope she apologized.'

Rosie frowns, threads her fingers through her salt-stiff hair and says quietly, 'She didn't, actually.'

Anna tuts, rolls her eyes.

'You think she should?'

'Ro – she had sex with your husband. More than once. Yes, she owes you a bloody apology! She owes you a thousand apologies and it still wouldn't be enough in my view.'

There's a part of Rosie that likes Anna's interpretation of all this, part of her that wants to be the uncomplicated victim.

Anna leans towards Rosie, eyes gleaming as she asks in a whisper, 'Did she say anything about being a prostitute?'

'Umm, not really.'

'So she said something about it . . .'

'Anna.' Rosie holds up her hand to get her to stop.

'Too much, you're right, too much. Sorry, Ro.'

They sit in silence for a moment before, again, Anna's had enough and asks quietly, 'So, did he find her online?'

Rosie nods. She sees them all again, all those thrusting, parading, hairless women cooing how much they love sex; how Seb must have, at some level, believed they were waiting desperately for him. It was pathetic. Laughable. The lies they were all telling themselves.

'Yes, and about a thousand other prostitutes.' Rosie feels a fresh slap of rage as she says the words out loud, but why shouldn't she? Why should she protect him? 'Another thing he lied about.'

Anna actually gasps. 'He didn't just see Abi?'

Rosie shrugs because, really, what the hell does she know about her husband any more?

'Where did you find this out?'

'On his computer.'

'The one from school?'

Rosie nods and notices how Anna's eyes widen and her mouth clenches like she's stopping herself from shouting something out loud.

'It's the premeditation that really hurts,' Rosie says, more to confirm the fact to herself than to share it with Anna.

Anna nods like she understands, but she doesn't because she repeats, 'Premeditation?'

Rosie looks away, waits for Anna to twig.

'Oh, you mean the planning that went into it. Booking the time, buying the train ticket, making sure you were busy so you wouldn't be suspicious, taking the cash out . . .' Rosie holds up her hand again to show that's enough. Anna's made her point.

'You're right,' Anna says, reaching for Rosie's cold hand. 'All that stuff, I can't imagine. It must make it so much harder.'

Anna doesn't need to explain herself. They both know what she's getting at. That what Seb's done is worse, much worse than what Eddy did. Even in infidelity there are hierarchies.

Rosie takes a sip of tea before saying, 'Then there's all this other stuff, like, at some deep level, Seb wants women to perform for him no matter the cost to them. I mean, how fucked up is that?'

Anna is back to shaking her head and says, 'It's so disturbing. It's all deception and suffering, when you think about it.'

Rosie has the unsettling feeling that her friend is looking at the same problem but from a different angle to Rosie. She takes another sip of tea and Anna does the same.

'Have you had a chance to think about what you want to do?' Anna asks. 'If you want to kick him out for good or . . .'

Rosie shakes her head and remembers asking a sobbing Anna something similar two years ago, before Anna adds, 'Take your time, love. I'll support you, help in any way I can. You do know that, don't you?'

Rosie nods, feebly, and Anna, apparently energized from the tea, asks with renewed vigour, 'Listen, there's something specific I need to talk to you about, something I feel I have to do, but before I ask, I just want to check you got the link I sent through for the clinic?'

'Clinic?'

'The STI clinic.' Anna mouths the 'STI' bit even though there's no one around to hear them.

Rosie must look blank because Anna says, 'I know it's probably the last thing you want to think about, and I know you guys haven't had sex for a year, but still, I heard that London is smothered in gonorrhoea these days, so I really . . .'

'What did you say?' Rosie leans forward, feeling blood rush, hot and sudden, back into her face.

'Yeah, there's this really nasty strain of gonorrhoea . . .'

'No, the bit before – about me and Seb, about us not having sex. Who told you that?'

Anna's eyes dart around Rosie's face again, searching for the right answer. 'Eddy told me, so Seb must have mentioned it to him.'

Rosie feels like her eyes have fallen out of her head and are rolling like marbles across the tiled floor. The cafe spins as her heart gallops.

'Rosie, what's wrong?'

Rosie stands and Anna clamps her hand back around Rosie's arm, but this time it doesn't feel good. This time it feels like Anna's trying to restrain her. Rosie wiggles free. 'He's been talking, has he? About our sex life, or lack of sex life, blaming me for paying a prostitute . . .'

The teenager behind the counter looks up from her phone. Anna's eyes are wide, appalled by this sudden, unexpected turn. 'No, Ro, I mean, I don't know what that man's doing but . . .'

'He's trying to justify what he did by blaming me, saying he had to go and pay for sex because I wasn't giving it to him for free – that's what he's doing.'

Anna looks disappointed that her meeting is being so badly derailed but Rosie feels light with anger, and it feels good, like she's high.

'I've got to go,' she says, turning towards the door.

'Wait, let me come too. I need to tell you about . . .'

'Anna, please, just let me go.'

'Oh, Ro, I'm sorry, I'm really sorry . . .'

Rosie doesn't hear the rest because she's already walked out of the cafe, the door banging behind her as she runs back to her car.

She parks badly outside their house and rushes inside. Seb's sitting at the kitchen table, hunched over his computer that still carries all those women inside. How fucking dare he be sitting there so normally, so untouched by everything he's done, while her world has blown up like a fucking bomb?

'You pervert,' she says from the open doorway.

'Rosie!'

Seb's cheeks pink in surprise. He looks at her, taking in her soggy, bedraggled appearance, and stands up from the table.

'Rosie, how was your . . .?' He moves towards her, like he wants to tame her, just like Anna.

She pulls away and growls, 'Don't you fucking come near me.'

'Just . . . Ro, please, tell me what's happened because I . . .'

Behind her, the front door bangs back on its hinges. In her hurry to get to him she didn't shut it properly and the wind has blown it open. Seb hurries to close it. She wants to hit him then, hit him because she knows he'll be worrying about someone overhearing them, someone hearing the truth she can feel bubbling up, about to burst out of her.

When he's standing back in front of her, head slightly tilted, he asks again, 'What's happened, Ro?'

She laughs. 'It's so easy for you, isn't it?'

'What is?'

'Lying.'

Seb doesn't react. Instead, he waits, knowing she'll keep talking, which of course she does.

'You weren't shown Abi's website at that awards thing, were you? You went searching for her. Literally, *shopping* for a woman.'

Seb's eyes swivel away from her and she knows what he's thinking.

'You didn't delete your laptop history, you idiot. I saw everything.'

Seb closes his eyes briefly; his cheeks and the scar above his lips redden. It feels fucking wonderful. But it's not enough. She swivels his laptop towards her on the table; it's still unlocked, and she navigates quickly to the history and opens up one of the sites. There's a close-up of a tongue licking an erect penis: 'The best oral without condom in London for only £80!' She scrolls down, stops at a woman's face – she's smiling, licking her top lip while her hands cover her bare breasts. Rosie points to her. 'Tell me something, Seb – do you think she actually wants you? Are you that delusional? Honestly, I think you're sick. Either you're mentally unwell, believing that a woman like that wants to have sex with you, or you're sick because you don't give a shit that that poor woman is obviously lying because she's desperate for money and you don't care about her pain. You'll just fuck her anyway!'

She starts scrolling again, down to a GIF of an arse in a G-string wiggling back and forth.

Seb closes his eyes again and Rosie has to resist the urge to peel them open with her thumbs, force him to look at what he's done, but instead gets closer to him and says, 'But that's not all, is it? You've been telling people about us, our sex life, that I hadn't had sex with you and that's why you hired Abi . . .'

'What? No, no, of course I haven't,' Seb interrupts, shaking his head, which makes Rosie erupt.

175

'Then how the hell does Anna know we haven't had sex in a year?'

Seb freezes, caught out, and Rosie feels a rush, the thrill of being right, her anger justified, so she keeps shouting, 'This isn't *The Handmaid's Tale*, Seb – a woman has the right not to want to have sex!'

She's expecting his head to drop, for him to become all meek and hangdog like he's been for the last few days, so it's a surprise when, jaw flexing, he takes a step towards her. 'And what about what I wanted? I tried, I tried everything I could think of, but you turned me away again and again. I didn't want to never have sex again. It was driving me mad, Rosie, completely insane.'

He taps his finger to the side of his head, his voice getting louder and louder, the scar on his lip getting redder. 'Perhaps I am delusional but at least I know what I want. I only ever wanted to have sex with you, my wife, the person I love, but that wasn't allowed, so what should I have done instead? I'd love to hear it.'

'No one should ever be forced into having sex!'

'And no one should ever be forced into celibacy!'

Rosie remembers the nights Seb tried to talk, the marriage counsellor she always found a reason to avoid, the gifts of lingerie Seb bought her, but she kicks the memories away. She won't let Seb derail her now, not now her anger is still fizzing through her. 'You've weaponized our intimate life to justify your own disgusting perversion. I never thought you'd sink so low, Seb, truly.'

Seb is shaking his head at her in disbelief. 'What intimate life? We didn't have an intimate life, Rosie, because you didn't want one! That's the whole fucking point! I told . . .'

'Every time I close my eyes, Seb' – Rosie moves closer to him, close enough that he can see her revulsion; she doesn't care as spit from her mouth flies at him – 'I see you fucking her! Do you have any idea how messed up that is?' She closes them now briefly, as though to demonstrate, and there they are – naked, Abi sinking her lovely mouth on to his, Seb desire-drunk and clumsy, Abi gasping at the cold press of his wedding ring in her vagina.

Seb doesn't see it, of course; he's too obsessed with his own pain as he shouts, 'And you have no idea how messed up it is feeling like your body is slowly starving, literally dying, Ro . . .'

Through his shirt she can see his muscles moving in and out, the chaotic beat of his heart, but she doesn't, she won't soften – not in front of him, anyway. Suddenly she just feels so exhausted. As though her whole energy quota for the day has been used up in the last few seconds, it takes all her effort to move close to him again as she says, 'I want you to go now Seb.'

He stares at her with dull, expressionless eyes before he starts packing up his disgusting laptop and his notepad and pens. Rosie watches him numbly and just before he heads towards the door she says, 'Don't you dare tell anyone anything else about me. Or try and make out like you shagging a prostitute is my fault. If you do, I swear to God I'll happily let everyone know the shit you really are.'

And just before he walks away, a part of Rosie expects to hear him say her name, apologize or even try to touch her again, and a bigger part of her is terrified when he does none of those things.

Chapter 14

Seb's body is bright with adrenaline. He slings his rucksack on his back, leaves the house he isn't sure he can still call home and walks, as fast as he can, back to Eva's. It feels like he's pulling his slimy heart, heavy with shame, along the pavement behind him. Rosie had looked at those websites. She knew that he'd lied to her again. He can't even really remember why he lied in the first place, but he remembers the moment he made his choice.

It had been after another one of their awful arguments last spring, when he was preparing for the head teacher interview. He'd opened his laptop to watch porn but, at the last minute, clicked on an advert for another adult site. He felt like some kind of beast that had been starving for hundreds of years finally being fed. He'd gone back again and again when the hunger to feel something with this body of his overwhelmed him. First at home in the early hours of the morning. Then at work, and then whenever he started to feel angry or afraid or unlovable, which he did, most of the time. He scrolled through thousands of pouting, beautiful women. More and more. Some pushing their breasts up, some with their arses aimed at the camera, some dressed up in corsets, some naked, some tall, some white, some Black, some strong, some thin; the array was dizzying. All of them told him through their plump, moist lips the same thing, the thing he needed to hear more than anything. The thing that Rosie wouldn't – or couldn't – seem to ever tell him. They told him that they wanted him. When he looked at them, he stopped worrying about Rosie. They wanted him, day or night, and whatever he wanted, they wanted. Whenever he wanted them, they wanted him too and, for a few short minutes, Seb felt less alone.

They were better than porn, these women; there was a realness to them, knowing they were just a train ride away. Some of them urged him to pay them to dance for him. They wanted him to pass over his card details so they could tell him all the stuff they longed to do to him, but Rosie tracked their credit card statement online and always asked Seb if there was a payment she didn't recognize. It was enough, for a while at least, knowing that he could pick up the phone and just call one of them.

Until the night that Rosie told him she'd cancelled the counsellor he'd booked for the second time. They'd argued, ugly and loud, and Rosie had told him again that she didn't care, didn't fucking care what he wanted, what he did, and had disappeared into the bathroom. Seb had taken his laptop downstairs, his entire body electric with rage, and he'd opened the websites to scroll, to lose himself in flesh, to disappear for a while in the aching fantasy of being with one of them. But that night, they stopped working. Where usually they'd move him from anger to desire, he just felt numb. He was still hungry. They all felt too fake suddenly, the screen of his computer and his limp dick in his hand too real. Shame flooded him, Rosie's words ringing like a bell in his ears.

I don't give a shit!

Rosie had made it clear again and again that she didn't want him, and now these women online weren't working either. He felt the great maw of loneliness opening for him, but he wouldn't, he couldn't turn towards it. So instead he picked up his phone as he opened the website for one of his favourites – a Brazilian in West London. Moving faster than his doubt, he called her, but the line was dead. He tried another favourite, and another, until finally one of the women who'd only existed in the abstract opened her mouth and said, 'Hello, Emma speaking.'

Back at Eva's he goes straight to his room like a moody teenager and hardly sleeps. He walks back to Rosie and the kids as the sun comes up. The morning is the usual combination of routine and frantic rushing; Seb's the last to leave as he pulls the front door closed behind him and steps out into the bright morning. The kind of morning that makes the promise of winter seem like a bad joke. Martin is there again, across the road, standing on the pavement, his two girls on their bikes staring back at their dad impatiently, while Martin pats himself down like he's lost something.

'Morning, Martin. Hi, girls.' Seb waves as he crosses the road towards his neighbour. 'You all right, need some help?'

'Seb,' Martin responds.

'What have you lost?' Seb asks but Martin looks away and says, 'It doesn't matter.'

'Daddy left his phone at home,' says the older girl, bored by her dad's prevaricating.

'I can keep an eye on these two if you want to run home and get it?' Seb offers.

Martin's eyes widen, like Seb's just suggested they run away together. 'No thanks, Seb, that's fine.'

'Really, Martin, I'm not in a rush, I don't . . .'

'I said no, Seb. OK?' Martin pushes past Seb and, waving his hands, calls, 'Come on, girls, let's get going.'

The younger girl narrows her eyes at Seb, her mouth open. 'Is he the man you and . . .?'

But Martin, flustered, interrupts her, 'Come on, I said let's go!'

He grabs her bike between the handlebars, pushing her forward, leaving Seb standing alone on the pavement.

It's nothing, Seb tells himself as he turns left to take the longer way to school again. Martin has always been over-friendly, too keen. His wife has probably finally drummed it into poor old Martin that he needs to be less eager, that's all. Seb keeps walking and as he approaches school he realizes that he's being left strangely undisturbed. A parent whom he recognizes as a friend of Rosie's passes him but keeps her head down, feigning absorption in something her son's telling her. Vita, usually so overwhelming, keeps her eyes fixed on her phone, smiling and pretending not to notice him as he passes; another parent glues herself to a wall to avoid him. It's like it's his first day on the job at this school and no one knows who he is. The students seem normal, some calling out, 'Hi, Mr Kent,' while others totally ignore him.

As he walks through the school gates Seb falls into step with Mr Clegg.

'Morning, Ben.'

Ben nods and Seb notices how his eyes widen. 'Seb, hi.'

'Have I got a massive boil on my face or something?'

Ben's lips curl into a half-smile on one side of his mouth

181

as he replies, 'You haven't checked your work emails yet, have you?'

Coldness creeps through Seb but he forces himself to shake his head and Ben, smiling properly now, says, 'I think we'd better have a little chat.'

Ben steers Seb into the SEN room, a home office-style shed, separate to the rest of the school. Seb puts the 'session in progress' sign on the door so they won't be disturbed. As soon as the door is closed, Ben hands Seb his work phone. It's open on an email and Seb immediately recognizes the Action! website – an organization that hosts and facilitates online petitions. Seb has signed plenty in his time; he remembers one against a huge development just outside Waverly. He looks at the headline for the one Ben's showing him.

Petition to Remove Sebastian Kent from Waverly Community Secondary School

Seb feels the initial shock of recognition, the sting of his name so formally written, and then every vein in his body seems to tighten and tighten as he reads on.

Since September, Sebastian Kent has been head teacher at our beloved school. But recently some disturbing truths have come to light that reveal his true nature. It transpires that Sebastian Kent has dubious moral standing and his values do not align with those of the school. He has recently been involved in disturbing, transgressive and immoral behaviours and we are very concerned for the safety and well-being of our children. We do not feel that he is safe to be around.

Seb can't read any more, forcing himself to look at the bottom of the page. The petition to destroy him already has forty-two signatures.

His hands shake as he passes the phone back to Ben.

'Well then,' he says, having to stop to swallow, 'at least that explains why no one said hello this morning.'

Ben looks serious as he asks, 'Do you know who wrote it?'

Seb breathes out. Anna loves this website, often emailing links to various petitions.

'I have a good idea.' He adds, 'Do you know who's seen it?'

'I don't know any staff member who hasn't, I'm afraid, and it's . . .' Ben looks at his watch. 'Not yet quarter to nine,' he says before hurriedly adding, 'We're all hoping there's nothing to it, of course.'

Seb looks directly at him. 'Do you think I'm unsafe?'

'Seb, we've worked together for almost a decade. No, I don't think you're *unsafe*, but the rumour mill is in overdrive. There are already accusations flying around about secret drug issues, that sort of thing.'

Ben's doing his best to ally himself, but Seb can still feel his eyes on him, uncertain, ready for Seb to twitch or give any sign that there might be some credence to the gossip.

'I see.'

'Maybe if you tell us what it is about, then all this insane speculation will come to an end . . .'

'Maybe.'

'So go on, then,' Ben says, narrowing his eyes. 'Have you gambled with school money?'

Seb feels like he's going to vomit as Ben raises one eyebrow and asks, half joking, half not joking, 'Or do you have a secret life no one knows about?'

Seb realizes he's run out of energy to defend himself. He won't do it, he can't. Ben's face drops as he sees that Seb can't return his smile. 'Thanks for filling me in, Ben. I'd better get going.'

'Yeah, don't want to add to the rumour mill. Mr Clegg and Mr Kent discovered in the SEN shed!'

Seb doesn't acknowledge Ben's lame joke, lets the door bang closed behind him as he leaves.

By midday the petition has seventy-two signatures and has been viewed hundreds of times. Seb heads out into the sunshine and walks quickly to the far end of the playing fields, behind the crumbling sports pavilion, just over the school boundary, where the older kids come to smoke and snog under the protective boughs of an ancient oak tree. He thinks about going to see his mum, but he can't bear the thought of telling Eva about the petition. She is strong and clear-sighted, yes, but she isn't immune to anguish. Feeling her shame at this new twist would uproot him entirely.

He takes out his phone, hovers his thumb over Anna's number. It'd feel so good to call her and scare her, to tell her how small and pathetic she is, but talking to Anna would be like trying to unpick a hook from his own kidney. It would be agonizing and only make everything worse.

He scrolls down to Rosie's name; he'd love to hear her voice. She must have seen the petition. But what if she hasn't seen it, what if there is still a chance that he could keep it from her?

He presses the call button, and she picks up immediately. She's walking somewhere fast, slightly out of breath. 'Just when we thought things couldn't get any worse!' she says without greeting, and his heart sinks. She's seen it.

'It's Anna,' he says, his voice heavy.

'Of course it's Anna,' she snaps back. 'I thought you were going to talk to Eddy, get him to calm her down.'

'Yeah, that didn't go so well.'

'Evidently.'

He hates how they sound more like Eddy and Anna than themselves. They'd listen to their friends argue like this, Seb raising an eyebrow at Rosie, Rosie smiling back, both feeling smug because they weren't slowly destroying each other, their relationship was better. Steadier. That's what he always believed. On the other end of the line Rosie sighs.

'You OK?' he asks, worried, and she snaps again, 'Of course I'm not fucking OK! I've just had Lotte and Vita calling, both telling me how worried they are, that they're here for me, and then digging, trying to find out what it is you've done. They're both secretly delighted, of course.'

'Shit.'

'Well, what do you expect? It won't take them long to figure out it was Anna who wrote the thing, and she'll buckle and tell them as soon as they put any kind of pressure on.'

She pauses, sniffs, before adding, 'She's got a point, of course. After all, you were using school property to book whores. It's a total ticking time bomb. I started looking up flights to Australia this morning right after reading the petition.'

Seb holds his breath and waits for Rosie to clarify, which she does, 'For me and the kids, I mean, obviously.'

He doesn't say anything.

The pause turns into silence. Wherever she is, she's stopped walking. She sighs again before she asks, 'Do the students know?'

Seb clears his throat to cut the vision of his kids boarding a plane to the other side of the world without him and manages to say, 'Not yet. There's a part in the email where she advises parents to keep their kids out of it until a "resolution" is reached, but it won't be long until someone lets it slip.'

He wonders if Rosie, like him, is thinking about Abi, about Lily, but neither of them mentions their names.

Instead, Rosie asks, 'What does she mean, "resolution"?'

'The only one she suggests is my resignation.'

Rosie sighs again.

'Do you think that's what I should do? Resign today?'

'I don't think you have any choice, and if the students are about to find out, well, you'll have hell to pay . . . I'm thinking about Sylvie, mostly.'

Sylvie is supposed to be joining the school next September. There's a brief silence, both trying to imagine their daughter starting secondary school with everyone knowing about Seb. It would be impossible. He won't let it happen. Rosie is right: there is no choice.

'I'll write to the governors and resign today.'

'Fine,' she says wearily. 'Anything else?' She asks like they're writing their weekly shopping list.

'No. I guess I might be back earlier today.'

'Go to your mum's,' she says sharply before hanging up.

This is it. Forced to give up everything that he's worked for for over twenty years. The job he adores, the work he is good at, the kids he's watched grow, the kids he believes in. He kicks the base of the tree with the toe of his shoe before sitting on the grass, his elbows resting on his splayed knees. He holds his head and cries until his throat is raw and he feels his scar beating with blood. He stops, and is about to get ready to go again when he hears muffled laughter coming from the other side of the pavilion. He walks slowly around and watches Ethan and a couple of other kids whose backs he doesn't recognize running away, across the playing field, back to school.

Back in his office, he opens a new document on his computer and, eyes still stinging, he types:

To: Chair of Governors

Dear Harriet Carvin,

I am writing to formally announce my resignation as head teacher at Waverly . . .

There's a knock at the door. Seb considers pretending he's not in; he can't take another confrontation. All he wants is to write this shitty thing and go back to Eva's, lock the door and never unlock it again.

'Mr Kent?'

Seb looks up from his computer. Mrs Greene has opened the door and pushed her grave face into the gap. 'Can I come in?'

Seb desperately doesn't want anyone near him, but it's Mrs Greene and the school, he knows, means everything to her. He suspects she'd be lost without it. She deserves an apology if not an explanation. Seb lifts his hands away from the keyboard. 'Of course.'

She shuffles in, closes the door deliberately firmly behind her and stays standing, staring before she asks, 'What is all this nonsense about, Mr Kent?'

What would Mrs Greene say if he told her the truth? She'd tell him to resign, that's certain, but would she fly into a rage?

Either way, nothing would change if he told the truth, but he would at least have treated Mrs Greene with honesty, with respect.

'If I tell you, Mrs Greene, I want to ask you to please remember the children – both the students here and my own children – and keep this information to yourself.'

Mrs Greene nods, a little impatient, a little irritated, because she's known for her discretion.

Seb looks at her, this woman who has always had such faith – such misplaced faith – and he hears himself say the words, 'I betrayed Rosie.'

'You had an affair?'

Seb shakes his head. 'No, I had sex with someone else. Someone I paid.'

He waits for it. The moment her belief in him shatters. She becomes very still, tilts her head, before saying plainly, 'You had sex with a prostitute.'

Seb hangs his head and then lifts it up again in surprise because he thinks he hears her say, 'OK.'

There must have been some communication issue.

'Sorry, what did you say?'

Mrs Greene shrugs. 'I said, OK. This is based on the assumption, of course, that the woman was working legally, of her own free will.'

'What?'

She moves forward and sits in the chair opposite Seb's desk, breathes out like she's just taken something heavy off her back. 'I've been worried it was something much, much worse. Honestly, the things they're saying in the staff room.'

Mrs Greene shudders and Seb feels as though he's banged his head hard and woken up to some alternative reality.

'Mrs Greene, you did just hear what I said?'

She looks up at him; her mouth flickers, suppressing a smile. 'It might surprise you, Mr Kent, to hear that I don't live under a rock, and it might surprise you even more to know I've lived what my parents always called a rather colourful life. Not many people know that about me – well, people here at school, anyway.'

She looks away from him for a moment, allows herself a little smile. Seb suddenly sees her as a child of the seventies. Long hair, baggy clothes, hitch-hiking somewhere exotic . . . but the image blurs. Seb doesn't know what to say; he just stares.

'Now, obviously I'm not going to start applauding your behaviour, but, well, people are people, and we all have . . . needs. And I do think this awful petition is completely wrong. What goes on in your marriage should, in my opinion, be between you and Mrs Kent. That's it. The person who wrote it clearly doesn't understand that what interests the public and what is in the public's interest are two completely differ-ent things.'

Seb opens his mouth to say something but shuts it again. He just wants to listen.

'Now, back to that resignation letter I think you've started writing. My advice to you is to delete it immediately.'

'But . . .' Seb starts before realizing he doesn't know what to say so instead squeaks, 'Why?'

'Because, believe it or not, Mr Kent, this is a golden opportunity.'

'What?'

Perhaps she's gone mad. Mrs Greene leans forward in her chair, towards Seb, and says, 'Us adults get this wrong time and time again, don't you agree? We think we have to be perfect, blemish-free examples for young people but it's complete nonsense!' She throws her arms wide. 'What young people need more than anything are role models who get things wrong, who mess up catastrophically, and when they do mess up, they need to see those authority figures apologize, accept their failings and try as hard as they can not to let people down again. They don't need to watch you be hounded out of your position, tail between your legs, full of shame – especially not when your mistake should stay where it belongs: in your private life! These kids need to know that when they inevitably get something wrong or let themselves and others down, their lives are not over.'

As she says the last bit Mrs Greene's eyes fill and she turns her head for a moment, pausing as though to tend to a private battle, before turning back to Seb.

'You could be an excellent head teacher here for many years to come. You know it, I know it. But you're going to have to fight this one tooth and nail. You're going to have to decide who is more important: the young people at this school or what your friends, colleagues and acquaintances think about your choices in your personal life.'

They sit in silence for a moment. Seb feels like he's taken a hallucinogen, each one of Mrs Greene's words like a tiny drug lifting him into a new world of technicolour, an un-visited place of courage and possibility. She's right. He is going to have to disappoint some people, but it's up to him to decide which people he lets down. Mrs Greene stands slowly and says, 'Well, that's my two pennies' worth. Hope I didn't say too much – I do get riled up sometimes. It's my half-day today so I'm heading off home now. Don't forget the cleaners will be in later, so lock all confidential stuff away, and I very much hope to see you back in tomorrow.'

Chapter 15

Abi's grating cheese for Margot's packed lunch when her phone buzzes with a new email. This time it's from Sebastian Kent and the title is 'A Response to the Petition'. The timing feels intentional; the petition was sent at a similar time yesterday morning and has passed around countless WhatsApp groups since – including one for Lily's class that Abi is part of. After just a couple of minutes the thread was covered in horrified emojis and 'WTF?' comments. The school gates have been fizzing with speculation and Abi knows, being new and still an unknown quantity, she doesn't hear the worst of it. She feels like her lungs are collapsing again as she opens Seb's email. She reassures herself that she can still whisk her daughters away if she needs to, if this is the moment Seb has cracked and given up her name to distract attention away from himself. She reads it hurriedly, one palm flat, pressing against the countertop.

Dear Parents, Guardians and Carers,

I'm writing to invite you to a school assembly this morning at 9.15 a.m., when I shall deliver a response to the petition that was posted about me yesterday morning. The students will also be in attendance, and I hope you are able to join us in the main school hall. I'm aware this is all last-minute and I apologize for any disruption caused, but it feels important to respond to the petition quickly. For those unable to attend, or for those who do not wish to come this morning, I would be happy to arrange another time to meet in person at your convenience.

With best wishes,

Sebastian Kent

'Don't grate your finger again, Mummy!' Margot says, taking a fistful of grated cheese before Abi can stop her.

'Margot!' Abi whips around to face her grinning daughter, the grater clattering to the floor along with most of the cheese. 'It's not funny! That's the last of the cheese – you're not going to have a sandwich now.' A thin strip is stuck to Margot's pouting bottom lip. 'And you're still in your pyjamas – come on!'

The cheese starts to quiver on Margot's lip and drops to join the other strips on the floor before Margot erupts into tears and turns and runs away. Abi is left rummaging under the sink for the dustpan and brush, guilt setting in fast, and wondering again if she can pack them up today, get them all on a train back to London, back to anonymity tonight.

After she drops Margot at school Abi walks to the park and tries to call Diego, but it's far too early for him to be awake, especially as he was in the restaurant late last night. Her phone is still in her hand when it buzzes with a WhatsApp from Lily.

> U heard about this petition about Mr Kent? SO wild! U
> coming to assembly thing?

Abi replies with a shocked emoji face and is about to type out a proper reply when her phone buzzes again, this time with an unsaved number.

> Hi Abi, I just want to reassure you that I will never mention
> you in connection to any of this school stuff and I'm sorry
> things have escalated in this way. Seb.

Abi stares at Seb's message and decides that, no, she still won't go to the assembly. She deletes his message. It would be awful. Rosie will of course be there, as well as Anna and Eddy. Her presence could send them into a rage and Anna is already unpredictable; it's too dangerous. Abi picks up pace and is walking towards the restaurant when someone starts calling her name.

'Abs! Where do you think you're going?' Lotte's voice is a pithy whine.

'Morning, Lotte. I was just heading into work, actually . . .'

'Oh no you don't!' Lotte smiles like she's about to hand Abi a great, delicious treat. 'We're going to go and find out what naughty Seb has to say for himself.'

'I thought I wouldn't . . .'

'Don't be mad, of course you're going! As your boss I command it!'

Abi wants to slap her away but instead she lets Lotte take her arm and lead her back along the path, towards the school.

'I just spoke to Anna; she's absolutely spitting feathers. She'd just arrived in London when she got the email. She says he planned it; knew she goes into London early for work on a Thursday. She's waiting to jump straight on the next train back to Waverly, but still, she won't arrive back into the station until ten-ish, so she'll miss the whole assembly. God, it's all just so exciting!'

Mrs Greene is at reception ushering them all in as Abi hangs back, letting the other parents go before her.

'Ms Matthews, good to see you,' Mrs Greene says to Abi. 'Are you planning on joining us or not?'

There are no seats left so Abi hovers with a small herd of parents standing at the back, to the right of the hall. There are Halloween decorations up, cut-outs of pumpkins and cats stuck to the walls. It's unbearably tense, the room like a giant can of fizzy drink, shaken and ready to explode. The teachers look nervous; most have given up telling their students to stop talking and a Mexican wave of chatter ripples around the echoey space. Parents smile at their kids, give them the thumbs-up, and their kids either ignore them or wave quickly back before their mates can see. Abi stands on her tiptoes to look for Lily but can't find her; instead she spots Eddy standing on the other side of the hall with Patrick and Vita. His arms crossed, he looks bored by whatever Vita's telling him before his eyes find Abi. She looks quickly away but not quickly enough to miss how his top lip curls, his eyes narrow – somewhere between horror and awe.

The stage is completely bare and as soon as Seb walks out, the room goes silent, like everyone in it shares one great lung. Together, they hold their breath. She can't see Rosie anywhere.

Seb isn't carrying anything. He stands in the middle of the stage and takes a moment to look at everyone staring at him.

He looks fairly composed but Abi recognizes the flash in his eyes – fear, uncertainty. There are a few nervous coughs, a couple of giggles, a teacher shushing some noisy students before he begins.

'Morning, everyone, and thank you for coming at such short notice. I know the parents here this morning understand why we're here. But some of the students might not, so I'm going to first explain the events of the last twenty-four hours. Yesterday, a petition was published and sent around your parents and guardians calling for me to resign. The petition made it clear that in the author's opinion I am not good enough to be your head teacher. It accused me of immoral, transgressive behaviour and asked for your parents and guardians to sign to show that they agree that I should resign.'

As he talks Abi feels the whole packed hall breathe out. Seb is clear, controlled. He is not a lunatic. He still sounds safe.

'I've asked you all here this morning to try to explain why I'm choosing not to resign, and I hope you'll allow me this opportunity and think carefully about what I have to say before you make up your minds for yourselves.'

He pauses, swallows. 'I want to stand here in front of you all and tell you that I did something wrong. I made a mistake in my private life that has hurt my wife, Rosie, very, very deeply and for which I'm so sorry.'

A parent in front of Abi gasps, another shakes her head and whispers to the person next to her, while another shushes them.

Abi's never heard anyone, let alone a man, apologize like this. She knows bullshit when she hears it, after all; her instincts were one of her few defences against the brutal and mad. But she doesn't hear the lilt of lies today. Seb, she thinks, really is sorry.

'I know there's a lot of speculation about what it is I did, and I want to first take the time to assure you all that it wasn't anything illegal. Beyond that, I will not share any further details, because it is a private matter and has no bearing whatsoever on my professional life as your head teacher, a role I adore and take very seriously.'

There's a rumble of discontent among the parents, pissed off that Seb isn't going to tell them which of their theories about him is correct. Seb notices it and pauses to let it run its course before he continues, 'The petition is right. I am in a position of great responsibility, and it is precisely because I take my role so seriously that I'm choosing not to resign. As a colleague reminded me yesterday, we all have the right to make mistakes and I do not want you – the students, the most important people in this school – to think that when you make mistakes in life – which you will – you must quietly disappear. I am hoping that by not resigning you will recognize that I'm doing what I think is required of a head teacher. I hope to show you that sometimes doing the right thing requires you to be a bit courageous. It requires you to refuse to hop on the bandwagon. To sometimes take the rougher, less travelled road. I'm accepting my mistake, asking those I have wronged for their forgiveness. I will not make the same mistake again. Instead, I'll keep working hard for you and for the school we are all a part of. I urge you to think carefully about all of this and please email me or arrange a time to talk if you have any further questions. Thank you for listening.'

Everyone's so quiet that even Abi, from the back of the packed hall, can hear Seb's footsteps as he walks off the stage. A self-conscious hush clouds the room, then a little group of parents stand up to clap. Others join in, because that's just what you do, while others turn to their neighbours to exchange wide-eyed, stunned expressions. The man next to Abi starts texting and then, inevitably, the students start to chatter. They all stand and walk out of the hall and that's when Abi sees her. Lily. She's smiling, standing right behind Blake, and as they start to walk, Abi notices that their fingers are briefly entwined before gently falling away from each other.

'Bloody hell!' Vita has somehow managed to twist and push her way across the hall and is now standing next to Abi, waiting in line to shuffle out of the room. 'Since you came to town things have got a lot more interesting!'

Abi's stomach squirms like a bucket of eels. 'Oh. Ha!'

Vita doesn't smile, just looks confused. 'Did you miss all that?' she asks, waving towards the stage. 'This is the most exciting thing to happen in Waverly since, well, since the Battle of Waverly in sixteen something or other . . .'

'Listen, Vita, nice to see you but I'm actually going to be late for work . . .'

'Your boss won't mind if you're late, not today.' Vita nods towards Lotte, who is standing in a circle of parents; she's shaking her head, appalled, at something a man is saying, the picture of wide-eyed virtue.

'What's your theory?'

'Theory?'

'About what he did.'

'Oh, I . . . I don't know. I haven't really thought about it, and I agree that it's actually no one's business what he does privately.'

Vita, ignoring what she just said, stares at Abi carefully like she doesn't believe a word of it. 'It's obvious,' Vita adds, 'that it was some kind of affair, don't you think? Otherwise, why is Rosie not here? A group of Year Ten parents reckon he's into, like, really hardcore gay BDSM stuff, but I also heard that Mrs Croughton – the head of English – is saying he had an affair with someone he met online, a girl way too young for him – *borderline* legal was the implication – and it's her parents who have exposed him, apparently . . .'

Vita looks to Abi, expecting her to react. Abi stares at the bald patch of the man in front, willing him to move faster, and keeps her face impassive as Vita says, 'Well! Whatever it is, you can bet Anna won't be able to keep it to herself for long, especially now. You coming to the cafe?' she asks with a patronizing smile that makes Abi's spine feel like it could crumble and collapse on itself.

'Cafe?'

'A group of us, including your boss, are going to have a coffee and discuss all this stuff. Anna's coming straight from the train station and hopefully she'll at last give in and set us all straight about what really happened!'

Abi surges forward towards the door and shakes her head. Vita's smile widens. 'Pity,' she says. 'Listen, we should sort out a play date soon, shouldn't we? Luca would love to have Margot . . .'

They're finally through the door and, without another word to Vita, Abi starts walking quicker, past the reception, dodging people. She has to get away from here, from Vita, from all of them.

Chapter 16

Eddy doesn't want to go to the cafe. What he really wants is to go home, get into bed and hide until this whole shitty episode is over. But Anna is, as his phone keeps telling him, heading straight to The Pot, a busy cafe in the middle of town, and she *needs* him to come. There's a group of them walking there now and Eddy is being bundled along like some reluctant celebrity spouse. He tried to squirm away, decided perhaps he could leave Anna untethered, let her figure out what to do with the mess she's engineered. He'd muttered something at the end of the assembly to Vita about having to get home for a work call, when he saw something that made his heart stop. Blake was stroking the hair behind Lily's ear, and Eddy could almost feel the electric pulse between the two of them, remembered the charge himself, the almost unbearably exciting moment as skin touches skin for the first time.

This was a complication they didn't need. He'd been hoping that Blake would change his mind about Lily, move on to another girl, like Eddy did weekly at fifteen. But judging by their shining eyes and the private, blissful smiles, they are both very much still stuck on each other. Anna doesn't know, of course; Blake hasn't told her. Eddy knows this because had she known, Anna no doubt would have told everyone about Abi in a bid to keep Blake as far away as possible from both Abi and Lily.

As they walk to the cafe, Eddy pretends to listen to Lotte and Martin talking some bullshit about all of them advancing on Seb's office together, an insurrection to demand the truth, and tries to think through how best he can protect his son – and, by extension, Lily – in all of this. If everyone knew that his new girlfriend's mum was a sex worker who had had sex with their head teacher, Blake would at best become a laughing stock and at worst might have to change schools, which would be a disaster.

By the time he's arrived at the cafe, Eddy knows he must protect Abi's identity, that his son's happiness, his fragile teenage confidence – once shattered, so hard to rebuild – depends on it.

When they arrive at The Pot, Anna is already there in her neat work suit, standing when she sees them all, her eyes sparkling, opening her arms to their little group, a strange corporate Jesus welcoming her disciples. 'Honestly, guys, the audacity of the man! He's got to go.'

Eddy knows they're in for a fight.

'It's the arrogance that blows my mind,' Anna says, settling down behind her large cappuccino. The group lean in closer towards her, hanging on her every word, desperate not to miss any clue she could let slip about what it is Seb's done.

'He's the one who's done this terrible thing and now he gets to come out of it like some knight in shining armour. It happens again and again. Just like Trump. It makes me so bloody mad.'

She blows the frothy top of her drink.

'The thing is, I'm not sure it's even ethical to let us go on speculating like this, Anna,' Lotte says, sipping her flat white but keeping her eyes fixed on Anna. 'I mean, it could be harmful, couldn't it – might start to impact the kids? That's what I'm worried about . . .'

'Me too.'

'And me.'

Others chirp because, of course, they're all saints here.

Anna nods like she understands but Eddy recognizes the wildness in her eyes; she's losing her grip on her plan, can feel the solidity of it slipping away. 'You guys have to understand that the reason I'm not revealing the truth is out of respect for Rosie. You know we're good friends. Trust me, I'm not protecting him, I'm protecting her. And their children, of course.'

Her hands shake, her coffee spills as she takes a sip; she's full of adrenaline but she's getting a little desperate, too, worried that the smiles surrounding her could quickly sour and curdle.

Eddy knocks the small coffee table with his knee as he stands. 'Anna.' She glances at him. 'Can we go and have a quick chat outside?'

She nods, shrugging her shoulders at the others, before following Eddy out of the door.

It's started to rain, so they're huddled in the cafe doorway.

They turn towards each other and just as Eddy's about to open his mouth she gets there first. 'I know what you're going to say, Ed, but I'm going to have to tell them what he did.'

'Anna, you promised . . .'

'No, I said if he did the right thing and resigned then I wouldn't say anything. I never promised anything if he didn't resign.' She opens her hands innocently. 'Lotte told me that a couple of people are saying that maybe I've made it all up, or have made it into something much bigger because I have some personal vendetta against Seb . . .'

'Well, that's ridiculous.'

'Of course it is,' Anna snaps, 'but it's also totally unfair. I'm not going to allow my integrity, *our* reputation, to be called into doubt because of his mess.'

Eddy feels like pointing out that they're a family not a business, that these kinds of phrases shouldn't apply to them, but Anna's already turning towards the door, ready to go back inside. But Eddy hasn't got what he needs yet – safety for Blake – so he takes her arm, turns her back to face him as he says, 'Promise me, Anna, promise me you won't mention Abi's name.'

She looks at him, shrugs and says, 'I don't see why I should have to bring her into any of it . . .'

'That's not a promise.'

Anna narrows her eyes at Eddy, mistrust blooming. Those suspicious neural pathways in her brain like well-trodden tracks. 'Why are you so concerned about her, Ed?'

He has no choice.

'I think Blake has a crush on Lily.'

'What?'

'I saw them, together, at the assembly. They looked close.'

Anna looks away from him, as though staring into some appalling future – her boy with a prostitute's daughter. 'Well, he's not . . . he's not allowed!'

Eddy can't help it, he laughs, and Anna's eyes flash, furious at him.

'He's not a toddler, Anna.'

'We have to get her away from him. Get them to leave town, preferably.'

Eddy winces. 'No, Anna. Lily seems like a lovely kid; we need to protect them both, and the only way we do that is by letting this whole thing just blow—'

'Anna, hi!' They both spin around to a tall, attractive woman pulling back the hood of her raincoat, smoothing her hand across her hair as she asks, 'It is Anna, isn't it?'

She smiles, Anna nods and the woman extends a hand. 'I'm Millie; my son Isaac is the year below Blake, totally idolizes him.'

'Hi, Millie.' Anna smiles. 'Yes, I've seen you around.'

Millie seems grateful to be recognized. Eddy's never seen her before.

'Listen, I know you must be busy, so I'll be quick: I wanted to ask if you'd be up for coming on my radio show later today? Well, I say "my show", but I'm just the producer. It's a local live show about issues and politics that have a special interest in the area, *I Heart Sussex*—'

Anna nods along, interrupting Millie, 'I've heard of it.'

'Great!' Millie beams. 'I was just in the assembly and, honestly, this thing with Mr Kent is just so interesting, so important. Everyone's saying that you wrote the petition . . .'

She gives Anna the opportunity to deny it, which she doesn't, so Millie keeps talking. 'I knew I'd be kicking myself if I didn't ask you to join—'

Anna beams back; she interrupts her again. 'I'd be delighted, Millie. I was wondering, after Mr Kent went so public this morning, how best to respond and obviously social media is just so . . .' Anna pulls a face; Millie nods along to show she totally gets it. 'Your show, I think, would be perfect.'

'Wait, what kind of things are you going to ask?' Eddy steps forward. 'I'm Eddy, Anna's husband.'

'Hi, Eddy.' Millie glances at Anna, recoiling slightly at how this conversation between two women is being usurped by a man.

'Eddy,' Anna intercepts, embarrassed, 'I'm sure Millie and I will talk about all those details later, before the broadcast.' Eddy recognizes Anna's tone; it's the one she uses when their cat has done something disgusting.

'Listen, Millie, we've got people waiting for us inside, so why don't you take my number and let me know where and when you need me, and I'll see you then? I've taken the whole day off work so I can be available whenever suits you.'

'You're amazing.' Millie nods her head, beaming again at the wonder of Anna, before they exchange numbers and Millie gives her the Waverly address where they'll be recording, adding, 'Anna, you're a dream. You'll be our big opener, so we'll need you in about an hour, say from twelve thirty p.m.? I'll call you shortly to confirm. Thank you so much and see you soon!'

Millie pulls her hood back up and walks away into the sheeting rain.

'Was that the radio producer?' Lotte's thin face appears behind the door and Eddy's about to tell Lotte that they haven't finished, that they'll be in in a moment, when Lotte swivels her eyes to Anna and says, 'I think you should come and see this, Anna.'

As soon as they're back at the table, one of the women waggles her phone at Anna. 'I just got this through on our Year Seven WhatsApp; there are a couple of really dubious parents in the year, annoyingly. Anyway, it's not particularly nice – a complete invasion, I'm afraid – but I thought you should know.'

Anna shakes her head at the woman and says, 'What is it, Clarissa?'

Anna looks like she wants to take Clarissa's phone, but Clarissa holds it tightly and clears her throat before reading out loud, 'I'm surprised this is all coming from a person who was close friends with Seb and who was, a couple of years ago, the object of some humiliation following her husband's affair. Surely, she'd be the first to understand that marital issues should stay in the home . . .'

Eddy feels his skin burn as all eyes turn right at him.

'Who said that?' Anna snaps. 'Eddy has nothing, absolutely nothing whatsoever to do with this thing with Seb.'

Eddy, still rushing with shame, knows he should probably say something, opens his mouth and starts, 'That was a mistake, a one-time . . .' before Anna grabs his arm, her fingernails a sharp reminder that this is her show.

'Listen, everyone. That woman I was just talking to outside is Millie from *I Heart Sussex*. I've agreed to go live on her radio show in about an hour. This bullshit . . .' She gestures to Clarissa and her phone, like they are the same being. 'Seb is clearly leading some kind of smear campaign to completely undermine me and make me look like a fool. I wanted to do what he didn't – protect his family – but now my own is being attacked. He's left me no choice but to share the facts about what he did.' She pauses for a moment. To everyone else, she'll look like she's finding this all incredibly hard, but Eddy knows she's already made up her mind. Nothing galvanizes Anna's anger like humiliation. She keeps talking.

'I think it's only fair that you – the parents – get to make up your own minds.' Everyone at the table nods encouragingly because they're close now, so close.

'Anna, please!' Eddy warns, desperate now. 'Think about the consequences for B!'

He won't say his son's name, can't risk someone other than Anna picking up on it.

'That's exactly what I am doing!' Anna stays defiant and Eddy stands again; he wants to shake Anna, tell her that these people aren't her friends, her friends are the people she's about to completely eviscerate. She just glances at him sadly before shrugging and turning back to the table, adding, 'Please, remember poor Rosie and her kids and please don't share it online or on any groups for now.'

The nodding heads are becoming even more furious in their agreement. Eddy knows that in this moment they'd probably give up their firstborn to get what they want. He wants to leave but something keeps him there, some instinct to protect Blake and even protect Seb and Rosie. He knows that if he leaves now, they'll all be completely alone.

Anna takes a deep, theatrical breath in, sighing out immediately. 'We . . .' Anna glances at Eddy, changes her mind and says, 'I . . . found out that on two occasions, Seb paid for sex with a prostitute.'

Lotte's hands fly up to her mouth while Vita lets hers hang open, her eyes swivelling, reptilian, to catch the others' reactions. Martin murmurs, 'Oh my God!' And someone else goes a few steps further with, 'Fucking disgrace!'

Anna's eyes are wide, righteous and apparently full of sorrow that this heavy burden has been placed on her shoulders. She opens her mouth to say more and seems a little

207

surprised that no one's looking at or listening to her any more. Instead, they're all luxuriating in their own shock, their own delight.

'What a complete arsehole!' Vita says.

'Didn't he say that what he did wasn't illegal? Is that even *true*?' Lotte spits.

'I think it is legal, it just depends on, like, the circumstances,' Clarissa explains. 'Like, if the woman is being controlled or whatever. If it was between two adults and was consensual then I don't really see what the . . .'

A couple of women recoil, their eyes thin slits of disdain. One of them says, 'He's a *head teacher*, Clarissa!'

Anna is holding up her hands, saying, 'Guys, guys, I know it's upsetting . . .' But, for the first time, she's ignored.

'It's a position of responsibility, respect. How can we possibly respect him now?'

'Yeah, but he isn't always a head teacher, is he? Like he said in the assembly, he has a right to live his life outside of the school, doesn't he?'

'Ah, yes, he does, but,' Anna interrupts, 'I'm afraid it gets worse.' Eddy watches as eyes widen, become livelier with possibility – imagining all the titillating, exotic, disgusting things Seb could have done to make it worse.

'He used a school laptop.' The eyes become blank; brows furrowed. Anna ploughs on, 'To look for her, I mean. He searched for prostitutes using school property and most likely while he was at school. Which means, as a public employee, we are literally paying for him to spend his time fuelling a cruel and abusive industry.'

Everyone's listening again now; Anna is on to something. 'That's what I was alluding to when I talked about him being unsafe, that he was putting our kids at risk. I mean, imagine if one of the children saw some of the sick things he was looking at on his *school* computer in his *school* office?'

Clarissa is the first to look away, her face twisted in thought. 'Sounds pretty unlikely that one of the kids would see,' she says, but the others ignore her because Lotte suddenly looks like she's about to burst into tears as she says, 'He's a monster, an absolute monster.'

Vita turns to hug Lotte, who whimpers over her shoulder for a moment before pulling away and saying, 'I can't believe I trusted him, really. I thought he was so safe, so wonderful.'

Others coo, pat and soothe Lotte, who first checks her mascara hasn't run before looking at the whole group and, shifting with impressive agility from sadness to venom, saying, 'He's a pervert. We need to get him away from our children.'

Anna looks up at Eddy and for a moment he sees that she's scared and alone. The realization settling in that she's doing this. That she's done this. She reaches for his hand, and he lets her take it. Their palms are cold; there's no warmth between them any more. He pulls his hand away. He wants to get out of here, wants to go home and guard Blake and Lily. Even though Anna hasn't mentioned Abi's name she's just one slip away.

'It's toxic patriarchy, is what it is – men abusing women for their own gratification and . . .' She doesn't get to finish because Lotte's voice is louder.

'No, it's complete perversion. Dangerous. He's a pervert and a pervert has no place anywhere near a school.'

'Oh, that's a bit strong . . .' Martin counters. 'I mean, I thought the same at first, panicked – especially when I heard those rumours that children were involved – but, you know, we live opposite Rosie and Seb, and I always thought he seemed like a good guy. Always stops for a quick chat.'

'Would you be comfortable leaving your girls in his care knowing what you now know?' Vita asks, lifting her eyebrows at Martin.

Martin looks away, says nothing, which Lotte interprets as a 'no'.

'There you go, then. You just proved our point. We don't know what other perversions he's hiding.'

Eddy moves quickly, in case Anna notices him leaving, calls his name for him to stay. He doesn't want to be anywhere near her, because she's chosen her own righteousness, her own anger above their son's fragile heart. Eddy isn't sure what he can do to protect his boy, but he knows he can't be here, by Anna's side, any more and so he walks quietly, back out into the rain, alone.

Chapter 17

Rosie sits at the kitchen table after the assembly. Upstairs, there are clothes all over the kids' rooms, half-packed suitcases for all three and for herself. She's wanted to leave so many times, but the truth is she can't think of anywhere they could go. Her parents would ask too many questions; they'd find the kids too noisy, too messy. Rosie has been out of touch with old friends for too long to ask for refuge for the four of them, and the thought of staying in a cheap hotel is soul-crushing and still way too expensive.

She'd flipped, laughing hysterically, when Seb told her yesterday afternoon that he wasn't going to resign, that he was going to hold an assembly to face the petition head-on instead. When she saw that he wasn't laughing along with her, she'd told him he was selfish, that he wasn't thinking about the impact on her or their kids, that he should just quietly resign, but even as she'd said the words, she'd known, of course, that that wouldn't be the end. There would still be endless speculation about why he was resigning. The petition was just too noisy to let him slip away quietly. There was also a belief swelling up in her, a momentary pulse of possibility, that Seb was right: he wasn't dangerous and of course he had a right to make private mistakes. But she'd stamped on these thoughts like they were on fire.

He'd wanted her to go to the assembly and she'd pictured herself standing by his side, limp and pathetic, like some insipid shamed politician's wife. She'd shoved him in the chest and called him all the worst things she could think of.

Later that night, lying sleepless in bed, she'd imagined not going to the assembly, not knowing what he said, another blank spot for her imagination to colour in like it did every time she thought of Seb and Abi. This morning, when Seb had suggested again that Mrs Greene could sneak Rosie into the hall at the last minute, that Rosie could listen, unseen, behind the curtains at the side of the stage, she'd nodded and reluctantly agreed.

She'd watched Abi as she hovered by the entrance to the school, unsure whether to go in or not. She'd seen how Mrs Greene said something cursory to her and how Abi had stumbled forward. She'd felt Abi's isolation, seen her bravery as she went into the hall, like she was eager to participate in her own downfall. She wanted to hate Abi, but she couldn't because out of all the people there, the people Rosie counted as friends, their voices bouncing excitedly to each other, Abi was the only one who understood. The only one who arguably had even more to lose than Rosie but was going in anyway.

Mrs Greene pointed, wordlessly, to where Rosie should hide. She saw Eddy standing, nodding, as Vita babbled in his ear. Then she found who she was really looking for in the crowd: Abi, smiling briefly at the people next to her, but not talking to them. Rosie watched as Abi scanned the students and knew she was searching for her child. Rosie had to fight the urge to go and stand by her side. What would happen, she wondered, inside Seb if he looked up from his place on the stage to see them, Rosie and Abi, standing together?

While Seb talked, Rosie mostly watched the reactions of the students. Some chattered and laughed, becoming quiet and still as Seb talked about making mistakes, about trying to do the right thing. One boy looked at his hands in his lap, as though thinking about all his future fuck-ups. She was glad for these kids, glad they were having this experience so young in life. She watched their eyes widen in surprise. She thought perhaps they'd never heard an adult talk like this, and then she realized that she'd never heard anyone do anything like this before, either. She looked at her weary, ragged husband, the bright lights highlighting how alone he was. She saw all the faces of the parents, their jaws snapping in judgement, and was surprised to find herself crying, because it was such a relief to see him stand before all that judgement and dis-belief. To see him standing flawed, fallible and so incredibly real, and suddenly her heart felt like it had tripled in size.

She was spotted walking away from the school after the assembly. A couple of mums asked if she was OK, if they could do anything to help.

'It's brave, I think, what he's doing,' one of them said. Rosie looked up at her and, even though she didn't say anything, the woman's words were like milk on a burn and Rosie realized that she agreed. Her husband was still a liar, still an arsehole, but at least, she thought, this time he wasn't a coward.

*

It was raining, so she decided not to go to the beach and instead drove home. She's sure she's only been sitting at the table numbly for a few minutes, but her tea is stone cold when she hears a key in the front door lock. She sits up, stares as Seb comes down the few steps into the kitchen. He looks hollow, all the confidence he'd shown on the stage totally spent. They stare at each other for a moment before he slowly pulls up a chair, close enough to touch Rosie, but careful not to. He sits, his hands between his knobbly knees. She looks at him as he looks at her. She sees his distress, his panic and sadness, but she also sees something else in him now, something quiet but determined, a commitment to the truth. But, she can't avoid it; the anger and humiliation are still alive in her. She moves a little away from him. He keeps his eyes down as he says, 'I just want to say thank you for coming this morning.'

She clenches her jaw to dam any tears.

'I also want to say that if you decide that you need to end our marriage, I would understand.' He looks up at her as he says, 'You don't deserve any of this, Ro. None of this is your fault.'

She nods, but his admission doesn't feel as good as she thought it would. Her teeth ache as she presses them together. Neither of them says anything and it's a relief for a moment just to be with him in silence.

They both startle when Seb's phone rings loudly in his pocket. He pulls it out to shut it up, muttering, 'Sorry,' but then he looks up at Rosie and says, 'It's Mrs Greene.' Rosie shrugs; she doesn't mind if Seb wants to accept the call. He stands and clears his throat before he answers, 'Hello.'

Rosie can't hear what Mrs Greene is saying on the other end, but she gets the gist.

'Yes, I expected as much. I've just come home to see Rosie,

but I'll start replying to them all as soon as I'm back, OK? Yes, please tell everyone that I'll be in the staff room over lunch, they can ask me anything then, that's fine.'

He's about to hang up when Mrs Greene says something else, making Seb pause for a moment before adding, 'Which radio show?'

His gaze is restless as he listens to her response, before becoming still on Rosie's face again. 'Ah, OK. I see. OK. I'll see you soon, then, Mrs Greene.'

He hangs up.

Seb swallows again, puts his phone in his pocket before sitting back down.

Rosie looks at him, lifts her eyebrows slightly for him to explain.

'Apparently it's all over the school WhatsApp groups that Anna is going to do a kind of response to my assembly, one p.m. on East Sussex Radio.'

Rosie closes her eyes. 'Oh no.' They're the first words she's spoken since he got here and they make Seb wince.

'I know. I'm so sorry, Ro.'

She nods, taking his apology quietly. She'd been so focused on trying to understand her feelings after the assembly, she hadn't thought about what would happen next.

'I think this is going to get worse, much worse, before it gets better.'

Rosie nods slowly.

'Listen, if you think it's best to get away for a while with the kids, I would understand.'

'I don't want to do that.' Her words are clear, and she adds, 'I don't know what I want, but I know that for now, at least, we're staying here.'

215

Seb nods; a couple of tears fall from his eyes. She doesn't want to touch him and doesn't want to say any more so she just watches him cry until his phone starts ringing again and she says, 'You should go. We'll speak later.'

He nods, wipes his eyes and does as she says.

Rosie considers not listening to Anna on the radio, but she has no idea what else to do with herself. The interviewer – Lydia someone – is in the middle of explaining to the audience about the petition, describing in her low, silky voice that it now has over three hundred signatures, and outlining Seb's decision not to step down and his subsequent address to the students and parents earlier that morning.

'Welcome, Anna Mayhew, author of the aforementioned petition, to *I Heart Sussex*.'

'Afternoon, Lydia.' Anna sounds calm, well prepared. 'I'm very happy to be here.'

'I understand that you and Sebastian Kent are good friends, have been for a long time – is that right?'

Anna's voice bounces. 'I think probably the past tense is more applicable now.'

'Ahh.' Lydia clarifies, 'You aren't any more?'

Anna patronizes her. 'I can't be friends with someone so lacking in basic human decency, someone who would put children at risk.'

'You're referring to the "disturbing, transgressive and immoral behaviours" you allude to in the petition?'

'That's right, Lydia. I was hoping he'd have the courage this morning to say exactly what it was he did so parents could decide for themselves, but I'm afraid he managed to dodge the issue.

'I've decided that he's left me with little choice but to tell the truth. I didn't want to, I wanted to protect his wife and his children whom I adore.' Anna's voice takes on a sorrowful edge; Rosie bites her bottom lip, mutters, 'Bullshit.'

'I've thought about it deeply, and I feel that I have a duty to the other parents and their children who attend the school. They have the right to know that the reason I wrote that petition was because twice, in the last few months, Sebastian Kent paid a woman for sex.'

There's a pause before Lydia says, 'Do we know if the woman was working legally and of her own volition?'

Rosie wonders if Lydia's thinking about how many times her little radio show will be listened to, how many shares it'll get online. If she is, Lydia does well to keep the excitement out of her voice.

'Yes. That is what he's been saying. But we can't be sure that he only saw one woman.'

'As far as you're aware, this woman consented, so this isn't a matter for the police?'

'As far as I'm able to gather at this stage, it was legal, but just because she consented doesn't mean that people in power should be able to do whatever they like to people with less power!'

'I see your point. And how did you find out this information?' Lydia keeps her tone neutral.

'Seb told my husband and then, well, there were other clues. Look, the point is that he's not fit to be headmaster. What I really want to encourage people to think about – especially parents with kids at the school – is what kind of a man treats women – and here I include both the prostitute and Sebastian Kent's poor wife' – Rosie bristles, swears again at

217

the radio – 'as playthings, either paying them for his own gratification or lying to them time and time again. As a feminist,
I don't want this kind of person anywhere near our sons and
our daughters.'

'You think he's unsafe?'

'Possibly. He's a man who used a school computer to search
for prostitutes. Most likely he searched for them during school
hours in his office. I don't trust him and that means I don't
think he should be anywhere near kids.'

'Ahh.' Lydia's voice drops a note. 'Do you have evidence
to support these claims?'

There's a beat; it lasts too long, making any conviction
sound hollow.

'I do.'

'I can see how that might change things for—'

'Of course it changes things! He was using school property
to look at sex sites on time that is being paid for by us, the
tax-paying public.' Anna starts galloping away again, relieved
to be on firmer footing.

'Hmm,' Lydia replies, careful not to add to Anna's specula-
tions but probably thinking about those all-important listener
numbers as Anna keeps going.

'I actually grew up in Ruston, so I've already experienced
first-hand how prostitutes and drug users invite crime and
tear a community apart. I've seen young lives destroyed by
this so-called "work" and I will do everything in my power
to stop that from happening here in Waverly.'

'Interesting,' Lydia says, a little vague, trying to steer Anna
back to the issue. 'It seems Sebastian Kent's not without his
supporters, though. He has a strong level of support, especially from the students themselves at Waverly Community.

They've taken to social media, with some calling him "the best head teacher" and "a really cool example", and there are a few mentions of them organizing some kind of response. It seems they're making up their own minds and some parents are behind them, too. I'm interested, as you have a son at the school – I wonder what he thinks about it all?'

Anna replies immediately, 'He's really upset, quite frankly, horrified that this has happened, and those other supportive students you mention are a tiny minority. The vast majority agree with me and my son that a head has a responsibility to uphold basic moral standards and not pay some poor woman so he can abuse her.'

'Thank you, Anna, that was really illuminating. As you can imagine, our phone lines have been going crazy, so I'd like to ask if you could stay with us a little while longer so we can hear what a few of our listeners have to say.'

'Of course,' Anna replies, full of generosity, 'I'd be delighted.'

'Our first caller is Carol from Withington, near Waverly. Hello, Carol.'

'Hello, Lydia. Hello, Anna. I just wanted to say how horrified I am hearing this news. My own kids went to Waverly Community and they loved it. In fact, just the other day I was talking about my son's plans to move back to Waverly so his daughter, my granddaughter, can go when she's old enough, but let me tell you, there's no way he'll be doing that now. No way. After all, like you said, if he can treat women like things, then what other perversions could he be hiding? Don't forget Jack the Ripper! All I can say is thank God there are still people out there, like you, Anna, putting our children and our community first. God bless you.'

'Gosh, thank you so much, Carol,' Anna gets in immediately, her voice throbbing with feeling.

'Yes, thank you, Carol,' Lydia adds, a little taut. 'Now we've got Lucy on the line from an undisclosed location. Hello, Lucy.'

'Good afternoon.' Lucy's voice is strong, like she'd shout if she wasn't on live radio. 'I'm a sex worker and have been working in and around Waverly for – wow – almost twenty years now, and although I've never called in to any radio show, today I felt I had to after listening to Anna.'

'Hello, Lucy,' Anna says, warmly, but Rosie recognizes a little wariness in her tone.

'Hi, Anna. I'm wondering how many sex workers you actually know. How many have you spoken with?'

Anna doesn't say anything; Rosie can practically hear her frown through the radio.

'Just as I thought . . .' Lucy continues.

'Well, obviously, I know one!' Anna blurts, desperate to claw back some authority.

'For fuck's sake, Anna!' Rosie shouts at the radio, missing whether it's Lydia or Lucy who asks, 'Who?'

'The woman – Seb Kent's prostitute – has moved to Waverly.'

Suddenly Rosie feels like a mosquito is trapped, whining inside her head.

'Poor woman!' Lucy mutters.

'Is that confirmed information?' Lydia asks, in an uncertain tone.

'It is,' Anna replies, and Rosie knows from her clipped tone that Anna will be jutting out her chin, trying her best to ignore the doubts that will already be poking her conscience. Rosie remembers Lily and Margot sitting around the table she sits at now. She thinks about the repercussions for them of this, Anna's fifteen minutes of fame, and kicks the table leg.

'Have you talked to her much about her life and experiences?' Lucy asks Anna.

This time the silence stretches on longer, turning into a clear 'no'.

'Because you seem to think you know an awful lot but there are a few major things, in my humble opinion, that you're missing.'

Lucy quickly clears her throat, not giving either Lydia or Anna the chance to interrupt. Rosie sits up to listen better as Lucy starts talking again.

'Firstly, I do this work even though I have other options. I don't love it. I do this work because it pays the bills better than anything else I've found.'

Lucy talks like a woman who has been unplugged, who has been forced to hide her real thoughts and feelings for too long. Rosie feels something chime within her, clean and clear: Lucy isn't a victim. 'Secondly, it's not sex workers or drug takers themselves that destroy communities. It's poverty. It's critical services like nurseries and mental health support groups closing. It's benefits decreasing as everything gets more expensive. Most sex workers are just women, many are mothers – and some men, I might add – trying to survive in these completely untenable circumstances – like most of the population. And lastly, I must admit I swore pretty loudly when you called yourself a feminist. You're not a feminist, Anna, you're a middle-class woman on a completely stupid, hare-brained crusade. My guess is you're bored as anything, possibly angry about something as well. Because how else could you delude yourself into thinking you're helping anyone by further stigmatizing an already vulnerable group – us sex workers – and perpetuating centuries-old lies and propaganda about us to the non-sex-working community? It just makes no sense. No sense at all. You are more dangerous to me, Anna, than the men I let through my door.'

For the first time, Lucy pauses, and Lydia jumps in with, 'Thank you for your views, Lucy,' before adding, 'I'd love to know what you think about Sebastian Kent, the head teacher who has been engaging sex workers.'

'Listen, I've got regulars who are teachers, GPs and, yes, I've seen more than one politician in my time. Even police officers. An urge to have sex is very, very human and cannot and should not be legislated against. Furthermore, I think this public shaming thing is awful. Who hasn't done something in their private lives they don't want everyone knowing about?'

'You don't think he's done anything wrong?'

'Well, I think he's been stupid using his work computer and doing it on work time. But we don't know if that is even true, given all the other misinformation Anna's spouting out today, and I don't want to give her any more oxygen until her claims have been proven.'

'One final question, Lucy,' Lydia asks. 'What about those women who aren't like you, working out of choice – what of those people forced or coerced into it?'

Lucy sounds weary as she replies, 'Look, I'm not claiming to have all the answers, but I will say we should start with decriminalizing sex work so sex workers can enjoy the same rights as everyone else, like the right to work free from discrimination and violence. That would be a good start. Then I'd look at the root causes of why some people end up in terrible circumstances – poverty and lack of opportunity, to name a couple. But really, please, just start listening to us and not to people like Anna.'

'Some strong feelings there from Lucy – thank you, Lucy. Anna, in the final few seconds, have you got anything you'd like to say in response?'

'Umm.' Rosie can hear Anna squirm; she clearly has no idea what to say, but not saying anything isn't an option. 'I just want to thank Lucy for her opinions and I want to remind listeners that Sebastian Kent is still in a position of huge trust and influence and has behaved completely inappropriately, given his unique position. We know he hired a vulnerable woman for sex. It is absolutely in the public interest to know these things.'

'OK. Thank you, Lucy, for calling in, and thank you, Anna, so much, for joining me today.' Lydia's voice is all smiles.

'Thank you, Lydia.' Anna sounds a bit lost, distracted, like she's forgotten the final few points she really wanted to hammer home, but Lydia's already moved on.

'Well, I think, listeners, we can all agree this is a very fiery start to our programme today. As ever, comments welcome, so please do text or leave us a message on our socials at *I Heart . . .*'

Rosie clicks the radio off and settles back into her chair. Almost immediately her phone starts ringing. It's Anna. She must have just got out of the recording room, Rosie her first thought. Rosie rejects her call. She can't listen to her apologies, her justifications.

Seb's laptop bag is still on the kitchen floor where he'd forgotten it earlier. She's made her decision before she's even stood up from her chair and pulled the computer out of the bag. Suddenly, where she once felt anger and repulsion at what Seb has done, she feels a great aching loneliness. She still has no idea what the future holds for them, whether she'll be able to look at him without seeing Abi twisted around him, without seeing the empty eyes of all those naked women, but she does know, in the same way she knows she loves her children, that Seb is not a danger to anyone. She opens up the laptop and follows the steps to delete the search history. Her finger hovers for just a moment above the return key and as she presses the button she feels a great rush of warmth. It's unusual and she's not exactly sure where it comes from, but as she closes the laptop, she realizes that the feeling isn't for Seb or even for the kids; the warmth is from Rosie to Rosie. A small gift of appreciation for listening at last to what she knows to be true.

Her phone buzzes on the table. Anna is calling her again. This time, too, she rejects her call; she doesn't want to talk to Anna. She picks up her keys, feeling strangely energized as she ignores the third call from Anna, and walks out of her home to find the other person she should have been listening to all along.

Chapter 18

Abi doesn't answer her door immediately. The intercom for the flat is old and there's no video so she doesn't know who is ringing. Best-case scenario: it's Diego, apron still on, and he has run straight over from the restaurant after reading the desperate text she sent him just a few minutes ago. Worst-case scenario: it's Lotte, Anna and a band of furious women who have figured out it must be Abi. Lotte will fire her on the spot and Anna will tell her that Lily and Margot are being told their mum has lied to them all their lives, that their mum was a whore.

She's been through worse, Abi tells herself fiercely, remembering the man who put his hairy hand around her neck, his weight pinning her, his red face above, spittle flying. That had been bad, but at least her home wasn't under siege, at least her kids were well away.

Whoever it is outside, they're not going away.

Her phone lights up with a message:

It's Rosie, Abi.

They haven't spoken since Rosie kicked Abi out of her car.

Please, I just want to talk to you.

She could hide, of course, pretend she's not home, but hiding has never in her experience made anything better. She walks slowly down the stairs and opens the front door. It's stopped raining but the air is rich with the smell of wet, slowly decaying leaves.

Rosie's standing on her doorstep, looking nervous. 'Can I come in?'

Abi opens the door a little wider. Rosie has to bend low to clear the fake cobwebs the girls have laced across the door and Abi gestures. 'The kitchen's straight ahead.'

They turn to face each other in the tiny kitchen. Something has shifted in Rosie because she's not looking at Abi with revulsion or pity. She's not looking at her like Abi's mum did, when she found out. Rosie's eyes are gentle, softer than Abi's seen them before.

'You heard the radio show?' Rosie asks, her voice steady.

Abi nods, looks to the ceiling briefly. 'Thank God for Lucy, hey?'

Rosie nods, breathes out. 'I'm sorry, Abi.'

Abi's first thought is that this is a sick joke, that Anna and the red-faced pitchfork crew are about to burst through the door, but Rosie is looking at her so steadily, her voice calm. 'I'm sorry about everything. I'm sorry you haven't got the change you wanted for your family, the chance you deserved. I'm sorry I didn't try and understand, and I'm sorry people like Anna . . . well, I'm sorry about Anna.'

Abi holds on to the side of the kitchen countertop, presses her fingernails into the cheap surface, but it doesn't stop her eyes filling with tears. She clears her throat to try to keep the aching in her heart out of her voice as she says, 'They'll be trying to figure out who it is Anna was talking about and I don't think it'll take someone like Vita long before my name is mentioned . . .'

Rosie reaches forward, like she wants to touch Abi, but decides not to. Clasping her hand around her own upper arm, she hugs herself instead. She doesn't say anything, just nods.

'I'm going to tell Lily the truth.' She says the words quickly, so she can't change her mind. Rosie opens her mouth to say something but, whatever it is, Abi doesn't want to hear. She holds her hand up to stop Rosie because there's no other choice. The only thing worse than the prospect of telling her daughter is the thought of Lily finding out some other way.

'I told Mrs Greene that Lily's got a last-minute appointment this afternoon and with everything happening at the school today I don't think anyone will mind if she comes home early. She'll be back soon.'

'How are you going—'

Abi cuts her off. 'I have absolutely no idea.'

Abi's not lying – she has no idea how she's going to tell her daughter that she's accepted money from hundreds of men in exchange for sex – but she doesn't tell Rosie that she's thought about it every day since Lily was a baby. That she's started thousands of conversations in her head, conversations that were hard enough to start but almost impossible to end.

Rosie's watching her; she looks sad, but she could just be relieved that at least her situation isn't as bad as Abi's, that she doesn't have to confess a lifetime of lying to her child.

'When we met last time, in my car. There was something you were going to say, something about not being a threat to our marriage. I wasn't ready to hear it then, but I am now. Will you tell me?'

Abi looks away. God, she's so tired of being everyone's

plaything. But Rosie didn't ask for any of this, any more than Abi. 'I was going to tell you that I think Seb came to see me because he wants to stay married. He needed some affection, and I think he chose to get it in what he thought would be the least messy way possible. It doesn't, of course, make him Husband of the Year, but at least you know I don't have any feelings for him, and I never will. Just like he doesn't have any feelings for me and never will. We never flirted or thought about running away together. It was an exchange. It was that simple.'

Opposite her, Rosie swallows and nods.

They're quiet again for a moment before Rosie says, 'I think Lily will, in time, come to understand all this. I think she'll understand you have nothing to be ashamed of.'

Which makes Abi laugh even as her tears keep rolling because what the fuck does Rosie think she can teach Abi about shame? But Rosie is shaking her head and saying, 'No, I mean it. I've seen you with your girls, seen the way you listen to each other, the connection you have with them. You're an incredible parent. Honestly, when my kids are teenagers, I'd love to have the kind of relationship that you have with Lily.'

While talking, Rosie's moved closer to Abi, and this time Abi hasn't pulled herself away because she wants Rosie to keep talking. She needs to hear this, desperately needs to hear these words no one ever says to her, these rare words: that she's a good parent.

'What if she . . .' Abi's crying properly now, overwhelmed as she's about to say out loud the words that have haunted her for so many years: 'What if she hates me because of it?'

Rosie nods, accepting Abi's fear. Braver now, she reaches forward again and this time Abi lets her gently hold her bicep.

'Yeah, I get it. She may get upset, but don't forget she's been raised by a strong, capable, free-thinking woman. I think she's more like you than you know. Don't underestimate her.'

'But the lying, Rosie, the lying is just so shit.' Abi swipes at a couple more tears as Rosie briefly closes her eyes. Yes, Rosie knows about lying.

'Yes, it is. It's shit. You had good reason to lie, Abi. You were protecting yourself and your daughters from people.' Rosie pauses before she decides to add what it is she's really thinking. 'People who don't know you and believe too strongly in their own prejudices. People like Anna and a lot of other people in this town. People like me.'

'Like you?'

Abi senses the threat of a trap again.

'Well, maybe I'm finally waking up. I'm trying to unlearn a lot of stuff.'

Abi nods, looks away. She can't figure out whether she should tell Rosie, whether it would sound trite. It doesn't feel like the moment to hold anything back. Fuck it.

'Look, I don't know if this will help but, well, he talked about you, you know. Seb. When we met. He asked me what he could do to make things better.'

Rosie covers her face with her hand briefly before looking at Abi. 'Really?'

'Really.'

'Why?'

It should be obvious, of course, but Rosie needs to hear it, just like Abi needed to hear that she's a good parent.

'Because he loves you, Rosie. Because he only wants to be with you. I think he came to see me to find out if someone else could cure this thing between you, but it didn't work. He needs you.'

'But how do I . . .?'

Ha! The irony that now Rosie is asking her, the whore, how to fix their marital issues.

'Find a way to forgive him . . .' Abi replies, aware how stupidly easy it is to say those words, how they belie the enormity of the task. Aware too, painfully, how this is exactly what she's going to be asking of her own daughter. For Lily to find a way to forgive her.

She glances at the clock. That's it, that's all Abi can offer. 'Lily is going to be home in a few minutes . . .'

'I'll get going,' Rosie says, rubbing her face again and starting to make her way to the door before pausing and turning back to Abi. 'Thank you for listening to me, Abi. I appreciate it.'

It feels awkward suddenly, like the honesty that just passed between them must be zipped, packed away before they can continue blundering through the dishonest world. Abi says, 'Yeah, that's fine.' Before adding, 'Thank you for coming over. Can't have been easy.'

They walk the few paces to the front door in silence, where Rosie turns back to Abi and, looking her in the eyes, says, 'Good luck,' before closing the door behind her.

Less than a minute after Rosie has gone, Abi is listening to her daughter trying to open the sticky lock on their front door. She must have decided not to have lunch at school. Abi thought she'd have another half an hour to prepare herself, but suddenly the door opens and Lily, school skirt swinging against her thighs, is now pulling hard at her key which is stuck in the lock. Automatically, Abi wants to move forward to help her, but she stops herself. Rosie was right: her daughter is more than capable.

When at last Lily has got it free, she startles when she sees Abi. 'Mum, why are you just staring at me?' But she doesn't wait for a response; instead she moves towards Abi, her eyes shining, popping with excitement as she kisses Abi on the cheek before moving past her into the kitchen, all the while chattering away.

'This is the wildest day ever, isn't it? First there was the assembly, and then have you heard about the radio show? I haven't listened to it yet, but everyone at school is buzzing about it. Can you believe Mr Kent? It's, like, so wild and so gross. Blake is mad – so, so mad – at his mum. He was saying he's going to go home early to have it out with her. He thinks she had no right to do that to Mr Kent or this woman – the prostitute, I mean . . .'

Abi turns away from Lily, anguish overwhelming her briefly, before smoothing her features and sitting down at the Formica kitchen table.

'You OK, Mum?'

'Yeah, I'm just trying to take it all in, that's all.'

Lily bends to open the tiny under-the-counter fridge, but she's too excited to eat so it sighs shut. She stands back up and, turning to look at Abi again, says, 'Mum, you know Blake?'

Abi feels the skin around her mouth crack into what she hopes is a smile and Lily beams back, her voice full of wonder, as she says, 'Well, I think he likes me! He asked me out and we're kind of getting quite close. But poor him – I mean, his mum has gone properly mental.' She hardly pauses for breath before she adds, 'Oh my God, and you'll never guess who

I just saw – Rosie! She was walking like she's some kind of celeb who doesn't want to get caught. Poor woman. I didn't say hello, I know she saw me, but she looked totally broken. Do you think it's OK that I didn't say hello? I don't want her to think I'm being cold, but Blake's right, I reckon, it was no one else's business, not really.'

Abi feels her heart beating too hard, like it's trying to escape.

'What's this appointment I'm back for, anyway? Mrs Greene said something about the optician?'

Abi can't answer.

Lily's forehead pleats and she steps closer to Abi. 'Mum, why are your eyes all red?'

Abi touches her face; it's wet.

'God, Mum, are you crying?' Lily is nervous suddenly; Abi can't remember a time when she would have seen her cry. Lily takes her hand and pulls her up into her arms so she can hug her. Her daughter is so strong. 'Mum, Mum, what is it? Is it something about all the stuff going on today? I saw you in assembly, I . . .'

Then she stops again, finally tuning into Abi, into the atmosphere swelling thickly in the tiny kitchen. Abi wants nothing more than to let herself go at last, she wants to sob in the arms of her daughter and beg, beg her forgiveness. But that is what Abi wants, that is not what Lily needs, so she stops herself. Abi turns away from her briefly to breathe and Lily moves closer to her, touches her arm.

'Are you sick, Mum? Is that it?' Lily asks, panic lacing her voice.

Abi takes one last big breath, the breath that could ruin them forever and, turning around to face her daughter, she looks her in the eye as she says, 'It's me, Lil.'

Lily stares at her, frowning.

'It's me they were talking about on the radio. I'm the woman. The woman Mr Kent paid for sex.'

Lily's shaking her head, like she's trying to shake the words away. 'Mum, what are you talking about? You were a therapist, Mum, a therapist . . .'

'Lily, please sit down . . .'

Lily is still shaking her head and starts backing away from Abi. 'Is this some kind of sick Halloween prank?'

Abi doesn't say anything and Lily's freckled face fills as she thinks all the worst things Abi has ever thought about herself. 'No, Mum. No . . .'

'Lily, please, let's sit down. I want to explain, I want to explain everything to you . . .' But Lily won't sit, instead she's shaking her head, and when Abi reaches out to touch her she shrieks, 'Don't! Don't touch me!'

Abi can't stop crying but she forces herself to calm down enough that she can say, 'I'm sorry, Lily, I'm so sorry for lying to you.'

Lily starts backing away again; she's still shaking her head, and she points at Abi, her mouth twisting, as she says, 'You're disgusting,' before she turns and runs out of the flat.

For the first hour, Abi waits for Lily at home. Lily, she knows, needs space. Abi thrums, numb, around the flat. She messages Lily that she loves her, that she's sorry. She deletes the message because, again, she's writing it for herself, not for Lily. She tries to cook but her hand is shaking too much to chop. She messages Lily that she'll answer all her questions, just to *please* come home. She deletes that one, too. She slumps on the kitchen table, which is where she's still lying when her phone starts ringing. She grabs for it – Lily, please, please let it be Lily. She almost throws her phone across the room when she reads her friend's name instead.

'Abi,' Diego says, his voice tense. 'Tell me you're on your way?'

Oh. The restaurant, her shift tonight.

'D . . . I . . .'

'What, what is it?' He's angry, his tone like a rough shake.

'D, I can't come in now.'

'What the fuc—?'

'I told Lily, D, I told her what I used to do, that I lied to her.'

'Jesus,' Diego says in English before continuing in rapid-fire Spanish. 'Is she OK?'

'I don't know,' Abi says before adding, 'Well, no. She's not OK, but I don't know where she is; she ran away somewhere, she's not answering her phone. I'm going to have to go and get Margot soon; she's gone trick-or-treating. I'm sorry, D, but I can't come in to work until I know they're both OK . . .'

'Fuck!' Diego shouts. 'This is our first week, Abi, almost our second weekend open, and you're not fucking here!'

'Look, I might be able to come in later, but I need to make sure the girls are . . .'

'Yeah, yeah, I know, I know you do. Look, sorry. We've got a full house tonight and the staff here are just . . . well, let's just say they're not London-trained, so please, for the sake of our careers, come in as soon as you can, OK?' He sounds like he wants to hang up straight away but mutters a quick, 'I love you all.'

She doesn't know how much time passes before she hears Lily's key in the lock for the second time. She pulls herself off the table. She's never been so nervous, more afraid in this moment of her own daughter than she ever was of any strange man.

Lily pulls her key away from the lock slowly. She's aged a decade since Abi last saw her. Her pale skin is puffy, her blue eyes bloodshot. Abi longs to hold her but there's a new force field around Lily and she senses that she doesn't want her too close, so she holds on to her own arms instead and says, her voice quiet, her words simple, 'I'm glad you're home, Lil.'

Lily looks at her, nods slowly. Her eyes are set and unblinking, her new world still blurry and out of focus.

'I promised I'd get Margot,' Lily says plainly. 'I thought we should talk a bit before.'

She walks into the kitchen, not looking at Abi, and sits down at the table. Abi feels a tug of temptation to fall into logistics, to tell Lily that of course she doesn't need to collect Margot, not today, Abi will collect her from outside the school as arranged by the parents taking the class trick-or-treating, but they both know that collecting Margot isn't the real reason Lily is back. Abi sits quietly opposite her daughter and waits. When she starts talking, the words come slowly at first before flowing into a great flood.

'You know, pretty much every one of my friends in London and here moans about their parents. They say their mums either embarrass them, want to be their best friend or boss them around, never trust them.' Lily shrugs, runs her thumb along a scratch on the table Margot made with some scissors, and keeps talking. 'But I never join in. I thought you, our relationship, was like my superpower. Our incredible secret. I might not have a dad, not really, but you know what? I never really cared because I had you. I have always known that I was loved, respected, important . . .'

235

She looks up; there's more she wants to say, of course, and Abi nods, gently, steadily showing Lily she can say it. Lily's strong enough to say it.

'I've always known that I was loved, respected, important. Until now.'

It hurts like hell, the heavy truth.

Abi nods again, puts her hands together on the table in front of her. Lily keeps running her thumb along the scratch as she says simply, 'You've been lying to me my whole life.'

Lily has the courage to say the truth, so Abi has to find the courage not to deny it.

'I have.'

Lily looks up from the scratch to meet Abi's eyes as she says, 'You were a prostitute.'

Abi nods.

'Why?'

Abi isn't ready; she's liquid and unprepared. These words feel too huge, too big for her body, but she forces them out. 'I wanted you and your sister to have better choices.'

'Why did you lie?'

'I wanted you and Margot to grow up free from the stigma of my choices. Free of my mistakes.'

'Do you regret it?'

'I regret that I had to lie but, no, I don't regret what I used to do for work.'

'Why?'

'Well, because I made a better life for you and for me and your sister. I created my own work, so I was always there when you woke up and was always the one to put you to bed at night. I had other options, other things I could have done – of course I did – but there was no way I could have done those things and been the kind of parent I have been. And the reasons for me to lie to you – well, they're more complicated.'

Lily nods for Abi to keep talking.

'There were . . . whispers, gossip about me on the estate. I mean, there was about most people. I didn't let it get to me until . . . well, it was true. The gossip. My mum heard stuff about me, asked if I was a sex worker, and when I told her I was she got really upset and kicked me out.'

What Abi doesn't say is that her mum hadn't called Abi a 'sex worker', she'd called her 'a fucking whore', and that it hadn't been just Abi she'd kicked out and said she never wanted to see again, but also Lily who was asleep in her pram.

'That's why we never see her,' Lily says quietly.

Abi nods, adding, 'I'm sorry.' Because she knows Lily would have liked having a granny. 'But honestly, I don't regret it because here you are, sitting in front of me, the most honest and brave person I have ever known. Having one of the hardest conversations we'll ever have. You are entirely yourself and I couldn't be prouder of you. It's all been worth it.'

They stare steadily at each other for a while before Abi says, 'You can ask me anything about it. I promise I'll tell you the truth.'

Lily nods – she believes her – but she looks away, her hands fluttering in her lap. 'Yeah, maybe. Not now I—'

A buzzer goes on Lily's phone, the reminder she sets whenever she's picking Margot up. Lily silences it and Abi says, 'I'll go,' not feeling ready to leave Lily, never feeling ready. 'You feel like painting or maybe having a bath . . .?'

Lily scrunches up her face before she says, 'Nah. Margot's expecting me. I'll come with you, if that's all right.'

'Of course, Lil. I'd like that.'

237

They both stand, the shock of the truth still pulsing through Abi. She's not sure exactly how to be now that Lily knows the truth, but there's no stiffness in Lily. She moves normally to her room to get a jumper for the walk to school.

Lily's back a moment later, her phone in her hand. 'I've just got a message from Blake,' she says. 'He's kind of upset about everything his mum said on the radio and he's asking if we can meet up in the park in a bit. Is that OK?'

Abi's never been so glad to be asked such a normal child-to-parent question. It's not full acceptance but at least it shows, Abi thinks, that Lily wants to try.

'Of course it is, sweetheart. Say "hi" from me, won't you?'

Her hand feels cold as she takes Lily's warmer one and squeezes it, gently, before Lily moves towards her, and they're the same height now so when they wrap their arms around each other, tightly, there's no imbalance, they hold each other.

It was all worth it.

Chapter 19

Seb hasn't left his office for hours. Apart from a brief respite around lunchtime when everyone was listening to Anna on the radio, he has been in meetings with either teachers or parents all afternoon.

Some were angry, telling him they were taking their kid out of the school immediately. Some were personally writing to the governors to have him fired, giddy with their own sense of power, their belief in their rightness. Others winced, struggled to keep their smiles under control. One dad Seb has never liked didn't bother hiding his amusement, his shoulders shivering with laughter before he leant across Seb's desk, offering his hand: 'Who'd have thought it, mate, honestly, the balls on you!'

He didn't seem to notice or care that Seb didn't call him 'mate' in return, that he immediately showed him – still laughing – to the door. What all these parents had in common, Seb realizes later, was that they were there for themselves, the kids just a convenient excuse to get a good, proper look at him. They wanted to see if he really was sorry or if he really was a pervert as others suspected. It was all coming out.

One mum started crying, shaking her head and patting a

ragged tissue under her nose. Seb wasn't able to look at her while he listened because her sorrow was between her and her past; it wasn't about him, not really.

Another, Adele, had already started a WhatsApp group 'to help the sex worker'. She told Seb in a soft voice she wanted to ensure the woman was looked after, that she could access any resources she might need. Adele had special training in working with vulnerable women; Adele was entirely on her side but she needed to know, she asked, pen raised, who it was who so badly needed her help.

Now Seb is waiting nervously in his stuffy office for his godson.

Blake had – as Seb thought he might – been one of the first to put his name down for the student appointments Mrs Greene made available to the older years. Now Seb stands as Blake knocks gently at his door. He wants to hug his godson, to feel if there might be any forgiveness softening his young, strong body, but Blake keeps himself bowed over, his eyes flicking; he doesn't look like he wants to be touched. His hair stands up from his head, like it has been raked many times by anxious fingers. Seb offers him a seat in front of his desk. Maintaining eye contact with the carpet, Blake sits, drooping in the chair like a plant deprived of sunlight and water. Seb pulls his own chair around the desk, so there is nothing between them, and waits, trying to gauge if Blake wants to talk first. Just when Seb is about to ask him how he's doing, Blake mumbles, 'It's shitty. What Mum did, I mean.'

Seb feels his stomach drop.

'Ethan and me listened to the radio show online at lunch.'

'Blake, you don't have to . . .'

'She's being an idiot, Uncle . . . I mean, Mr Kent.'

'How about I'm just Seb right now – never mind the head teacher bit?'

Blake nods, glances briefly at Seb, nods again, before he looks away.

'Blake, your mum is doing what she thinks is right.'

'Yeah, but she's talking bullshit. She said on the radio I was, like, fully behind what she's doing, that I was angry with you, which . . .' Blake shrugs again. 'Which is a total lie. She's never even asked what I think. It's like you said in assembly: we all mess up, it's about how we deal with it – that's the most important bit.'

'Blake, I really don't want to upset anything between you and . . .' Seb splutters.

'I know you don't, but Mum and her band of witches are saying how they're trying to protect *us* from *you* when actually the only people we think we need protection against is *them* and their small-minded views.'

Blake keeps his eyes on Seb as he says, 'I want to help, if I can, and I know you'd feel the same if you were in my position.'

Seb wants to agree, wants to nod and say, 'Yeah, course I would,' but he can't because he'd never have had Blake's courage. Had Seb been in Blake's position, he'd have done whatever he thought most people wanted him to do. Guaranteed. He wouldn't have rocked the boat; he wouldn't have stood up for what he thought was right. He'd have tried to be the person his dad had asked him to be. Solid. Safe. Good.

'Listen, Blake, whatever happens between your parents and me, I want you to know that if you ever need me, I'll be here for you, OK? I'm really proud to be your godfather and I'm so sorry you're tangled up in all of this.'

'What do you think I should do about Mum?' Blake asks, his eyes narrow.

Seb thinks about the years of friendship. The holidays they've shared. The countless bottles of wine and long, laughter-filled evenings. The way Anna comforted him when he was so full of grief after his dad died, the way he did the same for her after Eddy's affair. Had everything been so fragile between the four of them all along? It all seems like such a sorry waste of time. But Seb's sorrow for their friendships won't help Blake.

'Your mum's angry, which is fair enough. I think she needs to be angry and then, I hope, in time she'll see the difference between what I did and who I really am.'

'Yeah, but what should I *do*?'

'I can't tell you that, Blake.'

Blake groans, kicks his foot, annoyed, so Seb adds, 'Just remember that whatever she says or does, she loves you and she's trying her best, in her way, to protect you.'

Blake looks away for a moment, weighing things up, before turning back to Seb and asking, 'I don't understand why she forgave Dad, but she can't forgive you?'

Blake was only twelve when Eddy had the affair, and spent a lot of time with Rosie and Seb in the days when Eddy was banned from going home. Seb talked to Blake about it because Eddy was in too much of a state himself. God, it would feel good to agree with his godson.

Instead, he nods and shrugs his shoulders, hoping to show that he gets it but that he's not the person Blake should be asking.

Blake pauses again, his voice softer, before saying, 'Do you think you and Dad will be friends again?'

Seb breathes out; his thoughts blur. They were like brothers growing up, but that's over. They're fully grown now. Seb doesn't want to spend any more of his adult years trying to keep his childhood alive. They've been trying too hard for too long. The old jokes just aren't funny any more and the old ways of coping no longer work. Ignoring those changes kept them ignorant. Now, there's no turning away, no denying it. It's time to accept they've grown up and grown apart.

Seb answers quietly, truthfully, 'I don't know.'

There's a gentle knock at the door and Seb wants to tell Mrs Greene that he'll talk to her later, that his godson is more important. But Blake's already unfurling his long limbs, ready to go. Seb's about to put his hand on Blake's shoulder but he doesn't get that far because suddenly Blake reaches for him and, pulling him close, they hug, chest to chest. And over his godson's shoulder, Seb's eyes burn again, because he thinks that whatever else they've fucked up, Eddy and Anna, they made this beautiful human and that counts for more than anything else.

Less than a minute after Blake leaves, Harriet walks in, stiff and upright as the rulebook she seems to have swallowed.

She tells Seb that the petition and 'more than a few' complaints have been officially presented to the governors. They want to avoid a tribunal, but there is pressure, immense pressure, Harriet tells him, from the parents; they want to be involved in the decision about Seb's future. 'You see, they feel you involved them with your assembly, and I rather take their point. It feels incorrect to sideline them now.' She sniffs and blinks blue-veined eyelids over blue eyes.

'What are you suggesting – some kind of parent forum?'

'Precisely,' she says, unable to meet his eye. 'We've taken advice from the local council and we're going to invite parents to present their views publicly, and then us governors will have a separate, closed meeting – according to the school constitution – when we will decide whether your employment here is still in the best interest of the school or not.' She glances at him quickly before looking away. 'As time is of the essence, Mrs Greene will send out an email informing parents as soon as possible. It'll be held on Monday afternoon, after school. We'll have the governors' meeting later in the week and then present you with our final decision.'

The parent forum is unexpected, especially so soon, but everything else is as he thought it would be, even down to the way Harriet looks: tight-lipped and frowning, never once straying from her script.

By four p.m. the school is relatively quiet. Seb calls Rosie, but there's no answer. He aches to be with her, with his own kids, but he can't ignore it any more, he knows he has to do it eventually. He sits and picks up his work phone; he hasn't looked at his emails since Anna's radio performance earlier and as he opens his inbox his teeth clench together and his jaw immediately aches.

There are over a hundred emails waiting for him. Most of the subject lines are written in screaming capitals, many with exclamation marks – one is simply titled, 'SHAME!' He knows he should open them methodically one after the other but instead he clicks, almost greedy, trying to move quicker than the acid he can feel rising up in a wave from his stomach, heading for his throat.

Dear Sebastian Kent,

My daughter, Ada Barton, will never again attend Waverly Community while you are head teacher . . .

The next contains a link to testimonies from women coerced into prostitution, men paying their traffickers to rape them.

You exploit these women's desperation so you can abuse their bodies. Let's hope this doesn't happen to your own daughters, you disgusting man.

The next is a porn clip, the photo of Seb from the school website grinning, stuck on top of the male actor's face as he has sex from behind with a bored-looking woman filing her nails.

There's one from a group called Men Stand Strong! telling him he should be proud of himself, that wives should provide sex for their husbands – isn't 'with my body I thee worship' in the marriage vows after all?

There are a few from email accounts Seb doesn't recognize, each one progressively worse than the last.

Do your kids a favour, *Mr* Kent, get rid of yourself. Sooner the better.

I hope you never see your own children again, you sick fuck.

Me and my mates are coming to arse rape you until you die. Ha, ha, ha!

He reads them all and when he's done, he puts his phone screen-down on the desk and sits back in his chair. He should, he thinks, feel something. Rage, perhaps, horror or fear. But he's strangely empty where feeling should be. It's peculiar:

these furious strangers – people in general – suddenly mean nothing to him. Like he's unclipped himself from everyone else apart from a very few. He just wants to go home. He wants to go home very, very badly.

He looks out of the window and decides it's just about dark enough to leave, and he hurries down the little path that leads to the car park. He studies the ground as he walks close to the wall, avoiding the lights, and as soon as he's out of the school grounds and on to the pavement he feels something solid and too close. Out of nowhere he sees an arm reaching out for him, trying to shake his hand, and hears a voice saying, 'Seb, Mr Kent, hi, I'm Mark! So glad I caught you. I was about to give up.'

Seb keeps walking. He doesn't owe this man anything.

But the man keeps talking. 'I'm a producer for *The Talk Show* – you know, on BBC Radio Sussex.'

Seb shakes his head. 'No, no, I'm not interested.'

Seb starts walking away but he's not quick enough as Mark trots like a companionable dog beside him. He should tell him to go, to leave him alone, but up ahead there's a group of kids dressed in cheap synthetic black and lurid greens, comparing the sweets in their little pails. They could have siblings at Seb's school; a couple might even be old enough to be at the secondary school already. Seb can't risk someone recognizing him, especially if there's a bit of commotion getting Mark to leave him alone; besides, with Mark gesticulating by his side, Seb thinks people are less likely to recognize him. If he keeps his eyes on the pavement, they'll seem like a couple of commuters on their way home. Seb moves himself to the inside of the pavement, away from the road, and keeps his head down, nodding occasionally as Mark blabs away. 'What I'm saying is that obviously our website has blown up with comments after the *I Heart Sussex* show about you and your . . . umm . . . situation and, well, we want to give you the chance to respond, especially as some of them mention your dad, so . . .'

Seb stops walking. It's worked. Mark has his full attention now. 'What, what do they say about my dad?'

'Have a look yourself, mate.' Mark's come prepared; he hands Seb his phone with the BBC Radio Sussex page already loaded.

The screen shines in the darkness as Seb automatically scrolls through the words before him:

'The late Prof. Benjamin Kent was a colleague of mine and I have to say he would be appalled at his son's humiliating and shameful behaviour.'

The next reads, 'Agreed. I'm glad he doesn't have to live through this. Benjamin always led by example and it's such a pity his son has failed to do the same.'

Shame, not blood, throbs through Seb. The posts are anonymous, but still, they knew Seb's dad's name – they're legitimate. The thought that what he's done and this whole spiralling mess is tainting his dad's memory pushes Seb somewhere beyond shame, beyond feeling. Like all his emotional receptors have short-circuited and switched off. He looks up, briefly, at Mark, who is looking back at him, eyes wide, half his mouth raised, his expression a reluctant 'told you so'.

Seb scrolls down a bit on the phone to get away from those comments about his dad. He reads, 'Why are you so surprised? Privileged arseholes like Mr Kent have been screwing over hard-working people like this poor woman since time immemorial . . .'

Again, his thumb automatically scrolls down and down

and down; the words, the endless, endless words, blur on the screen. He stops at random: 'It's time the Head Cunt is taught a lesson, time for him to know what it feels like to be desperate . . .'

'See what I mean?' Mark asks, taking his phone gently back from Seb. Mark doesn't seem to notice that Seb hardly hears a word as he keeps talking. 'It's bigger than you think, this thing. Not quite viral but heading in that direction. Bacterial, maybe?' Mark snorts at his own stupid joke before he appeals to Seb again. 'Look, everyone has something to say about your story – everyone, that is, apart from you. Which is where I come in.'

It's time for Mark to go.

'I'll think about it,' Seb mutters.

'The show is on tomorrow afternoon; it would literally be perfect timing in terms of—'

'I said I need to think about it, OK, Mark?'

Mark pulls back, slightly chastened. Seb notices how young he really is, guesses Mark was probably the kind of kid at school to always try his best but never quite make it on to that podium. The kind of kid Seb adores, so he adds, more gently, 'Look, why don't you give me your details and I'll be in touch.'

Mark brightens and flicks a card into Seb's hand. They say goodbye and even though Seb is desperate to get into the safety of his childhood home, he forces himself to stay still as Mark leaves, so he can't clock which number Seb's mum's house is, before walking away himself.

Only a few houses on St John's Terrace have gone big on the decorations this year. There's the house at the end of the terrace which projects the same video every year on to the side of the building – a group of cartoon skeletons dancing in top hats, holding canes. Last year Seb's kids sat on the wall opposite, eating sweets and watching until Greer said she was going to be sick. Another couple of houses have jack-o'-lanterns lit, sticky-looking fake webs dangling from their doors. Eva's stuck the spiders she cut out with the kids on to the inside windows, but other than a plastic pumpkin that's about to run out of battery, that's it for decorations.

As he puts his key in the lock, someone calls his name behind him. He turns towards a man in a black waterproof and beanie, who holds up his phone – snap, snap, snap – before he says, jarringly cheerful, 'Fucking prick,' and, chuckling, walks away.

Seb scrambles to get inside and only starts to breathe again once he's heard the click of the door behind him. He holds on to the handle for a moment. Presses his cheek against the cool metal. He's still sinking, falling away inside himself, knowing that now when the name Benjamin Kent is mentioned, in lecture halls or among his dad's old students, the first thing people will say is, 'You heard about his son?'

'Sebastian?' Eva calls from somewhere inside.

He stands upright slowly and finds her in the kitchen, stirring the stew that has become a Halloween tradition. For the last two years Eva has gone out with them trick-or-treating, everyone going back to her house for stew before bed. Last year, Greer – a tiny, exhausted skeleton – had fallen asleep next to her bowl on the table. It is one of Seb's favourite photos of her. Eva turns and smiles when she sees him but keeps stirring. She looks small in the black witch's outfit she's worn every Halloween since Seb was a boy.

'How was your day?' Eva asks, moving towards him, holding his forearms as she kisses her son's cheek.

Seb lifts his shoulders, shakes his head. How can he answer? He can't. She knows. He clears his throat. It doesn't work. He tries again. 'What can I do?'

He means can he set the table or steam some vegetables, but Eva doesn't take it like that. Instead she points to one of the armchairs – the one that used to be his dad's – positioned in front of the wood burner.

'You can sit down,' she says firmly, and Seb feels himself liquefy as he does as he's told. Picturing his dad's head leaning back against the headrest, he has the shocking thought that he actually agrees with that post. He's glad that quiet, dignified Benjamin isn't here. That he'll never know the truth.

'Tell me, what are you thinking about?' Eva sits opposite him. She's never asked him that before.

He looks at her, surprised, and lies easily: 'I was thinking about an email I need to send.'

'Tsk. What were you really thinking, Sebastian?'

Seb looks away from her, stunned. The lies, even innocuous ones, have lost their power. He has no choice. He'll have to try the truth.

'I was thinking about Dad.'

Eva nods slightly, asking him silently to expand.

'I was thinking how disappointed he'd be in me.'

The space between her eyes pleats and she looks away, towards the fire.

'True, perhaps, in a way,' she says sadly before adding, 'but also true that your dad suffered from the same thing as you. He was always trying to do the right thing as well. Trying, perhaps too much.'

Seb stares at her. They've never talked like this, neither one of them admitting any fault or flaw in Benjamin. He'd been good in his life, true, but death had made him invincible. She looks back at him; this time she doesn't have to ask what he's thinking. She knows.

'Your dad grew up thinking that his role was to sort of mute himself. His own desires, his own wants. You know he always wanted to write? He didn't, of course, because your grandparents thought that was ridiculous. Too frivolous and unreliable. That's why he became a professor. To appease them. His life became about responsibility, about not letting anyone down. It was only when he got cancer that he started telling me the things he'd wanted for so long. That's when he went on that novel-writing course.'

Seb doesn't remember the course, but he does remember the half-written novel in his dad's spidery hand still in the drawer by his bed. He hadn't been able to hold a pen or a thought for long enough by the end to finish it.

'Sometimes I wanted to scream at him, but I didn't know why, and it's only recently, with all this with you and Rosie, that I see something similar happening between the two of you to what happened with us.'

Seb's eyes widen and Eva suppresses a smile. 'No, I'm not talking about sex. We were fine on that front, but I mean the deeper thing. The thing that stopped your dad and now you from being OK with yourself just as you are. It's OK to want and need things, Sebastian, and it's OK for some people not to like you. It's the trying to ignore those things – I think that's what's tripped you up.'

Seb feels like he's shattering, breaking into hard, sharp pieces of himself.

'This feels like more than just tripping up.'

Eva looks at him again, not trying to stop herself from

smiling now because it's unavoidable and so absurd, and she shakes her head a little as she says, 'OK. You're right. It's a monumental collapse.' Her face becomes serious again as she leans towards him and puts her warm palm on his leg. 'I know it's uncomfortable acknowledging that even if we don't like certain things about ourselves, they still exist. We must learn how to be with them.'

'But how, Mum?'

'Stop living for others' approval. It doesn't work. Start living for yourself. Trust us. We will still love you.'

Her phone rings; she whispers something in Danish about bad timing as she moves back to the kitchen to answer it. Without hearing her voice or her name, Seb knows it's Rosie asking what time Eva's coming out to meet them.

When she comes back, Seb's crying into the palm of his hand and she doesn't try to stop him; she just lets him shake and wail. Because she knows that this, this falling apart, was what he needed all along.

By the time Eva leaves, witch's hat in the crook of her arm, to meet Rosie and the kids, Seb is staring fixedly at the flames in the wood burner. He feels solid with sadness, as if turning towards his sorrow has made it grow hard and brittle within him. If someone were to peer into his mouth they'd see it there, a great blockage of regret and fear. There's no thinking any more and there's no emptiness, either. There's just feeling.

Eva has left one of her huge plastic bowls full of the Danish sweets she imports on the front doorstep so Seb won't have to deal with the trick-or-treaters; he hears their whispers and giggles as they reach for greedy handfuls of sweets. Some of them might know this is Eva's house but they won't know he's staying here, that there's a real monster inside.

An hour or so passes before his phone starts ringing in his pocket. He feels another lurch, a strange fear as he answers, 'Rosie?'

'Seb, hi.' She waits for him to say something, but he doesn't trust himself so instead, slightly irritated, she keeps talking. 'Listen, it's started raining. The kids are getting edgy. We're going to come back in about half an hour, but I stupidly left the crumble at home and we're all the way over by Rectory Gardens. I really don't want to have to go all the way home with everyone to get the crumble before going back to Eva's – would you mind . . .?'

He coughs, forces a brightness he doesn't feel into his voice as he says, 'No, of course I don't mind. I'll go and get it now and see you all back at Mum's, OK?'

'Thanks,' she mutters before calling out, 'Heath, come on, leave your sister alone.'

'Actually,' she continues, 'we're all wet and cold. We're going to come now; we'll be about ten minutes.'

Seb stands. He wants nothing more than for them all to be here, with him, their cheeks pinking by the fire, their eyes smudged with Halloween make-up, smuggling extra sweets into their mouths.

'OK. I'll go now and be back just after you.'

There's more squabbling before Rosie says a curt, 'Fine,' into the receiver and disappears.

Seb walks quickly. It's dark and still raining, so no one recognizes him as he pulls his hood over his head and keeps his eyes on the pavement. Putting his key in the door, stepping over ballet pumps and muddy trainers, breathing in the smell of his family, he feels a great swell rise in him again. It's something close to sadness but as he pulls his key out of the door, he realizes it's not sadness but an aching love that fills him. He'd never felt how close the two were before. He wants to linger, to stare for hours at all the photos on the walls, to relive their wedding day, his kids' births, their holidays on the beach. He feels greedy for the past, wants it all again and again. But it's gone and he is alone, and he knows they can never be that family laughing so easily again. His phone buzzes with a message from Rosie:

Back at Eva's, are you coming?

Chapter 20

'What are you doing here?' Blake asks as he walks off the floodlit AstroTurf towards his dad.

Eddy shrugs. 'Thought we could walk home together. It's been a weird day. Thought it'd be nice.'

Blake narrows his eyes. 'Is this about those condoms I took from your drawer?'

'What?'

'Doesn't matter. Come on, then.' Blake takes long strides along the pavement, forcing Eddy to speed up. A power play Eddy recognizes, making him jog every few paces to keep up.

'How was football?' Eddy asks, thinking he'll go in gently before mentioning the events of the day.

'Fine.' Blake keeps his eyes fixed on the pavement in front of him. Eddy's already run out of questions.

'I noticed you were standing next to Lily in the assembly. Lovely red hair – pretty, isn't she?'

Blake's far ahead, but Eddy's sure his son rolls his eyes.

'She's smart, too,' Blake says, pausing so Eddy can catch up with him. 'Look, Dad, I'm up for talking to you but I'm not up for pretending that everything is normal, OK? I'll tell you what's . . .'

They're interrupted because across the road, waiting to cross, is Patrick, waving and shouting, 'Eddy! Eddy!'

He's in Lycra jogging bottoms, a water bottle sloshing about in his hand, earbuds curled like mollusc shells around his ears.

'Hey, Eddy, wait up!' he shouts.

Eddy reluctantly stops, pointing towards Blake's retreating back and calling, 'I can't, Patrick, I'll speak to you later, yeah?'

But Patrick is already dashing across the road.

'Look, mate, I'm actually with Blake now, so . . .'

'Oh?' Patrick looks down the road, but there's no sign of Blake. He's turned into one of the residential streets that lead to the park, prepared to take a longer way home to avoid talking to Eddy.

'Come on, mate, I've been trying to get hold of you!' Patrick puts his palm on Eddy's back, gently steering him in the direction he wants him to go.

They start walking and Eddy says, 'I know. Sorry, Patrick, I've been kind of preoccupied . . .'

Patrick nods. 'Haven't we all, mate, haven't we all. Vita said Anna's been amazing, really clear-sighted throughout the whole thing . . .'

Next to him, Patrick must feel Eddy flinch because he adds, 'I mean, live radio probably wasn't the best plan in retrospect, but that interviewer really pushed poor Anna into a corner, didn't she? And it's like Vita's been saying, our focus shouldn't be on Anna, really, it should be on the prostitute.'

Eddy turns to look at Patrick. He thinks of Blake, of Lily, and doesn't like where this is leading, but Patrick smiles a knowing smile and keeps talking. 'I know, I was confused too at first, but then Vita explained her thinking. She said it's been awful at the school gates; all the women have become suspicious of each other. The theory is that either the prostitute has come here to blackmail Seb or she's in some kind of trouble and needs Seb's help . . .'

'Or she – like you and Vita – decided Waverly was a good place to raise her kids . . .'

But Patrick's already shaking his head at Eddy. 'Unlikely, mate. Too much of a coincidence.'

'Really?' Eddy says, stopping to look at Patrick. 'Or is it that Vita and her crew are just loving the scandal so much they don't want it to end?'

Patrick stops walking, too, and keeps his eyes on Eddy; he can't believe what he's hearing. '*Her crew?* You do realize you're talking about *your* wife, the woman who started this whole thing . . .'

Eddy feels his whole body deflate like a balloon because in that moment he realizes that Patrick is right. Anna has put him in this impossible position. She is essentially forcing Eddy to choose between his best friend and her, his wife. Eddy feels himself start to spiral within and, as he falls, he gasps for air and has to put his hands on his knees.

'Take it easy, Ed, blimey.'

Patrick passes Eddy his water bottle, but Eddy shakes his head.

'Just getting over something. I'm fine. I'm fine.' And as he lifts himself back up to stand, Patrick's watch beeps.

'Uh-oh, I've got to keep moving. Heart rate.' He waves his wrist in the air and adds, 'Martin, Rich and I are going for a pint tonight if you fancy talking about all this a bit more.'

Eddy's about to reply that he'd rather eat glass but Patrick's already jogging away.

*

Eddy thinks about walking a bit more on his own to gather himself before going home, but he doesn't want to risk bumping into anyone else so he feels in his pocket for his keys and looks up at his house, their house. It's the first year he can remember that Anna hasn't decorated it like all the other houses. He thinks about walking through the door, imagines Anna inside, curled on the sofa, tapping away at her phone, and he decides that he does need a moment before going in to her. He props himself against the wall, staring at the blank face of his home. He thinks about Anna, and where there used to be a kind of spreading warmth in his chest when he thought about her, there's just a kind of internal itch, unsettled, unpleasant. His mind fills with Seb and now there's a new sensation pouring deep in his belly, a dull ache, a kind of umbilical tug towards the friend Eddy's always loved most.

This afternoon, Eddy had given into temptation and looked at some of the Waverly forums. People had been uploading photos of Seb like spying on him was a new hobby for the whole town. Seb walking, head bowed, down the pavement; Seb pushing his key into his mum's front door, his face turned towards the camera, eyes bright with shock. Eddy stared close at Seb's pixilated face and tried to stir up some outrage within himself, to feel whether he could align the comments 'PERVERT!' and 'Abuser!' and 'disgusting man' with the ashen, hollow face of his oldest friend. But he couldn't. He just saw his friend scared and alone and wished he could climb into those pictures and put his arms around him.

As soon as Eddy opens the door, he hears voices in the kitchen, too many and too female to be his family, and he knows that even here, in their own home, they are not alone.

Lotte and Vita are sitting at the kitchen table. Lotte in a long white dress, with gappy sleeves, a thread of fake blood running from her bottom lip to her chin, and Vita a ragged kind of Wolverine, as far as Eddy can tell. There are three wine glasses and a half-empty bottle of red between them and it's a while before the women notice Eddy. 'Eddy, hi!'

'Where's Anna?' Eddy doesn't care if he sounds rude.

'Well, hello to you too!' Lotte scolds, playful.

'She's upstairs, checking on Albie,' Vita replies.

Last year Albie got so freaked out by a plastic severed hand on Martin's front lawn he had nightmares for weeks and swore he'd never go trick-or-treating again.

Eddy nods and takes a fourth wine glass out of the cupboard before he reaches over to rip his stupid, grinning face off the fridge. His carefree past mocking him.

Where is Seb right now? Could Eddy go to him?

'You all right?' Vita asks, one side of her mouth lifting. 'Pat messaged, said he'd just run into you and that you seemed . . . unwell.'

Eddy shakes his head, wonders what kind of language Patrick used – 'off' perhaps, 'mental' maybe. Eddy keeps his eyes on his wine glass as he says, 'I'm fine.'

Lotte slinks up to him with a flirty look as she sloshes wine into his glass. She takes his arm and pulls him gently back towards the table with her. 'We just popped over to show Anna our little list of suspects . . .'

She slurs the 's' and Eddy realizes she's a bit pissed.

'Suspects?' Eddy winces as he looks down. On a pad on the table is a handwritten list of five women's names. The final one, in different writing to the others, is 'Abi Matthews'.

'She's on there, isn't she?' Vita asks, keeping her eyes fixed on Eddy.

'Who is?'

Vita rolls her eyes, exasperated. Eddy exasperates everyone. 'Seb's prostitute.'

Lotte's hand is back on Eddy's forearm, her acrylic finger-nails drumming slightly against his skin. 'You must have heard that poor woman on *I Heart Sussex* today?'

Eddy looks at her blankly. Lotte shakes her head at him and says, 'I'll send you a link. She came on as a kind of response to that happy hooker type who called in during Anna's show. Lucy? Anyway, this woman today made me *cry*, Eddy. Actual tears, because this poor woman was tricked into prostitution by her supposed boyfriend. Said she coped by teaching her-self not to feel anything, to totally disconnect from what was happening to her. She's got severe PTSD now, as you can imagine, can barely leave the house. Listen, we're not doing this for our own benefit. We want to stop these awful abuses, prevent things like that happening here.'

He agrees but says, 'Don't you think things like that are a matter for the police?'

Lotte nods and rolls her eyes, like she knew he was going to say that. 'They should be, of course, but who is a young, vulnerable woman more likely to trust? Her boyfriend or the police?'

'But if she wanted help, this woman, surely she'd come forward?'

Lotte shrugs and shakes her head at the great, sad mystery of the world and the people in it. Vita is keen to get the con-versation back to the matter at hand. The list.

260

'You know Zoey Richards?'

'Who?'

Lotte rolls her eyes again, talks a little slower so Eddy can keep up. 'The woman who moved here, like, a year or two ago – you know, the one who always dresses a bit . . .' Lotte twists her face to Vita, looking for help in finding the right word, as Vita says, 'Slutty.'

Eddy has no idea who or what they're talking about.

'Then there's Jenni who, you know, is totally mute, never gets involved in anything, just hovers in the background like a ghoul.' Lotte shudders before adding, 'Then, of course, there's Abi.'

'Hang on, don't *you* employ Abi, Lotte? How can she be . . .'

'We don't know her. Not really, and besides, she's a bit . . .' Lotte scrunches up her nose. 'A bit out there.' Her eyes flicker to Vita, excited, before she turns back to Eddy and says, 'You know, she claimed Margot, her second daughter, is a sperm donor baby? I mean, imagine? She was already a single parent, had Lily when she was a teenager, and then she decides to have another? I mean, I don't like to judge but that's pretty extreme – if it's even true. Makes you think what else she's capable of . . .'

'Lotte, surely the fact this poor woman hasn't come forward should indicate that she wants privacy and not this . . . this crazy . . .'

'Come on, Ed, don't give us that,' Vita says. 'This is about protecting our community as well as protecting the woman. Anna's told me what happened in her own childhood, that there was literally a brothel next door to their house, that she had to step over used condoms on the way to school, that no one saw it coming in Ruston either . . .'

'But it's got nothing to do with you!'

261

'And that's precisely why places like Ruston go to shit! Because no one is prepared to protect . . .' She stops and they all turn as Anna comes back into the kitchen, a little guilty, like it was wrong of them to talk about Ruston without her approval and participation.

'Oh hi, Ed, you're home,' Anna says, looking tired but reaching for her wine glass.

'What is this, Anna?'

'Like Lotte said,' Vita answers for Anna, reaching back to the table for her list, 'we're here because we have a right to know who she is. It's wrong to keep it from us. As mothers we need to protect our kids . . .' Eddy must have heard these words a hundred times in the last week but as Vita talks something crystallizes in him. Yes, their kids need protecting, but not from Seb or even Abi. He looks towards the back door for Blake's trainers, his football kit, signs that he's home, but there's nothing. He could have stopped at one of his mates' houses or perhaps gone to the park for a bit to clear his head. His boy needs him to do the right thing.

He looks at Lotte and Vita as he says as calmly and politely as possible, 'I think you should go now.'

'Eddy!' Anna scolds, because even now being a great host-ess is the most important thing. 'Sorry, guys, I don't know . . .'

'No, I mean it. Please leave.' Eddy walks towards the front door and holds out his arms, showing them the way, standing firm as they splutter, mouths downturned, shaking their heads but still moving in the right direction, squeezing past him in the hall. Anna doesn't protest, just keeps apologizing, prom-ising to message them later, even as she waves them goodbye and out into the dusky night.

*

'Well, that was rude,' Anna says as he follows her back into the kitchen. Eddy notices how dull her eyes are, how she holds on to the table, how weary she is, how scared.

'Anna, what are you doing?'

Anna shakes her head, rejecting any blame. 'I didn't tell them anything, Ed!'

'They're not going to stop – you know that, don't you? If you give them Abi's name, you'll be destroying her life here, but you'll be destroying ours too.'

Anna splutters, shakes her head, but she doesn't say anything, so Eddy does. 'It's ironic, isn't it? Our home, our private space being invaded like this.'

Anna shrugs and mumbles something indecipherable as Eddy sits down heavily at the table and rubs his hands over his face, tugs again at his beard.

He feels his heart suddenly expand, like an airbag filling his chest, as his body again makes contact with the truth he's been trying so hard for so long to ignore.

'I can't do this any more.' He says it quietly but clearly.

'What?' Anna snaps.

'This whole thing, this mess we're in – you're not doing this to protect the kids or Rosie, and it's not even about what happened between Seb and Abi, is it?'

He looks up at Anna, takes her hand in his own, feels an overwhelming tenderness towards her as he whispers, 'It's about us.'

She frowns, but too late; he saw the break, the crack in her eyes. 'No, it's not.' She pulls her hand away.

'You haven't forgiven me for Singapore – that's what this is really about.'

'Oh God, Ed!' she shouts now, slaps her palm down hard

on the table. 'You always have to make everything about you, don't you?'

She's angry and that's fine. Eddy just feels tired and sad. His swollen heart stunned that he is at last listening to its frantic beats.

'I can't go on like this.'

'You mean, you're tired of being wrong the whole time.' Anna tries to scoff, sound dismissive, but it's unconvincing.

'Yes, I think you're right,' he agrees. 'I am tired of feeling wrong the whole time.'

'It's hardly my fault we haven't moved on!'

'No, you're right. It's not your fault and I really, wholeheartedly believe that. But I don't want either of us to wake up one day, eighty years old and still angry, still full of bitterness.'

'What are you saying?'

Eddy feels like he's pushing a pin into the airbag of his heart as he says, 'I want to move out.'

Anna looks horrified. 'That's not fucking funny, Ed,' she growls and Eddy, his cheeks suddenly wet, shakes his head and says, 'Anna, darling, I'm really not joking.'

She lifts her hand and for a moment he thinks she might slap him – she has before – but instead she says, 'You're crying. Why are you crying? You never cry.'

She takes a step away from him, like she's frightened of his tears, and he shakes his head because he really can't believe it either.

'Blakey!' Anna says, too loudly, moving swiftly towards her son, play-acting normality, as Blake walks in his slow, languid way through the back door. Blake puts his hand out to stop her getting any closer; she freezes, surprised. 'Have you been out trick-or-treating?'

He doesn't move and ignores her question. 'I just met up with Lily, Mum.'

Her arms droop slightly.

'Who, Lily Matthews?' She's pretending she doesn't know about the two of them, trying so hard to act normal.

Blake nods.

'Why on earth did you go to see her?'

'Because I like her, Mum, because I really like her, and I wanted her to be my girlfriend but you've fucked it up. Totally fucked it.'

Anna looks briefly to Eddy, perhaps wanting him to say something about Blake's swearing, but he won't. Anna shakes her head and says, 'No, Blake, you don't understand.'

Blake's fingers become claws by his side. 'She told me just now, Mum! She doesn't want to go out with me any more and I know it's because of the bullshit you said on the radio. She's acting calm but I can tell she's really upset. She doesn't want to get mixed up with the whole thing.'

Anna looks again towards Eddy who's standing now, next to the table. She's frantic for support but he shakes his head. He won't do it. He can't defend her in this.

'I didn't know you liked her . . .' she lies weakly.

'No? That's because you were too busy trying to ruin everyone else's lives instead of listening and looking after us.'

'That's enough!' Anna is shouting now. 'You don't get to talk to me like that, Blake! I'm doing all this – ending friendships, putting myself on the line – why? To keep you and your brother and every other kid in this town safe.'

Blake is shaking his head; he's got fire in his eyes. 'Mum, Uncle Seb messed up! He admitted it! Have you never asked to be forgiven for a mistake? Is your life so pathetic that you can't move on?'

'He used school property, Blake, he . . .'

'You buy all kinds of crap on your work laptop! You're such a fucking hypocrite!' He shoves past Anna, ignoring her ranting behind him, and is heading towards the stairs when he glances at Eddy, and Eddy catches the moment his boy sees the tears that are still streaming down his face, settling and glistening like dew in his beard.

'What's going on?' he asks Eddy, suspicious suddenly. 'Why are you crying, Dad?'

Eddy tries to smother the tears with his hand but it's too late.

'You guys have been arguing, haven't you?'

'Blake, this is a really crazy time, there's so much going on . . .' Eddy mumbles but Blake won't have it, won't have any more bullshit.

'Are you moving out again, Dad? Is that why you're crying?'

Eddy can't answer, all he can do is cry and say his son's name. Anna tries to take Blake's arm but he shakes her off again and, keeping his focus on Eddy, he says seriously, 'If you leave, I'm coming with you.'

'Blake, no, that's not . . .'

'Fine. Well, then Mum should go; and you, me and Albie stay.'

Then their son looks at Anna with an expression Eddy has never seen from him before, lips curled, eyes narrow as he says, 'She's the one who's ruined everything for us and for Uncle Seb and Rosie. She's the one who's publicly lying about me, her own son! She isn't safe to be around any more. You hear that, Mum? I don't trust you and I don't want to be around you.'

Then, before they can see his sorrow crest through his

266

anger, Blake walks through the kitchen and back out, into the night, and Eddy has to hold Anna back as she cries out his name again and again.

They sit silently in the wreckage of their marriage, Eddy untethered by the simultaneously shocking and grounding revelation that Blake has chosen his side. The doorbell ricochets around the stillness and despite everything Eddy still puts on a show – wolf mask on, snarling and growling – for the trick-or-treaters. Just as Eddy closes the door and goes back to Anna, he hears it. The noise of a plane about to crash. A high-pitched whine of something unnatural, something that is about to explode and cannot be contained, something that shouldn't be so close, something that is about to change everything.

Chapter 21

Seb hears the first scream from the fireworks as the front door clicks closed behind him, Rosie's crumble tucked into the crook of his arm.

It doesn't sound real at first. It's a TV turned up too loud, the neighbours' Halloween projection going wrong, maybe a teenager trying to freak out their friends. But then it comes again – the long howl followed by staccato bangs that Seb feels deep in his heart is unmistakable. It's a sound that belongs in soggy fields, up in the night sky, with the satellites and weather and other things Seb doesn't really understand. It's a sound no one should ever hear so close.

But the idiot setting off the fireworks is doing it in town.

From the top of the steps in front of his house Seb can see a pop of colour lighting up the sky just above the houses a few roads away, a tail of smoke lifting lazily into the air.

A bolt – painful and sudden – cracks down Seb's spine.

What the fuck is happening? Why is the sky right by his mum's so bright?

He jumps down the steps. The movement shakes him awake and he starts running down the rain-slicked pavement, the crumble shattering where he drops it on the tarmac.

As he runs, he passes a group of people in the middle of the road, Halloween masks lifted from their faces, their eyes wincing as they ask each other the same muffled questions.

'Was that . . .?'

'No!'

'Fireworks? What the hell!'

Seb takes the same route he took just a few short minutes earlier, but this time he doesn't care who sees him, who might shove a camera in his face and call him a pervert.

And as he runs he tries to ignore the images his brain keeps insisting he must see. Eva flicking lights on in the sitting room before walking into her kitchen to heat the stew. Rosie kicking her boots off in the hall, the kids following, limp with exhaustion behind her.

Back at Eva's, her message said. *Are you coming?*

He almost knocks a woman over, a hand over her mouth, staring at the flashing sky. She swears at him but he doesn't care. He's just a road away now.

He runs faster.

And as he runs he sees Rosie bending down on one knee to help Greer take her boots off. The older two with coats still on, slumping down in the armchairs in front of the wood burner, their teeth gummy with cheap sweets, wiping sticky fingers on the furniture, their Halloween make-up smudged.

I'm coming, Ro, please wait, I'm coming.

But as he runs he watches Rosie look up, surprised, as behind Greer Eva's letterbox creaks open and the first fizzing firework is shoved inside, just behind their little girl.

He skids on some leaves, almost falls as he turns into St John's Terrace. But he doesn't stop or even slow.

He runs. His body strains against its own limitations. Air

is forced into his lungs. He makes himself go faster as more and more fireworks are shoved inside, screaming, louder even than his children's screams.

And then it's in front of him. The neat, familiar little row of houses.

His mum's is popping, alive with colour. The windows are bright, shattering as gaudy pink and blue fountains spill and shriek and turn crazy corkscrews up, up into the night sky while the body of the house, already in flames, spits and crackles like it's in agony.

Inside. He's got to get inside.

There are more people here. Some of them are crying but most are silent, awed by the horror in front of them.

He won't stop until he's inside with them, until he can trade places or lie down with them. There is no other choice, no other way. He is desperate for the heat on his own skin, for the smell of himself burning, the smoke polluting his lungs.

He tries to pull his arm away, but it's weighted, someone hanging off it, slowing him, and as tries to shrug them off again it takes longer than normal to recognize the voice.

'Dad!'

There he is.

'Daddy!'

There they are.

His boy, his daughters crying and clutching Eva. He reaches for each one of them, pressing his hands against Greer's cheeks, kissing Sylvie's face and pulling his son tightly against his own heaving body before drawing his mum close too. He needs to feel the solidity, the realness of them, because what if this is his brain's way of tricking him, telling him they're safe just to stop him from going inside?

It's Sylvie who pulls away first, the fire flickering against her skin, her face frozen. 'Mum went ahead of us, Dad. She went ahead.'

Seb looks at Eva but her face is a mask of anguish and he realizes that if she weren't inside, Rosie would of course be here, with them. He pulls away from them almost as quickly as he drew them towards him.

He's running before they can say anything.

I'm coming, Ro.

He won't let her leave them, he won't let his children grow up without her, because this fire is for him, not her, and as he runs closer, he glances up briefly to the sky, to the unfathomable mystery, and makes a kind of cosmic promise. *Me for her, OK?*

Me for her.

The house has stopped thrashing now, giving in to the roar of the flames, resigned to its end. All that's left are great rolling waves of fire cresting and breaking from the blue, quiet heart of the fire. He pictures himself pushing Rosie out to safety, her ribcage filling with clean, nourishing oxygen.

There are noises behind him now, shouts and screams for him to stop but he doesn't, he won't. Smoke rasps through him; he feels his skin prickle as though blistering already. He runs through the gate; the fire is dancing around the front door, so he follows the path to the back but again someone grabs his arm. Harder, rougher this time, pulling him to a stop. It's a firefighter, bulky in all their gear, but Seb can just make out their eyes, they're trying to tell him something and then he hears her, he hears her, Rosie shouting his name, but he can't trust it. He needs to see her before he can stop. Again, the firefighter pulls his arm, rougher this time, forcing Seb to turn. Rosie is behind him, pressing against another firefighter, still calling his name like it's the only word she knows.

His heart is a wild thing as he moves towards her, slowly, like he's worried she'll vanish. He takes in her face first, streaked with black, eyes lively with shock. Terrified, but unharmed. He looks over the rest of her and she's saying, 'I'm OK, Seb, I just burnt my hand, I'm OK.'

He glances up, again, to the sky.

Thank you. Thank you.

'I thought, Rosie, Jesus Christ, I thought you were inside, I . . .'

And through it all – the shouts from the people watching, the roar of the fire and the wail of alarms – there's perfect silence as Rosie looks up at him, her face filled with something transcending fear or relief or even love. It's only later that Seb will find the right word. Acceptance. They reach for each other at the same time and in the flickering light as so much is destroyed Seb knows that something more precious has also been saved.

Chapter 22

The kids wrap themselves around Rosie and Seb, the five of them in a shaking huddle, before they're moved away by firefighters in bulky coats and gloves, the visors down on their yellow helmets. It's their show now.

Rosie is so grateful for Greer's weight in her arms, her daughter's legs squeezing her waist. Heath and Sylvie either side of Seb, his arms over their shoulders. They form a protective semicircle around Eva who stands, solemn but strong on her own, turned to face everything she's losing. The police move them back, further away. There's nothing for them to do now but watch this strangely intimate moment. They stand, watching tiny deaths play out in front of them as the physical pieces of Eva's life, Seb's childhood, Rosie's kids' childhoods lift and disappear into the night sky. Goodbye, family photo albums. Goodbye, Eva's childhood diaries. Goodbye, map with Benjamin's phone number.

Even though there are so many people, firefighters with their hoses and police with their radios, it feels like it's just the six of them standing there, watching. The children are quiet, reverent. Greer strokes Rosie's cheek. The children seem to understand that what is happening here is terrible but also sacred and Rosie knows in the pit of her that it's right for the children to be here. To witness what mustn't be avoided, to see what can never be properly described.

Next to her, Rosie feels Seb and she presses herself against the side of him. There is no one else, no one else she could stand next to and witness all this destruction with. She feels like she too is on fire as so much between them floats up, up, away into the night sky. He came for her. That's all that matters. It's no longer about who is right and who is wrong, it's no longer about all the things they should have done earlier and the things they should not have done at all.

A police officer approaches Eva. 'Mrs Kent? Are you Mrs Eva Kent?'

Suddenly the protective casing around their little group is broken and now there's someone else, an ambulance worker in dark-green scrubs next to Rosie asking, 'Hi, Mrs Kent, I'm Katerina. Can I take a look at that hand for you?'

Rosie feels Greer's legs around her soften like she's about to release, but Rosie holds her little one tighter, wrapping Greer's legs around her waist again, and says to the woman, 'No, no, thank you, I'm fine.'

Katerina asks again to look at Rosie's hand and she reluctantly passes Greer to Seb.

Seb puts his hand behind Rosie's head and for just a moment they stand, foreheads touching, his tears so close to her own. Rosie pulls away first as Seb whispers, 'I'm going to take the kids home and then I'm going to come back for you, Ro.'

Rosie shakes her head. 'No. You stay with them, Seb. They need you more than I do. Stay with them.'

Seb agrees with a brief incline of his head before he glances towards Eva, who now has two police officers in front of her, taking notes, and Rosie knows without having to be told what he's asking.

'Of course. I won't leave her on her own.'

Seb swallows and nods again before the four of them start walking slowly away. Rosie watches them and for the first time she notices how many people have gathered now. Neighbours, acquaintances, some strangers in Halloween costumes, some in dressing gowns and slippers, all turned towards the bonfire made from her mother-in-law's life. Some of them notice Rosie looking at them, and they nudge their neighbours so they too can turn to stare at Rosie. As Katerina leads her towards the open rear doors of the ambulance, Rosie looks back at all those faces and where she would once have felt shame grip, wringing her stomach like a filthy dishrag, she feels a wonderful lifting gentleness because none of them understand anything. None of them really know anything at all.

Inside the ambulance it's jarringly bright but Katerina's eyes are kind, the hand guiding Rosie soft. Rosie sits where she's told to sit and answers all the questions she's asked. No, she doesn't feel dizzy. In fact, she feels clearer than she's felt for weeks. Any nausea? She shakes her head. Her pulse is raised but Katerina lifts an eyebrow and says, 'Under the circumstances, I think we can let that go.'

Katerina gently turns Rosie's palm so it's facing up and, placing glasses on her nose, she peers down. Rosie winces and Katerina says, 'Sorry, sweetheart,' before asking, 'Can you tell me what happened?'

Rosie's about to tell her simply that she burnt her hand but as she starts to speak, she realizes that's not right. That's not right at all. Rosie must say the words, not just for Katerina, but also for herself. She must start trying to understand why she's sitting here with this kind, gentle woman tending to her while outside the fire roars.

'I'd gone back to Eva's a little before the kids. They were getting ratty, you know, hungry, and I just needed a moment.'

Katerina looks up at Rosie, nods. Rosie guesses she's a mother too.

'I'd just got into the kitchen, turned the oven on, when I heard the letterbox bang. Then I fell to the floor. I thought I was being shot at but then another one came and flew straight through into the kitchen, landing so close to me. I don't know, I just reached out my hand like I didn't believe it; I thought it was fake. That's when I got burnt. I ran outside after that, just as the whole place started going crazy. The fire brigade arrived soon after.' Rosie falls into silence.

The rest of the story is only for her and Seb.

'We drove past your husband on our way here.' Rosie keeps her eyes on her hand, unsure where this is going.

'He was running like a madman.'

Rosie feels Katerina's eyes flicker, land on her face.

'You can probably imagine, I see all sorts in this job, but I've never seen a man run like that.' She chuckles quietly, gently, before finishing her bandaging and telling Rosie that she should go to A&E tomorrow, but tonight she's free to go.

When she steps outside the air is smokier now.

Eva is standing alone once again. She stares at the fire, her face solemn, like she's determined to say goodbye to it all. Rosie moves to stand next to her, slides her undamaged hand into Eva's. She feels it all in her mother-in-law, the electric pulse of her shock, the blank newness of a future none of them could ever have predicted. Eva doesn't cry but she does sometimes hum. It sounds old and achingly sad, but Rosie hears it as a kind of hymn to change. It brings Rosie back to Benjamin's hospice bed where Eva stayed by his side for those final days and nights, humming, as he slowly, slowly went on his way.

Rosie has no idea how long they stay like that but by the time Seb comes back, it's like the fire has settled into the main course. All the soft things are gone, the fire grinding its jaws now against the bones of Eva's old furniture, the wooden window frames and beams. Eva's humming again so Rosie and Seb move away slightly to talk.

'They're asleep,' Seb tells her. 'They're exhausted, worried about you and Granny, but otherwise I think they're OK.'

'Who's with them?'

Seb's eyes widen a little. 'Eddy came over.'

'Eddy?' Rosie's voice lifts with surprise.

'Yeah, he'd been here and saw me leaving with the kids. I suppose he figured out that was a way he could help.' Seb shrugs his shoulders, breathes out, coughs a bit at the smoke before he says gently, 'Listen, Ro. The police came over. They're waiting, in the car over there. They want to ask both of us some questions about who could have done this.'

Rosie feels blank for a moment. She'd been so consumed by everything that happened, she hadn't given any thought to how they got here in the first place. She has no idea what she'd say to them, but she nods at Seb. 'OK.'

It's after midnight when Seb and Rosie walk the short distance home.

It feels strange being home. Rosie feels guilty – with Eva by her side, because look, here's their kitchen table, their sofa, their shoes all intact. All still here. Rosie runs upstairs to see the kids. They're as Seb described, all asleep together, a pile of puppies in Rosie and Seb's bed. Sound asleep. She kisses them, her heart swelling with gratitude for their sweet breath, for the life in them, before going back downstairs.

Eva is sitting in the kitchen, Eddy sheepish and uncomfortable opposite, a pot of tea in the middle. If it wasn't for the police officers also sitting at the table and the grim line of Eva's mouth in her ash-stained face, they could just be having a late-night chat.

Eddy stands as soon as he sees Rosie. His eyes are red; he's been crying. He hugs Rosie tightly, wrapping his arms fully around her, and says, 'I'm sorry, I'm so, so sorry, Ro.'

His apologies confuse Rosie because what is he apologizing for? This fire that wasn't his fault or all the stuff before that was?

She mutters, 'Thank you for being here, Ed. Thanks for . . .'

He waves her gratitude away and once they've promised to let him know if there's anything else that he can do, Eddy hugs them both one last time and leaves.

Now it's just the five of them. The woman introduces herself again, her name – Sarah Wilcox – coming after a series of letters that Rosie immediately forgets, and her colleague, Nathan, who is quiet with dark circles under his eyes.

Once introductions are over, Sarah Wilcox tells them it's important they act quickly, because acting quickly improves the odds that they'll actually find the person or people responsible.

Rosie and Seb nod and take it in turns to recount their version of what happened. The trick-or-treating, the forgotten crumble, the first blood-freezing shriek. Sarah Wilcox leaves the note-taking to Nathan and keeps her eyes fixed steadily on Rosie and Seb.

When they run out of things to say they look at each other, and Seb cups his palm over Rosie's hand where it rests on the kitchen table. Sarah Wilcox's eyes flash.

Her tone becomes a little cooler. 'We're aware you've been going through a . . . complicated time, Mr Kent, but we need to know: is there anyone who immediately comes to mind who might have reason to want to harm you or your mum?'

Seb looks briefly at Eva, who looks tiny now she's away from the fire. She moves her head in an almost imperceptible nod to show Seb she's OK. She can hear what he needs to say.

'I'd been getting threats. Death threats. Emails saying some ugly things. And there were people – parents, mostly – who were angry. Really angry. Some of the kids at school, I know, had really lost faith in me, but I don't think, I honestly don't think it would have been any of them . . .'

Rosie stares, horrified, at Seb.

Death threats?

'OK. OK,' Sarah Wilcox says, like this is all as she expected. 'We'll go to your office to have a look into all of that tomorrow, but I think that's all for now. Thanks for your help and, again, I really am so sorry.'

Her eyes flicker again towards Seb and Rosie holding hands before she looks up one last time, at Rosie. Sarah Wilcox's sharp face is full of questions and suddenly she looks more woman than police officer. Like she can't believe after everything Rosie is still here, because if her husband had done what Seb has, there's no way she'd stick around. No way she'd be

279

made a public fool. Rosie feels all of this but still she doesn't move her hand.

'OK, then. Well. Thanks for your time. Hope you manage to get some rest. We'll be in touch tomorrow.'

Rosie shakes their hands and wonders, briefly, if this is just another work night for them. Another family drama. For Sarah, Rosie and her family aren't so special, not really. Tomorrow trouble will come for someone else in flashing lights and impossible conversation, and so it goes on. How vulnerable they all are. What an extraordinary act of faith it is to keep going, keep living, when at some point, odds are, those blue emergency lights will wail and flash for you or, worse, for someone you love.

Once the police have gone, it's Seb who starts crying first.

He presses his fingers to his temples.

'I promised Dad,' he says to the empty space on the floor in front of him. 'I promised Dad I'd look after you, Mum . . .'

Rosie holds his hand tighter as his heart breaks. And even though she looks bone-weary, her body painful, Eva stands and says, her voice gentle but clear, 'How many times have I told you, *min skat*, promises are completely absurd.' But then she moves towards him, to cradle his head in her arms, and bends to bring her mouth to his ear as she starts whispering in Danish. Rosie can't understand, but that doesn't matter because the sound of a mother comforting her child is the same in every language. When she's finished, still with one hand around the back of Seb's head, she reaches for Rosie with the other.

They stay like that for a while and Rosie feels a strange lightness, a kind of lifting. Because Eva is right. Promises are absurd. They cannot stay the same as everything else changes.

They too, in turn, must become dust and blow away. Making them free to choose, if they wish, to try again.

Both Rosie and Seb help Eva upstairs and into Sylvie's room. They're all surprised to see the spare little bed made up already.

'Eddy?' they whisper to each other, doubtful because it was such a thoughtful thing. Eddy?

They hold each other again before Seb and Rosie quietly close the door behind them. As they gather sheets and a quilt to make up the sofa downstairs they hear Eva start to sob, and it's the saddest, strongest sound Rosie has ever heard.

They use sofa cushions to make up a kind of bed on the sitting room floor. Seb looks a bit unsure as Rosie starts to get in.

'You want me to go in Heath's room, Ro?'

Rosie shakes her head. 'No, I want you here, next to me.'

They're too exhausted to say anything else to each other tonight. That will come. Tonight has been about everything they've lost, and tomorrow they can talk about what they might be able to save, but right now all she wants is to know that he is there, breathing, warm and alive next to her.

Chapter 23

Abi puts on sunglasses and steps outside with Margot, Lily still in bed. Abi won't suggest school to her older daughter today. It's a beautiful morning, the kind that makes everything feel new, transformed – apart from, Abi realizes, a godawful smell, ancient like something's been burning for a long time. It's the somnolent smell of an ending, the chemical tang of things that were never meant to burn, burning. Like the cars the joyriders used to set on fire on the estate.

Margot takes Abi's hand as they walk, chattering about one of the girls in her class who has a swimming pool *at home*. A parent Abi hasn't spoken to before catches her eye as she crosses the road to Abi and Margot's side of the pavement.

'It's awful, isn't it?' she says, sniffing the air like a rabbit, her tone suggesting that actually what she means is not 'awful' but 'wondrous'.

Abi must look blank because the woman is smiling now, making her green eyes wide, showcasing surprise. She looks to Margot and back up to Abi as she says, 'You haven't heard, have you?'

Margot looks at the woman, reaches for Abi's hand again.

'What . . .?' is all Abi needs to say.

'Mr Kent – you know, the headmaster who shagged a prostitute? Well, someone burnt down his mum's house last night!'

'Oh my God!'

The woman nods.

'Was anyone hurt?'

The woman shakes her blonde head. 'Not really, nothing serious. But I have heard rumours' – the woman moves in, closer to Abi – 'that it was the prostitute who did it. Have you read some of the stuff they're saying online about her?' Then she glances at Margot and starts apologizing for talking about it with 'small ears around'.

The woman spots a friend soon after, thank God, and pretends she has to cross the road again to get to her.

'What does "shagged" mean?' Margot asks next to Abi, watching the woman leave, and Abi squeezes her hand and says, 'I'll tell you later,' and Margot, satisfied, goes back to the more interesting topic of her friend's pool.

'They found a frog in it once . . .'

Behind her sunglasses, Abi manages to avoid eye contact with anyone else at the school gates. Margot runs into school, pausing like always to give Abi a quick thumbs-up, and as soon as she's gone, Abi walks away. Ignoring the clutches of parents standing in small circles, bouncing the news to each other, like Seb and Rosie's personal life is their favourite new game.

But still, Abi isn't immune. She too wants to see what she can smell, wants to know if the rumours are even true. She doesn't know exactly where Eva lived, but she has a vague idea from when Rosie pointed it out once. As she walks, it becomes obvious which way to go from the people shaking their heads and walking in the opposite direction. She over-hears one of them, turning worried eyes towards the man next to her: 'We've got a fire alarm, Harry, haven't we?'

The road itself is still cordoned off. A policeman, lightly holding on to the plastic tape, answers questions from people standing on the other side. He sounds bored by the questions, but Abi can hear a little thrill, too, like he's puffed up with responsibility.

'I can't tell you any more, no,' he says to one.

'Only residents are allowed through,' to another.

And finally Abi hears, 'Well, today you'll have to find another route.'

Abi stays at the far end of the cordon. Eva's house, once in the middle of the terrace, looks like the stubby, blackened remains of a tooth, rotten down to the gum, in an otherwise healthy mouth. Abi stares and stares, transfixed by the smell, the smoke, the nothingness. Abi has never met Eva, but she remembers Rosie talking about her, that day they walked up to the viewing point.

She's interrupted by a man next to her who, in a loud voice, enunciates, 'Is this' – he points towards the smouldering wreckage of Eva's home behind him, before turning back to gaze into the blank round eye of a video camera – 'a random Halloween prank gone wrong, or is it, as we're starting to believe, an appalling expression of the anger and resentment that has been building in this usually mild-mannered place? This is Sam Beresford for BBC News, Sussex.' Sam Beresford freezes, holding his sad, benign smile for a moment, before dropping it entirely and anxiously asking the squatting man holding the camera opposite him, 'How was that?'

*

Abi closes the door to the flat and calls up the thin stairs, 'Lil?'

She hears Lily clattering from her bedroom before she appears at the top of the stairs, cradling the laptop they're supposed to share under her arm and asking, 'You've heard? About Mr Kent's mum's place?'

Abi swallows, nods.

'I can't believe it,' Lily sighs. 'Poor them.'

Abi realizes Lily is the first person she's met this morning to express any sympathy, any real feeling out loud.

Lily's long red hair shudders as she thuds down the stairs towards Abi. Abi opens her arms to her, but Lily doesn't move in for a hug, so Abi has to be satisfied with putting her hand briefly on her shoulder as Lily moves past her saying, 'Come into the kitchen with me? I want to ask you something.'

Lily puts the laptop on to the round kitchen table. It wobbles, so Abi bends down to adjust the piece of cardboard she's rammed under one leg while Lily puts the cereal bowls Abi and Margot used for breakfast into the sink.

Lily sits at the computer and Abi pulls up a chair next to her so she can see the screen as well.

Before Lily opens the laptop, she looks at Abi and says, 'You're probably not going to like this but I needed to know, wanted to know more about your . . . um, old job. So . . .'

She opens the laptop and there in front of them are a dozen or so thumbnails of women's faces, tits, crotches, legs wide open like butterfly wings. 'Sex mad!' one of them cries. '34GG all natural!' 'Hungry whore!'

Abi stands up like one of the women has slapped her. She wants to slam the computer shut, shout at Lily for looking at this stuff, send her with a disgusted face and pointed finger to her room.

But, of course, Abi can do none of those, would do none of those things; she just stares at her daughter, who stares back at her, noticing the angry flush Abi feels rising up her face, the sudden tension in her body, the taut way she asks, 'Why are you looking at that shit, Lil?'

Lily's cheek twitches. 'I'm just trying to understand, Mum.'

Abi looks away, up towards the ceiling. She hates this. Hates the thought of Lily's green eyes flickering over that pumped, pressed and airbrushed flesh. These women who, in London, Abi used to think were just like her. Women doing what they could to improve their lives suddenly seem so desperate to Abi, so vulnerable and one-dimensional, in this little, privileged town. Context really is everything.

Lily keeps her eyes on Abi and waits patiently, until Abi sighs and asks, 'You were looking for me, weren't you?'

Lily nods.

Abi looks away, up to the ceiling again, in the vain hope gravity will pull the tears she feels building back into her ducts. But it doesn't work so she wipes her hand across her face and reminds herself that no matter how hard this is for her, it's harder for Lily. She must get this right. So she looks back, into Lily's wide-eyed, freckled face and, sitting back down, next to her daughter, says, 'What do you want to know?'

Abi starts by typing in the password for her old website. She'd spent an afternoon before they moved down to Waverly removing links to www.theladyemma.com which she paid other websites for, before taking it offline completely. Without any sadness or regret, she thought that she might not ever see it again. It feels like years since she took it offline but it must be fewer than ninety days because she still has access. She watches Lily's face, her heart frantic; it feels like something trapped inside her as Lily reads to herself the words Abi still knows so well:

'Hello, I'm Emma. Your open-minded, discreet and passionate companion based in central London . . .'

The text is set in front of photos of Abi, images of her naked back, her clavicle, her feet lifted in the air, crossed at the ankle, some of her tattoos airbrushed away. She'd been proud of her website when she made it so many years ago, pleased she'd taken the time to get the wording, the tone exactly right. Diego helped a bit but she knew he worried about her, so she didn't ask for him to be too involved.

When Lily's finished reading, she turns to Abi and asks, 'So, you were, like, um, high end?'

Abi looks at Lily. She has no idea what words to use, no idea how to tell her daughter that, really, it didn't feel that different to Abi whether her arse was pressed up against the stale upholstery of an old car or against cold marble in a five-star hotel. The exchange was the same.

'I suppose so, but really I was just careful to be safe . . .' She thinks about how many times Lily, just by existing, saved Abi. Lily needed Abi so Abi had to be careful. She couldn't ever risk any time in a hospital bed or a police cell because she always had to get home for Lily.

'I learnt over time the kind of client I wanted to attract . . .' Lily is looking at her quietly, frowning in that way she does when she's concentrating hard. But there's no disgust in her face, there's no longer even any shock. She does, like she said, just want to understand. It's the best response Abi could have hoped for, really.

Abi keeps talking. 'I learnt a hell of a lot doing that job. I learnt how to market myself, where to advertise, how best to try and dodge time-wasters. I even learnt about boring stuff like bookkeeping and tax. But probably the most important thing I learnt was about boundaries.'

'Like what you were prepared to do and stuff?'

Abi nods, remembering how she was pinned down once, only fifteen, Lily's age now, by her friend's older brother. He'd been unzipping his jeans, Abi crying beneath him, when Abi's friend burst into the living room.

'I actually found that it was clearer with clients than it was with other partners I had outside of work, because, you know, we'd discuss what we were going to do before meeting.'

Lily frowns. 'Come on, Mum, what are you talking about, "other partners"? You haven't been on a date in . . . Well, have you ever been on a date?'

Abi grimaces, widens her eyes, innocent, exclaiming, 'I don't have time!'

'That's what you always say.' Lily glances back at the website and asks, a little sadly, 'Is this the real reason why?'

Abi breathes out, rolls her lips together and says truthfully, 'Perhaps. In part.'

Lily is quiet for a moment. Abi wants to stroke her hair, but senses Lily's not done talking yet and she doesn't want to disturb her.

'How did you start? What happened?'

She'd anticipated this one.

'You were six months old. It was the first time your dad had you for a night, looking after you at his mum's place, which was on the same estate where I grew up. Anyway, I was pretty antsy, worried. An old friend from school was working in a bar in King's Cross. She said she could smuggle me a couple of free drinks, so I decided to go along and distract myself from missing you. I met a man at the bar; he kept buying me drinks. It turned out he was staying at the hotel and . . . well, when I woke up, he was gone but he'd left cash on the side.'

He told her his name was Claude. He was probably in his forties, muscled and short, sunburnt although it was February.

'So that's it, you started doing it from then?'

Abi nods. Maybe, in time, she'll tell her about how she went back to the hotel and was kicked out by the smirking security staff, the shifts she worked in a Finsbury Park brothel, the other women sneering and competitive. Maybe, one day, she'll tell her how sometimes a girl working in the brothel would disappear without explanation. Deported? Kidnapped by a boyfriend? Arrested? The rest of them would ask briefly as they adjusted each other's bra straps before never mentioning her name again. But she won't tell her any of this, not now, not yet. Instead, she says, 'I really am sorry, you know, for keeping all of this from you.'

Lily nods, accepting her apology before she says, 'Well, I suppose all this bullshit with Blake's mum going for Mr Kent just shows why you couldn't be open about it.'

Abi nods; Lily's right.

'Does Uncle D know?'

Abi nods. 'But even we don't really talk about it.'

'Why?'

'I don't know, really. Maybe talking about it makes the whole thing more real somehow. Like I said, he used to worry. It's why he always kept me in the loop with his restaurant work, always wanted to help me find my way out when the time was right.'

Lily sits back in her chair, tilting her body slightly towards Abi as she asks, 'What are you thinking now, Mum?'

'About . . .'

'Waverly, all the gossip and stuff.'

Abi sighs again. 'Honestly? I was looking at flats this morning.'

'Where?'

'London, mostly.'

Lily makes a face, shakes her head. 'I don't want to go back to London.'

Abi isn't surprised. The cramped city with its noise and filth had never suited her dreamy, space-seeking girl.

'The thing is, Lil, I'm not sure it's safe for us here any more.'

'You mean after last night?'

Abi nods and pictures their own flat desecrated. The girls standing outside, freshly homeless.

'Brighton?' Lily asks and Abi smiles.

'Brighton could work.'

'I want to keep going to school here, though. The art department and . . .' Lily doesn't finish her sentence, but Abi is pretty sure she was about to say Blake's name.

'That's fine, Lil. I understand. We'll find a way to make it work.'

Lily nods and reaches over for her mum's hand. Abi feels an almost overwhelming rush of love. A love flavoured with something else now, something new. Respect, deep admiration.

'Are you going to tell everyone?' Lily asks, lightly.

'What about?'

'That it was you, Mum, who had sex with Mr Kent.'

Despite everything she's just shared, those words from Lily are still a shock.

'I . . . um . . . no, no. If we move to Brighton there'd be no point. We'd be mostly away from it all.'

'Hmm. I suppose.'

Abi draws Lily closer then, towards her, puts her hand behind Lily's silken head, kisses her face and says, 'You're amazing – you know that, don't you?'

Lily looks her mum right in the eye, their faces still so close Abi can feel Lily's tea-sweetened breath on her cheek as she says, 'I know.'

Lily doesn't know it but it's the best response. She moves to stand, closing the laptop before Abi says, 'Mind if you leave that here? I want to have another look at flats.'

Lily smooths her hair behind her ear and says, 'Course. I'm going to go upstairs and give Blake a call, OK?'

Abi feels like her heart has trebled in size as she squeezes her daughter's smooth hand one last time, smiling as she watches her leave.

She sits for a moment, stunned by Lily but also by a new feeling of wholeness. It isn't bringing Emma into her real life, exactly, that's making her feel this way, but rather the absence of something else. The release of the deep, smothering fear that the rest of the world was right, and she was wrong, that the things she's done are a sort of stain on her soul. A failure of goodness in her. Now, it doesn't matter. The rest of the world be damned; they can think whatever they like because Lily knows. Lily knows and she will still sit next to her and listen and hold her hand and call her 'Mum'. Lily hasn't only offered Abi her acceptance, she's given Abi something even more powerful. She's given Abi her freedom.

Abi and Lily eat lunch together at home – a creamy lemon and clam linguine, one of Lily's favourites – before Abi walks to the restaurant. The burning smell is less obvious now, but still sulphurous, like decomposing eggs. She'd messaged Diego earlier to say that she was coming in and he'd replied with a thumbs-up. He hadn't been in touch to tell her how the previous evening had gone, and she hasn't yet asked. Lotte had messaged, a cheery one-liner: 'Hope you're feeling better!' Followed by a stream of green-faced sick emojis.

Abi stops outside the restaurant just to look at it for a few moments. The gold lettering she chose with Lotte glints like fish scales in the sun, 'PLATE' glittering but still elegant in its simple, bold font. Staring at the place she'd had such hopes for, she starts to feel like secret doors within herself are slamming shut. Where just a couple of hours ago she felt a kind of awakening, she now feels like she's being wrapped in layers of suffocating cling film. Wrapped and restricted like she needs protection against seepage and spoiling. She'd wanted it to work here so badly.

Through the window, she sees movement inside the restaurant. Diego stops whatever he was doing and, sensing her, turns. He smiles immediately, lifts his hand before he frantically beckons her inside.

'Tell me now. Before Madam arrives,' Diego says. 'How is Lily?'

They're sitting at Abi's favourite table, a little two-seater tucked into the far corner by the window, drinking coffee.

'She's completely blown me away, D. I . . . I underestimated her.'

'Hmm. Perhaps. But she is who she is because you are who you are. You must see that.'

Abi rolls her eyes, shakes her head. 'Oh, I don't know. That's . . .'

'Too much to hear right now?'

Abi wrinkles her nose, nods, but she does smile. Diego squeezes Abi's forearm where it rests on the table between them. She places her palm on top of the back of his hairy hand and they both know what is coming. The words they must say next.

Diego goes first. 'So, look, *abuela*, we survived last night without you but, honest to God, I can't, I won't survive another service like that.'

He tells her about the waiter who left in tears, no one knowing why, the main courses that had gone cold, the errors on bills and parties being seated at the wrong tables, among many other mistakes. They'd had to comp five starters and three main courses.

'I know you can't,' she says, looking right into his dark chocolate eyes, 'and you shouldn't have to. But . . .'

'Ah.' Diego winces. He knew there'd be a 'but'.

'But I can't be here any more, D. It's not good for me, and after what happened last night it might not even be safe.'

Diego blows out through his mouth. Abi knows he thinks she's overreacting; he grew up in Mexico City – what happened last night was mild as milk compared to the things he's seen.

'I can't work here any more, Diego,' she says, plainly.

'You won't go back, will you?'

She knows what he's asking; he's asking if she'll become Emma again. And it's a good question but not one she can answer – not yet, anyway – so Abi lifts and drops her shoulders.

'Lily and I were talking about moving to Brighton. I'm going to go and see a flat there tomorrow.'

'Hmm,' Diego says, lifting his hand to scrub his palm

against the stubby bristle on his jaw. His eyes seem to journey elsewhere suddenly; she can't tell what he's thinking, whether he's already scrolling through his internal Rolodex, trying to think of any contacts who might be able to replace Abi, or planning next week's menu. It's a surprise when, blinking, he returns and says, 'A recruitment guy – someone who works in finding chefs, that sort of thing – contacted me a while back asking if I'd be interested in Sabor, that new place in Brighton.'

Abi nods, she knows it; the reviews weren't ecstatic, but they were fine. The food is much less exciting than Diego's, but she will need a job and likes where this thinking is leading.

'I have his number somewhere; I could call and ask if they're looking for someone?'

Abi doesn't need to say yes, she just smiles at her friend and says for the second time that day, 'You're amazing.'

Diego nods, pushes out his bottom lip and looking sadly at Abi says, 'I'm going to miss you here.'

And suddenly Abi feels herself crying again because this place, that for so long represented a new freedom for her, has become not a jail exactly, but a closed room, and she feels like she's just found a way out.

'Come here,' she says to her old friend, their shared dream lying crumpled at their feet as they hug.

Lotte arrives soon after with a large bag.

'Ooff,' she says, pointing at the contents. 'Candles.'

She stands, pressing her palms into the small of her back, and looks at Abi, a little sly, a little suspicious. Abi remembers Lotte giving her the same look during her interview months ago. Lotte had been worried about Abi's lack of recent references on her CV, but she knew she was going to have to overlook the issue if they wanted Diego. Which they did. Badly.

Today Lotte squeezes Diego's shoulder and turning to Abi asks, 'You feeling better, Abs?'

All Abi has to do is smile and nod before Lotte, due diligence done, looks away from Abi and, pulling out her phone, addresses Diego as she says, 'Oh, guys! I was interviewed this morning! By the Beeb! So exciting – my fifteen minutes . . .' she adds, lifting her eyebrows like she actually believes she's worth – no, owed – much, much more than just fifteen measly minutes.

She frowns at her phone as she searches for the link and, holding the phone away from herself and gesturing to Diego to lean in, she presses 'play'.

Lotte is standing outside the school gates, her hair neatly arranged over her shoulders, her lips shellacked, her expression one of studied seriousness. Abi immediately recognizes the reporter standing next to Lotte: Sam Beresford, the guy she overheard outside the remains of Eva's house earlier.

'I'm standing outside Waverly Community Secondary School, joined by Lotte Browning, a parent whose son attends the school where Mr Kent is head teacher. Good morning, Lotte.'

Lotte looks briefly at Sam before, smiling, she turns back and says direct to camera, 'It's not, Sam – no, not a good morning. I'm afraid me and my family along with the rest of our community here in Waverly are still trying to comprehend what happened last night.'

Lotte, transfixed by herself on the screen, mouths along, repeating the words silently as Lotte in the video says them.

'We're all in shock and our hearts go out to Eva and her family.'

Sam moves the microphone back under his own chin as he says, 'Does that include Sebastian Kent, Eva's son?'

Lotte frowns, smiles and shakes her head gently at Sam. 'Of course it does!' Before she adds, 'Listen, it's important that everyone understands the community here doesn't have a problem with Mr Kent as a person. We would never condone or want to incite violence against anyone.'

'Yes, but last night . . .'

'The terrible things that happened last night were the mis-judged actions of . . . I don't know, a few crazy people. But they do at least highlight the strength of feeling here. We've seen it happen in neighbouring towns and villages, the slow corruption of a once beloved place. We will protect our community. And part of that means ensuring the people who are at the forefront of our community – the leaders or elders, if you like – share our values. Which Mr Kent clearly does not. It's as simple as that.'

'And what about the woman who supposedly recently moved to Waverly – what would you say to her?'

'Mr Kent's prostitute, you mean?' Lotte checks. Sam nods, his eyes flaring, unsure whether that is a banned word on air, and Lotte turns back, fixes her eyes once again, straight on the camera. She breathes out, sadly. 'I'd say first that we're sorry. I'm sure none of this is your fault and, please, if you need help, we're here. We are here,' she adds more softly, before her plastic mouth lifts into a saccharine and carefully produced smile.

The video ends with Sam thanking Lotte.

Diego sits back in his chair, his jaw hanging open. Lotte

leans forward, thinking his reaction is something other than what it is – shock, worry for Abi, bemusement.

'What do you think, D? Did I talk too quickly? Did I smile enough?'

Diego can't meet her eye as he stands up from his chair and says, 'Wow.'

'You liked it?' Lotte asks, a little shy.

Diego looks at Lotte, his dark eyebrows closer to his hairline than Abi's seen them before, and he says, 'You're something else, Madam, you really are.'

And because Diego is Diego and because he calls her 'Madam' and because this is just his adorable Mexican way (isn't it?), Lotte beams at him before he says, 'I'd better get back.' And as he turns, heading towards the kitchen, he looks at Abi and she knows in that moment that he understands. He fully understands and even though she never needed his permission, not really, to leave, she has it and their friendship will continue.

When he's gone, Lotte starts unpacking her candles, telling Abi how she and Richard are having a security camera fitted outside their front door because, 'It just feels like we can't trust anyone any more, you know?'

She doesn't notice Abi staring at her, wondering what it'd be like to be so fearful of things she knows nothing about. Because what, really, does Lotte know about threat and violence?

'Lotte, I need to tell you something . . .'

'What was that?' Lotte asks, adding, 'Look at this. £10.99 for a candle and they stick the price over the wick!'

'I'm handing in my notice, Lotte.'

Lotte looks up sharply then, her eyes little knots of disbelief, betrayal.

'What?'

'I'm leaving the restaurant.'

Lotte squints at Abi. 'That's insane. Diego's going to get us a star next year – why on earth would you want to—'

'I don't want to be here any more.' It's the truth, Abi thinks, why complicate things?

'We've only just opened! And Diego, oh God, he's not going too . . .'

'No, no. It's just me. He already knows. I'll work this weekend and then we can figure out my leaving date. I'm still in the first three months of my contract and we agreed, didn't we, that either party can terminate with immediate . . .'

Lotte isn't listening; she's too invested in her own sense of betrayal. She comes towards Abi, hands at her waist, her face a twist of rage. 'I defended you, do you know that?'

'Lotte . . .'

'To Anna and Vita – they both wanted to keep you on the list. Especially Vita . . .'

'List?'

'No, no. It doesn't matter. Don't come in this weekend. We don't need you. In fact, don't ever come here again.'

Abi stammers, but Lotte's face is blanched with anger, and she starts walking towards Abi again, forcing her backwards and saying, 'Get out. Go on. If you don't want us, then we sure as hell don't want you.'

Chapter 24

Saturday is crisp and sunny. It's the kind of weekend when Seb would get everyone out. 'Family bike ride!' he'd call upstairs, or, 'Come on, we're going to the woods!' But Seb doesn't leave the house. They don't talk about it but there's a tacit agreement between the three adults that Seb should never open the front door, just in case it's not a well-wisher but a reporter, or worse. Rosie, often with a child or two coiling around her, leaps up whenever it rings. Which it seems to every few minutes with some ashen-faced neighbour. When they've run out of vases and jam jars and there's no fridge or freezer space left, Rosie heaps their offerings on the kitchen table. By the afternoon, the table looks like one of the kids' games of shop. Flowers propped up, nestled against each other in their plastic cones. Lasagnes and home-made bread and cakes. There are clothes for Eva, and not just ones destined for the charity shop – angora jumpers, jeans that fit her perfectly – and one of Eva's old walking friends passes Rosie a discreet bag that is full of new cotton underwear, socks and bras.

They all say a variation of the same thing, these friends and neighbours, these ex-colleagues and choir members.

'We're so sorry. How is she, dear Eva?' Before, more quietly, like they're not sure they should say his name at all, 'And Seb? How's everything with his *situation?*'

Seb hangs back from all of them, freezing even though they wouldn't be able to see him from the doorstep.

While she's waiting for the kettle to boil, Rosie silently hands Seb her phone. It's open on the front page of a local newspaper website which reads:

Head teacher Sebastian Kent: how yesterday's villain became today's victim.

Rosie touches Seb's arm briefly before she takes a mug upstairs for Eva, who is once again waiting on hold with her insurance company. Alone in the kitchen, Seb scrolls down to the comments section of the article. The comments reflect the headline, how quickly the tide of public opinion can change. Where once there was only vitriol, now some comments seem genuinely sympathetic:

'That poor, poor family.'

While others are still completely delusional:

'A nurse friend said he was so badly burnt saving Rosie – he's going to be permanently disfigured!'

There are still many that laugh:

'Ha ha! He got what was coming to him!'

And:

'How do you feel now your precious family are the vulnerable ones, *sir?*'

Seb types the truth:

'Helpless . . .'

But then he hears his kids laughing in the den they've built in Heath's bedroom and he deletes the word and goes upstairs to hide with them.

Eva spends all Saturday either on the phone or in bed. Seb sits with her, and the kids bring her home-made cards and snuggle into bed with her, but for most of the day she keeps her face towards the window and when she needs to be alone she says, 'I think I'll have a little sleep now.'

She doesn't sleep, she cries. Sometimes Seb cries with her and sometimes, knowing she wants to be alone, he just listens to her crying behind the door. The saddest tears he's ever known.

During the afternoon Rosie takes the kids to a beach an hour's drive from Waverly; they're less likely to bump into any one they know there. When they get back, cheeks pink and smelling like new air, the opposite of smoke, Rosie tells Seb the kids want to go back to Eva's, that they want to see for themselves what the fire has left.

'Do you think we should?' Rosie asks, taking a biscuit from a tin delivered by someone Seb didn't recognize.

Seb wants to say no. He pictures his children picking over the crunchy charcoal, like children from a war zone. Imagines Heath rummaging through the mess for any sign of his favourite football cards, the ones he kept at Granny's. Or Greer just standing bleakly, alone in the desolation.

He turns to Rosie and nods. 'If that's what they want. It might help them get their heads around it.'

Rosie sighs.

'OK,' she says, 'OK. I think you're right. I'll take them.'

He reaches for her good hand then and she lets him hold it. Somehow she seems to know that Seb wants to fall to his knees in front of her, that he wants to tell her over and over how sorry he is. Sorry for all this mess, all this destruction, and sorry for not loving her better. Because he does: love her, so very much. She knows he wants to say these things, but she shakes her head at him. 'No, Seb. Now is not the time.'

She gently lets go of his hand before going to tell the kids to put their wellies on and walking them over to Eva's.

While they're gone, Seb finds Rosie's iPad. He felt strangely compelled to see pictures of what is left, after the fire, to see what his kids are going to see. But as he turns it on something else automatically fills the screen.

Students' petition to keep Mr Kent as head teacher at Waverly Community.

The words wobble in front of Seb as he reads.

We, the students of Waverly Community, are writing this petition to voice our complete support of Mr Kent. We know many parents and other adults think they know what is best for us. But none of them have asked us or bothered to listen to what we think. So, we're telling them here.

Mr Kent did something wrong. There's no getting away from that and we're not pretending it didn't happen. But that doesn't mean he is all bad. We want to learn from someone who is willing to admit they get things wrong. We want to learn from someone who is willing to try and gain back the trust our parents keep saying he's broken. We're told that it's OK to make mistakes, that everyone does from time to time. Well, now it's time to prove it.

It's our school, our education, and it should be our choice.
We want Mr Kent to stay!

It's been signed 120 times. The first signature is Blake's and the last is Rosie's.

Rosie and the kids come back about an hour later, wide-eyed and quiet, their hair flecked with ash. Heath leaves a small, sad tray of blackened things they rescued outside on the doorstep along with their wellies, soles stained black. The kids watch a film while Rosie tells Seb that the homes next to Eva's have also been badly damaged by smoke and water from the hoses. That the people who live there have been moved into hotels. She tells him that she spoke with Detective Sergeant Sarah Wilcox who said they haven't found any camera evidence of who might be responsible or any other clues. She intimated that she thought they were probably local, that they seemed to know which residential roads to stick to in order to avoid cameras. No witnesses have come forward.

'It's strange,' Rosie says, 'I thought I'd be angrier, like, want to find them more, but . . .' She shrugs.

Seb gets it – it isn't about retribution. All he wants is for his family to be safe. What he doesn't tell Rosie is that Sarah Wilcox and her colleagues are looking in the wrong places because the person who did this isn't out there, walking the streets. He might not have lit the fuse but still, the person responsible is right here. In front of Rosie, inside him. Inescapable.

Rosie and Seb put Heath and Greer to bed together and as soon as the younger two are asleep they go to Sylvie and sit side by side on her bed.

'You're OK again, aren't you?' Sylvie asks. Seb looks at Rosie, who glances briefly back at him. She's confused too. 'You guys, I mean.'

Seb sits on the edge of his daughter's bed and feels a tug, deep, towards the old ways, a desire to tell Sylvie that of course they're fine. But he looks at his girl and sees for the first time that she's not OK.

Seb experiments with the truth again. 'We're getting there, Sylv. I think we're getting there.'

Sylvie nods seriously before smiling, satisfied, as she snuggles down in bed, and both Rosie and Seb kiss her forehead again and tell her they love her. Sylvie's asleep before they've even tiptoed out of her room.

Seb follows Rosie downstairs and finds Eva, in one of Rosie's nightshirts, stirring something in a pan on the stove.

'Oh good, they're asleep,' she says when she sees them, before turning back to the pan. Still stirring, she asks, 'Now, have you got any cinnamon?'

'Eva,' Rosie says, 'we've had so much food brought over, you shouldn't be . . .'

Eva shakes her head. 'I needed to do something. And besides, I really fancy a dhal.'

They eat together quietly. Eva was right: the dhal is perfect. Seb can practically feel the spicy goodness of it warming his cells. When they've finished, Rosie stacks their bowls by the sink and sits back at the table.

'I've been thinking,' Seb starts, quietly, but his voice clots in his throat so he clears it and tries again. 'I've been thinking, Ro. I'm worried something else might happen, that it's not safe here . . .'

'You think we should go away somewhere?'

Seb nods.

'Where? Where could we go?'

Seb looks away.

'Center Parcs?' Rosie asks, sarcastic, the thought of a holiday now totally absurd, before adding, 'We're staying here, Seb. The kids want to be here. I think they want, need, things to be as normal as possible, to go to school . . .'

'Well, I'll go away. For a few days. It's me they . . .'

Rosie is shaking her head again and Eva says, 'Rosie's right, Sebastian: you need to stay here.'

He looks at them, the bravest people he knows. They can tell he needs them to explain.

'There's the parent forum on Monday. If you leave Waverly, it'll be like you're running away,' Rosie says and Eva nods, agreeing.

'She's right. The fire didn't burn all that stuff away. You still have to face everyone; you still have a responsibility to the kids.'

'No, no, I'm resigning. There's no way . . .'

'If you resign now then you're right, Sebastian.' Eva's voice is steady but firm. 'You are in danger. In danger of all of this being for absolutely nothing. Of going through so much and buckling anyway. The kids' petition is all the proof we need. They need you to hold on.'

She puts her warm palm on top of his before adding more gently, 'And don't forget what your dad always said. Chaos often precedes change. That's the way of things.'

Her voice cracks and Seb wonders whether she too is thinking about everything they've lost. They only have a small handful of photos of Seb's dad now, just one or two from

Seb's childhood and none of Eva's family or her own youth. A young police officer had brought them over in a small tray, along with a bronze dolphin figurine and a couple of bits of pottery they'd been able to save from the wreckage.

'I don't know how . . .' he stumbles, feeling the full impact of his weakness, the rush of his helplessness.

'None of us do. It's OK not to know and it's OK not to succeed but it's not OK, when you've come so far, to just give up.'

How many times has Seb delivered a similar speech to his students over the years? Twenty? Fifty? A hundred?

He still doesn't know if it's the right thing but, then again, he doesn't even know if there's any such thing as 'the right thing' any more. Was there ever? It seems to Seb that all there is, all there ever was, is trying. Trying. The rest is out of their control.

He nods and says, 'If it's what you both want.'

'I don't think either of us *wants* any of this, Seb,' Rosie replies, a little sharp, before adding, more gently, 'But there's no avoiding it's where we are.'

Eva goes back up to bed after supper. Seb and Rosie sit next to each other on the sofa in the sitting room. It's dark but neither of them makes a move to turn on the lights and a part of Seb wishes they could stay like that, just the two of them, in the darkness and silence. Just sit like they did before Anna's radio appearance. But he knows he might not get another chance to say the things he's not sure she'll believe.

'I don't know if I can ever tell you how sorry I am, Ro.'

Rosie turns to him, her face calm. 'I don't know if you can ever make it better,' she says, before adding, 'Tell me something, Seb. Would you do it again? Pay a woman for sex, I mean.'

Before, he'd have acted shocked, probably have said, 'No! Of course not!'

He's different now. They both are. So, he says, 'If we weren't together any more? Maybe.'

She doesn't seem either sad or angry. If anything, she seems relieved. Like she can feel on a subtle, pheromonal level that he's telling the truth.

'But what I can tell you,' he says, his voice almost a whisper, 'is that for as long as we're married, I will never betray you again.'

Rosie's crying now, her tears silent and silvery in the evening light. 'I thought we weren't making promises any more.'

'That's not a promise, it's just something I know.'

Rosie looks away from him for a moment, before turning back again. 'How can we know that we won't just end up in the same place, Seb? I can't just make my body do things I . . . I'm worried we'll follow the same patterns, lying to ourselves, to each other again . . .'

'We won't because neither of us wants it to go back to how it was. We'll make a new agreement. Not one based on promises that might destroy us and each other in our efforts to keep them, but an agreement based on an intention to always be truthful.'

Rosie breathes out, squirms next to him with embarrassment. 'You make it sound easy.'

'I don't mean to.'

'I think I need help figuring out who I am now beyond, you know, being a wife and mother. And I guess that means physically, too. I need to know who I am inside this body, and

I think that'll help me know how I want to experience this body. Does that make sense?'

Seb nods. It makes sense, but still, his mind reels. What they'd both been experiencing all along were different manifestations of the same thing. They'd both been trapped, alone, trying to keep an inordinately complicated show on the road. The weight of it had been too much, struggling as they were, separately. It was never sex that he craved, not really. It was this. It was honesty. It was connection. It was believing he could still be loved in all his ugliness. That his most hidden, shameful parts, the parts that quaked with fear and loneliness, could still be welcome, still be loved. Shame, he realizes now, loses its power when it's not hidden away but brought out, into the light.

They're suddenly interrupted, both turning towards the porch light as it flickers on, the sensor disturbed by someone walking up the steps. Next to him, Seb feels Rosie brace; he reaches for her. But it's not someone with a brick for the window – it's Anna, her hand clamped at her sternum, carrying a small plant in a pot. She sees them, through the window, at the same time as they see her. For a moment, Seb thinks she's going to say something to them, mouth through the glass. She doesn't. Instead they all just stare, surprised, observing the shapes of each other. Anna looks away first and they see her stoop to place the pot down, by the front door, and, without looking at either of them again, she turns and disappears, back into the night.

It's Rosie who stands first, walks quickly to the front door, runs down the three stone steps, Seb following behind, and calls into the crisp darkness, 'Anna!'

Anna stops but doesn't turn around right away, until Rosie moves closer to her and says her name again like she's trying to wake her old friend up. 'Anna.'

The street lights are bright but Anna's face is still full of shadows. They stare at each other and Seb senses that now Rosie has Anna's attention she isn't sure what to do with it. In the end it's Anna who steps forward and, speaking directly to Rosie, says, 'I just wanted to keep us all safe, to stop history repeating itself. That's all.'

Seb watches Rosie nod; she knows. They stand there for a few seconds longer, the three of them, and it feels like they all know this isn't an apology and neither is it forgiveness. This is a goodbye.

He moves a step closer to his wife but doesn't touch her as Anna turns and walks away from them for the last time.

Chapter 25

Abi hadn't planned to go. She'd deleted Mrs Greene's email
and neither Lily nor Abi had mentioned the parents' forum
to the other. They had agreed on the first flat they saw in
Brighton, but they'd had to sign for it immediately, so they
didn't lose it. It meant going into savings to pay double rent
for at least a month, but freedom, Abi figures, is worth it.
This morning, at breakfast, Abi is blank when Lily asks, 'Is
the meeting today in the pavilion or the hall?'

Abi's toast hovers between her plate and her mouth.

Lily rolls her eyes. 'Tell me you're going, Mum.'

'Going where?' Margot asks.

'Lil, I really don't think it's a—'

'You don't think it's a good idea? Mum, come on, you've
got to go!'

'What are you talking about?' Margot drops her spoon,
porridge and honey landing in a splat on the floor.

'Mum, you have to show you're not ashamed, that you've
done nothing wrong . . .'

She casts Lily a warning look towards Margot.

'What?' Margot asks again, looking from her mum to her
sister and back again.

She thinks Lily is going to tell her to defend Seb, to stand up for what's right, so when Lily says simply, 'I told Blake,' it feels like she's been kicked in the stomach.

'Why is no one listening to me!' Margot runs with a great extravagant huff out of the room.

Abi will go to her later. Right now, she can't move.

'You told Blake,' Abi asks, both a question and a statement, 'about me.'

Lily nods.

Abi feels like she's been electrocuted. 'When?'

'Last night.'

Abi gets up to find her phone. The screen comes alive, but she has no new messages, there have been no phone calls. No one shouting, 'Whore!'

Lily is looking at her steadily but it's like Abi can't find a safe place to land. She wants to kick things, throw the fucking bowls across the room. Instead she just pulls her hair away from her scalp and almost shouts, 'Why the hell did you do that, Lil?'

Lily shrugs, enraging Abi even more. 'You're a part of my story and I've decided to give things a go with Blake after all, but I don't want any secrets between us.'

She is heartbreakingly, shockingly naive. What does Lily know about romantic relationships? Abi hasn't had a boy-friend since Lily's dad fifteen years ago and that was a complete mess. When it came to relationships, the Disney channel had been her educator.

'That's not . . . Lil, that's not good enough . . . You and Blake, you're not going to be together forever, it's . . .'

'You said you weren't ashamed of what you'd done, the choices you made . . .'

'I'm not!'

'Then why are you so scared?'

Abi turns away from Lily; she doesn't want to scream at her. This fight is not between the two of them. It's between Abi and the world that never understood her, never even tried.

She stays still, her hand covering her mouth, even as she hears the thump, thump, thump of Margot jumping down the stairs.

'I'm still cross!' her little voice calls from the hall.

Yes, Abi thinks, *me too, sweetheart, me too.*

Later, feeling calmer, she thinks Lily was probably right. They might be moving town, but the school is still going to be in all their lives for years to come. She'll go if only to see what people are thinking; she'll go to make sure Lily is still safe; she'll go because not being there could mark her out, put her back on Lotte, Vita and Anna's list of suspects.

The pavilion has the tense, excitable atmosphere of a New Year's Eve party or – Abi imagines – a political party awaiting results on election night. There's a long queue of people waiting to get inside, Mrs Greene at the front checking names, ensuring as best she can that everyone entering really is a parent and not a member of the press who hover by the school gates, smiling at parents, competitive and sly. As she walks through the gates Vita is talking to a friend, but her eyes fix on Abi.

On the stage at the front of the pavilion, Harriet sits behind a small desk, with two microphones on stands at either side. There are about twice as many parents as there are seats, so they spill up the aisles, a mess of chatter and expectation against every wall.

Lotte must have got there early as she's in a prime spot on a chair at the front, holding Richard's hand but leaning across him to talk to a couple of other people Abi only vaguely recognizes. Anna sits on her other side, her phone in her lap, staring blankly at the floor in front of her. Lonely in the noise around her. She glances up, like she can feel Abi looking. Abi looks away.

There's no sign of Rosie and Seb.

The woman next to Abi accidentally elbows her. 'Sorry!' she says laughingly, before adding, 'God, now I know how sardines feel!'

Abi smiles back at the woman, too nervous to trust herself to say anything.

On the stage Harriet moves to the nearest microphone and says, 'Right, can you all hear me . . .?' But no one can until someone at the back turns something and heads snap up as Harriet booms, 'Afternoon, everyone. Good, that's better. Thank you for being here. I think the incredible turnout demonstrates how committed we all are to ensuring our children have the best possible education, which is great to see.'

'I think most people are here because they love a good gossip,' the woman next to Abi talk-whispers as Harriet ploughs on.

'As per my email we are holding this parent forum so we, the governors, can canvass opinion among you, which will influence our closed-door meeting when we shall decide whether Sebastian Kent has a future at our school. I want to reassure you that we are working closely with an advisor from the council who is here today, to ensure we follow procedure. Now, it's critical that I remind you all that this meeting was scheduled before the awful fire last week, which is a police matter and not for discussion here. Understood? Good. We thought about cancelling in light of the shocking act of violence, but we governors must still make a decision for the children, and it feels more pressing than ever to do so in a timely manner. So, I'm asking that we please stick to the matter at hand, namely, whether Mr Kent should be asked to permanently leave his position after allegedly using school property during work hours for his personal' – a few sniggers – 'activities.'

Harriet looks up sharply.

The woman next to Abi mutters, 'I heard there was no evidence at all – he'd wiped it, of course – so that computer stuff is just Anna's hearsay. But then again, she hasn't been wrong in any of this so far, has she?'

The man next to the woman looks down at her, arms crossed, frowning.

'Oops!' the woman says, running her thumb and forefinger across her mouth as though zipping herself up, and turning back to face Harriet who says, 'Now. We have an hour, and I'd like to invite any of you up to the microphone here to voice your opinions, but please keep them short. I will stop you if you talk for longer than two minutes and if any of you go wildly off track.'

Harriet's eyes cast around the packed pavilion like she's doubtful anyone will have anything useful to say, before she moves back to her chair.

A wave of nervous energy ripples through the parents before a man sitting at the back gets up and, looking grimly determined, walks to the microphone.

'Hello, I'm Tim. We have two daughters at the school. Now, before all of this, I was very liberal in my thinking, open-minded. But over the last few days, I've realized there's a big difference between theory and practice. We can all be as liberal as you like when it's just theory, but when it actually happens, when it's your own kids who are being taught by someone you consider a sexual transgressive, then all theories are out the window. It's my understanding that his laptop had been wiped clean, but he's never come out and denied it, has he? I don't trust the man any more and I certainly don't want him anywhere near my daughters. We'd like him gone.'

Abi wonders what Tim gets up to when he's alone. Pictures him for a moment in stockings and high heels. She should never have come. She looks towards the exit; she'd have to walk past so many people to get out. Everyone would see, but that might be better than standing here listening to these people bullshit about things they know nothing about for the next hour.

Tim going first has broken the seal; there's now a small queue of people waiting their turn for the mic. A few echo Tim, adding their own sentence or two about sexual and power imbalances and how, in their mind, Seb orchestrated his own downfall. Then a woman, her cheeks pink and clashing furiously with her red dress, says, 'I think he's an absolute disgrace,' and Abi realizes it's not nerves making her shake, it's rage. 'What he's done – *buying a woman's body* – is deplorable. He's broken his marriage vows and his sacred promise to God. We have no idea what else he's capable of. Good riddance, I say.'

There are a couple of claps from her supporters in the audience, people growing bolder. It's the strangest thing, almost comical, hearing people talk about her body. *He never bought my body*, Abi thinks, *because look, here it is, just below my head. Like always.*

Harriet reminds everyone to please keep to the matter of Seb using school property. 'This is not' – she glances at someone, off stage to her right – 'about his personal choices.'

Next up is a tall, angular woman. Abi tenses but immediately relaxes as the woman says, 'I just want to say that I find Mr Kent's humiliation, his shame, very relatable. It's many of our worst nightmares, isn't it? The kind of thing that would keep you up at night, something hidden in your personal life becoming so public. Now, I'm not Christian, but while I've been sitting here, listening to others mention Christian values, I keep thinking of that bit in the Bible that says something like, "Those without sin throw the first stone," and none of us can, can we?'

Abi wants to clap but no one else does so she keeps quiet as the woman stands down. Lotte is next, smiling, Vita behind her in the queue. Abi feels every one of her cells shrink back as Lotte, eyes cast down, takes the mic lovingly, like a jazz singer, and bringing it towards her lips says, 'My friends and I are very concerned for the well-being of the woman, of the "sex worker".' Lotte enunciates the quotation marks. 'We feel it's only in hearing her side that we can be reassured that she was, as Mr Kent *claims*, "choosing" to work legally and independently, free of any coercion.'

Abi reels. The woman next to her mutters something, but she doesn't hear, she's too adrenalized. Abi thinks about how her mum called her a whore before making Abi and Lily homeless, and she thinks about a brothel owner who said if she offered him 'freebies', Abi would get more work.

Lotte steps down, allowing Vita to step forward. They whisper something briefly to each other before Vita nods and moves to stand behind the mic.

'That's one side of our concerns.' Vita looks out at her

316

audience before starting to talk more quickly, not knowing how long it'll be before she's shut down. 'The other is that this woman came to Waverly with the express intention of blackmailing Sebastian Kent for his shitty betrayal, but she lost all her bargaining power when Anna went public, telling everyone that twice he'd hired a woman for sex, so . . .'

'Stop at once!' Harriet grabs the other microphone, but it's not working and, besides, no one else wants Vita to stop. A few phones are waved, high in the air.

'. . . enraged, it was her, the prostitute who put those fireworks through Eva Kent's letterbox. Think about it, it makes sense, we're not only looking for a prostitute but also for an arsonist!'

Harriet's apoplectic now and a couple of teachers are bustling up the pavilion, trying to get to Vita. Everyone is talking at once, everyone enthralled by Vita's audacity, high on their own shock. Vita's microphone has been turned off and she hands it to a red-faced teacher before taking a step back, chin lifted high. Harriet, now with a working microphone in her hand, tells them all that she'll end the meeting if there are any further – she turns dagger eyes towards Vita – unwelcome disturbances. It's amid this chaos that Abi sees her mum's expressionless face the last time she saw her, and hears the security guard sneer, 'Fucking whore,' as he shoved her out of the hotel. She sees the faces of the men who spat at her, and her friend's brother who almost raped her. Where once she felt the throbbing ache of powerlessness, now a great calm rises in Abi. She can end this. She's the only one who can actually end this. She starts pushing herself forward; she's almost at the front of the queue now and she has no idea what she's going to say, but now the only person she can see is Lily and it's like Lily is leading her, showing her the way.

317

Chatter still ripples around the room as the man in front of Abi hands the microphone to her without saying a word. It's heavy, shaking in her hand. She thinks again of Lily. How Lily refused to be ashamed. 'I don't know any of you or this town or Mr Kent well . . .'

'Get on with it!' A loud shout comes from the floor. Vita's outburst has energized the crowd. But the man shouting at her has turned an engine on inside Abi. She feels herself vibrate with heat, like she's about to burst open.

Her voice is calm but stronger than she's ever heard it as she addresses the man. 'I know you,' she says. 'You're the man who thinks he can talk for me, about me, instead of me.' She turns back to address the whole room as she says, 'You all do, don't you? You've been doing it for centuries, people like you talking about whores like me.'

She looks at them, all their little faces turned towards her – did she just say what they think she said? Eyes clicking from ambivalence to interest, some lift their phones slowly into the air again. Even Harriet has frozen on her way to grab the microphone from Abi.

'Look at you – you're like children, asking to be told what to think, how to feel, listening to any idiot who talks loudest. Well, at least now, for the first time, I'm the one with the mic. It's your turn to listen. I do not want to tell you my story and I certainly don't want your pity or need your help. All I've ever wanted, all I ever hoped for when I moved my family here, was the basic dignity of making changes in my life – in my own time, on my own terms. That's it. That's all.'

She feels like she's staring into each and every one of them individually as she talks directly from her guts.

'But now I know that's not possible. Not here. Not with

people who enjoy watching someone fall, enjoy it even more when the person falling had been trying to climb. So that's it. You don't get to say you got rid of me because, right now, I'm ridding myself of you. And just to be really clear – I consented to every man I had sex with in exchange for money. I don't regret any of them. But this' – she casts her hand around the pavilion to indicate all of them – 'trying to be a part of this community – that, that I do regret.'

Her hands shake as Abi clumsily passes the mic to the man closest to her, but with adrenaline, not fear. Everyone is staring; those closest move back to give her space to pass before a few hands reach out for her. Someone shouts, another laughs, someone else starts clapping, slow and rhythmic, their neighbours dumbly joining in so by the time Abi reaches the back of the pavilion it sounds like half the audience is with her, but all Abi can hear is the blood rushing in her ears. She does notice how Mrs Greene smiles as she opens the door for her, respectful, like Abi's just done something Mrs Greene has wanted to do for a long, long time. She wonders, briefly, about the older woman's story. And now Abi is outside and people start calling her name, start clamouring and reaching for her; she breathes in one deep, chill breath and she knows that at last she is truly free.

Chapter 26

It's a week after the parent forum and Eddy is helping Anna pack. So often it has been the other way around, her carefully folding his shirts into a suitcase before a business trip, but now it's Anna who is incapable of making any decision alone.

She is going to stay with her sister in the Lake District for an unspecified length of time. They are calling it a 'few days' but Eddy suspects – hopes, even – that she might take longer. Because whatever is happening to Anna, she needs time to heal properly. This is not a wound that can be plastered over. It needs air, it needs rest, it needs time.

It was Anna who suggested the trip. She'd come back from the parent forum too stunned to talk. Eddy didn't know what the hell had happened until Blake showed him the video of Abi. He'd felt like punching the air watching her. As soon as it finished, he watched it again. Blake standing, his arm over his dad's shoulders, grinning by his side.

'What about Lily, is she . . .?' Eddy asked his son, worrying about the repercussions, but Blake's smile only got wider at the mention of her name.

'She's . . . yeah, well, she's amazing,' he said. Eddy got the impression that wasn't the first time he'd used that adjective to describe his new girlfriend.

'You really like her, don't you?'

He looked away then, shy but still smiling. 'Yeah, Dad, even more now.'

Lily's refusal to be shamed had completely deflated the few bullies who taunted her online and at school. Her dignity made them seem ridiculous, isolated, sad.

Blake still wasn't able to forgive Anna. He was still angry, still walked out of the room as soon as she appeared and would only talk to her if absolutely necessary. Normally this kind of thing would make Anna crazy with anger but mostly she just seemed fearful. She'd become paranoid that who-ever had burnt Eva's house down was now planning some kind of retribution against them. She dreamt of bricks flying through their window, her sons' blood spilling through gaps in the floorboards. Eddy, who was sleeping in the spare room now, tried his best to keep her calm, would go upstairs and try to help her go back to sleep after a nightmare. But it was hard, almost impossible, when she was getting messages from disguised numbers telling her how dangerous and how fuck-ing stupid she was. Eddy was still on enough community WhatsApp groups to know that Vita and Lotte had effectively absolved themselves of any wrongdoing, Lotte claiming and pointing out – as she'd said publicly in both a BBC interview and at the parents' forum – that she'd always only had Abi's best interests at heart. Vita's defence had been harder, meaner. She'd said at the forum she'd merely been relaying Anna's theory, that she was just the spokesperson and not the ring-leader – she wasn't, after all, the person who had started the witch-hunt, announcing what Seb had done on live radio. Vita didn't say Anna's name because she didn't have to. Everyone was just relieved to have someone new to blame.

This morning Eddy had suggested to Blake in the kitchen that he take the day off school; he'd wanted to see if he could broker some kind of peace between Anna and Blake before Anna went away. Blake shook his head at Eddy's hopeful suggestion. Instead, he looked directly at Anna, his gaze full of scorn. 'No, Dad. I need to go to school. I want Uncle Seb to know he has my full support. Ethan and me – we made a poster.'

He went out of the back door, leaving it open so a few leaves from the sycamore tree in the garden blew into the kitchen, Anna staring, unseeing, after him.

Now Anna sits meekly on his side of the bed that has for the last few nights been only Anna's bed, and Eddy holds up two pairs of woollen socks. 'Which one?' he asks. She points to a red pair and Eddy throws them into the open suitcase. They don't have long.

'Do you think he'll come home to say goodbye?' she asks, picking at the skin around her thumb.

'I hope so, love, I really do.'

But Blake has already messaged Eddy telling him he's going to one of his football teammates' houses after school. That Eddy shouldn't expect him home until much later. Eddy didn't know how to reply, so he's just left it for now. Anna nods, head bowed; she knows he isn't coming.

'I wonder how long you'll call me that,' Anna says, lifting her head to look at Eddy, who is now counting out pairs of her pants.

'Call you what?'

'Love.'

Eddy stops counting.

'You don't have to answer. I suppose there's going to be a load of stuff we can't answer for a while at least.'

He drops all the pants on top of the red socks in the suitcase. Suddenly it feels perverse, packing her up like this, like she's been fired from all their lives and is gathering her paltry belongings into the sad cardboard box of the immediately dismissed.

He sits next to her. Puts his hand on her forearm to pull her poor ragged thumb out of her teeth.

'Come on, Anna. We said we wouldn't talk about what's going to happen between us just yet; you need a rest, a break from here, from everyone. You'll be feeling so much better in a few days and then, when you're home, we can make a plan.'

'We don't have to separate, do we, Eddy?'

She strokes his head, twiddling his curls around her fingers in the way he likes, but he gently takes her fingers out of his hair and says, hating the words but feeling the truth of them in his whole body, 'Yes, Anna, sweetheart. Yes, we do.'

She starts crying again then, but softer and sadder this time.

He leaves Anna in the kitchen, writing notes for Blake and Albie. He fetches her headphones and a snack for her long train ride before carrying the case downstairs. She starts telling him what food they have, the meals he could defrost for the boys, as he rushes her out of the front door, remembering to grab her rain mac at the last minute.

Even though the train station is only a few minutes' walk from home, they drive, Anna sitting low in the passenger seat like she's trying to smuggle herself out of town.

Eddy spots some of Blake's friends walking along in a group after school, Lily among them, laughing. One of them recognizes Eddy and points his finger as they drive by, his mouth an exaggerated 'O' of excitement as the others turn to stare in their direction.

They pull into the station car park; Eddy's about to find a spot but Anna points towards the front of the station and says, 'Just drop me off here, Ed.'

'No, I'll . . .'

'Please, Ed, just go,' she says softly.

Eddy winces; his stomach slips. 'You sure you're going to be OK?'

Anna shrugs her shoulders and her face looks like it's about to break, but she manages to keep her voice steady as she says, 'I'm a big girl, Ed. I'll be fine.'

'You'll call when you get there?'

She nods and they hear an announcement for her train to London where she'll need to change to head up north. Anna reaches for the car door handle, but Eddy stops her, drawing her into a hug. It's uncomfortable, awkward – they both have to twist – though it's not as bad as the moment when usually they'd kiss on the lips but now they just look at each other, blank and clumsy. Who knew one of their last times together as a couple could be charged with so much regret, the opposite of all that hope Eddy remembers from their first joyous dates so many years ago?

Eddy feels something rise in his throat and he leaps out of the car to retrieve Anna's suitcase, tries to swallow the feeling back down. When he hands her the case they kiss on the cheek; her skin is salty and he squeezes her hand, like they were just good friends, really, all along. Her train is already pulling into the station as she walks away.

Eddy parks around the corner from school and waits for as long as he can for most of the parents and kids to evaporate before jogging towards the school gates. He's nearly there, arms crossed and head down, when he collides with someone who is also walking quickly. The woman is smaller than Eddy, holding a little girl's hand, and Eddy automatically holds his own hands out, palms open to show her he didn't mean it.

'God, sorry! Sorry!' Eddy repeats as the woman glances at the girl to make sure she's OK first, and that's when Eddy recognizes her. She's wearing a beanie over her short hair and an oversized raincoat, but Abi makes no effort to hide her face from him. Instead, when she looks up, right into him, she's neither smiling nor shying away. She looks weary but clear. The words – the automatic apologies for not looking where he was going – freeze in Eddy's throat. He breathes out and so does she and the little girl says, 'Who's that?'

Eddy will never again get this chance, these brief seconds to say the words he should have said much earlier. When he opens his mouth, they come gently, slowly, like he's talking from a part of him he didn't even know had a voice, 'I'm sorry.'

Abi just keeps her eyes on him, nods and turning towards her little girl says, 'Oh, he's just someone who needs to get better at looking where they're going,' as the two of them walk away, hand in hand.

As soon as Albie is in the back seat and they're driving away from school, Eddy tells him that Anna has gone away for a few days. His head tries to steer him towards the emotional convenience of a lie – that she's gone on a fun trip – but he battles against it.

'The thing is, Albie, she needs a bit of space and time,' he says. 'She needs a break.'

'Is she not feeling well?'

'No. No, she's not.'

Albie nods and glances out of his window and says, 'I'll make her a card,' and Eddy's about to tell his sweet boy that that's a wonderful idea when Albie adds, 'If Mum's away, does that mean we can get fish and chips?'

Eddy smiles – he's a chip off the old block – and says, 'Absolutely.'

There are roadworks on the way home, the traffic's bad, so they take a different route and it's only when Albie points out of his window and says, 'There's Uncle Seb's car,' that Eddy clocks where they are. Unusually for this busy road, there's a generous car space right outside Seb and Rosie's place. Eddy finds himself suddenly indicating right and parking. He looks through the mirror at Albie in the back seat as though hoping his eight-year-old will be able to explain to him exactly what the hell he's doing. That brief moment with Abi has emboldened him. Now is the moment for magic, the time for forgiveness and, besides, he hasn't seen either Seb or Rosie since the fire.

Albie just blinks back at him and sensing another opportunity asks, 'Can I wait here and play games on your phone?'

The curtains in the front room are half drawn but as Eddy approaches the front door he sees Sylvie and Rosie through the side pane in the bay window. Rosie notices him looking at her almost immediately, like she was expecting him. Eddy raises a hand and Rosie nods back, says something to Sylvie and walks out of the room. Eddy moves closer to the front door, but that feels too close; he steps back again. He rakes his fingers across his damp palms, tugs at his beard. He tries to think why he's here, what he's going to say, but his nervousness seems to have smothered all rationale.

He's expecting Rosie so it's a small shock when the door opens and Seb is standing there, opposite him. They haven't been alone in so long. Eddy steps forward, his body forgetting everything because it just wants to feel the familiarity of his oldest, dearest friend. But Seb flinches back, away from Eddy, slightly.

'Eddy,' Seb says, a note of caution in his voice. 'I didn't know you were coming by.'

'No, nor did I . . . I was just passing so . . .' Panic sparks down Eddy's spine. 'Albie saw your car and I wanted to say, I just thought . . .'

Seb looks at Eddy, waits patiently, but he makes no effort to make this easier for Eddy. Seb's calm makes Eddy flounder, so he blurts the first thing that comes to him. 'Anna and I are separating.'

Shit. Eddy's making it about himself again, so he adds quickly, 'But you don't need to worry about that; I'm not, like, expecting anything . . .'

'I didn't know,' Seb says simply. 'That must be hard. I'm sorry.'

He doesn't say, 'That's got nothing to do with me,' or, 'I don't give a shit,' or try to close the door on Eddy. He doesn't even look like he's thinking any of those things, but he doesn't reach to hug Eddy or open the door to invite him inside like he normally would.

'Yeah, well, just thought I should let you know. She's gone away for a bit so . . . if you . . . anyway, I . . .'

Seb keeps looking at him before he says, 'I've been meaning to be in touch, Ed. I wanted to thank you, properly, for being here. That night. The fire. It was good of you to stay here with the kids. Thank you.'

'Oh, Seb, of course, of course. Least I could do. I . . . How is Eva?'

Seb moves his head from side to side. 'OK, under the circumstances. Been better.'

'Any update on who did it?'

Seb shakes his head like he never expects there to be an update. Something's different about him and Eddy's not sure he likes it. Seb seems flat, a little absent, not even trying to make this less awkward, less icky. He's putting no effort in, and Eddy starts to panic. It's been too long since either of them said anything. This is going badly. Then Eddy lights upon the thing he'd forgotten – he'd known there was something!

'Oh shit! Seb! The governors' meeting – how'd it go?'

Seb breathes out, nods slowly and says, 'Well. That's been another surprise. We just found out yesterday. Because there was no proper evidence that I had used a school computer, they told me I can keep my job.'

'Wow!' Eddy opens his palms in celebration. 'That's amazing news. Congratulations!'

'Yeah.' Seb nods but he seems unsure whether it is good news or not. 'Yeah, I suppose it is.'

'You don't sound happy about it?'

'I don't know, Ed. I'm just having a day where it feels like we've all lost so much.'

Eddy puts his hand on Seb's shoulder, but he feels his muscles stiffen against his touch. He takes it away and desperately tries to steer the conversation back into warmer waters as he says, 'The kids must have been pleased?'

Finally, Seb smiles properly and Eddy, encouraged, adds, 'Blake told me about the poster.'

'Yeah.' Seb's smile broadens; he laughs a little. 'I think some of them were pleased. Blake kept on giving me high-fives.'

'I bet.' Eddy smiles with him, and for the briefest moment he can feel the two of them coming together again, like before, but almost immediately Seb starts to fall away again and Eddy, desperate, searches for a way to bring him back. 'Listen, Seb, I was thinking maybe you and me could find a time to pay old Court Five a visit. I'll bet she's been missing us . . .'

Seb is gently shaking his head. 'I don't think so, Ed.'

'C'mon, Seb. Don't make this into something bigger than it needs to be. We both made mistakes. If we can acknowledge that, accept it, then I don't see why we can't go back to how things were before all of this . . .' Eddy stops talking because Seb's still shaking his head, harder now.

'Ed, no. That's just it, I don't want things to go back to how they were.'

'Well, how do you want them to be?'

'I honestly don't know. But I think . . . I think it'd be good if you just give me some space to figure it out.'

Eddy steps back. He knows when someone is breaking up with him; he's had enough experience. Eddy bows his head and grabs his beard just as from inside the house a little voice – Greer, Eddy thinks – calls, 'Daddy! Daddy!'

Seb turns back inside, calling, 'One moment, sweetheart!' before coming back to Eddy and motioning with his head. 'I've got to go.'

Eddy says too loud, 'Sure! Yeah, of course!'

Seb knows Eddy makes himself upbeat, jolly, because he doesn't know what else to do with this awful sinking. Seb knows it but again he does nothing to try to make it better before he says, 'Bye, Eddy.'

And just like that, Seb closes the front door.

Eddy stays there, on the top step, for a moment longer and feels his new aloneness swelling around him, and it hurts, but mostly it just feels strange. And he's surprised that he can still turn away from the door he loves, still full and aching with the feeling, walk back to his car and say to his son, 'Come on then, Albs. Next stop, fish and chips.'

Chapter 27

Six weeks later

Abi's already arrived, sitting on a bench on Brighton beach in front of a cafe blaring out Christmas carols and blowing on a cup of something hot between her hands. They haven't seen each other properly since Rosie went over to Abi's after the radio show, although Rosie had messaged her after the glorious parents' forum. She'd felt worried for Abi and then a strange light had seemed to fill her chest – forgiveness, perhaps.

Rosie stops walking just to watch her for a moment. She looks the same as she did when they first met – messy on the outside, but still, there it is, that rooted strength in her eyes.

She's wearing the same denim jacket but this time with a thick scarf and jumper. She watches the rolling sea and the people around her calmly, like she doesn't expect anything from anyone. She isn't trying to change anything. And looking at her now, Rosie realizes it was never Abi herself she found so dizzying. It was Abi's self-reliance and clarity that drew her in, because it was what she most yearned for herself. Abi knows how to be a good friend to herself and now, slowly, day by day, Rosie is learning too.

She is even gradually starting to feel gentler towards her own body. Greeting it like an old friend when she sees herself undressed in the mirror – hello, stretch marks; hello, wobble. She'll hold her hand over her tummy to feel the warmth of herself. Her own skin to skin. Last night, for the first time in years, Rosie and Seb had a bath together.

Rosie watches a family walk past Abi. Abi smiles at one of their kids and then she looks up, straight at Rosie, and they stay there, just looking at each other for a moment, before Abi lifts her drink to Rosie and Rosie smiles, raises her hand and walks towards her.

As she gets closer, Abi looks at the bag Rosie's carrying, the towel poking out of the top. 'Don't tell me you're actually going to go in.'

Rosie shrugs and rotates her shoulders. 'Haven't decided yet.'

Abi doesn't stand to greet her, she just shakes her head, takes another sip from her cup, but she's smiling as she mutters, 'Maniac.'

She shuffles up the bench so Rosie can sit next to her.

Rosie isn't sure how to start this. 'So, how's it going?' feels like the language of yesterday. Instead she trusts the silence and listens to the sea sighing its lovely sigh as it rolls back and forth.

'I come down here most days now,' Abi says, nodding to the sea like she's visiting an old friend. 'It's one of the best things about living here.'

Rosie turns to look at Abi briefly, smiles. She remembers their walk up to the viewing spot in Waverly. She'd been so full of expectation of their friendship then, fantasized about the two of them going on weekends away together, their kids having sleepovers, how they'd become so close they wouldn't be able to imagine life without the other. It was like she'd known even then that Abi was going to have an important role in her life, and she hadn't, of course, been wrong. Abi had been bigger, more explosive than she could ever have imagined, just not in the way she'd planned.

'I saw Lily collecting Margot the other day. She said she comes down here to sketch.'

Abi laughs. 'Yep. Early Sunday mornings are her favourite. All those confused, dehydrated Saturday night ravers, their wide, crazy eyes immortalized in charcoal.'

They laugh together and it feels like they've been laughing together their whole lives.

Lily decided to stay at school in Waverly. Rosie heard people mutter words like 'extraordinary' and 'so impressive', but Lily loved her mum. That was all. She knew how to be sad and angry at the years of lying but she didn't know how to be ashamed of Abi and she liked her school. For Lily, it was that simple. Margot, still too young to know the truth, was happy to stay too. Besides, Rosie figured, even if they went some-where new, there was every chance that someone in the new school would have read about them online or in the papers. It reminds Rosie of the article written for a left-leaning Sunday supplement that Seb emailed her a copy of a couple of weeks ago. It was the only interview Abi had agreed to because, unlike all the other media, the focus wasn't on Abi or Seb – it was on the adult industries and made the case calmly and clearly for the decriminalization of sex work. Regulating the whole industry to keep everyone a little safer. The journalist had sent Seb, on Abi's request, a copy of the article before it went to press.

'I enjoyed the article, by the way.'

Abi nods. 'Yeah, well, they did a good job. I wasn't sure for ages whether it was the right thing but, I don't know, there was so much rubbish being written about me it felt like a wasted opportunity not to try and make some good come from all the attention.'

In the article Abi had called herself 'Emma' and Rosie wonders again, as she did when she read the article, whether Abi has resurrected Emma, whether she's started working again from Brighton. But where once Rosie would have felt fluttery, almost anxious with not knowing, now she just feels mildly curious before the question fades, like that particular query never really belonged to her in the first place.

Abi turns to face Rosie again and asks, 'Seb's last week at school. How are you all feeling?'

Rosie breathes in deeply, the cold sea air sharp and bright in her lungs. The governors' verdict – that there was no evidence that Seb had used school property to look for sex workers and that he hadn't broken any rules of conduct – had taken them both by surprise. They'd nodded and smiled weakly at each other; this was good news! But Rosie's stomach had twisted, and her chest felt heavy, bricks piled on the delicate scaffold of her ribcage. One evening, Seb had turned to Rosie, his face white, his brow rippled, as he said, 'I don't think I want to be head teacher any more.'

And she'd cried with relief.

Seb agreed to stay in post until Christmas, help ensure a smooth handover to the current deputy head, Mr Clegg. They haven't packed a single bag, but their flights are booked for Boxing Day and they've found a small house to rent in what Maggie says is an up-and-coming Sydney suburb. It is happening.

It had been Seb's idea. He'd suggested it in one of their weekly couple's therapy sessions and so Rosie had messaged Maggie that evening to find out if her offer of work was still on the table. Maggie had immediately arranged a Zoom with Rosie and by the end of the call they'd already started talking about Rosie's salary. It was like a kind wind was propelling them along, blowing them all the way gently to the other side of the world.

Next to her, Abi is still waiting patiently for an answer and Rosie widens her eyes and smiles without trying. 'Excited. I mean, we all wobble sometimes, of course – the kids will miss their friends – but, yeah, I think we need an adventure together. It feels right.'

Abi nods; she's smiling too. She gets it.

To be new they need to go somewhere new. In Australia, they'll only have each other to rely on and Rosie is strangely looking forward to that. To a simpler, less peopled life. Maybe they are running away from Waverly, but she doesn't care because it also feels like they are running towards each other.

'How about you – are you going to miss your friends?' Abi asks.

It's a bold question and Rosie doesn't know how to say, 'What friends?' without sounding self-pitying or dramatic. She shrugs and keeps quiet. But it's the truth: Rosie no longer has friends here; not the kind of friendships she really yearns for, anyway.

She's only seen Anna twice since she got back from staying with her sister in the Lake District. They talked briefly, their conversations clipped but weighted by everything they were not saying. Perhaps they'll talk properly before Rosie and Seb leave, but maybe not. Rosie feels too interested in the future to linger for long in the past. When she thinks of Anna and those other friendships with Lotte and Vita, she feels that old messiness, the old internal pacing creeping back. She told Seb and he said he felt the same about Eddy. It wasn't over forever, he'd talk properly to him at some point, he was sure, but when that would be he didn't yet know and that was OK. Their phones ring rarely now and neither Seb nor Rosie misses the sound.

The plan is for Rosie to work full-time with Maggie and for Seb to homeschool the kids for the first six months, by which time they hope to have a better idea of where they want to be longer term. Eva is going to rent their house with some of the insurance money while her own is being rebuilt. She's booked a flight to Sydney too and will be staying out there with them for the whole of February.

'You know the weird thing,' Rosie says, looking at Abi again. 'I feel like thanking you for fucking up our lives.'

Abi breathes out and rolls her eyes before her face softens again and she says, with a smile, 'Same here.'

Rosie, ignoring the sounds of other people around them, tunes back instead into the rolling sighs from the sea again for a moment before picking up her bag. She stands and says, 'Come on, then. I'd better get this over with.'

And it feels good to move towards the sea across the shingle, not touching each other, but still, the two of them, walking side by side again.

Epilogue

Abi is going into the kitchen to check on the roast chicken when she hears a car pull up outside the flat. She stays away from the window because she doesn't have to see her to know it'll be Anna. Blake will already be reaching to open his door even though the car hasn't come to a complete stop yet; he likes to come to Brighton at the start of Anna's week, when she stays in their old family home with the kids. Lily only goes to their place when it's Eddy's week at home. Abi suspects Blake would rather get the train from Waverly to Brighton but maybe letting Anna drive him is part of their agreement. He can go, but only if he lets Anna drive him – twenty minutes just the two of them. She pictures those journeys, Blake staring blankly out of his window as the dual carriageway rushes by, answering Anna's pre-prepared questions with monosyllables.

Abi feels a wave of sympathy for Anna as she listens to Blake's car door slam shut. Imagines the shock as Anna's shoved back into silence, alone again. Her car engine is running but still Anna lingers for a moment so she can watch from the other side of the road as the front door to their flat flies open, Lily standing there, beaming, before Blake has a chance to ring the bell. Anna must see the way their children's eyes are both brimful of light as they kiss and hug and check in with each other.

And in that moment before the other mother drives away, Abi feels the chasm open again between them, because how can Anna not be moved by this, not want to protect and delight in this beautiful thing that is happening to these beautiful young people?

As Abi moves fully into the kitchen towards the oven just under the window, Anna drives quietly away.

The flat is exactly how she likes it today. Full and noisy. Diego and Stephen are in the little sitting room teaching Margot a new card game; she hears Margot call out in her high voice as Blake and Lily join them, 'Yay! Blakey can be on my team!'

The chicken is ready, the skin turning a delicious light brown. Even Diego won't be able to find fault. She leaves it to rest on the side as she takes the miniature roast potatoes, fragrant with rosemary, bubbling with olive oil, out of the oven and drops a curl of butter on to the veg.

Then next door, above the voices, Abi's phone starts ringing and she hears Lily say, 'Hello, this is Abi's phone.'

Lily makes her way across the tiny hall to the kitchen, tucking her red hair behind her ear, a concentrated, inscrutable look on her face as she silently hands Abi her phone.

'Who is it?' Abi mouths but Lily just stares at her, her frown deepening, her mouth slightly open before she turns away, back towards the laughter and warmth.

Abi lifts the phone to her ear.

She recognizes her breathing immediately before she even says, 'Abigail?'

Abi feels something disintegrate within her at the sound of her mum's voice, but she also remembers Anna sitting in that car on her own. She reminds herself that forgiveness must work in all directions. She walks slowly out of the kitchen, out of the front door and into the needle-sharp air to listen to her mum and so she, too, Abi – at long last – can be heard.

Acknowledgements

I've said it before and I'll say it again, signing the contract with my agent, Nelle Andrews, was without a doubt in the top three good decisions of my life. Her dedication, tenacity and mama bear instinct for her authors is second to none.

Another top-drawer decision was saying 'I do' to James Linard, the best person I know. Living up to the 'tricky second album' stereotype, this book has been hard to write at times. There have been many (entirely necessary) revisions which have led to many morning-chorus panics, cancelled holidays and James emptying the dishwasher for the 4,503rd time in a row. While I've wept and wailed, James has been steadfast and clear-sighted. Thank you so much, always, my love.

Our boys, Otis and Quinn, have written their own books alongside this one and have helped by getting me out of my own head – mostly by wrestling or leaping on me from a great height or handing me a worm to rescue. Thank you, sweethearts, for always reminding me of what really matters. I love you guys so much.

I would never have believed it possible to actually write for a living were it not for the constant unwavering love and belief of my parents, Sandy and Edward Elgar, both of whom inspired a love of literature in me and my sisters.

Thank you to my excellent bros-in-law, nieces, nephews and God-kids. You are the best.

Thank you to my wonderful friends both old and new. If my characters had friends half as good as you, they'd never end up in such terrible states.

Halfway through writing this book the brilliant Frankie Gray left Transworld for pastures new. Thank you, Frankie, for steering the early ideas and for gently making me understand why the first full draft had to be totally rewritten.

I was nervous working with someone new halfway through a novel, but I'll never forget Thorne Ryan, my new editor, saying, 'Don't worry, we're going to get on.' She was bloody right. Thorne's instinct for a great story and her incredible brain power blows me away. I feel very, very lucky to work with someone I admire so much.

The first time I met Ola Olatunji-Bello she made such considered, brilliant editorial suggestions, I knew immediately she was another complete natural. Thank you both for your incredible patience and care.

I'd also like to heartily thank the excellent Anna Carvanova and Anna Nightingale, both of whom I have no doubt have amazing careers in books ahead of them.

Thank you to Eloise Austin for being at the marketing helm. Huge thanks to publicist Becky Short – surely one of the most engaging and fun people in publishing.

Barbara Thompson has been incredible on copy-editorial, spotting things that totally passed me and others by – thank you. Thanks also to Viv Thompson, Holly Reed, copy-editor Eleanor Updegraff and proofreader Rachel Cross.

In the sales team I'd like to thank Deirdre O'Connell, Phoebe Llanwarne and Rhian Steer.

In international sales, the appropriately named Cara Conquest – thank you.

In production, hearty thanks to Phil Evans. I'm indebted also to the brilliant Beci Kelly for the amazing, dizzying cover design.

I'd also like to thank my old boss and friend Del Campbell, who offered me a job even though I'm sure I seemed entirely unsuited to the role. Your early belief in me in my former role and now as a writer has meant more than you probably know.

Thank you to all the service users past and present. The ones who love what they do, the ones who feel indifferent and those who want to leave the industry. I hope the two former groups can work safely, legitimately and free from stigma and discrimination. For the latter group, I hope they find any support they might need to leave and do something else.

Finally, thank you so much, reader, for coming all this way with me.

Emily x

After studying at Edinburgh University, **Emily Edwards** worked for a think tank in New York before returning to London where she worked as a support worker for vulnerable women at a large charity. She now lives in Lewes, East Sussex, with her endlessly patient husband and her two endlessly energetic young sons. Her previous novel, *The Herd*, was a number one bestseller.